THE GATES

-HELL BEGINS-

BY IAIN ROB WRIGHT

The Gates

Hell Begins

ISBN-13: 978-1518801846
ISBN-10: 1518801846

Cover art by Stephen Bryant
Edited by Autumn Rose Speckhardt
Interior design by Iain Rob Wright

www.iainrobwright.com

Give feedback on the book at:
iain.robert.wright@hotmail.co.uk

Twitter: @iainrobwright

First Edition

Printed in the U.S.A

For my son, Jack. Thanks for keeping me on my toes.

Also thanks to my Advanced Reader team for helping me whip this monster into shape. Couldn't have done it without you.

PART ONE

"Every war has its demons."

— Richard Engel

-ELIZABETH CREASY-

DEVONSHIRE, ENGLAND

E LIZABETH CREASY FROZE.

The mother bird and her fluffy grey ducklings marched single-file from the hedge on one side of the road to the embankment on the other. When the mother noticed Elizabeth, and her agitated cocker spaniel, Boycie, she picked up speed. Her brood, in turn, picked up their speed—a cute little army marching on the double. Their feathery advance took them into the long grass where they promptly disappeared.

Elizabeth grinned. "Oh, what a lovely day, Boycie." Boycie looked up, tongue lolling out, but said nothing.

It was indeed a lovely day. The greens were green, and the sky was blue as a crystal ocean. If not for a slight thickness to the air heralding a possible storm, it was the perfect afternoon.

Two years retired now and yet to become restless, Elizabeth's daily jaunts through the fields and farms surrounding her home never failed to exhilarate her. After decades toiling in an office, she'd all but forgotten the benefits of simple fresh air, and it'd been an invigorating experience reacquainting with the joyous beauty of nature. If only her beloved Dennis were still alive to enjoy it with her, but that was not to be. At fifty-eight, an aortic rupture had snatched her husband away while he drove his evening bus route. The ensuing low-speed crash had not injured anyone, but Elizabeth had been left a heart-broken widow. She lamented on the time they could have spent together— 'cuddling' in bed all morning and spending the afternoon feeding ducks by the lake. Simple pleasures sure, but oh, the absolute best.

She hadn't been with a man since her beloved Dennis had passed, but Lord knows she had felt the need. Lately, she'd even been considering joining an online dating site just to get a man between her legs. Only so much batteries and plastic could do for a woman of her age—and Colin Firth wasn't cutting it anymore. She needed a real man, with real man parts.

Up ahead, the little knoll she enjoyed climbing came into view. Twelve-months ago, the act of hiking up it would have assaulted her knees, but now she could assail it briskly. From atop she could gaze right across the rolling fields to the sleepy village of Crapstone where she kept a modest two-bedroom cottage. The house in Torquay she had shared with Dennis had been too painful to keep, so she'd sold up a year after his death to purchase the cosy home her and Boycie now lived in.

At the bottom of the hill, she wheezed a little. The muggy weather made it harder to breathe and she was getting out of breath. Her daily hike would have to be a little more leisurely today. You could never be too careful at her age.

"Come on, Boycie, up we go."

Obedient as always, her cocker spaniel started up the hill at an ambling pace matching her own, and together they trampled the thick, green grass as they progressed towards the top. Birds chirped, and the sunshine was so potent that it seemed to massage her shoulders with invisible hands.

She started singing—"All things bright and beautiful..." Boycie barked.

"Settle down, Boycie. I don't want a duet."

Boycie barked again.

"Now, now, Boycie, settle down." The cocker spaniel hopped from paw to paw, floppy brown ears twitching. Elizabeth was about to scold him when she saw what had got him so worked up. "Hmm, that wasn't there yesterday, was it, boy?"

The smooth black stone was the size of a football, and out of place up on the lonely hill. No other rocks or boulders lay around, and certainly none that were jet-black like this one. It more resembled volcanic glass than anything that should be found in the English countryside. If not for the delicate grey veins snaking over its surface, it would have resembled an old-fashioned bowling ball. The closer she got to it, the less smooth the stone appeared—like how a television picture degraded when you went right up to the screen.

Boycie tugged on his lead, hard enough he almost yanked free of her grasp. She gave it a swift tug and brought the spaniel back to heel. "Behave, Boycie! What's got in to you?"

The birds stopped chirping and the warmth of the sun disappeared, yet it was still so muggy that it was hard to take a breath. A distant roll of thunder, but not a single cloud hanging in the sky.

Elizabeth's eyes fixed on the strange black stone. The word 'obsidian' popped into her mind. She reached out to touch it, not knowing why other than something inside of her demanded it. Her fingertips were just about to make contact when Boycie bit her.

"Damn it!"

The leash slipped out of her grasp and Boycie fled, running down the hill full pelt like a greyhound chasing a rabbit.

"Boycie, come back here!"

"Damn it." Her hand throbbed something terrible; a purplish-blue blotch forming where one long canine had crushed her skin.

Boycie had never snapped at her like that before. Never. What had got in to him?

Then came more pain.

Thwump thwump thwump...

Elizabeth turned and clutched her forehead. The delicate grey veins on the stone's surface had started to pulse and vibrate. It was calling out to her. She couldn't help herself. She reached out.

Pressed her fingertips against the stone.

Ice cold. Like running her hand down the inside of a fridge. It felt... wrong. Unnatural.

Elizabeth was just about to pull away when something

seized her. Her fingertips fused against the stone's icy surface. A powerful force snatched her mind and showed her unbelievable things. Distressing images seared themselves into her soul and boiled the blood in her veins.

She saw horrors—exquisite tortures of the worst kind.

A vast legion of monstrous creatures.

She saw Hell.

The pictures in Elizabeth's mind were so wondrous and

terrifying that her eyeballs melted inside her skull and leaked down her cheeks while her heart burst in her chest like a pin pricked balloon. When her sixty seven year old body slumped to the ground it was an empty husk and her days of ambling through fields were over—her retirement irrevocably ended.

The cold black stone went back to sleep.

~RICK BASTION~

DEVONSHIRE, ENGLAND

WHEN RICK'S SONG CAME ON THE RADIO he winced and pulled out the plug. Few things upset him more than hearing his number 1 hit, "Cross to Bear. It was fingernails on a blackboard, and its title had become more than a little apt. Its existence was his cross to bear.

Sitting in the kitchen of his vast country home, he poured himself another whiskey and switched on the wall-mounted television. Evening had not yet arrived, and the only programmes airing were a couple of convoluted quiz shows and a mock-court case with Judge Kettleby. Today, the gesticulating gavel-wielder heard a case about a stolen Xbox. Riveting stuff.

Rick slid off his stool and took his whiskey into the living room, where he ambled over to the sleek black piano in the corner. Despite the melancholic feelings playing always stirred in him, he never lost affection for his beloved parlour grand. He'd saved six long years for it back in the days before he'd acquired his fortune. The sense of achievement of finally making enough money to buy the beautiful instrument had made him cherish it even more. Now he could buy a piano worth twice as much, but it wouldn't mean half so much.

Sitting down at the piano, Rick placed his whiskey on the coaster already on the shiny black lid. His fingers began to play automatically.

House of the Rising Sun.

Closing his eyes, he slipped away and became a vessel through which the music flowed. It was impossible not to smile against the haunting onslaught of well-played piano music. It was that feeling of peace and calm that he felt as he caressed the keys that had first attracted him to the music industry. Life contained so much misery, so if he was going to devote his life to something, it would be this—creating beauty with his fingertips.

A bum note.

He lifted both hands away from the keys in horror. The uninvited C Major had been unmistakable. His ears did not lie.

The doorbell rang again.

He sighed.

He hadn't played a bum note after all—someone had pressed the doorbell in the midst of his playing.

He leapt up with a grunt. Unannounced visitors were not something he often received, thanks to the imposing iron gate that stood at the end of his long gravel driveway. He had no idea who would be calling on him now.

The security panel in the entrance hallway illuminated and the CCTV-controlled video feed had activated. The LCD monitor showed a man outside, dressed in a suit and tie, despite the balmy weather.

Rick activated the intercom and spoke into the microphone. "Who is it?"

The suited gentleman spotted the CCTV camera and waved. "Don't you recognise your own brother? That tiny bit of fame must have gone to your head."

Rick groaned. "Long time no see, Keith. Come on in." What the hell was his brother doing here?

He pressed the gate release and then went and unlocked the front door. He waited on the front step while a burgundy Range Rover crunched up his pebble driveway. It'd been an age since he and Keith had seen each other, so this unexpected visit was rather...unexpected.

The Range Rover pulled up next to Rick's imported Mustang in front of the property's detached double garage where Keith switched off the engine and got out. He looked smug and proud for no reason, but that was ordinary for him. "Hello, brother," he said.

"Nice motor," said Rick. "I remember you always wanted a Range."

"Best thing England ever made. Got her last year after a particularly lucrative month." He patted the bonnet lovingly then shot a thumb at Rick's sky-blue 2009 Mustang. "I don't know how you can drive that foreign abomination."

"Seemed a good purchase at the time." Truth was, Rick had never been much of a car fanatic and only got the American import because it felt like something rich people did. For the amount he drove it, it'd been a waste of money, but it was nice to look at and roared like a dragon on the highways.

Keith didn't wait to be invited. He stepped through the doorway into the entrance hall where he glanced around nosily. "Place is a little big for just you, isn't it?"

Rick glanced at his property and considered the truth of it. The Edwardian mansion, with its rough stone floors and gnarled mahogany beams, was perhaps a trifle grand for a single, essentially unemployed man, but it was also the only thing that reminded him of the success he'd once been. Win or lose, he'd made enough money to live in a massive house like this. He shrugged. "I like it here. Doesn't feel so big after a while."

Keith nodded, but said nothing.

They both went into the living room, which was modern compared to the rest of the lower floor which still retained its Edwardian charms. They gave each other an awkward hug.

"It's good to see you, Keith. Take a seat, I'll get you a drink."

"Nothing for me, thanks. Marcy and I don't much touch alcohol these days."

"Really? Good on you both." Despite his brother's refusal, Rick went and retrieved his whiskey from the piano and gulped it down, then poured himself a fresh measure from the bottle in the kitchen. Back in the living room, he found Keith spread out on the couch like it was his own.

Rick perched on the other couch. "So, you really don't drink?"

"Well, you know how it is. We don't want to raise Maxwell thinking that booze is an ordinary part of life."

"You mean like dad raised us?"

"Oh, come on, Rick. Dad was never as horrid as you make him out."

"You'd gone to university by the time he was really bad. I was thirteen. I'm the one who got to see the bastard he turned into— I'm the one who got to watch him knock mum about."

Keith sighed. "Mum and dad's marriage was nothing to do with us."

"Anyway," Rick changed the subject, "how is Maxwell? He must be—what?—four by now?"

"Four in October. He'll be starting school soon, though I think he's ready now. He's so smart, Rick. I tell you, he'll be Prime Minister one day."

"Must take after you. You've always been driven."

Keith looked smug, and Rick chided himself for kneading his brother's ego. Rick could be King of the Universe and Keith wouldn't give him the slightest congratulation, so why was he throwing his brother a bone? Rick still remembered the look of devastation on Keith's face when he'd signed his record deal. No happiness, no pride in his younger brother's accomplishments— just resentment and anger. Rick became the rich and successful brother, and Keith detested it. When it'd all inevitably gone down the pan, Keith's transparent glee almost ended their relationship. Perhaps it should have, but Rick had allowed himself to fall back into the old routine— Keith turning up his nose at everything he did, and him trying to act like he didn't notice.

"So, why are you here, Keith? I haven't seen you in over a year—since Tabitha got married."

"Tabby's already divorced. I could have told you it was on the cards the moment they said their vows. He was a carpenter."

Rick frowned. "So?"

"Just saying. Chap didn't have much going on. Tabby wanted more."

"She told you that, did she?"

Keith shrugged. "It was obvious."

"So why are you here?" Rick demanded. "Not to talk about our cousin's divorce, I'm sure."

"Can't I just drop by to see my little brother? I wanted to check in on you, make sure you hadn't hanged yourself in this big empty mansion."

"Why would I hang myself?"

"Because... Well, you know."

"What? Because I lost my record deal and haven't been able to get another one? Or because they make funny videos on the Internet about how cheesy my one and only hit song was. Rick Astley called me the other day and thanked me for replacing him. Should I just hang myself?"

"I never said that."

Rick knocked back his whiskey and went to get another one.

"Maybe I'll kill myself when my money runs out. Fortunately, I made a shitload of it, so that will probably never happen. Least I'm a stinking rich failure, huh?"

"Rick, come on..."

Rick stormed off into the kitchen. Once he'd poured himself a fresh drink, he placed his elbows on the counter and held his head in his hands. If Keith thought he was depressed, it was because he damn well was. Suicide, though, had never crossed his mind. As much as he hated the sour turn his life had taken, he had made it once. He'd been top of the charts and saw his face printed on the cover of Rolling Stone Magazine. Most musicians only dreamt of getting a shot like he had, and whether it had lasted or not, Rick had been lucky. For that reason alone, he was proud. It was just difficult finding self-respect when you were a one-hit wonder. If a man made a fortune by selling a business and retiring at thirty, he was forever successful, but if a musician got rich off one song and then hung up his guitar, he was a joke—his short career became a punchline. People enjoyed watching celebrities fall—it was modern blood sport—and while Rick had been a celebrity for all of five minutes, he had fallen hard.

"...grizzly scene discovered just outside the Devonshire village of Crapstone."

Keith walked into the kitchen. "Hey, Rick, I'm sorry if I upset you."

"Quiet a second. They're talking about something that's happened in Crapstone. That's only a few miles from here."

Keith pulled up a stool next to Rick, and they both watched the television while the news report continued. There was a female reporter standing at the base of a grassy hill surrounded by police tape. Several men and women in latex gloves hurried around, working on something out of sight.

"Atop this small hill, the body of pensioner, Elizabeth Creasy—a retired local businesswoman—was found dead; her eyes badly mutilated in what police are suspecting was a premeditated and personal attack."

Rick scrunched up his face. "Poor lady."

"She must have annoyed the wrong person," said Keith. "Most bizarre," the reporter continued, "is the presence of

a bizarre object found beside the crime scene. A smooth black stone was discovered right next to Mrs Creasy's body, but all attempts so far to collect it have failed. In fact, several attempts to interact with the stone have resulted in further casualties as two police officers, first to arrive at the scene, both suffered fatal injury shortly upon touching the object in question. A team of geologists from the University of Exeter are now examining the stone, but their initial studies are yet to provide any insight into its nature. Police are hesitant to draw any conclusions, but this has been a strange and brutal attack in one of the country's most idyllic locations. I'm Kimberly Wilkins, back to the studio."

Rick pulled a face. "Horrible."

Keith shrugged.

"Somebody mutilated her eyes, Keith. I don't know how a

person can..." He sighed and took a nip of whiskey. "And that stone they were talking about... They said they couldn't collect it. What does that even mean?"

"That it's heavy. Who cares?"

Rick wasn't sure why he cared. Perhaps it was because he often felt so isolated and vulnerable here on his own. He sometimes lay in bed at night hearing noises and worrying about robbers creeping around downstairs. That might be why the thought of an old lady being mutilated and murdered just miles away from his home was more than a little unnerving. "I just find the whole thing sad," he said. "Why would someone do that to a pensioner?"

Keith chuckled. "You always think too much, Rick. I remember when our dog, Cassie, died. You cried in your room for a week. You were such a funny child."

Rick topped up his whiskey and exhaled into his glass, then took another long swig. He clonked the empty glass down on the counter and took a moment to study his older brother—a slightly plumper, slightly balder version of himself. His previously jet-black hair had lightened towards grey and his nose seemed bigger. "What do you want, Keith? Will you tell me why you're here? I know it's not because you missed me."

Keith rubbed a hand against his stubbled chin. It was unlike him not to be clean-shaven. "Maybe I should have that drink after all, Rick. I'll have whatever you're having."

Rick poured his brother a whiskey in a fresh glass and slid it towards him. "Why are you here for God's sake? Will you just tell me?"

Keith wrapped his fingers around the whiskey glass and stared down at the oak-coloured contents. "Because I have no place else to go. I need to stay here tonight, Rick. Maybe for a while."

Rick closed his eyes. He could not have got a worse answer.

~MINA MAGAR~

OXFORD STREET, LONDON

"COME ON, MINA," SHOUTED DAVID. "We need to get there before the others. There won't be room to swing your elbows soon, and I need those shots."

Mina kept a firm grip on her camera and fought to keep up. She was fifteen years younger than David, but when there was a story to be had, the man could move like the wind. His yellow hair flowed behind him like a thoroughbred's mane, and he slipped through the crowd like water through a sieve. All Mina caught were brief flashes of his Argyle socks. She, meanwhile, bumped into people almost every step, and received more than a few dirty looks. She couldn't help but apologise profusely.

Even on a slow day, Oxford Street was one of the busiest spots in London, and today people were teeming through it like ants. They packed together in small groups, lining the road on both sides. The police were massively outnumbered and struggled to maintain order. The large gathering lacked the festive spirit of, say, a Royal Wedding, and instead held an atmosphere more akin to a kindling riot. People had a look of mischief about them, and several lampposts were skewed as people hung off them like chimps.

David shouted again. "Come on, Mina. I can see those buggers from The Chronicle already there. We can't let them hog the headlines."

Mina fiddled with her camera while trying to run. She wanted to have the settings ready for when she started snapping. Her pictures would be used in the Slough Echo, but if she produced something noteworthy, it might spread to bigger outlets, or even go viral. Maybe if she achieved that her father would finally see she was good at her job, and stop telling her to quit all the time.

Not looking where she was going, Mina collided with the square back of a man. The shaved head turned around and glared at her. "Watch where you're fuckin' goin', luv."

Mina backed up. "Sorry, I'm so sorry."

When she heard the man mutter the words, 'Fucking Paki,' she was stunned. How dare he! She wasn't even from Pakistan. How could people be so hateful?

"Come on," David shouted for the third time. "Get moving."

Mina wanted to say something back to the snarling racist, but instead she ended up smiling nervously and moving on. Much as she would've liked to confront him, she wasn't that person. Even the thought made her stomach churn. So she put the experience behind her and focused on her job.

"I'm right behind you, David," she shouted as she dodged around a woman with a pram loaded with shopping bags instead of a child. Up ahead, the historic Selfridges building loomed unhappily. Its sleek interior was devoid of shoppers, and the bus shelter out front had been smashed and twisted by enthusiastic oglers trying to climb it.

David pointed ahead, still dodging through the crowd with fluid ease. "We need to hurry, come on. We can't afford to miss anything."

"I'm right behind you," she shouted, even though she was six steps back. They were heading for the Soho Street intersection on the east end of Oxford Street, but they had been forced to get off the tube at Bond Street as Oxford Circus and Tottenham Court Road were closed. It was a long walk on a normal day, but today was a nightmare. It was like squeezing through a corridor of hot, sweaty people, and when she saw Newman Street coming up on her left, she let out a moan of joy. They were only one street away.

"There! I see it," David shouted.

Mina caught up to him and saw it too. They had arrived at a police cordon outside McDonald's. A dozen scientists milled around inside the tape as if they hadn't even noticed the thousand-strong mob surrounding them. They were focused on the strange black stone, curiosity at the forefront of their minds. Mina was fixated on it too, surprised at how unremarkable it was.

Since the first stone had been discovered last night in the village of Crapstone, hundreds more had materialised. Business began as usual that morning in the City of London, but it soon became evident that something strange was afoot. At seven-thirty, a double decker bus had struck a bowling ball-sized stone in the centre of Oxford Street and broken its axle. The driver got out to investigate, and died of a massive and explosive heart attack a second after touching it.

News circulated rapidly after that—panic spreading thick and fast. Identical stones appeared all over the United Kingdom, from Inverness to Plymouth to Norwich to Hull, and Glasgow too. Wales had identified more than a dozen within its borders. Word spread that anyone who touched the stones would immediately die of a heart attack, and that had been the nugget of news to set the nation on edge.

The stones were a threat.

Public alerts were issued: Do not approach the stones and report any discoveries immediately. A hotline was set up too, plastered at the bottom of every news report. New discoveries came in every minute.

The stones were everywhere.

"It's just a rock." Mina heard the disappointment in her voice as she spoke. "I was expecting something more... I don't know. It's just a rock."

A leathery-skinned old woman grabbed Mina's arm, madness in her rheumy eyes, and barked at her. "It's aliens. They've sent 'undreds of meteorites to Earth to colonise us. That stone is gunna crack open like a coconut and spill its load into the atmosphere, you mark me words. We're all dead!"

Mina yanked her arm away and rubbed the finger marks left on her skin. She clung to David, but he paid her no attention, focused only on making it past the police cordon. Mina covered her mouth in shock when she saw him knee a child out of his way. The little boy fell to his knees, got up, then went crying to his mummy, arms outstretched and begging to be picked up.

"David, you just hurt a child."

"The brat shouldn't have been in the way. Ah, here we are, finally."

They made it over to a burly police sergeant with a clipboard in his hands. He was grinding his teeth and taking slow, deep breaths. His wide eyes examined David and Mina with suspicion. "Stand back, please."

"We're with the Slough Echo," David snapped.

The sergeant ran a finger down his clipboard and nodded. "Okay, step inside the cordon, but don't go within six feet of the object."

David swooped beneath the police tape without another word. Mina took a moment to thank the sergeant before doing the same.

The black stone sat in the middle of the road.

Mina's tummy churned. It wasn't hunger—she'd grabbed a hotdog less than an hour ago—it was something else. The mysterious object, just ten feet away from her, had killed people.

It was dangerous. She'd been so intent on getting to Oxford Street, that she'd not stopped to consider the peril she was placing herself in. Had the stone been tested for radioactivity, toxicity? Was she in danger just by being close to it? The dozen scientists surrounding the thing did little to assuage her fears.

A tug at her arm pulled her away from her fears. It was David. "Get snapping, girl."

"Yes, right." Mina raised her camera and started snapping away, altering and fine-tuning her settings as she went. It was difficult to know how the best photograph would look until she examined the digital reel on her laptop, so she followed the photojournalist's credo and just kept on snapping. The more pictures she took, the better the chances of getting something valuable. Different angles, different settings, different lenses, but just keep snapping.

David interviewed the police officers, scribbling away furiously on his notepad while they spoke. Usually he would use a tape recorder, but police officers were notoriously shy around recording equipment, and they gave much more away when faced with a simple pencil and pad.

While Mina tried to do her job, a pushy photographer from The Chronicle fought with her for the best angles, hustling her out of the way so often that it almost felt malicious. Mina knew she should hustle the older woman right back, but it wasn't something she was used to. The other woman carried herself with such confidence and authority that it was hard to resist her. The police officers all smiled and chatted with her, while they had only disapproving glances for Mina. She started to wonder if she would ever find her feet in this job.

Satisfied that she had got as much as she was going to get, Mina placed her spare lenses back into her hip bag and let her camera hang around her neck. Now that she no longer stared through a viewfinder, the black stone in the centre of the cordon seemed to be alive—less a detached photographic subject, and more an imposing presence that demanded attention. From six feet away, she could see that the surface of it was not jet black, but streaked with delicate grey veins. She wondered what it would feel like if she touched. It could kill her, she knew that, so why was she so eager to approach it? It was that same feeling she got whenever she stood on a high balcony and peered over the edge. That same voice in her head that always dared her to jump: Just do it!

A batch of shouting broke out behind Mina and made her turn around. The burly sergeant who stood outside the cordon had dropped his clipboard and had begun fighting with a lad in a red hoodie. A skinny girl batted the sergeant with both fists, yelling at him to leave her boyfriend alone. The profanity she used was impressive.

The sergeant applied a headlock, yanking the lad around. "I told you to bloody get back."

The lad twisted and squirmed, trying to break free. "You have no right, pig! People deserve to know what's happening!"

The sergeant released the lad's neck and shoved him backwards. "Move away or I'll bleedin' place you under arrest."

"Fuck you, pig," the girlfriend shouted. "Go suck a dick," said the lad.

"Okay, that's it." The sergeant reached to his belt and pulled out a canister of CS gas. He pressed the nozzle and gave the young man a full dose in the face that sent him stumbling backwards, coughing and spluttering. The lad's girlfriend screeched like a tomcat and pounced on the sergeant with her claws out. The sergeant restrained her easily with his meaty arm, and let her have a dose of the CS gas too. She fell to the floor weeping and scratching at her eyes.

The crowd ignited in anger. Hundreds of yelling voices merged into one, singular accusatory howl.

"Nazi!" somebody shouted.

"Fuckin' pig," came another.

The sergeant was on his radio, calling for backup, but

before he got a call through, somebody threw a milkshake that exploded against his chest and covered him in pink mess. His face grew red with fury, and he started throwing punches at whoever was near. The lad in the red hoodie was pulled back by the paternal crowd, which then surged forward as a single, massive organism. Mina winced as she saw the same snarling racist who had called her Paki punch the sergeant in the face. The loud crack was like a cricket ball hitting a bat, but the stunned police officer remained on his feet and continued swinging his fists madly.

But it was a battle lost before it'd already begun.

The crowd dragged the sergeant to the ground, and the racist thug kicked his head like a football. Somebody else stamped on his testicles. Mina was glad the sergeant was unconscious through most of it. She was also glad that she had not confronted the racist. That could have been her head being kicked like a football.

The two police officers within the cordon raced to their colleague's aid, but could not get near. The crowd was a pack of lions guarding its prey until it was well and truly dead.

"We need to go," said David, clutching Mina's arm.

"We need to help."

"No! We need to get out of here before they do the same to us."

Mina shook her head. "Why would they attack us?" "Because we're on this side of the cordon. Now come on."

Mina allowed herself to be dragged, but found herself unable to take her eyes off the black stone. She got the feeling it was staring right back at her.

Police cars raced down Oxford Street, sirens blaring, but they had to stop when they encountered the thick mass of bodies. Within seconds, the squad cars tilted and rocked as people laid siege to the trapped officers. The windscreens cracked as people climbed up on the bonnets and, within seconds, the police cars had disappeared in a sea of bodies.

"This is insane," said Mina. "They're acting like animals."

"Just keep moving, and don't make eye-contact. Things are about to get nasty."

"They're already nasty."

David grabbed her arm again and pulled her close. "People are afraid, Mina. And when people are afraid, their inner cavemen come out. There's no rationality in a man when he panics. Just keep your head down and don't stop moving."

Mina dodged around an old woman who had fallen in the road. She wanted to stop and help her, but the crowd was a living thing, and swallowed the pensioner up before there was any chance to offer help. David dragged Mina beneath the awning of French Connection to catch a breath.

"What do we do, David?"

"We wait for the first gap in the crowd and then get the hell out of this city."

"David, there are hundreds of those stones. What if this is happening everywhere?"

"There are thousands of them," he corrected her. "You were there when Carol got the report. Thousands of them all over the world. I don't think I understood the chaos they would cause until now. Hundreds of years ago, people's superstitions kept them in line. Now, in the age of science, people don't tolerate things they can't understand. Until someone makes sense of these stones, things are going to get ghastly."

Mina swallowed. "I'm afraid, David."

"So am I, but there'll be time to be afraid later. We need to get out of here."

"And then what?"

"We give the public the news, and hope they don't riot."

~TONY CROSS~
IRAQ-SYRIA BORDER

THE PATCH OF SCRUB DESERT AT THE IRAQ-Syria border was the worst hell British Army Staff Sergeant Tony Cross had ever visited—and he'd visited many. The air was so arid that it seemed to dry you out from within, and every breath was like swallowing sand.

And there was the isolation.

Nothing but sand, rubble, and rocks for a hundred miles in every direction. The nearest town was Rutba, but the people there were as frightened of British soldiers as they were of the fanatical members of the ISN—Islamic State Nationalists. They feared the West because they might be accused of being in league with terrorists, and they feared the ISN because they might be accused of being in league with the West. The ordinary people of Iraq were perpetual victims of religion and money, and neither served them well. Tony felt sorry for them in the same way he felt sorry for cows in the field—they didn't realise how much their lives were not their own.

Lieutenant Ellis stood with his hands on his hips and stated the obvious, "Looks like this fence has been tampered with."

The gap in the border fence was twenty metres wide, and either end of it had been rolled aside so neatly that they resembled a pair of decorative pillars. Sabotage—but from which side?

"What are you thinking, Staff Sergeant?" Lieutenant Ellis asked Tony, no doubt noticing his dubious expression.

"How far away is the border crossing? Two miles? Three? The only way the Iraqi Guard didn't notice a giant hole in their fence is because they're either useless, or they're letting the ISN stroll right on through."

Ellis stiffened. "We can make no such assumptions. The Iraq national forces were trained by our soldiers. They know what is at stake."

"Do they? To me their choice is pretty simple. Side with a group of men with the same religion and colour skin as them, or with a bunch of rich, white westerners with avarice behind their smiles."

Ellis strolled up to Tony and lifted his chin in a way the pompous git probably thought was authoritative. "Now look here, Staff Sergeant, I will not have you criticising our operations here. You have made it quite clear your feelings on our duties in this part of the world—and since I have served nowhere near as long as you have I will reserve my judgement—but please keep your disenfranchisement to yourself. The men need not hear it. We are here to do a job, so leave the moral quandaries to the politicians."

"That's the last bunch of crooks I'd leave it to."

Ellis placed his hands on his hips. "Am I understood, Staff Sergeant?"

"Perfectly, sir."

"Good. We can be fairly certain that this is the ingress point from Syria into Iraq, so our mission is as planned. We set up here, and ambush the next group that tries to come through."

"I don't think that's necessarily the best course of action, sir."

"Oh? Why not?"

Tony told him, "The first set of rebels we fall upon might be a bunch of wet-eared kids. We should hold off until we identify a high value target."

"And allow members of ISN to funnel through in the meantime? No, I'm afraid not. We are here to shut down this security breach for the Iraqi government and that is what we will do. We engage the first border-jumpers we see, and then get this fence repaired."

Tony didn't waste time arguing. This twenty-six year old, fresh out of Sandford Academy thought he knew everything and wouldn't bend from what he thought best. He wasn't the first arrogant little twerp to give Tony orders, and it was just part of the job. In the older days of war, Ellis might have got a bullet in the back, but those times were over. As they were carrying out a pretty low-risk mission in a conflict they were not officially involved in, Tony's only concern was keeping the lads from doing mischief. Ellis could play the simpering peacock as much as he wanted.

Tony snapped off a half-arsed salute. "I'll get the men dug in just behind that hill, sir. It'll keep us well hidden until the time is right."

"Excellent! See to it, Staff Sergeant."

Tony marched away, leaving the Lieutenant to stand with his hands glued to his hips. The young officer's expression made it look like he was planning a campaign to rival D-Day, but the truth was that there was probably very little going on inside his skull. With all the British Army's great progress into the modern fighting force it was today, it was still top- heavy with entitled idiots from 'military families' and well- bred fools looking for a jolly old jaunt in the forces. The real leaders of the Army were the sergeants like him.

Tony flagged down one of his corporals, a young Scouser named Green. Like his name suggested, he was a little inexperienced, but he was also bright and eager—which counted for a lot out here in the wastelands.

"Yes, Staff Cross? Do you have orders?"

"Get four men and dig a defensive trench on the rear of that hill." He pointed to the gentle slope that formed a moderate peak. "We'll dig in with a lookout position at the top. We'll see any border jumpers long before they see us. Have Corporal Rose help you."

"Right away, Staff Cross." Green marched away at the double, gathering men as he went.

There were fifteen of them assembled at the border, split off from a platoon of two hundred stationed at a temporary camp fifty miles way. Britain had decided not to take direct action in the Syrian conflict, or commit itself to any land wars, but it had compromised upon a small reactionary force to operate within 'friendly' Iraq. Any border jumpers could be dealt with as criminals, rather than terrorists, and that made things less politically precarious. After the decade-long nightmare of Al Qaeda, Britain did not want to draw the ire of another extremist group. It might have held an obligation to keep Iraq free of dangerous individuals, but it held no such responsibilities to Syria. Damascus could burn for all Westminster cared, so long as it was down to Syria's people or Syria's government. Tony didn't particularly disagree. How could the Arab nations ever hope to evolve and pull themselves up out of the dirt if the West interfered every time a government was threatened? There would be no United States if some disenfranchised Brits hadn't stuck their fingers up to the Crown. There would be no democracy in Britain if not for Cromwell and his armed uprising. People needed to overthrow governments and take control of their own destinies. The rest of the world should stand back and let them. The Arab Spring movement was the Middle East's first step towards positive change. Worst thing to do now would be to try and manipulate things from Washington, London, and Brussels.

Not that Tony held any respect for the ISN. Like all fanatics, they were monsters hiding behind ideals and traditions—they deserved whatever they got—but it was for the Arab world to deal with them. Only through their own trials and triumphs would the people of the Middle East gain the confidence needed to unite against extremism and join the rest of the world on equal footing.

While Private Green carried out his orders, Tony took a trek up the hill to double-check that it was indeed a suitable location to stage an ambush. The elevation alone should give them the better end of a firefight, but it never hurt to know the terrain. For instance, as he strode up the gentle incline now, he noticed that the ground underfoot was loose. It would become tough to see if a sudden gust swept dirt up into the air. The last thing the men needed during a battle was a face full of sand. It might be worth building a windbreaker out of any larger rocks they could find.

So Tony set about looking for those rocks. There were numerous fist-sized boulders, but few that were large enough to provide cover. The unit had brought jeeps with them— hidden nearby under sandy tarps about half-a-mile back—so it was possible to make a quick reccy to see what lay in the surrounding area, but before he had properly considered doing that, he spotted a large stone up ahead. A jet-black boulder, completely out of place amongst the browns and greys of the desert.

In fact, it looked very much like it had been placed there.

Tony squinted and muttered to himself, "What the hell is that thing?"

"Incoming," came a squawk through the radio.

Tony dropped onto one knee and swung his rifle up and around. Private Harris, a large brute of a man and the group's lookout, pointed toward the Syrian border. Lieutenant Ellis rushed to the bottom of the hill and signalled the men to gather up, but as Tony was on higher ground, he stayed right where he was. Ellis realised that his Staff Sergeant was in a better position and instead rallied the men to Tony's location.

"Who's coming? How many? And which direction?" Tony asked Private Harris before Ellis had time to interject.

"Vehicles—I counted four. Three cars, one van." "Dear Lord," said Ellis. "That's quite the convoy." Tony faced his commanding officer with urgency. "We

should get the men behind the hill and call it in to Command."

"Yes, of course. Everybody, form a firing line behind the hill and await my orders."

When the Lieutenant did nothing else, Tony frowned at him. "Are you going to call Command, sir?"

"No, it's unnecessary until we know what we're up against."

"When we know what we're up against it'll be too late."

"Nonsense. I don't want to put a call through to Command without good reason."

"There could be twenty armed men in that convoy."

"Pah, twenty rebels against fifteen British soldiers. In an ambush no less."

Tony gritted his teeth. He knew the Lieutenant wanted to call Command after successfully taking out a rebel unit so that he looked like a competent leader with initiative, instead of an officer who called everything in to get orders from above on how to proceed. "Fine," Tony relented. "Let's just be ready."

The men scurried behind the hill and bedded down, spreading themselves out six feet apart and forming a well- spaced firing line. Closer to the top of the hill, Tony peeked over the crest to see what they were up against. It was bad.

Four cars and a van—not three as Private Harris had reported. If the vehicles were full of rebels, there would be a serious firefight. The ambush would have to be executed flawlessly, because if it became a protracted affair, there would be casualties on both sides. Tony got on his radio, quickest way to speak to all fourteen men at once. "Everybody keep their 'eds down 'til either me or the Lieutenant give the word. When the shit hits the fan, we drop grenades on those vehicles and pin 'em down with gunfire. Hit 'em quick and hard enough and they'll drop their weapons and surrender. Radio silence until then. Over."

Tony remained at the top of the hill, pulling out his binocs and assessing the situation that was racing across the desert towards them. AK47 barrels protruded from the car windows like spines of a porcupine. The convoy was headed right for the breach in the fence, which meant they knew it was there. ISN rebels.

Ellis crawled up the hill and rested beside Tony. "You shouldn't have ordered radio silence until I had spoken. I may have had something to add."

Tony knew Ellis had nothing to add, but he nodded and gave an apology. "Just trying to do my best for you, sir. I've identified five vehicles; passengers armed to the bleedin' teeth. We need to be ready."

"We are ready," said Ellis. "My men are ready for anything."

"Let's hope our grenades hit the target. It'll improve the odds."

"Don't you feel that's a little excessive, Staff Sergeant? We don't know who is in those vehicles. There could be civilians. Would it not be better to be a tad more precise?"

Tony blinked at his superior. "They're illegally crossing the border and bearing arms. Our mandate is clear, sir. We take 'em out, and any civilians stupid enough to be in the middle only 'ave themselves to blame."

Ellis sighed. "Poor fellows aren't going to know what hit them. Fall back, Staff Sergeant, lest they spot you."

Tony nodded, then shimmied down the hill on his belly until he was a part of the firing line. If all went to plan, the men would rise up like something out of Braveheart and reduce the enemy in seconds. Tony had faith that the lads would be ready to act, but he was yet to witness any of them under fire. You could never tell how good a soldier was until somebody tried to kill him. If this didn't go fast, it would get bloody.

The convoy was still half a mile away. Nothing to do but wait. Tony tried to ignore the churning in his belly he still got before a fight. Even after fifteen years in the Army, you never stopped being afraid of death. Even suicides changed their minds in those final seconds before death. They all begged for a second chance as they dangled by their necks. Every soldier worried a bullet would find them without them even knowing it, and all of them begged for their mothers if they ever got hit. Tony had held the hands of more dying men than he cared to remember.

Movement in the corner of his eye.

Tony flinched and hoped he wasn't about to spot a sneaky rebel coming up on his flank—but all was well. It hadn't been movement he'd seen, but a flash of light. The strange black stone he'd spotted earlier seemed to be glowing. Its smooth surface danced with delicate sparks of light, like the static on an old-fashioned television. There was a crackling sound too. But Tony was a soldier, not a geologist, and his only focus was the enemy speeding towards him. Whatever the strange stone was, it would have to wait.

The din of sand-clogged engines arrived, and the British soldiers behind the hill became visibly on edge. Tony saw the tension in each of their eyes and knew exactly how they felt. For a man, controlling his adrenaline was an arduous task, and perhaps a soldier's biggest skill, and to run into danger instead of away from it was against every basic human instinct. It took training and courage to overcome the urge to flee.

Giving the word would be difficult, for Tony would have to rely on his ears instead of his eyes. He'd have to gauge when the enemy convoy was within range purely from what he could hear. Too soon or too late and things could go very wrong.

The engine noises grew louder.

Tony gave a hand signal to the men. Wait.

Grenades slipped from link straps. Safeties went off L85 combat rifles. All done in silence.

The men were ready.

Tony kept his hand where it was. Keep holding.

The engine noise rose in pitch.

The convoy was close.

Almost time. Almost...

"Engage!"

Tony flinched. His hand was still in the air, signalling for everyone to remain holding, but the men leapt out of cover and raced up the hill.

Ellis had his rifle pointed and was bellowing at his men like a lion. "Engage, engage, engage."

"You fool," cursed Tony, as he shouldered his rifle and ran up the hill. None of them could be sure what they would find there until they reached the top.

When Tony got there, he saw it was bad.

The convoy was still fifty metres away. The flat, hard ground of the desert had carried the engine noise and made the vehicles sound closer. If the men had waited just another five-seconds, the enemy would have been close enough to engage, but now, Tony realised in horror, they were screwed.

A volley of British Army grenades took flight, arced through the sky, plummeted back towards the ground.

Multiple explosions shook the air and kicked a cloud of dirt up off the desert floor. Nobody could see or hear anything. Confusion reigned.

Then the enemy convoy screeched to a halt just outside the border fence. Their vehicles were unharmed—the British grenades had missed them—and armed ISN soldiers spilled out into the desert, surprised, but in no way deterred. They used their car doors as cover and opened fire upon the hill. Private Green went down in a red mist as a bullet took off the top of his head. Two more privates and a corporal went down right next to him. Four men dead in a single second.

Tony zeroed in on the nearest car in the convoy—a banged up Toyota Corolla—and pulled his trigger. The first burst ricocheted and sent sparks off the bonnet, but the next round hit an ISN soldier in the throat and sent him cartwheeling to the ground.

The dirt kicked up two feet in front of Tony, making him turn and leap for cover, ducking down behind the hill. By that time, Lieutenant Ellis had already fallen back, and so had all the other men with half a brain.

"Our grenades fell short." Ellis stated.

"No shit!" Tony growled. "Why did you give the order?" "Because I felt it right."

"Well, it was sodding wrong."

Ellis cleared his throat. "We need to focus on our next move now, Staff Sergeant, not the past."

"I agree. We need to flank 'em. They have too much cover to keep trading shots back and forth like this. It'll degenerate into a case of who has the most ammunition, and we don't know what they've in the back of that van."

Ellis flinched as a bullet whizzed past his head, but he stayed calm and kept talking. "Okay, I concur. I'll split the men into two."

"No, we don't split up. Our only cover is here and that's where the unit needs to stay. I just need two men."

"You're going yourself?"

"Damn right I am. The men acted on a bad order and that's our fault."

The corners of the Lieutenant's mouth crinkled, and he looked offended at the implication, but he settled on a guilty look and nodded. "Take any two men you want, Anthony."

Tony chose the two men nearest, for it didn't matter whom. There were no heroes in the unit yet, just a dozen well-drilled kids. The two men he chose were Corporal Blake and Private 2nd Class Harris.

"We break south along the fence," Tony explained, "and try to get an angle on 'em. The fence will stop us from getting behind their cover, but if we can get at their flank, we can take 'em out while the rest of the unit suppresses 'em from the front. You be careful, Harris, you're big bloody target."

Both men nodded, a mixture of excitement and knicker-wetting fear on their faces.

"On my command. Ready...

"... Go!"

The three British soldiers raced down the hill, heads down and zigzagging. Tony was a decade older than Corporal Blake and Private Harris, which led to him falling back a pace, but he could still move at a decent clip—even at thirty-four. Gunfire bit the dirt around his feet, but he kept on going, outrunning his death by a factor of centimetres.

The border fence was just ahead. Corporal Blake was almost there, Harris right behind him.

Something caught Tony's attention, making him stop. The strange black stone came up on his left and had begun glowing brightly. His focus and urgency dripped away. He strolled towards it even as gunfire cracked from every direction. He was uninterested in anything other than the curious black stone. It seemed to call to him. The light coming out of it spread and started to form a border around a translucent layer that reminded Tony of the suds in the centre of a child's bubble blower. Something inside that translucent layer moved—something that seemed to stare right back at Tony as he approached it.

It's beautiful.

Before Tony could figure out what was happening, a bullet hit him in the back and dropped him to the ground.

Suddenly the bright light above the stone was replaced by darkness.

~SAMANTHA SMART~
CENTRAL PARK, NEW YORK CITY

S AMANTHA LOVED CENTRAL PARK IN THE summer. It was so alive. When people thought of New York City, they pictured skyscrapers, banks, and museums, but to Sam, Central Park was the real soul of the city. In the seventies, the park had been a dangerous place, like the city itself, but gradually, and in tandem, both the park and city had evolved. Now the Big Apple was one of the most welcoming places on Earth. A place where kosher delis sat alongside Italian pizzerias, Ethiopian restaurants, and LGBT bars. No racial underclasses here like there were in LA or San Antonio; New York was a place of acceptance. Gay or straight, black or white, it didn't matter in the Big Apple, which was why Samantha, a Lesbian from Utah, felt so at home. Sure, the hustle and bustle could give you a headache, and the traffic was pure torture, but that was why the park was so wonderful. Even in Manhattan, you could find tranquillity.

Today was different though. The park buzzed with excitement. Manhattan had gotten a new tourist attraction this morning.

The strange black stone had materialised outside the Central Park Carousel and killed three homeless people during the night. Now it was cordoned off, and mounted police officers trotted between the crowds, sharing what they knew and chatting with curious tourists. The stone was deadly, and no one could move it. A few hours ago, the City Council had attached a harness from a truck-mounted crane to the stone. The truck had tipped over before the stone had even shown the slightest hint of shifting. Three people had been crushed. In the last hour, the stone had started to glow.

The crowd grew anxious, but they would not disperse. In fact, the crowd only continued to grow. Thousands of people were now gathered in the park and business had ground to a halt as employees failed to return from their lunch breaks. Even Wall Street was deserted—and it usually took a bomb threat to drag those wolfs from their dens. Everybody wanted to be in the park.

New York was a city of togetherness, and people were gathering in mutual support of one another. This strange black stone had inserted itself into their city, and they would stand together until they understood exactly what it was. The citizens of New York were afraid, but they were consolidated.

An old man stood nearby. He smiled at Samantha as she slid from one gap in the crowd to another. "They're saying it came from space," he said.

"What, like a meteor or something?"

"Yeah, I don't buy it either. You looked tired, miss. Here, finish the rest of my coffee."

"No, that's..." She smiled, embarrassed, but took the cup anyway. "Are you sure you don't mind? I could actually kill for coffee right now."

"Sure, enjoy it. They give you such big cups nowadays that I can never finish."

Samantha sipped the hot beverage and sighed at the spreading warmth in her tummy. "Makes you wonder when they'll stop, doesn't it? One day we'll all be drinking from buckets."

The old man put his hands on his rotund belly and chuckled. With his white hair and wizened, grey eyes, he resembled Santa Claus.

"So, why are you so tired, miss?"

"I didn't realise I looked so bad. You can tell just by looking at me?"

"The bags under your eyes give you away. I used to work night shifts at a grain mill in Buffalo as a young man. I know tiredness when I see it."

"Wish I could say it was because I was hard at work all night, but it was irresponsible fun, I'm afraid."

"Partying with your boyfriend?" "Girlfriend."

The old man recoiled. "Oh, excuse me, I never..."

"No, it's okay. Sorry, I don't know why I felt the need to correct you."

The old man recovered and shrugged his shoulders. "Because I needed correcting, miss. Why should I assume that you have a boyfriend and not a girlfriend? I should have said partner. I'm afraid you'll have to forgive an old man for being old-fashioned."

Samantha grinned, again reminding herself how much she loved this city. If she'd told an old white guy in Utah she was gay, she might have been heckled in the street, but not by this old New Yorker. "You're forgiven." She smiled. "My name is Sam."

"Ha! Mine too. What a coincidence."

"No way! Your name is Samantha? How weird." She chuckled.

"You silly thing. No, my name is Samuel, but my friends call me Sam."

"This might become confusing."

"It just might be. Maybe we should go our separate ways, miss."

Samantha giggled. "Maybe. You staying to watch the glowing black stone from outer space?"

"It would feel wrong not to stay. It has a momentous feeling about it, don't you think? Like something is going to happen worth staying for. You heard identical stones are all over the country?"

Samantha nodded. "Yeah, but this one is ours. This is the New York black stone. I just hope it doesn't turn out to be anything bad."

Samuel patted her on the arm. "I have faith it won't be. All these people gathered... It must be for something good. I think we can all feel it. We're meant to be here. Something will happen soon, and things will make perfect sense. It'll be good, I know it. A gift from God."

A lifelong atheist, Samantha would usually object to such a claim, but the old man had accepted her for who she was, so she was certainly willing to accept him. "You might be right," she said. "Come on, Sam, let's go find somewhere to get a better look."

"Okay dokey, Sam. You lead the way." "Sure thing, Sam."

"Thank you, Sam."

"You're very welcome, Sam."

The old man chuckled. "You sure we shouldn't have gone our separate ways?"

"Too late now. Come on, Sam." "Okay, Sam."

* * *

They managed to find a spot next to an overcrowded hot dog vendor where Samantha bought them both a foot long. Samuel took his with onions and mustard, her without.

"Taste buds need a kick at my age," he explained. "Among other things."

Samantha rose on her tiptoes and tried to see over a large woman's shoulder. She couldn't see the black stone, but could see the light coming off of it, and that was what finally made her nervous. At the beginning, the stone had merely been peculiar, but now that it glowed, it seemed alive. Was it really from outer space?

"What can you see?" Samuel asked her.

"Not much. It's still glowing. I think..." She hopped up and down to get a better look. "I think the light is spreading out."

Samuel grinned. "It's happening. It's going to reveal its secrets."

The crowd hushed. Several thousand people stood in complete silence. The strange light was definitely spreading, the glowing loop becoming a frame within which a translucent layer shimmered. Sam could see right through it, but her view was distorted, like trying to read a letter underwater. Images flickered and danced inside the transparent layer, but she could make out nothing in detail.

"There's something inside," somebody in the crowd cried out.

"It's like looking through a lens," someone else added.

The bright archway continued to grow, rising twenty feet above the crowd. The translucent centre shimmered like the surface of a pond.

Samantha couldn't take her eyes away. "So beautiful."

"I see it!" Samuel shouted beside her. "Everything is about to change."

By now, the entire crowd was entranced; a thousand mouths hanging wide open, and twice as many eyes staring in amazement. The glowing archway continued to grow, towering over the nearby carousel. The translucent centre began to thicken and take form.

Samantha reached out for Samuel's hand and squeezed it. The miracle in front of her was starting to make sense. "I think... I think it's a gate."

A blinding explosion of light.

The crowd cried out in shock.

All hell broke loose.

The screaming started at the front of the crowd, nearest the cordoned off area with the stone. It was cries of fear at first, but evolved into cries of agony. Samantha stood too far back to see what was happening, but the crowd turned in on itself, people elbowing to get away.

"We need to get out of here." Samuel grabbed her arm.

Samantha shook her head in a daze. "What's happening? I can't see what's happening."

"Something came through," Samuel told her. "I was wrong. Whatever this is, it isn't good. It's not God."

The screaming continued; it never stopped for a single second.

Samantha glanced back. People flew into the air and crashed against the ground, arms breaking and mangled legs snapping. Something steamrolled the crowd—a charging rhino? Surely something explainable. Then a horrendous thing showed itself and put all hopeful notions of an escaped rhino aside.

A man, twenty feet tall and rippling with taught muscles, swiped at the fleeing crowd, breaking backs and caving in skulls with giant fists. He was naked save for a loose robe falling from his shoulder and around his waist. His bare back was pierced by spines of charred bones, and his face was a dark shadow of rage— yet flawlessly beautiful even in its ferocity.

Samantha watched in terror as the monstrous giant snatched up a police officer from his horse and tore him in two, like a Christmas cracker, his wet innards showering the crowd.

"We need to leave," repeated Samuel, grabbing her so hard on the bicep that she cried out in pain. She understood though. They needed to get away.

They took off towards the playing fields where the park opened up and bordered Central Park West. Maybe there they could get free of the mad panic and bloodshed. People were lying on the ground everywhere, trampled half to death by the fleeing crowd that was no longer united, but selfish and afraid. A young woman with two broken arms lay on her back sobbing, but no one stopped to help her. The crowd moved too fast for anybody to risk being a Good Samaritan.

As the two Sams entered the emerald grass of the playing fields, Samuel slipped and almost pulled Samantha down with him. He fell in a mess, but made it up again quickly. He tried to continue, but gritted his teeth and hissed.

"Samuel, are you okay?"

"My ankle's gone. I'm too old to be dashing around in blind panic."

Samantha reached out to help him, but it was just as a squad of teenage boys in football jerseys came ploughing along and barged right into them. Samantha hit the ground hard, cursing at the boys from on her back. "You fucking bastards!"

They'd ploughed into Samuel too. He lay on his back, moaning. Samantha dragged herself across the grass to him to check he was okay. The crowd continued its stampede, clattering feet dodging Samantha and Samuel only at the very last second. Soon somebody would not be paying attention and would crash right into them.

There was also the giant to worry about—currently stomping its way towards the playing fields.

"Samuel, get up. That thing is coming." "I can't," he whined. "My leg."

Samantha looked down at Samuel's leg and saw that his sprained ankle had developed into a broken shinbone. The glistening white shard poked out of his trousers and glistened with globs of blood.

"Those goddamn jocks."

Samuel sighed. "Don't blame them. They're just frightened. You go on, miss. Get out of here."

"I'm not leaving you, Samuel."

"You just met me. I'll forgive you."

"I wouldn't forgive myself."

"Better living with guilt than dying with honour, if you ask me."

Samantha glanced towards the edge of the playing fields. A group of police had assembled there and were discharging their weapons at the towering monster. The giant bent and swung a long arm, scooping them up as if they were matchsticks. The screaming police officers tumbled twenty feet in the air before gravity reclaimed them and smashed them against the ground. A dozen bullets had hit the giant, but it carried on without the slightest concern.

"Get out of here," Samuel grunted through his pain.

"I can't leave you."

"I can't let you die for me."

Samantha wished she'd met Samuel years ago. The instant connection they'd made was rare, but it was destined to go to waste. She shook her head, and fought back tears. "I'm sorry."

"I know you are, miss, but it's been lovely meeting you. Now get gone."

Samantha nodded, leapt up, and ran. She wanted to glance back at Samuel, but refused to allow herself. Nothing to be gained by a final look.

Police cars skidded in the grass up ahead, leaving long brown furrows in their wake. Officers leapt out either side in pairs, armed with shotguns and rifles. They wasted no time in heading straight towards the Beast of Manhattan.

The furthest reaches of the crowd had crossed the edge of the playing fields and were spilling into the busy thoroughfare of Central Park West. Traffic screeched to a halt as yellow taxis shunted into the backs of city buses, and unlucky pedestrians got caught in the middle, bleeding out as twisted metal pierced their vital organs. Horns honked so persistently that the individual sounds merged into one long, continuous blare. That seemed far away to Samantha, though, who was running across the playing fields. Her legs started to tire, and young men and thinner women overtook her on both sides. A helicopter zipped overhead, low enough to make the grass shimmer. The sound of machine gunfire arrived like something out of a Vietnam War movie. Samantha was still running as fast as she could when the hair on the back of her neck stood up.

She glanced back over her shoulder.

The Beast of Manhattan was right behind her.

The ground shook.

She was done for.

Something crashed into Samantha, cracking against her

skull and knocking her vision sideways. She hit the ground, and something crushed her. Her eyes remained open, but she saw nothing but darkness.

The Beast bellowed.

A stranger's hand covered her face as she lay there in the grass for several minutes, wondering why she wasn't dead. The stranger who had fallen on top of her did not move an inch. Was he okay?

Samantha slid the stranger's arm away from her face and tugged at their clothing until she found a belt. When she finally tugged the guy off of her, she managed to sit up. She gagged when she saw the caved-in face of a teenager lying beside her. The Beast must have struck him. His dead body falling on Samantha had saved her life.

The playing fields were quiet. Bodies littered the ground like confetti. The Beast had marched away into the city, where chaos was now visible. The epicentre seemed to be outside the Holy Trinity church, which had caught fire.

Samantha dragged herself to her feet, sobbing. The shock and utter bewilderment finally took a hold of her. The dead stranger's blood soaked her, and she tasted it on her lips. What the hell had happened? Why was New York always subjected to such horror? She'd been a child in Utah during 9/11, but she often imagined the terror in the city on that terrible day. Now she knew.

She almost fell back down to the blood soaked grass as her knees clashed together like cymbals. The smell of cordite assaulted the air, and from somewhere she heard the faint moans of the injured, but it was impossible to identify anybody alive in such a mess. So she took a walk in the park she loved, no longer pleasant and green, but grizzly and red.

It didn't take long to find Samuel. She'd left him at the edge of the playing field, and that was where he remained. It was unclear what had killed him, but his sagging chest spoke of badly broken ribs. A slight bruise on his temple might also have been the culprit.

"It was good meeting you, Samuel."

More moaning, but this time louder, and from many voices. Samantha glanced up and peered toward the carousel where the nightmare had started. The great glowing archway still hovered above the black stone with its shimmering, translucent centre. Whatever it was, and wherever it led to, it was still open.

Someone approached Samantha.

The hunched over man was hurt, his flesh singed and smoking. Flaps of blackened skin hung from his naked body and littered the floor behind him like gory breadcrumbs. His moans were desperate and pained—a walking embodiment of nerve-searing agony. Samantha hurried towards him, tears filling her eyes. "Oh God, I'll find you some help. Just...just sit down."

The burned man didn't accept her help. Instead, he snarled like an animal.

"It's okay. I want to help you. I-"

The injured man grabbed Samantha's throat with a crushing grip. "You should concentrate on helping yourself, whore." Samantha tried to wrench the hand away from her throat,

but her attacker was inhumanly strong. Every time she gained a grip, her fingers slid on loose chunks of burned flesh that sloughed away in her hands.

"Please," she begged.

"Your begging is a song the whole world will be singing. We bring unending torture and eternal slavery. Your cities will crumble, your children will weep blood and shit themselves in misery."

Samantha choked, the vice around her throat tightening. Her terrified eyes fell upon a legion of horrors.

An army of smouldering, blackened monsters marched across Central Park. A dozen at first, but then more and more. Soon there were hundreds. Burned monsters from some faraway, fiery pit.

Demons.

Samantha felt herself grow weaker. Her eyes bulged in their sockets as she kept on struggling, but it was no use.

Death beckoned, and she could not refuse its call. "Why?" Samantha managed to ask in her final moments. But she didn't live long enough to get an answer.

~GUY GRANGER~
LOWER BAY, NEW YORK

What the hell is happening over there, Captain?" Guy Granger's second-in-command, Lieutenant James Tosco, stared at him with piercing blue eyes.

Guy didn't have a clue what was happening. The view through his binoculars was difficult to make sense of. It was hard to see past Brooklyn from where the USCG Hatchet floated in the Lower Bay, but Manhattan was at the centre of something bad. The city was in panic. Fires had broken out everywhere, and the sound of chaos made it all the way across the Upper Bay. The Hatchet, a 263 foot U.S. Coast Guard cutter, had been approaching New York Harbour for routine maintenance when it had been halted by a state of emergency being declared. It appeared the terrorists had struck again.

This time there were no exploding planes or toppling buildings. The damage seemed smaller in scale, yet wider spread. The distance between individual fires stretched several blocks, and dozens of helicopters spiralled the skyline from Hell's Kitchen to Midtown East.

Tosco cleared his throat. "Captain?"

Guy lowered his binoculars. "I don't know what's happening, Lieutenant, but it's bad."

"Then we need to offer assistance."

"No. Command told us to hold firm, so we hold and await orders."

Tosco grunted. "The men are unsettled, Captain. Many have family working in the city. In the time it takes to wait for orders, people will die."

Guy said nothing, just examined his second-in-command carefully. Eventually, he said, in a voice that brooked no argument, "There are ten officers aboard this ship, Lieutenant, and sixty enlisted seamen. If you are suggesting we will have some kind of disruption on our hands, it would lead me to seriously doubt your credentials as my senior officer."

Tosco bristled, pointy ears twitching beneath the brim of his officer's cap. "Everything is under control, Captain. I just felt it my duty to inform you of the men's feelings."

"Noted, Lieutenant, but you're not running a union. You carry out my orders, not theirs. Go and perform a weapons check and put the crew on high alert. If we do get instructions to head into harbour, I want us to be ready."

"Aye, aye, Captain." Tosco snapped off a sloppy salute and stormed away.

Guy exhaled. His second-in-command was becoming a problem of late. Too ambitious and bull-headed to accept orders without complaint, James Tosco had reached a stage where he obviously felt he should be commanding his own boat. A strapping lad of thirty, smart and athletic, he certainly had the aptitude for command, but this was Guy's boat, and he did not tolerate insubordination, or a negative attitude from anyone. You let things slide once and you gave the go ahead to be undermined at every turn.

He would need to deal with Lieutenant Tosco.

Chief Petty Officer, and Guy's oldest friend, Frank Jacobs, gave him a sheepish grin that suggested he wanted to be of use. The man's chubby brown cheeks had sagged in old age and his once fuzzy black hair was now brittle and white. He looked older than usual, and worried.

"This isn't going to be a good day, is it, Captain?"

Guy placed his binoculars down on the desk and said, "I'm thinking not. We heard anything back from Command yet?"

"Nothing other than instructions to hold ready. They don't seem to understand what's going on either. Apparently, it has something to do with that strange black stone they found in Central Park this morning. It exploded or something."

"They say there are matching stones all over the country."

"All over the world," Frank corrected. "My aunt in Trinidad said there's one right in the middle of town, next to the laundrette."

"How is your aunt?"

"Eighty-eight and still growing her own strawberries. They're the most delicious things you ever tasted, Captain."

Guy grinned, then spoke more seriously, "What do you think is happening, Frank? Has New York been attacked again?"

"After 9/11, I don't see how any attack could succeed. Every inch of New York is covered by half-a-dozen security cameras. You only have to utter the word bomb and Homeland will turn up on your doorstep ready to water board you. Whatever this stone they found in the park is, I don't think it's the work of terrorists. I'm not sure if I feel better or worse about that."

Guy raised an eyebrow. "You're not one of those who believes it's aliens?"

"I don't know what I believe, just have a bad feeling, that's all. I'm an old man, Captain, and my waters tell me this will be a long day."

"Well, whatever happened is still going on. Is Tosco right, Frank? Should we be helping?"

"We do as we're commanded."

"Always?"

"Always."

Guy chuckled. "I've known you twenty years, Frank, and I don't think I've ever once seen you break a rule."

"I leave that to men like you. If you want to help, then help. Long as I follow your orders, I'm doing my job. It's for you to worry about what Command will think."

Guy looked back through his binoculars and was certain that the devastation had doubled in just the last five minutes. More fires had taken hold, and Army helicopters zipped across an ever expanding area like hungry buzzards. Brooklyn remained quiet, but Roosevelt Island was aflame and the chaos had begun snatching at the fringes of Long Island.

"Take us a quarter-mile into the Upper Bay, Frank. I want to see if our help will even make a difference before I think about lending it."

"Aye, Captain."

Guy left the pilothouse and headed down to the armoury. He expected to find Lieutenant Tosco there, but instead, he found two ensigns and a dozen enlisted sailors. They stood to attention when they saw him approach.

Guy waved a hand. "At ease. How goes it?"

Ensign Lucy Smith answered, "Lieutenant Tosco asked us to ready weapons and ammunition, sir."

Guy nodded, pleased that Tosco had carried out his orders as requested. "Good."

"How long until we enter the harbour, Captain?" "Who said we're going into harbour, Ensign Smith?" "Oh, I... My mistake, Captain. I just assumed."

Guy gritted his teeth. Tosco had been getting ahead of himself. "No decision has been made whether to head into harbour, Ensign, so do not pre-empt my orders."

"Sorry, sir."

"Do we know what's happening out there, Captain?" asked one of the ship's mechanics, Seaman Biggins.

Ensign Smith shouted at him. "Biggins! Do not address the captain unless you are spoken to."

Guy waved a hand. "It's okay, Ensign. Truthfully, Seaman Biggins, I don't know what's happening, but it's not anything good. As soon as Command gives an update, I will share it with the crew."

"Thank you, Captain."

"You're welcome. Now, where is Lieutenant Tosco?" Ensign Smith pointed towards the wide shutter at the end of

the storage area. "Out on launch deck prepping the Jayhawk." Guy gave a slight nod and marched away. "As you were, sailors."

He went over to the shutter and raised it. The wind came

rushing in, along with the sound of distant chaos from Manhattan. Tosco was indeed outside on the launch deck, sitting inside the Jayhawk rescue helicopter and running system checks. The main rotor spun and the rear prop propeller whirred in fits and spurts.

"Everything nominal, Lieutenant?"

"I'm still running checks, but aye, sir."

"Why did you tell Ensign Smith that we're heading into the harbour?"

"I said we need to prepare to go into harbour."

"You can see her confusion."

Tosco stopped flipping switches for a moment and stared at Guy. "It's only a matter of time before Command gives orders to head in. People are in trouble, and we're floating out here doing nothing when we should be helping."

"What we do is entirely my decision, Lieutenant. You give orders without my say so and you'll find yourself working a tugboat in the Arctic."

"Don't threaten me, sir."

"It's no threat."

Tosco hopped out of the helicopter and faced Guy down.

"Times have changed. The Coast Guard doesn't pull drowning fishermen out of the sea anymore. We fight drug lords and human traffickers. We are men of action."

"If you want to fight so badly, Lieutenant, I suggest you transfer to the Navy. They would be glad to have you." Tosco rolled his eyes. "I'm not interested in fighting

foreign wars. I am a Coast Guard because I want to protect the shores of my country. Right now, I am failing to do that. The citizens of New York need us."

"The men on this ship need you, Lieutenant. They need you to do your job and carry out my orders. Undermine me and you jeopardise the safety of the crew."

"Then don't give me a reason to undermine you, Captain"

Tosco went to walk away, but Guy stopped him by grabbing his arm. "Do you know what it takes to send a man to the brig, Lieutenant? My say so, that's all. It's been some time since I've had to lock a man up, but go and ask Chief Petty Officer Jacobs if I'm willing to do it. I once locked him up for six weeks without letting him out."

Tosco looked surprised as Guy hoped he would be.

He capitalised on the advantage by continuing. "That's right, Lieutenant. Frank Jacobs is my oldest friend, and about the straightest shooter you could ever hope to meet, but even he got on the wrong side of me once. Let's see how you fare if I deem you guilty of insubordination. Or even if you just piss me off."

Tosco licked his lips and kept quiet.

"I will take your silence as a good sign. I appreciate your initiative on checking the response vehicles. Carry on. I'll let you know if you're needed."

Guy marched away, just as the ship lifted anchor and began to turn starboard.

"Captain!" Tosco shouted after him.

"Yes, Lieutenant?"

"We're moving. Are we heading into harbour?"

"It's very likely, yes."

"Then why give me such a hard time if you agreed with me all along?"

"Because it's not my job to agree with you, Lieutenant. It's your job to agree with me."

***

"We're just coming up to a half-mile out," Frank informed Guy when he reached the pilothouse. "What do you want to do, Captain?"

Guy picked up his binoculars and took another glance at the city. From nearer shore, he could make out the snarled traffic and panicking mobs of people. There was full-scale panic in Manhattan, but it was still unclear why. People leapt from the docks into the water, or clambered into boats. Small pleasure craft joined giant transporters as a mass exodus headed for the sea. Those unlucky enough to miss a chance at boarding a vessel now flailed about in the river, heads bobbing under for several seconds at a time before reappearing. People were drowning.

Guy decided. "We're heading into harbour, but keep our approach slow. There's a lot of traffic coming our way."

"Tosco will think he got his own way," Frank commented.

"Aye, but he might reconsider his attitude going forward. I told him about the time I locked you in the brig for six weeks."

Frank looked at him and frowned. "You mean when I had a

staph infection and you had to quarantine me? And it was less than two weeks."

"Yes, but Lieutenant Tosco doesn't know that. He thinks I left the most honest man on board to rot. It should remind him who's in charge."

Frank chuckled. "With no time to spare too. Any more lip from him and I was going to throw him overboard myself."

"I can deal with Lieutenant Tosco."

"I know you can, but I'd hate to see you get your hands dirty. The crew likes the Lieutenant and they won't be pleased if you take a firm hand against him."

"They don't have to like it, Frank; only understand what happens when you question the captain of this ship. Now, take us into harbour, Chief Petty."

"Aye, aye, Captain."

***

They almost collided with a millionaire's catamaran on the way into harbour, but they eventually managed to navigate their way to the docks of the Hudson River. From there they had no need of binoculars to see the devastation. The senior officers, and a portion of the crew, were all standing inside the pilothouse, staring out the window at a scene none of them could understand.

In New York, shell-shocked victims staggered down the streets in various states of ruin, blood covering most of them and many mortally wounded. One old man carried his own severed arm around with him in a bewildered daze, while a sobbing younger woman held a bundle of gore-streaked rags that might have been a baby.

Tosco was shaking his head. "What in God's name has happened?"

Guy wished he had the answer, but it continued to elude him. All that was clear was that some disaster had befallen Manhattan—possibly, dare he even think it, something worse than 9/11. "Has Command come back to us yet?" he asked Frank.

"No, you want me to hail them?" "Yes."

Frank got on the radio. "USCG Hatchet to District Command. Over."

"District Command receiving you loud. Over."

"Requesting permission to carry out rescue mission in New York Harbour. Injured civilians identified. Over."

"Negative. Please change course to U.S. Naval Base Norfolk. Over."

Guy took the intercom. "Captain Guy Granger speaking here. Can you explain why I am to redirect the Hatchet to Naval Base Norfolk? Over."

"United States Navy has taken command of District Coast Guard. We are to relinquish authority to Norfolk immediately. Over."

Guy had a bad feeling. The Navy only took control of the Coast Guard during times of war or national emergency. "Command, there are civilians here who need us. Requesting permission to stage a rescue attempt before relinquishing authority to U.S. Navy. Over."

"Negative. Over."

Guy stamped his foot. "Goddamn it, man. People are drowning in the Hudson River. Are you telling me to leave American civilians to die?"

There was silence on the line. Then came a shaky reply, "You are in command of the Hatchet, Captain Granger. Do as you will."

The line went dead.

Guy clenched his jaw and thought things through. He didn't understand what had happened in Manhattan, but Command had ordered him to redirect to Norfolk. The Navy had taken control, and it would be foolish to disobey them.

People continued hurling themselves into the Hudson.

The Navy took lives. The Coast Guard saved them.

Guy made up his mind. "I want two teams of eight in Rapid 1 and Rapid 2. There are too many birds in the sky to risk launching the Jayhawk, so we concentrate on the people in the river. Tosco, get men on the .50 cals this second, but they don't start firing without my word. If there are enemies in the city, I want to be prepared."

"Aye, aye, Captain." Tosco saluted, turned on his heel, and raced to put words into action.

Guy turned to Frank next. "What are these people so afraid of? Do you have any idea what's happening?"

"I've never seen anything like it, Captain. There are people on the docks with limbs missing. It's a war zone."

It wasn't an exaggeration. Even now, Guy could see mangled men and women throwing themselves into the water rather than facing whatever was occurring behind them. They were drowning quicker than he could spot them. "We need to move fast."

Frank placed a hand on Guy's shoulder and squeezed. "Aye, aye, Captain."

* * *

Considering half the men serving aboard the Hatchet had never seen real action, they carried themselves well. The rapid response boats dropped down onto the water and were away in moments. Each sailor took a firearm, but only a handgun—rifles would only frighten the civilians more. If bigger weapons were needed, the boats would return to ship.

Within ten minutes, the two rescue crafts were packed full of half-drowned people and on their way home. The first groups of survivors were laid down on the launch deck and the ship's doctor, Gonzalez—a loaner from the U.S. Public Health Service—checked them over. The healthiest survivor was escorted to the pilothouse and brought before Guy. The teenage Avengers fan—judging by his garish t-shirt—was stained with blood and mucky with Hudson water, but he was free from injury aside from a superficial gash across his left brow. Blood had leaked into his left eye and dried so that it was now stuck half-closed. His long hair was so filthy that it appeared brown when it was probably ash blond.

Guy handed the kid a coffee. "What's your name, sir?"

"Simon."

"Hello, Simon. I am Captain Guy Granger, and this is my ship. You are currently in the care of the United States Coast Guard. Are you able to tell me what happened?"

"No. I mean... Yes, but you won't believe me. It's crazy."

"Allow me to be the judge of that. Please, tell me as best you can."

"Monsters."

Guy leaned forward to hear more. "Monsters?"

"Yeah, and I don't mean figuratively. That black stone in the park opened a big, glowing gate and something came through. A monster, twenty feet tall with wings."

Guy cleared his throat. "Did you say, wings?"

"Yeah, but they were all burned up and useless. Just bones, really, but you can tell they used to be wings."

"You're saying that Manhattan was attacked by a giant monster? Like, Godzilla or something?"

Nobody in the room laughed. There had been too much bloodshed. The kid telling the story was deadly serious, and because of that they were able to stay focused on what he was saying—as ludicrous as it sounded. "I know it sounds crazy," the kid admitted, "but it's the God's honest. That black stone opened some kind of gate, and the Devil came through. It's Lucifer, dude. The end of the world, and we're all screwed."

Guy exchanged a glance with Frank that told him they were both thinking the same thing. The kid was suffering with shock. Nothing could be gained by further questioning. "Okay, Simon," said Guy. "One of my men will take you back outside for treatment. We'll get you back on land someplace safe as soon as we can."

Simon nodded and stood up, but before he allowed himself to be led away, he turned back to Guy. "I haven't told you everything. After the Devil came through, there was an army."

Guy folded his arms and gave the kid his attention. "Tell me about the army."

"Men, like you and me, dude, but all burned up, like they just stepped out of a fire. They came right out of the gate in a big group and started attacking everyone. I was working at an office on 65th Street—sixteenth floor. I saw it all."

"Why did you leave?"

The kid looked sad. "Because my girlfriend works at the zoo. I wanted to get to her. I... I still don't know if she's okay."

Guy put his hand on Simon's shoulder. "Give your girlfriend's details to one of my men, and we'll see what we can do."

"Thanks, dude—uh, Captain."

"You can call me Guy."

Simon nodded, then allowed himself to be led away like a child.

"What do you make of the kid?" Frank asked Guy.

"I have no idea."

"It must be shock," Tosco added. "Unless we're to believe that the Devil has come to New York."

Guy actually chuckled at that, but then felt bad for doing

so. "Whatever the truth, we can assume it started in Central Park and spread from there. Perhaps that stone they found this morning really is to blame. It seems too much of a coincidence to be otherwise."

Frank groaned. "Then what of all the other stones they discovered? Is this happening everywhere?"

Tosco covered his mouth and gasped. "You're right! I need to call my wife. The men need to check on their families."

Guy shot him down immediately, even though part of him was desperate to agree. Guy had two kids and an ex-wife, and would love nothing more than to speak to them right now, but he had a duty as well. That duty was the reason Alice and Kyle barely spoke to him anymore. He hoped, one day, his children would respect him for his dedication to his job. "Lieutenant, our only priority is the harbour. We can help these people, but we can't help our families—we can only pray that they are safe."

Tosco looked to argue, but glanced at Frank and seemed to think better of it. "Okay, I'll go check on the progress of Rapid 1 and 2. They should be heading back with more civilians."

At that moment, the radio squawked. "Rapid 1 to Hatchet. Over."

Guy grabbed the intercom. "Captain Granger. Over."

"We're under attack. Repeat: we're under attack. Help. Hello. Over. Help. Over." The voice on the line was frantic and struggling to maintain radio protocol. Never a good sign.

"Who is attacking you, Rapid 1? Over."

"You can smell their flesh on fire, even in the water. They're in the harbour... dragging... dragging people under. Burned... They're so badly burned. They pulled Williams and Biggins overboard. We're returning fire, but they keep popping up out of the river... They keep grabbing us. Oh God. Ensign Smith is wounded, she needs help. Lost visual with Rapid 2.... Saw them being boarded. Permission to retreat. Over. Please help. Over. Over."

Guy opened all channels and shouted his command. "All units, get the hell out of there! Rapid 2, if you're reading me, get out of there now! All personnel return to the Hatchet ASAP! Return to ship immediately!" He turned to the Lieutenant. "Tosco put those MGs to good use. Over."

"He said they were burned," Frank said in a haunted tone. "Yes, I heard him," said Guy.

"So do we take what Simon told us as truth? He said there was an army of burned men."

"I think we have to take him seriously until we know different."

Frank shook his head and swallowed loudly. "Then does that mean the Devil really is stomping around Central Park?" "Either it's the Devil," said Guy, "or something that looks a lot like him."

~RICK BASTION~
DEVONSHIRE, ENGLAND

AFTER LEARNING THAT HIS OLDER BROTHER planned on staying with him for a while, Rick had needed some air. That was why they were heading on over to The Warren, a local inn just a short walk down the road from where Rick lived. It was early evening, warm and balmy, and so the perfect night for a pint down the pub. When Rick thought about it, he realised it had been months since he'd last had a drink outside his house.

The Warren came into view as they rounded a bend in the country road. The Tudor building was as quintessential as an old English pub could be, and the amber glow of the setting sun made it blur like an oil painting.

Braaaarr...

Rick and Keith had to hop back into the hedges as a red transit van whizzed past them. The limit was 30 mph, but the driver seemed to think otherwise.

"Someone's in a hurry." Rick tutted.

"Probably forgot to pick his wife up from spinning class," said Keith as they cautiously crossed the road and headed into the pub's car park. "So, you drink at this place often?"

"No, I haven't been here in a couple months. It's a nice place though. Wood burning fires and horse brasses, that kind of place."

"A dusty old relic, you mean?"

"What's wrong with the way things were?"

"Huh, you would say that."

Rick frowned. "What do you mean?"

"You're always looking fondly backwards instead of brightly forward. It holds you back."

Rick ignored the comment and headed inside the pub.

Warm shadows embraced him as he left the sunlight and approached the old oak bar in the centre of the room. A single barmaid stood behind the brass taps and smiled as he approached. "What can I get you gents?"

"I'll have a pint of lager, please. What do you want, Keith?"

Keith winked at the barmaid and said, "I'll have a large cognac, please, sweetheart."

There was a brief flicker of contempt in the barmaid's eyes, but she nodded politely and went to get the drinks.

Rick turned to his brother. "Thought you were off the booze."

"Got a taste for it after that tipple at yours." He leant on the bar and looked around. "You know, this might be my kind of place after all."

Rick followed his brother's gaze over to a suited businessman sitting next to an older man in a tweed jacket who was reading a broadsheet newspaper. "You mean, because the people who drink here are snooty?"

"Not at all, not at all. I just like the atmosphere. Bet it's lovely in the winter with the fires going. It must get all sorts in here—farmers, vicars, local doctors. Not like the pubs you get in the city. Yes, this is my kind of place all right."

The barmaid returned with their drinks, and Rick paid her. Then they headed around the corner of the bar to a seating area with sofas and a television. This part of the pub was busier, and a group had assembled in front of the plasma screen.

"Evening," said Keith, sipping his cognac before he'd even sat down.

"Sshh! Be quiet," someone chided.

Keith frowned at his brother. "Friendly place you've brought me to."

Rick glanced at the television to see what had everybody's attention and saw it was the news. Looked like something had happened in America. Possibly New York. A young brunette stood at the edge of the assembled group, arms folded and mouth wide in horror. Rick moved up beside her and gently got her attention. "What's happening?"

"There's been an attack on America. It's going on right now."

"Oh Jesus, really?"

The young woman nodded, then gave Rick that odd look of recognition he was used to, and always dreaded. "Do I know you?" she asked.

"It's possible," he said glumly.

Something seemed to click into place, and her face lit up. "You're that singer, Rick Bastion. Cross to Bear, right?"

"Yeah, that's right."

It surprised him when she said, "Cool song."

"Yes, if you like formulaic pop music," Keith butted in then offered his hand. "I'm Rick's big brother, Keith." "Sarah."

"Good to meet you, Sarah. Can I buy you a drink?"

Rick huffed. "Jesus, Keith. There's been a disaster, and you're hitting on a girl ten years younger than you? And while you're married, too. Nice."

Keith shot him a look of pure venom. "I was doing no such thing. Just being polite. Some people like to make friends. That might seem alien to you, Rick, seeing as how you choose to spend all of your time alone, but the rest of us are more social."

"You know nothing about me," Rick muttered. "Anyway, you still haven't told me why you turned up on my doorstep."

Sarah had been watching the short exchange, and now she rolled her eyes. "They say it's even worse than 9/11. It started in the park where they found one of those weird black stones."

Rick blinked. "Like the one in Crapstone?"

"Yes. The Police have been up on that hill all day, trying to work out what it is. Those stones just keep appearing out of nowhere, and no one can move them. It's scary."

Rick was glad the anxious churning in his stomach was not unwarranted, that others felt nervous too. "When I heard that old woman had been murdered right next to one of them, I got a bad feeling."

Sarah nodded, making a lock of hazel fall loose from behind her ear. She tucked it back again and said, "Me too."

"Ssshhhh, we're trying to listen," someone said.

Rick shut up and watched the television along with everybody else. Half of New York City was in flames. Cars piled up in the road, and bodies littered the streets. Unusual for the news to be so graphic, but there seemed to be nowhere to film that wouldn't show some level of bloodshed.

Sarah covered her mouth like she was going to be sick. "What are those things?"

It took a moment for Rick to spot what she was referring to, but once he had he couldn't focus on anything else. Amidst the chaos was a surging mass of inhuman creatures. They resembled men, but looked like they'd stumbled right out of an inferno. Like locust, they enveloped the city streets and eviscerated everyone in their way. The citizens of New York were so desperate to escape that they were launching themselves right off the docks into the river. Dozens and dozens of boats headed out to sea while a single

Coast Guard vessel slipped through in the opposite direction.

Rick tried to blink but couldn't. "It's a bloodbath."

Sarah was shaking her head, mascara running. "I've never seen anything so horrible."

"Least it's them and not us," said Keith.

Rick and Sarah both glanced at him in disgust. "Seriously, Keith, that's not a cool thing to say."

"I just meant, it would be even more terrible if it was happening here."

Rick pictured the strange black stone found near the body of Elizabeth Creasy and felt uneasy. Was a similar black stone responsible for what was happening in New York? If so, then what would happen to the village of Crapstone?

* * *

Twenty minutes later Rick and Keith had taken a seat around a small round table with a wobbly leg. They were joined by Sarah who, as it turned out, was a member of The Warren's kitchen staff. She was twenty-seven, but lived with her parents in the village since divorcing her cheating husband a year ago. Her job at the pub was temporary while she decided what she wanted to do. Rick enjoyed her company, but it also meant he couldn't quiz his brother about why he'd turned up out of the blue. Had Marcy kicked him out? They had always seemed so close—she was as pretentious as he was.

"I hate it when things like this happen," Sarah said to them over their second round of drinks. "Whenever something terrible happens on the news, I can't help thinking about the children— how frightened they must be. I imagine them getting taken into a room and told that their daddies won't be coming home, or that mummy has been hurt. It's just so horrible."

Rick sipped his beer, trying to pace himself. He was a sloppy drunk, which was why he usually drank alone at home. That didn't concern his brother though; Keith was ready for his next pint shortly after starting his last.

"I still don't understand what's going on," said Rick. "Those monsters were attacking like an army."

Keith rolled his eyes.

"No, he's right," said Sarah. "They were monsters. All their skin had burned off, like they'd come straight out of Hell."

"Don't be silly," said Keith. "There's no such thing as Hell."

"There is," said Rick, glancing at the television. It had been running the same aerial shots of New York City for the last twenty minutes now, and it was tough to endure. "I'm worried about the stone in Crapstone. What if the same thing happens?"

Nobody said anything, not even Keith. In fact, the entire pub was silent, except for the sombre tones of the television news reporters. No one knew what to say. Silence seemed the only fitting statement.

It wasn't until an hour later that anything new happened. "Help me!"

An injured woman staggered into the pub, her cleavage exposed and covered in ragged claw marks. The side of her face was so badly wounded that a section of her cheek was missing and revealed the teeth inside. No sooner had the woman made it inside the pub than she collapsed in the middle of the floor right in front of the bar. The businessman was the first to go to her. He dropped down and lifted the woman's head in his arms. "Somebody, call an ambulance."

The barmaid was on it, pulling a cordless phone from under the bar and making the call. Rick ran to help the businessman, but didn't know what to do. The ragged wounds on her bare chest looked as if a sharp fork had dragged through warm, flesh-coloured butter. Blood didn't squirt out so much as continuously oozed.

A coppery scent filled the bar.

"Do you know First Aid?" the businessman asked Rick. "No, I don't. We just need to keep her comfortable, I think,

until the ambulance arrives."

"It's on its way," the barmaid shouted from behind the bar.

"They said ten minutes."

The businessman shook his head. "I don't think she has that long."

"Let's just hope for the best," said Rick.

"Oh God," somebody cried out.

Rick arched his neck to look around. "What is it?"

It was Sarah. She was pointing at the television. "Look!" The news showed new scenes of devastation, but not of

New York. Another city was under attack—London.

The barmaid turned up the volume.

"Oxford Street has been cordoned off as disaster strikes the nation's capitol. Just moments ago, as a large crowd gathered, the unidentified black stone, located this morning in the city's busiest shopping street, began to emit light. What happened next was something right out of a nightmare. These scenes were captured less than five minutes ago."

The reporter disappeared, and video footage took her place. It showed a glowing lasso of light emanating from a black stone in the centre of the road. The lasso spread out into a wider circle and formed an archway. There was no loss in quality as the first creature emerged onto Oxford Street. It leapt at a nearby police officer and tore into the man's neck with blackened teeth. The crowd broke apart, screaming in terror, and people fought each other to flee as more creatures poured through the archway behind them. An endless stream of monsters appeared.

A legion of burned and twisted horrors.

The video ended and the news reporter returned. "This is happening in numerous locations. The mysterious black stones, recently discovered throughout the country and the world, have opened, what appears to be some kind of gateways, and an unknown enemy is pouring through. New York was the first city under siege, but we can now confirm similar attacks in several of the world's major cities. The Armed Forces are mobilising, as are those of other countries. The best thing to do right now is to stay indoors and stay tuned to your televisions."

Keith put his hands on his head. "Shit. I need to call Marcy."

"I need to call my mum," said the barmaid. "Jesus fucking Christ," said Rick.

Sarah fainted.

~MINA MAGAR~
SOHO, LONDON

L ESS THAN TWENTY FEET AWAY FROM WHERE Mina now stood, a BMW hit a shopfront at 50 mph and sent a shower of glass into the air. The driver got out, dazed but miraculously alive. People strolled around the wreck as if they hadn't even noticed it, and the only person to even react was a young boy who pointed and laughed.

"David, we need to get out of here."

"Mina, why aren't you taking pictures? We need pictures." Mina fondled the heavy camera hanging around her neck

and considered ditching it, but she just couldn't. It was a part of her, and had cost as much as her car—not that her decade-old Peugeot was worth much. She sighed and took a skewed photograph of the crashed BMW. The angle would add to the disorientating feeling of the accident. She made sure she got a snap of the shell-shocked driver, too. Next, she intended to take a photo of a burning coffee shop on the corner of the street, but when she looked through her viewfinder, she saw something that made her take notice.

A young girl lay trapped inside the building, crushed beneath an overturned table. She was screaming for help as the flames crept towards her.

Mina realised she was taking pictures of other people's misery instead of trying to help, so she let the camera hang around her neck and raced towards the burning coffee shop, even as David yelled at her to get back and focus on her job.

The young girl trapped inside had a broken leg—left foot pointed backwards.

"Help me, please," she begged, eyes swollen with pained tears.

Mina grabbed the edge of the table and strained to lift it. The fire was at the back of the room by the service counter, but it was hot enough to make her break out in a sweat. The girl screeched as the weight shifted against her ankle. Mina had to grit her teeth to keep from dropping the table, for it was heavier than it looked. Too heavy.

"It hurts, it hurts."

"I know it does," said Mina, straining with all her strength. "Can you get yourself free?"

"No, it hurts."

Mina's arms trembled—couldn't hold the table much longer. With a groan, she lifted it another few inches, but that was everything she had. "How about now...? Can you get free?"

The girl screamed in agony. "I can't. The pain..."

Mina's knuckles creaked. It was only a question of what gave out first—her hands or her biceps. "You need to move. I can't hold it!"

"It hurts."

The table began to wobble. Mina couldn't hold it anymore. The flames were getting closer.

She would have to drop the table and run. She couldn't help the girl. "I'm sorry," she said.

Suddenly the weight in her hands lightened.

"After three," said David, now standing beside her.

"One...two...three!"

Together, they shoved the table up and over. It fell free of the girl, and she screamed in renewed pain, but there was a hint of relief creeping into her cries now. They grabbed her under the armpits and dragged her out of the restaurant and onto the pavement. Nobody came to help or even paid much attention, for everybody in the crowd had some place to be, and it was unanimously away from here.

Mina and David had retreated from Oxford Street south into Soho when the gate opened, avoiding the initial slaughter, but they hadn't escaped the mass exodus from the city. Everyone in London knew they were under attack. That nobody understood by what made their panic even worse. They had made it as far as the Soho Theatre before they had slowed down, and then they headed west onto Meard Street to catch their breath

"What's your name?" Mina asked the girl, trying to stop her screaming and attracting attention.

"G-Gabby."

"A beautiful name. Gabby, we need to go. I know your leg hurts, but you need to hop as fast as you can."

"We can't bring her along," said David. "We have work to do."

Mina glared at him. "I'm not taking any more pictures, David. We have to get out of here."

David looked at her like she was mad. "This is the news story of the century—of all human history. Do you want to be a bystander, or do you want to be the photographer whose pictures remain in the archives of mankind until the end of time?"

"I want to be one of the survivors. Which is why I'm getting out of here and taking Gabby with me."

David flapped his arms and stamped his foot, almost comically. "You will regret this for the rest of your life, girl. Think about it."

"There'll be no rest of my life to live if I hang around here."

"We're all going to die," Gabby moaned. "They're coming to kill us."

Mina grabbed the girl's head and seized her focus. "Gabby, we will be just fine. Move as quickly as you can, okay?"

They continued south towards the theatre district, Mina propping up Gabby, and David following behind and complaining about what a mistake she was making. Part of her wondered if a real photojournalist would do as David suggested and continue taking pictures. War zone photographers stared death in the face every day, but she was choosing to run away. This felt different though. This didn't feel like a situation where reporters should be expected to hang around and document.

They'd not yet witnessed the invading creatures first hand, but the scattered survivors fleeing the city had screamed and wailed about burned monsters tearing people apart. One woman even barked at Mina about a giant angel come to smite them all. People had gone mad with terror. David tried interviewing some of them, but most of what he got was confused babble.

The roads were clogged with wrecked vehicles and broken glass covered the pavements. Slow-moving lines of exhausted survivors funnelled along where there was a gap, and uniformed shop workers stumbled side-by-side with executives and public servants. Several thousand refugees looking for a way out—and this was only one small part of the city. How bad were things? People were already starting to turn on one another. Mina saw a topless man strike a cyclist with a brick before making off with his bike. The previous owner still lay unconscious in the gutter outside a media office. David insisted on getting a picture.

Helicopters buzzed overhead but did nothing to help. Gunfire clattered in the distance.

Gabby moaned before they even made it to the end of the street. "I need to stop. My leg..."

"We can't stop, you stupid girl," cried David.

"I can't go on anymore."

Mina eased the girl up against the bonnet of a crumpled Royal Mail van and stepped back. "Thirty-seconds," she said, "but then we don't stop until we're safe. Do you understand, Gabby?"

Gabby nodded, fresh tears down her cheeks. "I'm not even from London," she muttered. "I live in Stroud. I only came here for a job interview. My mum will be so worried about me."

"Sorry," was all Mina could say.

David tapped his foot and generally looked pissed off. Mina did the only thing she could think of to oblige him—she lifted her camera and started taking pictures. She zoomed in on an old man lying beneath an overturned motorised scooter. There was a chance he was alive, but nothing anybody in the street could do for him. His head was smashed open and his brains were bleeding out. Mina had to cover her mouth to keep from throwing up.

The crowd began to thin out as they passed the Apollo Theatre, enough people having fled to the further reaches of the city leaving Soho mostly deserted. If not for David's constant lingering, they would have been out of there too.

Ominous grey smoke rose above the skyline back toward Oxford Street and across the river, the spiky summit of the Shard rose solemnly in the background. London burned, but the gunfire in the distance might have been the Army fighting back. Could the situation be dealt with? Could the city be reclaimed from whatever abominable horrors had spilled out onto Oxford Street?

Mina took her last picture—a snap of a dirty Labrador trotting down the pavement with a rolled up newspaper in its mouth—and was about to turn away when she noticed something in the distance. At first, her eyes only registered movement, but then she took in some of the finer detail. Something was definitely there.

Unsure of what she was seeing, she looked through her camera's viewfinder and zoomed in 12x. Something massive strode across the road several blocks back. The semi-naked figure walked like a man but was five lengths taller and had the remnants of wings on its back. Mina thought about what the crazy woman had barked at her earlier: A giant angel. Could such a thing be true?

Just as she started to accept what she was seeing, the giant creature disappeared into the next street and was gone as quickly as it had appeared.

David grabbed her arm. "Time to go."

"Did you see that?"

"See what?"

Mina shook her head. "There was... Nothing." A scream.

Mina and David turned to find Gabby on the floor. She crawled backwards as something stalked after her.

A creature had leapt up onto the roof of the Royal Mail van. It was so horribly burned that its nostrils had fused over and one eye socket was hollow. It leapt down on top of Gabby and seized her by the arms, hoisting her up off the ground like a child.

Mina went to help, but David grabbed her shoulder and twisted her around. "You already saved her once."

More creatures surged into the street from a side road up ahead. They leapt on any stragglers they could find, and agonised screams soon filled the air. Gabby screamed too, as the burned man gouged out her eyes with its blackened thumbs. It was enough to extinguish any hopes Mina might have had of saving the girl. There was barely a chance to save herself.

David was already running, but Mina caught up with him once she got a hold of herself. The creatures pouring into the street moaned in ecstasy as they tore the heads and limbs off screaming victims. One of them spotted Mina and gave chase.

"David, help," she screamed.

David tilted sideways at a sprint and pointed ahead. "Over there."

A pharmacy lay ahead, its door hanging wide open. David made directly for it, leaving Mina little choice but to follow if she had any chance of escaping the thing tearing after her. She leapt up on the pavement and sprinted.

The creature chasing her dodged around a shattered bus shelter and headed her off from the front. Unaware, David carried on running. To her astonishment, the creature spoke. Its charred lips cracked and peeled as they formed words.

"Nowhere to run, little girl. We are everywhere. The Red Lord will make you his slaves."

Before Mina could reply, the creature leapt at her, a roaring beast snatching out with skinless hands. Mina grabbed the only thing she could—her camera—and swung it as hard as she could. The heavy, digital SLR struck the burned man in the side of his skull and dropped him to the pavement where he went still. The strap broke and the expensive piece of equipment shattered on the ground.

Mina got moving, and made it through the pharmacy's door just as David was closing it. It slammed behind her, and David quickly tipped a display rack over to act as a barricade.

The streets filled with terrified screams.

"Quick, get back here," said David, crouching behind a service counter at the back of the room. Mina leapt over, and they both scurried to a storage area at the back stacked with pills and medicines.

David put a hand on Mina's shoulder and eased her back against the wall. "Did any of them see you?"

"Wouldn't they be in here by now if they had?"

"I saw that one attack you. I think you killed it."

"What? You mean you saw me in trouble and didn't help?"

"What could I have done? Besides, you handled yourself
     pretty well. If a little woman can kill those monsters, then the
Army should get this whole mess sorted out soon."

Mina bit her lip at the sexist remark. Too much had happened
to get into a petty argument. She wasn't good with confrontation
on a normal day—had been meek and shy ever since her mother
died and her father began home schooling her. She wanted to
sit in silence and try to make sense of it— but could the fact that
London was under attack by bloodthirsty monsters ever make
sense?

She thought not.

*　*　*

David pulled his phone out of his pocket and tried to make
a call. Several times he had tried in the last hour, but the mass
panic had caused the network to fail as thousands of people used
their phones at once. This time, however, looked promising as
David glanced at Mina urgently from where he sat. "Yes, hello?
Carol, is that you? Oh, thank God. Yes, it's David. I'm okay..."

Mina kicked out a leg at him across the floor.

"...Mina is with me too. We're stuck on a London backstreet
somewhere in Soho. There are monsters attacking—that's the best
way I can explain it. Do you want a quote from me? How about-"

Mina kicked him again. "Can she get us help?"

David rolled his eyes but took the hint. "We need help, Carol.
We're trapped inside a grimy little pharmacy, and I don't know
how we're going to make it out of the city. Things are bad. That
stone in Oxford Street opened some kind of portal." He paused
and listened, then said, "I don't know if it's aliens. They don't
look like aliens. They look more like demons. Carol, you need to
send help. In the meantime, I can conduct an interview over the

phone. Carol? Carol…?" David glanced at his phone and cursed. He immediately redialled but couldn't get through. "Damn it."

Mina honed in on something he'd said and mentioned it now. "Demons?"

David looked at her curiously. "What?"

"You said they look like demons."

"Don't they?"

"Yes, they do, but if they're demons then the gate that opened was…"

David finished her thought. "A gate to Hell."

Mina nodded. "That would make things a whole lot worse than we even thought."

"We're not being invaded by Hell, you silly girl. I won't even consider it. Heaven-Hell, it's all a load of codswallop."

"Well, wallop me a cod," said Mina. "Because those monsters outside are demons."

David huffed. "Aren't you a Hindu?"

"What? Because I'm brown? There're as many Christians in India as Hindus, but that's beside the point. Up until today, I was an atheist, same as you. Yet here you are, talking about demons."

David folded his arms across his chest. "Fair enough. You may still consider me still an atheist though."

"Even after everything you've seen?"

"Those monsters could have been anything. Escaped lab specimens for all we know."

"What about the…" Mina trailed off.

"What about the what?"

She knew David wouldn't believe her, but she was burning to talk about it. "I saw something else," she said. "There was a giant. It looked like a man with wings. It looked, I suppose, maybe, a little, you know, like… an angel."

David bellowed with laughter, then flinched and covered his mouth. "Sorry," he said in a whisper. "But you must be mad."

"Come on, David. You just don't want to admit the truth."

"The truth has a way of evolving, Mina. I'll wait until we have all the facts before drawing conclusions. Now, let's think about getting out of here."

"Go back outside? It's not safe."

"No, perhaps not, but we can't sit around here forever. You think those chumps from the Chronicle are holed up somewhere cowering?"

"No," said Mina. "They're probably dead."

David huffed. "It's gone quiet. Let's just take a look." Mina closed her eyes and had to summon courage to even

get up off the floor. When she eventually managed it, David had disappeared into the front of the shop and lurked behind the barricade. She hurried over to join him and dared to take a peek out of the window. The demons had gone. In their place was a carpet of bodies. Hundreds, maybe a thousand people dead. A fire had started at the end of the road.

It was Hell on Earth.

"We have to get out of here," said Mina, completely changing her mind about staying. "No one is coming to save us."

David glanced up from over the barricade and saw all the bodies. "I agree. Somebody has to tell these people's stories."

"You can't tell a story until it's finished," said Mina, "and this one hasn't even got started yet."

"I fear you might be right." David took off his jacket and placed it on the counter. He rolled up his sleeves and started taking down the barricade.

~TONY CROSS~
IRAQ-SYRIA BORDER

TONY LAY ON HIS FRONT GASPING. HE REACHED an arm around his back and prodded at himself until he felt the most pain. The most tender area was just below his right shoulder blade, and when he brought his fingers back, they were bloody. He'd been hit. First time in fifteen years. Hadn't even seen it coming. Because he'd been distracted.

No, not distracted—mesmerised.

That strange black stone. Glowing.

Rough hands grabbed Tony's webbing and started dragging him. Suddenly, he was sliding along the desert on his back. The person dragging him was out of sight, but in front of him, he saw the ISN soldiers advancing. They'd removed the handbrakes from their vehicles and were using them as rolling cover. A few of their number lay dead, but there was at least a dozen still engaging.

The ambush had failed.

Goddamn you, Ellis.

Tony's rescuer released his webbing and let him drop against the dirt behind the hill. Lieutenant Ellis appeared before him looking like a ghost with his pale and sullen face. "Anthony? You've been hit."

"You don't fuckin' say?"

Ellis frowned. "Not too badly, I see. Harris, help the Staff Sergeant up."

Tony grasped the meaty hand offered to him and made it up into a crouching position. The pain in his shoulder was bad, but he battled through it. "Sit-rep?"

"We've lost six men, but we're holding steady," Ellis informed him.

Tony groaned. Six young men dead. What a waste. He turned to Private Harris. "Why are you here? You were heading for the fence with Corporal Blake."

"Blake's dead. I saw you were down too, so I abandoned the plan and got you back into cover. You're lucky the bullet only winged you, Staffie."

The pain in Tony's shoulder didn't make him feel so lucky, but he patted the private on one of his massive arms and thanked him. "You saved my life, lad, but that means we're still pinned down without options."

Ellis clutched his rifle against his chest. "There must be something we can do?"

Tony couldn't think of anything besides a full retreat, but then his mind turned to something else. "The stone... Harris, did you see a strange black stone when you rescued me?"

The young private nodded. "Yeah, the thing was glowing. I almost took a bullet looking at it, so I had to get out of there."

"I suppose it's not important right now," Tony admitted. "We need to get our arses out of here."

The ISN soldiers were right at the base of the hill now— Tony could hear them. He popped his head above cover and saw them pushing closer. He also spotted that strange black stone. The odd glowing had distracted the ISN as well, and with a little luck it might just buy Tony and the others a chance to escape, but when he saw the rear doors of their van open, he feared the worse.

Two ISN soldiers appeared carrying an AGS-17—an automatic grenade launcher. Tony had seen the weapon only in training videos, but he knew it could spit thirty high- explosive frag grenades in about ten seconds. It would obliterate the hill and any men taking cover behind it.

"We need to get our arses out of here now!" Tony shouted. "Move!"

"They'll mow us down," Ellis argued.

"They're about to blow us up."

Ellis understood and grabbed his radio, but before he made a call, something halted the fighting. A blinding flash of light. A skull-piercing whine.

Tony cupped his ears, lifted his head from cover and saw what was happening. For a moment, he thought a grenade had exploded, but as his eyesight recovered, he saw that the enemy was stumbling around in confusion.

A glowing archway had risen twenty feet high above the black stone, and it now shimmered in the air like a cloud of vapour. It looked like some kind of gate.

Something came through. It materialised from the floating puddle and hit the desert as solid form. Whatever it was was barely human, hunched over like an old crone—more ape-like than person. It was naked and entirely bald, with two curled talons the length of chef's knives hanging from each arm.

Tony rose to his feet. "What the f-"

The ugly creature leapt into the air and came down on top of one of the ISN soldiers. It snatched away the soldier's AK- 47 and sliced through his neck with one of its razor-sharp talons. The cut was so deep that the victim's head fell back on his shoulders, and blood spurted out of the exposed neck stump like a fountain.

It thundered and rained with bullets.

The ISN opened fire first, a dozen soviet assault rifles chattering all at once, but the British soldiers were quick to add fire from their more modern combat rifles. The snarling creature reeled backwards. Chunks of flesh and dark red blood filled the air around it.

It hit the ground as dead as anything could be.

Silence fell upon the patch of Iraqi desert. Two opposing groups of men stood on opposite sides of a hill having just dispatched a mutual enemy. What had just happened confused everybody enough that the fighting ceased. Yet nobody dared break cover. Nobody dared lower their weapons.

The centre of the archway shimmered.

Another creature leapt out.

This time the soldiers were ready for it, and the creature was dead before its clawed feet settled on the ground. The ISN looked at its corpse, and then at one another. Fear and confusion adorned their faces. Tony had never seen Islamic extremists show fear of anything, but these men were shitting their knickers. To give them their due, not one of them tried to flee.

A dozen more creatures came through the gate.

Tony moved his finger back to his trigger but didn't fire. He found himself staring. They were honest-to-God monsters: clawed feet, taloned hands, and vile, naked bodies—some of them even sported obscene, dangling tackle between their legs, while others had nothing. One of them spotted the British soldiers behind the hill and raced in their direction.

Tony lopped its leg off with a burst of rifle fire, then re-aimed and blew its head to smithereens. The things were fast. The creature had been leaping and bounding towards Tony like an angry gorilla, and if he had missed his shot, it would've been right on top of him. Within seconds, a handful of the ISN had been taken down in a merciless attack. The creatures were so fast it was impossible to aim at them quick enough to keep them back.

They surged forward in a tide of deadly claws and teeth.

The Syrian rebels screamed as they began to fall.

Pushing through the border fence and encircling the base of the hill had brought death to the ISN soldiers. Their vehicles had been sitting just yards from the black stone when the gate had opened. The monsters had leapt out right on top of them.

"We need to help them," said Ellis.

Tony shot him a glance. "What?"

"They're being ripped apart by those monsters. We need to help them."

"We need to get our arses out of here. They can go fuck themselves. We've lost men."

"Yes, we have, but we will rescue the ISN soldiers anyway. We are better men, Staff Sergeant. We are British soldiers." Tony shook his head and cursed so loudly that the men heard it over the gunfire. "Fine, but the only chance we have is to head across the border into Syria. If we try to move off this hill back towards our vehicles, those things will head us off."

"Fine." Ellis got on his radio. "All men. On my command, we will abandon this hill and head for the breach in the fence. We are moving east into Syria until we can find a place to regroup. During our retreat, we will endeavour to assist the ISN forces below. They are assaulted by a common enemy and it is ignoble to use them as a screen for our escape. Over."

Tony watched the men groan at the mention of helping the ISN, but he knew they would do as commanded. The way things were going, it might not even be an issue. There were hardly any ISN soldiers left to save. The creatures had made it amongst the vehicles and were rapidly slicing the terrified extremists to pieces. One creature spotted Tony peering over the hill at them, but he shot it in the face before it had a chance to warn its brothers.

"We need to move before they come for us."

Ellis barked into his radio. "Men, on my word. Hold... hold... move!"

What was left of the British firing line crested the top of the hill and descended towards the border at a staggered sprint. They were met with no armed resistance, for the ISN were overwhelmed by the creatures. If there was any chance to aid them, it would have to be now.

Tony made a beeline for the bullet-battered ISN vehicles. One of the ISN soldiers saw his approach and took it as a threat, but before he had a chance to point his rifle, Tony shot him in the chest. He was there to help, but they were still enemy combatants, and if they pointed a gun at him they were going down. The flaring agony in his right shoulder made him firm about that.

Tony made it amongst the remaining ISN and shouted to get their attention. They glanced at him suspiciously, but he waved a hand of peace before any of them tried to shoot him. Eventually, they realised that the British soldiers were lining up behind them and adding their fire to the fight against the creatures. Together, the two groups of men were able to take out a dozen of the beasts in a single, quick, combined volley, and they were soon backing away towards the border fence.

Tony counted only three surviving ISN soldiers and a mere seven British soldiers—including him and Ellis. More than half the men on both sides were dead.

And the enemy were still coming.

The remaining men wove between the vehicles and broke into open ground where they all picked up speed towards the fence. Tony didn't want the ISN at his back, so he fell back and brought up the rear. In doing so, he left himself vulnerable to attack from the creatures. Glancing back, he spotted an army taking shape.

He spotted something else.

The ISN's van lay just ahead and lying in the dirt right beside its rear tyre, was the AGS-17 grenade launcher. Tony licked his lips and tasted grit. If he didn't do something, the creatures would chase them right into Syria. He had to buy them all a head start. It was a sergeant's job to look after his men.

Lieutenant Ellis spotted Tony as he ran in the wrong direction. "Anthony, what the blazes are you doing?"

"Not letting a big fuckin' gun go to waste," he shouted back.

Just about to reach the fallen grenade launcher, a creature leapt out in front of Tony from between two banged up Toyotas. He raised his rifle and placed a round right through its left eye, but by that time it had launched itself into the air. Its dead carcass came down right on top of him, and his injured shoulder raged with agony as he fell sprawling onto his back. It was all he could do just to kick the dead monster off of him and clamber away through the dirt.

More of the creatures raced towards him.

The other men continued their retreat towards the border. He was alone.

The AGS-17 was two feet away. He scrambled on his belly and grabbed it. The heavy steel in his hands reignited his confidence, and he leapt to his knees and deployed the tripod so gracefully that he could have been playing music.

The first grenade rocketed straight into a creature's face, and the massive explosion took out two more in the vicinity. All three creatures exploded in ludicrous gibs. Dirt blew into the air and peppered Tony's face, but he barely felt it, too much in that quiet, focused place that all soldiers went to in the heat of battle. He was on his feet without even realising it and firing more grenades at wherever the creatures were most congregated. Whenever one of them got too close, he would pull up his rifle and let off a shot, before returning to the grenade launcher in his other hand. The recoil should have taken him off his feet, but the weapons were a part of him, and he tamed them like wild horses.

Creatures exploded all around him.

One of the Toyotas flipped and came down on its roof when a grenade exploded beneath its chassis. It crushed several creatures and caused many more to leap out of the way. Tony became a one-man army, reaping destruction one grenade after another. His final volley hit the area in front of the gate and shredded a bunch of creatures that had only just passed through. When the grenade launcher finally ran dry, at least three-dozen creatures lay dead or mangled. Their piggish squeals filled the air.

Tony caught his breath for a moment, taking in the heady scent of singed flesh and burning metal. He threw the empty AGS-17 down on the ground and turned heel to race towards the border and re-join his comrades. He'd bought them some time. Hopefully it was enough, because he had a feeling that this was an enemy that was just getting started.

PART TWO

"If you're going through hell, keep going."

— Winston Churchill

~GUY GRANGER~

LOWER BAY, NEW YORK

A LL GUY COULD THINK ABOUT WAS ALICE and Kyle. Since the mobile phone amnesty, the men aboard the Hatchet had been coming to him with horror stories from all over the country. His Airman, whose job it was to pilot the Jayhawk, had wept as he'd spoken of his hometown of Carmel, Indiana, which was besieged. His auntie and two cousins were already dead. There were similar reports from enlisted men hailing from Boston, Tallahassee, Newport, and Marietta. Everywhere with a black stone was under attack.

Which meant the whole of America was under attack.

It was Guy's turn to make a call now, but he sat in his cramped quarters with his cell phone in his lap and hands shaking as he found himself unable to dial.

Just make the call, he told himself. You have a job to do, and this is the only chance you will get to speak to your family. Make the goddamn call, Guy. Find out if Kyle and Alice are okay.

He unlocked the phone and brought up his contacts. His hands shook, but he kept his forefinger straight enough to press his ex-wife's name and start the call. He placed the phone to his ear and waited.

"Guy, is that you?"

"Nancy, are you okay?"

"No, I'm not okay. What's going on? Brunswick is under attack. That's only the next town over."

"But Durham is okay?"

"Yes, I think so. The local police have gone to help in Brunswick, but things are okay here. They say those stones opened up some kind of gate and monsters are pouring through."

"I think that's correct," he admitted, "I've seen the monsters. They're real."

"Oh God."

"Nancy, where are Kyle and Alice? Are they with you?" "No."

"Jesus, where are they?"

"They're in London. You know that."

Guy's eyes went wide as he realised. "Damn it. Their school trip was this week?"

"And all of next. I can't believe you forgot. I suppose I should be used to it by now."

"Nancy, I'm not calling for an argument. I want to know my family is safe, so just tell me. Are the kids okay?"

"Guy, I haven't been able to reach them all day. The news said London is under attack." She sobbed.

Guy almost dropped the phone. His hands shook. "Nancy, when did you speak to them last?"

"Yesterday. It was night time there, but around midday here. They were having fun; said they were going to visit Big Ben in the morning."

That put Kyle and Alice in the heart of the city.

Guy closed his eyes and tried not to scream. "Okay, Nancy, don't panic. Give me the details of where they're staying and I'll contact the U.S. embassy; see what I can do from here."

"Thank you, Guy. Clark has tried to get in contact with the school, but hasn't gotten anywhere."

The mention of his wife's lover dispelled some of Guy's desperation and replaced it with anger. "Is Clark there with you now?"

"Yes, did you want to speak to him?"

"No! I mean, I don't have anything to say to him. Just stay together and don't leave home. Things are bad, Nancy, but at least it's not everywhere. If Durham is okay, then stay put. I'll try to find Kyle and Alice. Contact you as soon as I hear anything."

"Thanks, Guy. You stay safe." "I always do."

He ended the call and once again stared at the cell phone in his lap. Nancy was okay, and that was good, but nothing told him his children were safe.

There was a knock at the door.

When Guy opened it, he found Frank standing there.

"My aunt is gone," he said. "I tried to get a hold of her, but a nurse at the local hospital answered the phone."

Guy sighed. "I'm sorry, Frank."

"Thank you. Have you got a hold of your kids? Nancy?" "Nancy is okay, but Kyle and Alice are in London." "Their class trip?"

Guy huffed. "Now I really feel like an asshole. I forgot all about it, Frank. They're stuck on the other side of the Atlantic, and Nancy can't get hold of them. I... I don't know if they're okay."

"Of course they are. I've never known a thirteen-year old boy as grown up as your Kyle. He'll be looking after Alice even as we speak. They'll be okay."

"I hope you're right."

"I am. So what's our next move, Captain?"

"We head for Norfolk, as commanded. We can refuel and get new orders."

"Sounds like the smart move. You will have a problem on your hands though."

Guy tilted his head. "What problem?"

"Begins with a T."

"Tosco? What's my second-in-command up to now?" "Some of the men want to leave, go to their families. Tosco

told them they could."

"He said what? I'll throttle him."

Frank put his hand against Guy's chest. "Just stay calm.

You can control the situation best by making the most sense. Tosco's just another demagogue who thinks you run a ship by pandering to your men."

"Demagogue? Have you been studying the dictionary again?"

"Not a lot to do on board a ship but read. I'll get the Hatchet moving again. Sooner we leave New York in our wake the better, if you ask me."

Guy nodded agreement.

They marched up to the pilothouse where they found Tosco and a gathering of enlisted men. Guy was happy to see that none of his other officers had sided with Tosco and were all elsewhere, performing their duties. Tosco held his chin high and squared his shoulders as if he were about to put forward a great speech of noble cause.

Guy didn't give him a chance to utter a single word. "I understand that some of you want to leave," he said, wiping the smug expression from Tosco's face as he took the upper hand and addressed the issue before it had a chance to be raised. Tosco would not get the opportunity to play hero and put forward the concerns of his men. "But I would remind you of why you are here: You are enlisted men of the United States Coast Guard. You are not trained killers, like the Navy. You are not merchantmen or fishermen. You sail the Seven Seas not as pirates. Every man and woman aboard this ship signed up to be a hero, and today we saved over thirty civilians from a terrible fate. For that, they will thank us for the rest of their lives. You probably think that earns you the right to disembark this ship and go searching for your families. Perhaps it does. Yet, I ask you to think carefully, because the moment you step off this ship, you cease being heroes at a time when the world needs heroes more than ever. As long as people are in need of help, it is our duty to stay aboard this ship and do what we signed up to do. Something terrible happened today, and our country is relying on us to minimise the damage. If we fail to protect our homeland, then what do our families even have left to live for? America is a country forged by brave men and women. The moment we stop fighting for our freedom is the moment we lose it. I, too, have a family, but I will remain aboard the Hatchet and do my duty. I ask you to do the same. We are heading to Norfolk, and there we will rearm and refuel. What will happen beyond that, I do not know, but I suggest that those of you that pray do so now. Pray for us all."

Before anybody replied, Guy turned to Frank and gave his orders. "Sail us out of here, Chief Petty, and don't stop until I say so."

~RICK BASTION~
DEVONSHIRE, ENGLAND

RICK STILL HAD THE INJURED WOMAN IN HIS arms, but now Sarah had passed out on the floor besides him. Keith was frantic trying to call Marcy while everyone else in the pub paced up and down. The news report said they were at war—not just Britain, but the entire world. Where had the creatures come from? What did they want? Was it all some kind of media conspiracy? Other than what he'd seen on the news, Rick had witnessed none of it for himself. He'd walked to the pub only two hours before, and it had been a normal evening. It wasn't until this injured woman had collapsed in front of the bar he saw anything wrong first hand.

"The paramedics are here," somebody said, and Rick looked up to see a man and woman entering. Both wore green NHS jumpsuits, and were quick to rush over to help. There was no mistaking the haunted look in their eyes.

"What happened to her?" The female paramedic asked as she started examining the unconscious woman.

"I have no idea," said Rick. "She just ran into the pub and fell down."

"Something bad is going on," said Keith. "It's all over the news. My wife isn't answering her phone. Something's happened."

"We know," said the male paramedic, whose bald head was slick with sweat.

"What do you know?" asked Rick. "Anything we don't?"

"This woman is dead." The female paramedic said. She went to stand up. "We can't help her."

"What? You haven't even tried," said Rick.

"She has no heartbeat. I'm sorry. Usually, we might try to do something, but we had another seven emergencies called in on our way here. We're the only ambulance in the area, and we have to spend our time where it can do most good. This woman has been dead too long."

Rick looked down at the woman whose head he'd been holding for fifteen minutes and saw the truth of it. The amount of blood that'd leaked from her chest had formed a massive puddle on the wooden floor beneath her, and her arms were the colour of chalk. She was cold.

"Can you help Sarah?" he asked. "She passed out from the shock."

The female paramedic took something from her kit bag and waved it beneath Sarah's nose. She winced and began to stir. "She'll be fine. Just give her a few minutes to wake up."

"We have to go," the male paramedic urged.

"What do we do with her?" asked Keith, pointing to the dead woman.

"I'll inform the coroner," said the female paramedic. "Just place a sheet over her and wait for someone to come."

Rick eased the dead woman's head down onto the floorboards and stood up. He retrieved his pint from the table and downed half of it.

The paramedics disappeared out the door, which left the people inside the pub to stand around anxiously. Nobody knew what to do. Rick wondered if he should go home or stay where he was.

Screaming from outside.

Rick stared at his brother. "What now?"

"I don't know. Just close the door."

Rick nodded, went over to do so, but couldn't help glancing outside at the car park. The ambulance was parked right outside, its lights chasing away the shadows of approaching night. The paramedics were nowhere to be seen.

The screaming had stopped.

He took a tentative step outside the pub and looked around. The front of the ambulance faced him at an angle, its large rear doors hanging open. He couldn't see inside from where he stood, but the paramedics must be in the back.

Who had screamed?

"Hello? Is everything all right out here?"

The sound of movement from the ambulance drew him forward another few steps. It took a handful more until he had moved around sufficiently to face the rear of the vehicle.

Something horrible glared back at him.

It was a man, but also a monster. His eyes were cloudy and white, lips cracked and bleeding. He looked dead.

"Are you okay?" asked Rick, not knowing what else to say.

"I am your end," the dead man hissed. "I will use your hollowed skull as a latrine."

Rick noticed the bald paramedic lying on a gurney in the back of the ambulance. His neck had been twisted around and broken. This monster had murdered him and would do the same to Rick. He turned to run, but the dead man leapt out and grabbed him, cold hands seizing his throat. Rick fought back the only way he could—with his legs. He lifted his right foot and stamped down on where he hoped a kneecap would be, and the dead man howled and collapsed sideways. The icy fingers slipped from around Rick's neck and allowed him chance to stagger away.

The dead man bellowed. It reached out its hands to try and grab Rick again, but every time he tried, he crumpled to the ground as his broken leg folded.

"Is it safe?" came a voice.

Rick glanced upwards to see that the female paramedic was lying prone on the roof of the ambulance. A bad scratch parted her left eyebrow, but she seemed otherwise okay. "What are you doing up there?" he said. "Come down and help-"

The dead man tackled Rick around the waist, dragging him to the ground. Before he could react, his enemy had straddled him and was back to squeezing his throat. "Submit to slavery, worm, and you may get to live out your days as a foot licker."

Rick struggled, tried to bring his legs up to kick the monster off of him, but he couldn't get any leverage. Every second, the pressure in his head increased and made it impossible to focus on anything else other than trying to get a breath.

"Your men will be sodomites, your women whores."

"Well, doesn't that just sum up the 21st Century?" Keith appeared over the dead man's shoulder, holding what looked like an old iron fire poker. He brought the metal rod down two-handed, like a barbarian wielding a broadsword, and shattered his target's skull, caving it in at the top so that it resembled a grizzly heart shape.

Rick swatted the hands away from his throat and gasped uncontrollably, even as his brother and the paramedic dragged him to his feet.

"There are more coming," cried the paramedic.

Clutching his throat and still struggling for air, Rick glanced across the car park and saw that more of the dead men were indeed coming. They lumbered down the road like zombies, but were cursing and shouting threats. One of them brandished a tree branch like a spear.

"Get inside," Keith urged. "Now!"

The three of them hurried back inside the pub, closing and locking the thick wooden door behind them. The helpful businessman understood that danger was on its way because he quickly dragged a table over to act as a barricade.

Rick staggered over and finished what was left of his pint, then slumped over the table while Keith took charge. He told them what was coming and that they all needed to find weapons. It was good that he was being proactive, because nobody else was. Rick least of all. He could do nothing but close his eyes and wish it wasn't all happening.

"R-Rick?"

Rick opened his eyes and glanced to the side. Sarah had woken up on the floor and was propping herself up on her elbows. She looked bewildered. "What's happening?"

He knelt beside her. "We're in a spot of bother." "The monsters are here, aren't they?"

Rick nodded.

"Are we going to die?"

He looked at her face and couldn't bear to tell her the truth; so he lied. "We'll be fine. My brother already took care of one of them."

Sarah smiled at him, but she looked more likely to cry than laugh.

* * *

"Why aren't they trying to get inside?" asked the female paramedic, whose name turned out to be Maddy. She peeked out of one window through a gap in the curtains.

"Because they don't want to end up like their friend," said Keith, patting the iron poker that he had not put down since bashing the dead man's brains in. His bravado might have been masking the fact he still couldn't get through to Marcy.

"It's because they're smart," Rick muttered as he worked on his fresh pint. "They're figuring out the best way to get at us."

Maddy folded her arms. "Then we have to be ready."

The businessman, Steven, clutched an iron poker, identical to the one Keith had. He waved it in the air as he spoke. "Whatever is out there picked on the wrong people."

"This isn't time for bravado," said Rick, staring into his pint. "The thing that attacked me wasn't human. It was like a zombie, only it spoke. It hated me, hated all of us."

Sarah plonked herself down on a chair next to him. "We need to get help."

Keith pointed his poker at Maddy. "She was supposed to be our help."

Maddy sighed. "On our way here, emergency calls came in from all over. Only reason Tom and I made it here was because you people were the first to call. I wouldn't hold up much hope of getting any more help. I've got a feeling that emergency services are inundated right now. Poor Tom..."

"Then we stay here," said Keith. "We batten down the hatches and arm ourselves. The Army will get a handle on this eventually. That thing that attacked Rick was easy enough to kill. Wherever these things came from, they underestimated us."

"I need another drink, Diane" said Rick, suppressing a dire need to belch. The barmaid fetched him one.

"I don't think getting drunk is the answer," said Keith.

Rick held up his fresh pint. "You go ahead and be the hero. I'm going to get pissed."

Steven waved his poker again. "We need to stick together and stay focused. You'd be dead if your brother hadn't helped you."

"I would be too," said Maddy. "Thank you."

Keith lifted his chin and squared his shoulders. "Just doing what anyone else would have. I'm sure my brother would do the same."

Rick sighed. "So what do we do?"

"We get ready," said Keith. "Those things try to get inside, we do everything we can to stop them."

Maddy nodded. "Sounds like a plan."

Everyone agreed, and within minutes, they all had weapons. Rick, Steven, and Keith clutched iron pokers from the pub's three fireplaces, while Diane and Maddy wielded knives from the kitchen. Everyone else went with whatever they could find, ranging from jagged beer bottles to a baseball bat found hidden beneath the bar. It was just in time, too. The attack began not ten minutes later.

***

The fight came not to the front door, but to one of the windows. The thick double-glazing did not shatter, but crumpled inwards a piece at a time. Everyone formed up, weapons at the ready.

A window smashed at the opposite end of the pub.

"Damn it," Keith shouted. "Split into two groups, one at each window. Move, move, move."

Rick headed towards the other window, taking Sarah and Steven with him. To his dismay, they both looked at him like he was the one in charge.

The window shook in its frame, the curtains flapping as the air moved. "You both ready?" Rick asked.

Sarah nodded. Steven pulled off his blazer and threw it on the floor, rolled up his shirt sleeves, then gave a thumbs up.

"If they're anything like the one that attacked me, these things like going for the neck. As soon as they lunge, let them have it."

Large shards of glass fell loose and shattered on the ground. Rick tightened his grip on his poker, knuckles creaking. Sarah held her beer bottle near her waist, ready to stab.

Then the siege halted.

Both windows stopped cracking as the enemy outside stopped attacking. Rick looked at his brother at the other side of the pub, who replied with a confused frown.

There was noise. Rumbling.

Rick cocked his head. "Is that...? Is that the ambulance?" "It sounds like somebody is driving it," said Steven. Sarah shifted on the spot. "Those things can drive?"

"It looks that way," said Steven. "Why, though? If they want to get at us in here, why drive away?"

Rick had a thought. "Unless..."

Sarah looked at him. "Unless what?"

Rick heard the noise of the accelerating engine just in time to shout a warning. "They're going to ram us."

An earthquake shook the building and the barricade in front of the pub's door disintegrated as the nose of a speeding ambulance crashed through it. The heavy wooden door flew off its hinges and crashed against the bar.

"They're dividing us," Rick shouted. "They've split us in two."

The ambulance's rear doors sprung open and dead men spilled out. From the driver's seat, a corpse with long black hair slid out. It looked at the poker in Rick's hand and laughed. "I'll gut you with that thing before you ever get chance to swing it."

Rick defied his enemy and swung at a dead woman with mottled grey breasts. His head was fuzzy with alcohol, but he was glad to have the edge taken off now. Sober, he might have retched at the sight of her caved in skull.

Steven joined the fight and took out two dead men in quick succession. Sarah was less aggressive, and backed away until a dead woman was right on top of her. Desperation made her strike out, but she managed to slice her attacker's throat open.

From the other side of the pub, obscured by the crashed ambulance, the other guests fought for their lives. Rick worried about his brother and gritted his teeth as he connected a blow with a brunette's rotting skull. He fought his way to the ambulance, but dead men continued to spill out into the pub and blocked his way.

The fight had just got started.

Steven held his own. With Sarah huddled behind him and striking out at anything that got too near, they made a good team. Rick took out another attacker, gained several more feet towards the ambulance, but the black-haired dead man stood in his path.

"A valiant effort, worm."

He struck Rick in the chest with the force of a kicking horse and sent him flying into the air. He hit the ground in a crumpled mess, and it was only dumb luck that allowed him to keep a hold of his poker. He thrust it out in front of him as protection while he fought to get his breath.

"You are pathetic, worm."

Rick waved the poker, but was powerless on his back. "W-what are you?"

"A man."

Rick shuffled backwards. "You're not a man, you're a monster."

"Men are monsters."

Rick cowered, tried to get up, but ended up shuffling along on his backside some more. The dead man cackled with delight.

"Please," Rick begged.

"Your begging will not save you. You are—"

The dead man stumbled forwards in surprise, falling right onto the pointed tip of the poker that Rick still held out in front of him. His bloated stomach slid right down the length of the iron rod and left a slick trail on it. The poker went straight through him, poking out of his back. Rick shoved with all his might and sent the wounded monster to the floor.

Sarah appeared and helped Rick to his feet. Steven stood nearby with his tie flapped over his shoulder, and all around him lay the corpses of dead men. He was panting heavily, keyed-up and ready for more.

"We have to get out of here," said Sarah.

"Not until we help my brother."

Rick could see Keith swinging his poker desperately, as two creatures had him pinned against a strobing fruit machine. They grabbed him by the arms and wrestled with him.

Rick slid over the ambulance's bonnet and raced to help. He no longer had his fire poker—it was embedded inside the black haired dead man's torso—so he did the only thing he could think of and converted his speed into an attack. He aimed his foot at the nearest enemy and put so much force into the kick that the dead man flew into its partner, and the two of them smashed down on top of a table. Keith was quick to capitalise and rammed his poker down into them like a pike, impaling the dead men together like meat on a shish kebab. "Never piss off an accountant," he shouted at them.

Rick grabbed his brother's arm. "We need to leave. This place isn't safe anymore."

Keith looked at the broken windows and the obliterated doorway and nodded. "We need to get back to your house."

"What? No, we need to get help."

"You heard what Maddy said. There is no help. Your house is big and old, with big gates and alarms."

"Sounds good to me," said Diane, coming up behind them and covered in dark red blood that didn't belong to her. The baseball bat in her hands was snapped and caked in gore.

"Me too," said Maddy between pants.

Rick looked around and saw that they had won a pyrrhic victory. A dozen of their attackers lay dead or injured, but many of the pub's drinkers were dead also. Steven and Sarah were still on the opposite side of the ambulance, but they seemed to be okay. They were staring over the bonnet; expressions weary, yet exuberant.

"We made it," said Steven, sounding like he could barely believe it. "I've never been in a fight in my life before today."

"Well, you kicked ass," said Rick. "You were like a Viking."

Sarah patted Steven on the back. "I wouldn't have had a chance without you. You were amaz—"

Her eyes went wide. Steven turned to glance at Sarah and his eyes went wide too. He stepped away, startled.

Rick reached out across the bonnet, not understanding what was happening. "Sarah?"

She opened her mouth to speak, but blood passed between her lips. Gnarled black fingernails appeared around her throat, and then her face disappeared, replaced by the back of her head. The sound of her neck snapping echoed off the ceiling like a gunshot.

Her dead body slumped to the floor.

The black-haired dead man appeared where she had been standing, iron poker still sticking out of his torso. The grey flesh around the wound was scorched. "You think you can fight back, maggots? You will all die." He grabbed the poker in his belly and dragged it out with a slithery plop! then threw it down on the ground next to Sarah's head.

Steven took a swing, but was too slow. The dead man ducked the blow and struck Steven hard enough to launch him up and over the bonnet of the ambulance. Rick and the others ran to his aid, dragging him back to his feet and hustling him towards the exit.

The black-haired corpse laughed at their retreat.

Outside, it was fully dark and completely silent. Steven was groggy and struggled to walk straight, so Keith and Rick grabbed an arm each and marched him across the carpark as fast as they could. As they did so, Rick kept picturing Sarah's face. There one minute; snapped around and facing the wrong way the next.

Dead men walked the Earth, killing the living.

The apocalypse had arrived.

As Rick dared to glance backwards one last time, he saw the black-haired corpse strolling after them casually, apparently, in no hurry.

~MINA MAGAR~

MAYFAIR

I T WAS LIKE WALKING THROUGH A MOVIE SET for the grizzliest film ever made. The dead littered the roads like rubbish, their blood, the ancient city's latest graffiti. Tens of thousands dead. Mina made the assumption simply by extrapolating from what she saw on every street. Now and then, amongst the dead men, women, and children, she or David would spot a body that wasn't human. One laid in front of her now—a charred creature with clumps of flesh between its crooked teeth. Somebody had fought back and run it through with a skiing pole. The price tag still hung from the rubber grip.

"Every inch of its skin is burned away," Mina muttered, more to herself than David. "It's like these things walked right out of a fire."

David was busy making notes and using his phone to take pictures, but he heard what she said and replied. "Well, they say Hell is hot, if that's still what you're implying."

"I think these monsters used to be men and women once. What do you think that means?"

"Maybe they've been burning in Hell for all eternity."

Mina thought about it and found it grim to even consider. Was there really a Hell? Did people truly go there to burn for eternity? She'd never been a believer until now.

"The stones," David said flatly as he pointed his camera phone at a prominent blond, shaggy-haired politician he'd found tangled in the wreckage of a shiny bicycle. "Wherever they're from, the stones are the key."

Mina agreed. The stones had opened some kind of gate, but who had put them there? The monster she had killed outside the pharmacy mentioned 'The Red Lord'. Was that the Devil? Or something worse? Was the giant creature she had glimpsed the Red Lord?

"I wish you hadn't ruined your camera," said David. "We're alone out here and have the exclusive."

Mina groaned. "It was my camera or my life, and we don't have the exclusive. It's happening to everybody, so there's no need for anybody to report it."

"Nonsense. People will be too terrified to understand what is going on. We have a chance here to gain evidence and try to help piece things together. You already have your theory about Hell coming to Earth—as silly as I may deem it—and we can see if it holds water."

Mina took a moment to think about it. They were alone in the aftermath of a catastrophe, and perhaps there were ways to help, but, as she viewed the utter devastation of London, she felt powerless. She prodded the dead creature with her foot and grimaced when the toe of her boot came back sticky. The demons had attacked en masse and with complete surprise, but they could be hurt—and killed. They were ferocious and relentless, but as fragile as any human being. Maybe the Army and their guns could turn things around.

Mina's phone rang and made both of them leap. David had spoken with their Slough office multiple times since they'd left the pharmacy, but Mina had completely forgotten about her own phone.

She answered the phone and heard her father's barking voice on the other end. "Mina? Are you all right?"

"Yes, dad, I'm fine. I'm in London."

"London? Bloody damn it, Mina, why are you always in trouble? You could be at home safe with children, but instead, you are out in the middle of everything."

"I'm a journalist, dad."

"You are not a journalist, Mina. You take your hobby too seriously. I could have lost you today because of your irresponsible behaviour. You need to come home right now. Get away from that city. There is fighting."

"Yes, dad, I know. I saw it first-hand."

"Bloody damn it. You are where it happened? How did you stay safe?"

"I hid."

"Good girl. Now, I am wanting you home."

"It's not that easy, dad. Things are bad here." "That is why you must leave."

"I have a job to do."

"No, you do not."

Mina sighed and gripped the phone tightly in her fist. "Yes, I do, dad. I'm standing in the middle of a thousand bodies, and it's my job to do something to help. I'm not interested in being at home, raising children, and cooking dinner. I'm a journalist, so let me journalist...lise."

"Mina, you do as I am saying."

"I'm twenty-five years old. I'll do what I say." She put down the phone and switched it off, hands shaking.

"You okay?" David asked her.

She swallowed and nodded. "Yeah, I'm fine."

David looked at her, the first time he hadn't frowned or given her an order. "You were good on the phone. Didn't take any nonsense. Attitude like that will take you places."

Mina smiled. "Perhaps. More likely, my dad will make my life a living hell."

"Hell is already here, so what have you got to lose?" "Good point."

Movement ahead. A man stepped out of an alleyway and headed towards them.

"Oh no," said Mina.

David glanced at her. "What is it?"

Mina watched the racist thug heading towards them and felt her bladder loosen. "This guy is bad news."

"Do you know him?"

"More than I would like?"

"Give me that phone, luv," the man demanded once he was close.

"You forgot to say please," said David, folding his arms. There was blood down the racist's white t-shirt, and when he looked at David, there was murder in his eyes. "What did you fucking say to me, mate?"

David shifted a little, but there was too much pride in him to back down. "Manners cost nothing, my friend. You want to borrow my colleague's phone, then I suggest you ask nicely."

"David, it's fine. He can have my phone."

The racist grinned spitefully. "There you go mate, your little slag doesn't mind giving it up."

David strode forward, wagging his finger. "Now look here you-"

The thug punched him around the side of the head so hard Mina thought his skull might have cracked. Unconscious, he flopped face first to the pavement with not even his arms to break his fall.

Mina yelped in shock.

The bald menace sneered at her. "You're that Paki from earlier, ain't ya?"

"I'm not a... I am English."

"The fuck you are."

"I was born in Wigan."

"More like a fucking call centre in Mumbai." "Mumbai is in India, so how could I be a Paki?" "You fucking cheeking me, slag?"

Mina swallowed, tried to find whatever it was she needed to stand up to this beast. "People are dead. You shouldn't be attacking people. We all need to help one another."

"Which is why I want your phone. Give it."

Mina reached into her pocket and pulled out her phone. She was about to hand it over when she caught sight of David, facedown on the floor. Rather than scaring her, it made her angry. She placed the phone back in her pocket and shook her head. "It's my phone and I'm not giving it to you. You try to touch me and I'll scream. The monsters might come."

"Oh, you're going to give it to me, sweetheart, and you can scream all you like." He lunged forward and grabbed her, threw all of his weight on top of her so that she fell backwards and struck the pavement. The wind escaped her lungs and the man grabbed her arms. He bent over her and started to lick and bite her neck like a panting dog.

"Stop it! David, help!"

David remained unconscious just three feet away. "Never had a Paki before." Her attacker nibbled at her

earlobe. His fumbling hands went to the buttons on her jeans and popped the first one. "Gunna fuck the shite out of you, Paki."

Terror got the best of Mina and she screamed.

The beast cut her off by smashing his fist into her mouth. "Shut it!"

He was just about to punch her again when a small red hole appeared in his windpipe, followed almost instantly by a piercing snap! He looked down at her with an expression of utter confusion. The little red dot on his windpipe leaked blood and air, making a gargling sound. He slumped sideways and collapsed to the pavement.

Mina clambered to her feet as quickly as she could, moaning in a mixture of fear and relief. She turned around and saw a group of men in jeans and sportswear—not much more than kids. One of them, a black lad in a luminous green beanie hat, held a smoking pistol in his hand turned sideways. "Racist motherfucker," he muttered as he lowered the gun to his side.

Mina took a breath and said, "Y-you... you shot him. How...? Where did you get a gun?"

The lad gave her an odd look that made her feel stupid. "Ask me no questions, I tell me no lies. You all right, darlin'?"

"I... Yes. Thank you. You're not going to hurt me, are you?"

The lad glanced back at his friends, who seemed to bristle at her comment. Then he looked again at Mina but didn't seem happy. "I just saved your arse, luv, and you accuse me of bein' a mugger and shit. I ain't gunna hurt you. We ain't even like that."

"Oh," said Mina. "It's just that you all look so... scary."

The lad looked down at his baggy jeans and black hoodie, then surprised her by chuckling. "Just how we do on the streets, innit? You dress how you want, and we dress how we wants. Just clothes, innit?"

"Thank you," said Mina, truly meaning it this time. Her attacker lay dead at her feet, but she didn't care one bit. There were lots of people dead today, and the racist bully was among the most deserving.

"What's your name?" Mina asked her rescuer. "Vamps."

"Vamps?"

The lad gave her a wide grin, revealing his gold plated fangs. "Yeah, Vamps. These are my homies: Mass, Ravy, and Gingerbread."

The other three men nodded silently. The one she assumed was gingerbread—due to the gingerbread man on his t-shirt—was a huge white guy with curly ginger hair.

Mina shook all of their hands. "It's a pleasure to meet you all."

"You need to be careful out here," Vamps warned her. "There's some heavy shit going down."

"I know. I'm a journalist. David and I are trying to get out of the city. You should come with us."

Vamps looked down at David, who was finally beginning to stir, and then back at her. "Nah, I'm sound, darlin'. These are my streets, d'you get me? Me and the boys are staying put, and any of them fucked-up, Freddy Krueger bitches wansta come take us on, they welcome. This is our manor and ain't nothing gonna bowl up and make a mess of it. You take care, darlin'. Next time, just hand over your phone, innit? And 'ere, take this." He pulled a thin black stick out of his belt and tossed it Mina's way.

She caught the object and saw that it was a metal police baton. The weight of it in her hands felt deadly, and she immediately felt safer. She couldn't help it, she hugged Vamps as he was about to leave. "You're a hero," she told him.

Vamps eased her away, looking awkward. "Easy now. I ain't no hero. Don't you go writin' 'bout me in your paper. I ain't news friendly."

Mina nodded. "I promise. Take care."

"You too."

Then the group of young men disappeared, merging into the side streets as if they were a part of the city itself. The spirit of London had just saved her.

David managed to sit up and rub at his head. He saw the racist thug lying dead on the pavement, and then he looked up at Mina. "What the hell happened?"

Mina helped her colleague up and told him, "You wouldn't believe me. There are angels in this city as well as demons."

* * *

"Did you hear something?" David asked Mina about an hour later. Since setting off again, they hadn't encountered another soul. Mina had secretly been hoping to run into Vamps and his gang again, but they were long gone. David listened to her story about the young man's heroics, and was upset that she hadn't kept the lad around for an interview. He'd been grumpy ever since waking up, and it was hardly surprising, considering the angry red lump on the side of his head where the thug had punched him. He'd also grazed his forehead on the pavement when he fell. Mina, herself, had a fat lip.

"I said did you hear that?"

Mina clutched the police baton Vamps had given her and raised it by her side. "I don't know what it was, but maybe it's a bad idea, us being out in the open like this."

"Perhaps you're right."

The noise came again, and this time Mina spotted movement. It came from the top floor of a double decker bus. Someone was staring out of the window.

"Oh god," said Mina. "There's a kid up there."

David looked up at where she was pointing and gasped. "My word."

"I'll go get him." Mina hurried, but then slowed down. The last thing the poor kid needed was someone sprinting towards him with a weapon. She reached the bus and climbed the steps carefully. The seats on the lower deck were all empty and the driver's compartment door hung wide open.

"Hello? You don't have to be afraid. My name is Mina."

The sound of scurrying feet came from above her head, but no voice in reply. She worried what she had seen only looked like a child, but might have been something else—another racist bully, or a demon. She hated having to have the police baton at the ready, but she lifted it now and was more than prepared to use it as she headed up the stairwell behind the driver's compartment. When she reached the top deck of the bus, she saw more empty seats. Litter and abandoned possessions littered the floor, including a fat wallet with cash poking out of it.

A thatch of brown hair rose above the back of a seat, and a young boy peered at her.

"Hey there, little guy. Are you hurt?"

No reply. The staring eyes scrutinised her.

"My name is Mina. What's your name?"

"Don't come any closer."

"It's okay." She took another step, despite the boy's warning, and this prompted him to leap out at her and wave a claw hammer in her face. "I said step back."

Upon closer inspection, the boy wasn't so young—a teenager in fact, and probably as tall as she was. She took a step back. "I'm not here to hurt you. I just want to see if you're okay."

When the boy spoke again, she noticed his American accent. "I'm fine," he snapped. "Just leave us be."

Mina frowned. "Us?"

A girl popped up from behind another of the seats. Unlike her older brother, she had golden blonde hair. "Kyle? Is she another monster?"

"No, Alice. She's just a normal lady, but she's going now." "I don't want her to go."

"We have to stay here, where it's safe."

"It's safer if you come with us," said Mina.

The boy pulled a face. "Out there? Everybody's dead."

"I want to go home," Alice moaned.

Kyle placed an arm around her. "I know you do, Ally, but home is far away. We have to keep ourselves safe. I'll look after you, I promise."

There was the sound of footfalls coming up the stairs, making them all fret, but it was only David. He rounded the last few steps and entered the upper deck. "Crikey," he said when he saw them all standing there. "Two children? How did you both survive?"

"We hid," said Kyle, puffing out his chest. "We were on a school field trip—my entire grade plus a few from the grades below. We were all headed to the zoo, but we got attacked by a bunch of monsters. All our friends and teachers are dead. Only reason we got away is cus I had to take care of my sister. I got her and ran. One of our teachers was with us for a while, but he left us."

Mina gasped. "He left you?"

"Yeah, more of those monsters came at us from down an avenue and Mr Campbell ran into an alleyway. We didn't have a chance to follow him, so we hid inside a store—that's where I got this hammer—but then the store caught on fire and we had to run again. Alice spotted this bus, and that's where we've been for hours."

"We need to get you out of the city," said Mina. "David and I will protect you. We won't run away on you like your teacher did. Will we, David?"

"What? Oh, no, of course not. You're safe with us, lad. We're journalists."

Alice looked at her brother like a hungry kitten. "Please, Kyle. I don't want to stay on this bus anymore. The monsters are all gone. We watched them leave."

"I think it's safe for now," Mina assured them. "The monsters seemed to have gone someplace else."

Kyle huffed. "Yeah, but where? They didn't just vanish."

"Which is why you need to come with us," she said. "It's getting dark, and the monsters could be back any minute. You'd be all alone out here if they do."

Alice whimpered.

Kyle's expression lost some of its confidence, and the hammer he held so confidently lowered to his side. "Okay, we'll come with you folks, but only if you promise to get us back home to America. No offence, but London sucks balls."

Mina laughed. "It's certainly seen better days. Good to meet you, Kyle and Alice. This is my colleague, David, and I've already told you that my name is Mina."

"Pleased to meet you," said Alice, offering out her little hand and shaking Mina's.

"Are we ready?" David asked impatiently

Kyle raised his hammer and nodded. "I want to get my sister home."

***

They had headed east through Mayfair, planning on using the first working car they came across, but they were yet to find an area where the traffic hadn't snarled up into an impassable wall at every intersection.

Hyde Park was ahead, Marble Arch sat just a little way off in the distance. For now it was as good a place as any to head, so that's where they went.

"They say that's where you used to hang people," said Kyle, a macabre grin on his face.

David returned the boy's smile. "That's right, lad. They called it Tyburn in those days, and the elm trees here were used to execute condemned men. The most famous of them all, the Tyburn Tree, used to be at the site where Marble Arch now sits. Executions were entertainment."

Alice looked horrified. "They used to enjoy watching people die?"

"They don't anymore. Great Britain doesn't execute people in this day and age. America would be wise to follow our lead. It's uncivilised."

"America is the greatest country in the world," said Kyle.

"For now, yes," David conceded. "But the British Empire once ruled the world, and look at it now. All great empires are destined to eventual mediocrity and extinction. No dynasty lasts forever. Before the British Empire, there was the Ottoman Empire, and before that, the Holy Roman Empire. Before that-"

"We get the point," said Mina. "I think what David is trying to tell you, Kyle, is that you should never think yourself better than anybody else. We're all just people, and we should stick together. Especially now."

Kyle chewed at the inside of his cheek and seemed to consider the lesson being taught to him, which Mina thought was pretty level headed for a teenage boy.

"I like England," said Alice. "Even with the monsters. I like all the big statues and the palaces. America should have a King instead of a president. Presidents are rubbish."

"My mum says they're all crooks," Kyle added.

Mina smiled. "Are you sure you can't remember your mother's telephone number, Kyle? It would be good to call her."

"It's stored on my phone, but the teachers made us leave our phones in the hotel."

"Unfortunate," said David. "Where are you children from again?"

"Nebraska, originally, but our mom moved us to Maine. It's where Stephen King lives."

"Yes, I'm aware. What about your father?"

"He lives on a boat." Kyle said it contemptuously. "Don't see him much."

"He's a United States Coast Guard," Alice added. "He rescues people."

"Wow," said Mina. "I wish my daddy did something cool like that. My daddy runs a chip shop."

Alice frowned. "What's a chip shop?"

"It's where they sell English French fries," Kyle told her knowingly.

Mina smiled. "That's right."

"Can we have some?" Alice asked.

"Sure we c-"

David put a hand up to halt the conversation. "Oh, yes! Oh, bloody well thank the stars. We're saved."

Mina put her arms around each of the children and squeezed them tight as they all saw what lay ahead of them. "Soldiers," cried David. "It's the British bloody Army." Hyde Park was covered in a vast collection of military jeeps and trucks. Soldiers milled about like ants, and were setting up sandbag walls, or mounting scary-looking machine guns on tripods. Mina noticed other survivors wandering into the park from every direction, spilling out of side streets or stumbling out of nearby buildings. From out in the open, it was clear that London was burning, but this large area of grass and water had been spared. People were being rescued. This was salvation.

A squad of soldiers spotted Mina's group and immediately approached. The lead soldier's name patch read: MARTIN. "Identify yourselves," he barked.

David spoke on their behalf. "My name is David Davids, journalist for the Slough Echo. This is my photographer, Mina Magar. These children were unfortunate enough to be on a school trip from America. We picked them up on our travels."

"I'm Corporal Martin, good to meet you." The soldier looked at the two children and seemed sympathetic. "Your parents are back in America?"

They both nodded.

"Sorry to hear that. We'll try to contact them for you." He focused on Alice and said, "You're lucky you had your big brother watching out for you."

Kyle wrapped his arm around his little sister and stood proudly.

"Have you got everything under control?" Mina asked the soldier, nodding to the large military force spread out over the park.

Martin shook his head. "Not even close. The Army deployed in three sections of the city, but we all took a hammering. Orders came through to fall back either here or at Greenwich Park. We're concentrating on getting civilians out of the city. You're lucky you found us."

"We need to get to Slough," said David.

"No can do. We're choppering people out to Cambridge. They're setting up a refugee camp there, but it's not safe to go north or east."

"Why not?" Mina asked.

"Because London isn't the only place hit. Birmingham and Manchester are both under attack too, and so are Southampton, Swindon, Plymouth, and a shit-tonne of other places. The enemy are coming at us from all sides."

"Do we know what they are?"

"Not a clue. Some of the men have been calling them demons; said those glowing gates lead straight to Hell."

Mina caught David glancing at her, but she asked another question, "Where have all the demons in London gone?"

Martin shrugged. "We made a dent in their numbers when we caught them out in the open at Regent's Park. Choppers made a real mess of 'em at first, but then they took rifles off our dead squaddies and aimed them up at the sky. The RAF pulled out and left us to look after ourselves. Typical Crabs."

Alice tilted her head. "Crabs?"

Martin smiled at her kindly. "Yeah, sweetheart, the RAF pilots. Ask 'em to lend a hand and they crawl off sideways. That's why we call 'em Crabs."

Alice frowned and remained confused.

"Where are the demons now?" Mina asked.

"North of the city. The enemy army in Birmingham is

heading south—they took a battering as well—so we think they might plan to merge their forces. More of those creatures are pouring through the gates every minute, so we're doing our best to secure each one."

"So we're getting a handle on it?" asked David hopefully.

"Huh, hardly. We gave 'em a good seein' to, admittedly, but they outnumber our forces fifty-to-one. Eventually, we'll run out of weapons and men—most of our veterans are overseas and we've had to call in the reserves. This ain't like bombing a bunch of Afghans. These are our own cities, full of civilians. The only way we can fight back is by putting boots on the ground—but that's not something we can do indefinitely. People need to join the fight."

David frowned. "What do you mean?"

"I mean you civvies will have to start diggin' in instead of running and hiding. The only way we'll win this war is by matching the enemy's numbers. Everyone needs to get involved in this one, but the TV and radio are warning them all to stay in their homes. Not my call, but if you ask me, that will be our downfall. The Armed Forces can't win this war on its own."

"We're reporters," said Mina. "We can tell people to fight back."

David scoffed. "Against an army of demons, Mina? Really?"

Corporal Martin shot David a glance. "Either that or we all die, pal. Simple choice when you think about it. Come on into the camp. There'll be a chopper heading out in an hour or so."

"To Cambridge though," said Mina. "If you want us to tell people to fight, we need to get to our offices in Slough."

"No can do. The CO has already been begging the Press to rally the public, but they're getting their orders straight from the PM—wherever that cowardly bugger is hiding. The Government is trying to keep everyone out of harm's way—I understand where they are coming from— but they don't understand that they're dooming us all."

"We're from an independent paper," said David. "We don't have politicians pulling our strings. We can report the truth."

"At a piddling paper in Slough. Ha!"

Mina tried to get the soldier to see sense. "It's a start, isn't it? We have a website. Who knows who might read it? We say the right things and word will spread. What other chance is there?"

Martin rubbed at his chin and thought about it. "Okay," he eventually said. "I can't redirect a chopper for you, but I can spare a couple men and a jeep to get you out of the city. Slough isn't too far to take the risk, I suppose. If you can get some civvies to fight, I can hardly say no."

Mina and David looked at each other and smiled. They were finally getting the hell out of this city.

~GUY GRANGER~
NORFOLK, VIRGINIA

SOUND CARRIED WELL ACROSS THE DAWN waves, which was why the Hatchet's crew heard Norfolk Naval Station long before they saw it. The report of gunfire and explosions was an omen none of them appreciated, and when they came within visual distance, they encountered the largest collection of military and Coast Guard vessels any of them had ever witnessed. Frigates and cutters floated alongside monolithic destroyers and sleek gunships. Guy even spotted an aircraft carrier he was certain was the USS New Hampshire, not even due to be finished for another eight months. Completing the fleet were several dozen littoral combat ships and patrol boats—quick and agile craft with small crews. It was a veritable invasion force, but the battlefield had come to them.

All the ships in dock were playing host to enemy forces— those same burned creatures that had attacked New York. They were also under attack by a second army of animalistic creatures with deadly talons. Guy watched a massive group of them tear right through the crew of a Hazard Perry class frigate, like termites through a table leg.

Unlike the attack on New York, this latest enemy had a clear leader. The giant beast towered above the docks and looked like a man, but it had the twisted spines of broken wings on its back. A loincloth covered its waist, but it was otherwise naked. Long golden hair fell across its muscular shoulders.

An angel acting like a beast.

The giant was so strong that it lifted a petrol tanker parked on the docks and hurled it. The metal cylinder collided with the decks of the USS New Hampshire and conflagrated. Burning sailors scattered across the decks while a scorched hole appeared in the aircraft carrier's runway. A helicopter tilted over on its side and fell into the water.

"It's a massacre," said Tosco, standing beside Guy in the pilothouse.

Guy kept the binoculars pressed against his eyes. "They must have somehow known the Navy was assembling here."

Frank's eyes went wide. "You mean they hit us strategically?"

"Maybe it's a coincidence," said Tosco. "There could be a gate nearby. We need a confirmed list so we know where's safe and where's not."

It was a good idea so Guy nodded. "Lieutenant, can you focus on that going forward? Every time we get Intel, or an enlisted man calls home and finds out about an attack, make a note of it and stick it on the map."

"Roger that, but what do we do right now though? Should we retreat?"

Guy studied the battlefield and considered turning around and leaving, but ended up shaking his head. "I think it's time for us to start acting like heroes. Get the big gun ready, Frank. Tosco, get men on the MGs."

Tosco left the pilothouse while Frank passed orders to the ship's gunner, Petty Officer 3rd Class Carrie Bentley. The woman got to work, flipping switches and inputting commands at a rate Guy himself could never hope to match.

"Main gun online," she said after a few moments. "Give me a target and it's gone, sir."

Guy looked through the binoculars and tried to figure out where best to strike. The problem was that the battlefield was a melee; man fought monster at close quarters. There were few places to hit that would not result in casualties on both sides.

Then he saw his opportunity.

"Hit the big son-of-a-bitch."

Bentley looked at Guy. "Just to confirm, Captain, you're asking me to target that giant, winged, can't possibly exist, son-of-a-bitch we're all looking at right now but can't quite believe?"

"That's the one, sailor."

"Aye, aye, sir."

Guy stood behind Frank with a hand on the man's shoulder. "Take us in closer, Chief Petty, but not so close that we can get hit with anything that son-of-a-bitch throws."

The Hatchet forged ahead, all those standing in the pilothouse enraptured by what they were seeing. All those on the decks were busy as bees as they readied weapons and prepared to fight. Every ship lying in Norfolk's dock was a war zone, with men being torn apart in their dozens as they ran out of ammo and could not reload quick enough. The ships lucky enough to be at sea were relatively safe from the fighting—some were even leaving—but the enemy snatched assault rifles from dead sailors and fired at them. Anyone not smart enough to be in cover ran the risk of being peppered with 5.6mm NATO rounds. The enemy was smart.

It was a massacre.

The giant son-of-a-bitch bellowed and grunted his commands, directing his creatures like a medieval general. The monsters spread out over the docks like vermin, devouring everything in their path.

"I have the target locked, Captain," Bentley informed him. "Fire when ready, sailor."

The ship rocked, and an explosion followed. The shell was too fast to see in flight, but when it hit the son-of-a-bitch in the chest, everyone in the pilothouse cheered. Staggering backwards, the giant was stunned and off balance. A scorch mark on its chest released tendrils of smoke.

Bentley turned in her seat and grinned. "Hit confirmed, sir."

"Good work, Bentley."

The giant roared. It had not toppled, and was in no way beaten.

"Fire again, sailor."

"Aye, Captain."

Bentley let off another shot. Another direct hit.

Once again, the shell struck the giant squarely in the centre of its chest. This time, it dropped to one knee, but it was straight back up again, glancing around until it spotted the Hatchet and understood from where the shell had fired. It pointed its massive hand and bellowed.

"Sir, I think we pissed the target off," came Bentley. "Permission to shit my pants?"

"Permission granted."

The giant stomped towards the docks; as it picked up speed, it glared across the sea at the Hatchet.

"It'll never reach us," Frank muttered. "We're a half-mile out."

Guy grunted into his radio. "Tosco, open up the MGs." "Roger that."

There was an almighty rat-a-tat-tat as the Hatchet's two side-mounted machine guns unleashed on their target. The giant roared and swiped at the air as if surrounded by flies. It staggered again, but still did not go down, nor did it even bleed.

Frank had grown pale. "Its flesh must be made of iron."

Guy crossed his arms, narrowed his eyes. "Fire again, Bentley. Take its goddamn head off."

Bentley loaded up another shell and let rip. The impact knocked the target's head back with such force that Guy actually winced. The giant toppled backwards and fell to the ground, crushing its own minions beneath it.

The Hatchet's crew cheered and whooped.

"Eat that!" Bentley shouted in victory.

"Good work," said Guy, patting her on the back.

Then the giant leapt back up to its feet, so angry that it kicked a group of its own creatures up into the air like a petulant child kicking toy soldiers.

Guy swallowed a mouthful of dread. "We can't kill this thing."

"It can't reach us," Frank said again.

Silence descended over the pilothouse.

The giant sprinted for the edge of the docks. There was nowhere to go as the ground ahead disappeared and the water neared, but it did not slow down. When it reached the end of the dock, it launched itself into the air and came down right on top of the damaged runway of the USS New Hampshire. It sprinted down the entire length, knocking aside wounded sailors and stomping on inert aircraft. Then it leapt onto a nearby frigate. The smaller ship lurched, tilted, but stayed afloat. The giant kept on running.

"Get us out of here," Guy barked. "Full-turn-one-eighty, now!"

Frank took the controls, hustling men out the way. The ship vibrated as the engines went to max output. Everyone on board held on to whatever was bolted down.

The giant leapt from the frigate to a smaller patrol boat that couldn't bear its weight, so it leapt to another frigate. It would be right on top of the Hatchet soon, a clear causeway of Navy vessels all the way.

The horizon panned through the pilothouse window as the Hatchet turned to port full speed. No large ship could quickly perform a one-eighty, but Guy was satisfied that his crew was doing it as fast as possible.

But they were not going to make it.

The giant continued leaping from ship to ship, getting closer and closer. It would be on them any second, landing right on their decks and sinking them.

Guy had to do something. "Bentley, load another shell." "And fire?"

"Not until I give the command. Just keep a lock on the target."

"Aye, Captain."

The Hatchet carried on turning.

The giant kept on getting closer.

They were sitting ducks.

"Sir, if we don't fire soon, the ship will be pointing in the wrong direction, and I won't be able to hit the target." "Just hold, Bentley."

"But sir..."

"Hold!"

Several ships sank as they bore the giant's weight. Another ten seconds and the son-of-a-bitch would reach the Hatchet and sink it just the same.

"Sir, I must fire now." "No, Bentley, hold."

There was a tense silence. The men in the pilothouse clenched their fists and waited for the captain's orders.

The giant let out an almighty roar as it launched itself from the final stepping-stone, aiming itself right at the Hatchet's launch deck.

Guy threw out his fist. "Fire!"

Bentley launched the shell.

It hit the target in the middle of its chest and spun it in mid-air. The force of the blow had altered the giant's trajectory and sent it tumbling into the ocean instead of onto the rear deck of the Hatchet.

Guy turned to Frank. "Cease turn, full engines fore."

The Hatchet sped away.

The giant broke the surface of the water and roared, but it would never swim fast enough to catch them now, they were headed in a straight line. They left Norfolk Naval Station ablaze behind them, a hundred ships sinking to their doom.

"Where to next?" Frank asked once they had some breathing room. The crow's feet at the edge of his eyes had extended.

"How are we doing for fuel?" Guy asked.

"Almost empty. We can go about another six-hundred miles."

"We need to fill her up. Whatever happens we'll need to be on the move. I won't risk a situation where we need to get somewhere in a hurry and can't."

"There're refuelling facilities at Norfolk, Captain, but I guess that's out."

"Head down to Cape Fear, Frank. We'll refuel there." "Aye. It'll take a few hours."

"Good, it'll give us all time to come to terms with what's happening, and for Tosco to make a start on that list. Time to find out the state of our beloved country."

"Should we contact Command?"

Guy considered his last orders from Command, to head to Norfolk, and decided his men's welfare was better left to him. "No, Frank. Let them contact us."

* * *

As Frank had predicted, it took a few hours to reach Cape Fear, but the region on the south-eastern coast of North Carolina was as green and pleasant as ever. The civilian refugees took to the ship's railings to look out at the beauty, and it was obvious that for some, their worries were momentarily forgotten.

The Hatchet hugged the coast on its way down to the Coast Guard station, and during that time, it became clear that a great fear had fallen over the various towns and villages. People here were not under attack, but the country they loved was.

Tosco had compiled a list of confirmed attack sites, and it made for grim reading: Jacksonville, Los Angeles, San Francisco, Anaconda, Memphis, San Diego, Clearwater, Billings, Pittsburgh, Fresno, Atlanta, Omaha, Tulsa, Newport, Wichita, Seattle, Minneapolis, Honolulu, Riverside, Newark, Toledo, Irving, Richmond, Sacramento, San Jose, Norfolk, New York, Des Moines, Brownsville, Peoria, and Elgin. And the two that were likely the reason the residents of Cape Fear were so worried: Charlotte and Raleigh.

There appeared to be no discernible pattern to the attack locations. Some states had relatively few gates, such as Illinois, where neither Chicago nor Springfield had been hit. The Prairie State's biggest disaster site was Carbondale. California, on the other hand, was staging its own Armageddon with nearly every major city hit.

Although every bone in his body begged him not to do it, Guy had allowed his men free access to the radio, telephones, and internet. All the services were spotty, but it had soon become clear that mankind was at war. Every radio and television station had devoted itself to news coverage, but none could seem to agree on what was happening, or what to do about it. The theory that had the most supporters was that the gates to Hell had opened up and demons now walked the Earth seeking to destroy humanity. The second most popular opinion was that aliens were responsible.

It was difficult to draw any conclusions.

The giant the Hatchet had encountered was no anomaly. There had been sightings of similar winged creatures all over the world—including one in London where Kyle and Alice were hopefully still alive. Guy prayed they were. The general assumption was that the giants were Angels of Death come to smite mankind, but that was adamantly hand-waved by the religious-right who would hear nothing of it.

Guy hadn't made up his mind about the truth, but he decided it would be best to refer to the enemy as demons from now on, for efficiency's sake, if nothing else. If the men knew what they were fighting, they would be less afraid and more focused than if they were battling shadows and monsters. The fear on board the Hatchet was enough to incite desertion, and that was something that would need addressing soon. The crew could not be relied upon if their minds were set on leaving.

"We're coming up on the base now," said Frank. "I radioed in, and they're ready to receive us."

Guy blinked. "The Coast Guard is still functioning?" "There's a skeleton crew apparently."

"Good, take us in."

"Aye, Captain."

The Hatchet pulled up alongside the deserted docks, and a grey-haired old man in a navy blue Coast Guard jumper met them. The weather was scorching, but he hadn't seemed to have noticed. He saluted Guy as he appeared on deck and descended the gangway.

"Retired Captain Lund," the old man said. "Caretaker of the station here."

Guy shook his hand gladly. "Captain Granger. Thank you for receiving me, Captain Lund. How have you fared here?"

"Not bad, considering. Nearest attack is Charlotte, but that doesn't make it any less frightening for us here. Watching the news is like watching a horror movie. Command won't return my calls, and I just got word we lost a third of our domestic Navy in Norfolk."

Guy sighed. "We were there. It was bad."

"Well, I'm glad someone made it at least. All the Coast Guard vessels headed there last night to support the military. Some were friends of mine."

"I'm sorry. Some ships got out, but more were lost."

The old man took a long breath and let it out loudly. "You need fuel, I hear? Well, since I have no boats, you can have all the fuel you want. Heading anywhere in particular?"

"I have some ideas, but nothing set in stone yet. We'll head wherever we can find that's safe; unless we're needed somewhere else. From what I saw at Norfolk though, there's not a lot my crew can do but keep care of themselves."

"There're a couple young guys back at base," said Lund. "I'll radio 'em to come fuel you boys up in a jiffy. You wanna come inside a spell and have a cup of Joe?"

"I wish I could," said Guy, "but right now, I need to keep a tight leash on my crew. If I go wandering off inland, they might do the same."

"I understand, Captain. Let me know if I can make myself useful."

"You can count on it. Thank you, Captain Lund."

"You can call me Skip. Everyone else does."

"Thank you, Skip."

Frank came down the gangway. His expression was urgent,

and in his hand, he held a cell phone—Guy's cell phone. "You left it in the pilothouse," he explained. "You will want to take this call."

There was a knot in Guy's stomach, but he reached out and took the phone and placed it against his ear. "Hello?"

"Dad, is that you?"

"Kyle! Are you and Alice okay?"

"Yeah, dad, we're fine."

"Where are you? How did you get in touch with me?" "We're with some soldiers in London. I gave them our

address back home and they got a call to mom. She gave me your number and said I had to call you too."

Guy tried not to dwell on the fact that his son had not chosen to call of his own free will. "I'm so glad you're okay, Kyle. I've been worried. Are they looking after you?"

"Yeah. Things were pretty bad for a while, but then a couple of reporters found me and Alice hiding in a bus. They took us to an army camp in the park. The soldiers are going to put us in a helicopter and take us somewhere safe. I think they said it was some place named Kane Bridge."

Guy thanked God for the British Army. "I want to speak to one of the soldiers before you go."

"Yeah, okay. There's one here with us now—Corporal Martin. He's waiting outside the tent. He'll give you the details of where we're going."

"Good. You look after your sister, Kyle. No matter what, okay? Can I speak with her?"

"Sure."

There was a pause, then Alice's sweet little voice came down the line. "Daddy?"

"Hi, princess. I'm so proud of you for staying safe."

"It was really scary, daddy. There were monsters, but Kyle looked after me."

"I'm proud of him too. The nice soldiers will look after you now until you get home to mommy. Do exactly as they tell you, okay, and keep close to your brother."

"Mommy says there are monsters at home, too."

"Mommy is safe," Guy assured her. "You spoke to her earlier and so did I."

"Is Clark looking after her?"

Guy cleared his throat. "Yes, honey. Clark is looking after her."

"When can me and Kyle go home?"

"Soon, I promise."

"Will you come get us in your boat?"

"Daddy can't do that, honey. Daddy has a job to do."

"But the soldiers said that's over now. Corporal Martin said that we have to fight. If you come and get us, you can teach me and Kyle how to fight."

"What? No, Alice, I don't want you to fight. What else did this Corporal Martin say?"

"I heard him say we're going to lose. That there are too many monsters."

"Let me speak to him."

"What?"

"Honey, let me speak to Corporal Martin."

Alice sounded sad, like she knew she'd just caused trouble.

"Okay, daddy. I'll go and get him."

There was a clonking sound as Alice placed the receiver down, and then Guy could hear Kyle speaking, asking his sister what was wrong.

Then there was the sound of gunfire.

Guy shouted down the phone. "Alice? Kyle?"

There was a man's voice in the background. Guy could just about hear it. "Come on, kids. We have to get somewhere safe, right now. We're under attack."

"But I was talking to my da—"

The line went dead.

The cell phone fell from Guy's grasp and shattered at his feet. Frank caught him just as he was about to fall.

"Guy, what is it?"

"Alice and Kyle. They're in danger. Something is attacking them."

Frank didn't speak.

Guy wrung his hands together and started pacing like a caged cat. "I should be with them, Frank. I should be protecting them. Damn it."

Frank looked him in the eye and held him steady. "You told the men we're all just gonna have to pray our families are okay. Kyle and Alice have survived so far. You have to hope they can make it through. They will make it, Guy. We all will."

Captain Lund's boys arrived around the coast, piloting a fuel barge up alongside the Hatchet. The putt-putt of the engine echoed across the water.

Guy wiped the tears from his eyes and straightened up. "Get the men to refuel, Chief Petty, and then assemble everybody on launch deck—the civilians too. I have something to say."

Frank nodded. "Aye, aye, Captain."

* * *

The Hatchet's crew assembled alongside the civilian refugees on the launch deck, awaiting an address from the Captain. Captain Lund and his boys were also present as Guy had requested them also.

Guy stood on top of the ship's main gun emplacement so he was high enough to see the far edges of the crowd. The Hatchet wasn't a huge ship, and the massed gathering made it seem cramped. The civilians looked nauseous and afraid, unused to the sea and even less used to the fighting.

"Thank you for gathering," Guy began. "Some of you have served with me for a long time, some of you not so long, some of you are only catching a ride. Regardless of your position on this ship, we have all survived a terrible tragedy together, and for that, we are brothers and sisters—bonded through adversity and strengthened by courage. I am proud to captain this crew. All civilians are now free to go, and I hope that Captain Lund will assist you in whatever ways he can. New York is no longer safe, but there are still areas yet to be attacked. Cape Fear is one of those areas, so I suggest that you remain here for the time being.

"I also offer release to my crew. Many of you still have time left to serve, but I have come to realise that a man must protect his family first, his country second. In fact, by doing the first, we often serve the second, so go if you must, and find your families. There will be no repercussions, you have my word. Humanity is at war, and none of us can escape the days ahead, but I will hold no one on board my ship if they do not wish to be here. I, myself, will be crossing the Atlantic to find my own family."

There was a collective gasp from those who understood the magnitude of what he was suggesting. The Atlantic was a big ocean to cross in a ship not made for comfort.

Guy gave the crowd no time to settle and continued earnestly. "The Hatchet is just about fit to do the journey with a full tank of fuel, and it's the right time of year, so I'm going to London to find my children. I'll pilot the ship alone if I have to, but if anyone wishes to join me, I will welcome their company, not as enlisted men, but as volunteers."

"I've always fancied seeing Wembley Stadium," said Frank.

"You think it'll still be there?"

Guy looked at his oldest friend warmly. "Only one way to find out."

"I'll join you, Captain," said Lieutenant Tosco. His eyes were red and swollen, showing he'd been crying. "I just found out my wife is dead. If I can help you save your kids, then I'll sail to England with you."

Tosco had been the last person Guy had expected to join him, but he was more than thankful to have his second-in- command along for the ride. "Thank you, Lieutenant Tosco. I'd be glad to have you."

More hands went up as more and more enlisted men volunteered. Almost half the civilians remained as well. The final voice in the crowd was Captain Lund's. "I'd like to come too, if that's okay, Captain Granger?"

"Don't you want to run things here, Skip? The voyage will be long and uncomfortable."

"Don't consider things are going to be too dandy wherever I go. If I'm to risk my life, I'd rather risk it where I belong: At sea. I'll be leaving good boys behind—they'll take care of your civilians, but I want to join your crew, sir. One last adventure for a silly old man. I'll pull my weight, you can be mighty sure of it."

"I have no doubt. Welcome aboard, Skip." Guy looked for more volunteers, but none remained. About a third of the crew had opted to leave, but with the additional civilians, the Hatchet would end up being over-manned. They'd need to resupply before setting off, but that was a problem to be addressed later. For now, Guy just wanted to bask in the feeling of solidarity between him and his fellow sailors. He had truly expected to be making the journey across the Atlantic on his own. Even now, life could surprise him.

"Get some rest, sailors," he commanded. "We leave bright and early. Until then, think about your decision, and enjoy the land beneath your feet while you can. England awaits us."

~MINA MAGAR~
HYDE PARK, LONDON

MINA HAD BEEN SITTING ON THE MOONLIT grass listening to her father's angry voicemails when the first shot fired. It came from the edge of camp, over by Marble Arch, and when she looked up, she saw soldiers hastily gathering up their weapons and running to offer support. David had been sitting under a nearby floodlight, working through his notes and chatting to Carol on the phone. He came over now in a hurry. "Did you see what they're firing at?"

Mina got up and wiped grass off her butt. "It's too dark to see. The creatures must be attacking again."

David hissed, "Let's hope those soldiers know what they're doing."

The gunfire increased, lighting up the darkness like a celebration. Radios squawked everywhere as soldiers communicated with one another urgently. Explosions joined the mix and gave Hyde Park its greatest ever fireworks show.

"It's bad," said Mina. "The whole camp is getting involved."

Corporal Martin appeared from one of the nearby tents with Alice and Kyle hurrying behind him. "You need to take the children," he ordered. "I need to get over there."

Mina gathered the frightened children to her side, but didn't want to let the soldier rush off. "They're attacking again, aren't they? How many?"

Corporal Martin looked at her gravely. "Just one."

"One? I don't understand."

As if to address her confusion, a beastly roar echoed across Hyde Park, and something huge charged towards the camp. The giant scooped up a black taxi and launched it at the assembled soldiers, scattering them into cover. They spread out, pumping magazines full of ammunition into the creature and hitting it several times with grenades.

Nothing slowed the giant down.

A jeep skidded to a halt in front of it. When the soldier in the back manning a huge machine gun pulled the trigger, it sounded like a volcano erupting. The onslaught of automatic fire was enough to send the giant reeling, but it quickly recovered, dragged an elm tree out of the ground, and launched it at the jeep. The vehicle bucked, rolled, and ended up on its roof. The soldier who had been manning the machine gun fell awkwardly and snapped his neck.

David shot Corporal Martin an accusing look. "Your men are dying."

"Which is why I need to go help them."

Mina grabbed the soldier's arm. "No, you'll die. Your weapons aren't working on that thing."

"Uh, guys?" Kyle got their attention and pointed to the other side of the park. "There's something else coming."

Screams filled Hyde Park as an army of charred creatures arrived from a dozen side streets and fell upon the camp. Soldiers began to fall, clutching torn open stomachs and mangled throats. Meanwhile, the giant continued its devastating march, crushing all in its path.

"The battle is lost," said David. "We need to get out of here."

Alice cried. Kyle put his arm around her, but looked close to tears himself. Mina smiled at the boy and tried to let him know it would be alright—even though it wouldn't be.

In the centre of the park, two choppers started up their rotors, each one loaded full of refugees. The army of creatures made for them, but were held back by the last smatterings of resistance. If those soldiers didn't hold their ground, the civilians would be sitting ducks.

Corporal Martin grabbed his rifle and prepared to head off.

Mina grabbed his arm. "You're not seriously going to go fight, are you?"

"No," he said. "We're getting the hell out of here. Come on."

They raced after him as he took them across the playing fields towards the centre of camp. It was closer to the danger, but Mina understood the soldier's motives. The vehicles were all parked in the centre of Hyde Park, and reaching one was their only means of escape.

"Is that the thing you saw earlier, Mina?" David asked her as they sprinted towards the motor pool.

"I only saw it for a moment, but yes, that's definitely it." "It has wings like an angel," Alice said.

"It's not an angel," said Kyle. "It's a monster."

"A demon," Mina stated, as sure of it as ever.

"But it looks like a pretty man," Alice argued.

"It's going to bloody well kill us if we don't hurry up," Corporal Martin shouted at them all.

The burned creatures were no match for bullets and went down in clouds of gore whenever shot, but their sheer numbers gave them the advantage. They didn't seem to fear death and were happy to sacrifice themselves if it meant that their comrades would reach their target.

It was a Kamikaze attack. Unstoppable.

Mina and the others were almost at the jeeps. All around them, soldiers screamed and begged for their lives, but they received no mercy. The demons tore out their intestines and left them to die in agony—they seemed intent on maiming over killing. The gunfire became less and less. Floodlights tipped over and shattered, allowing the shadows to claim Hyde Park. Alice screamed and covered her eyes. She stopped running and refused to move."

Mina tried to grab the girl, but was clawed away. "I want to go home. I want to go home. I want to go home."

"Sweetheart, you have to keep moving."

Kyle came and knelt in front of his little sister. "Hey, Ally. It's going to be okay. Remember the bus? We were okay, weren't we? You promised to do whatever I said, and I kept you safe then. I need you to run towards the jeep, okay? Do you understand, Ally? I need you to run. I love you, and it will all be okay." Alice wiped away her tears and went to look back at the dying soldiers, but Kyle stopped her. "Don't, Ally. You just focus on running and think about what you're going to do when we get home. Mom and Clark will take us to Funtown, but first you have to get to that jeep over there, okay?"

Alice nodded and finally got moving again, but they'd lost time they could ill afford. Hardly any soldiers remained between them and the murderous horde of creatures.

The giant was now close enough that the ground trembled beneath their feet as they ran. A hundred metres away, the two helicopters hopped up into the air. They lurched away in separate directions, one heading south, the other heading north, but the chopper heading south passed right over the battlefield.

Right into danger.

The giant leapt up and swatted the helicopter to the ground. The fuselage crumpled and the main rotor broke free and cartwheeled across the park, taking out several soldiers and demons. There was a small explosion from the chopper's engines, but most of the damage came purely from the force of impact with the ground. Dismembered arms and legs spilled out from the wreckage. Mina's mouth filled with vomit, but she forced it back down. There was no time to for nausea.

Corporal Martin made it to the jeep first, but he didn't hop in behind the wheel. Instead, he hopped in behind the machine gun mounted on the back. "David," he shouted. "The keys are in the ignition. Get us out of here."

David stumbled. "What? I... I can't take the wheel. What if I crash? M-My nerves are shot."

Mina shoved him out of the way. "I'll drive, just get the kids inside."

David nodded, relieved. "Okay, Kyle, get in the jeep, quickly."

Kyle shook his head. "Alice first."

Alice was shaking and trembling, but she hurried towards the jeep as her brother urged her to move. David grabbed the little girl under the arms and launched her across the back seat, where she seemed to take comfort in clicking in her seatbelt. Once secure, she looked over at her brother and waved her hand. "Kyle, come on!"

"I'm coming, Ally." He took a step forward, but as he did something yanked him backwards.

David went to help, but then changed his mind and backed up against the jeep. "Kyle, run!"

Mina and Martin shouted warnings too.

Alice screamed.

But it was too late.

The demon had the boy firmly in its clutches.

Kyle was brave. He punched and kicked at his attacker, tearing away strips of burnt, tattered flesh, but the simple fact was that the boy just wasn't strong enough. The demon shook off the blows as if they were flies and thrust its skeletal hand right inside Kyle's belly, ripping out a pink, glistening bag that could only have been his stomach. Blood exploded from his mouth, and he made the most pitiful whine, but then he fell to the floor, dead.

Martin opened up the machine gun on the back of the jeep, and the demon danced as a hundred metal wasps stung him. Scraps of singed flesh flew into the air like ash, and tendrils of smoke appeared from every bullet hole. When the vile creature hit the dirt, it looked like a soiled rag.

Alice tried to leap out of the jeep and go to her brother, but David grabbed a hold of her collar and kept her inside the jeep. "He's gone, sweetheart. We have to go."

"Kyle, no!"

Martin shouted across to Mina. "Get us the fuck out of this city."

"Don't have to tell me twice." Mina stamped on the accelerator and took off at full speed. Behind them, Hyde Park descended into darkness and terror.

~RICK BASTION~
DEVONSHIRE, ENGLAND

RICK WAS GLAD HE AND HIS BROTHER hadn't got a taxi and travelled to drink somewhere further afield, for they were able to reach his home within ten minutes, and just as night fell. Keith led the group as if it were his own house they were going to, but Rick had no inclination to complain. After the losses at The Warren, their group now consisted of just him, Keith, Steve, Diane, and Maddy, but when they reached the thick iron gate that protected his property, they discovered a new survivor.

"What are you doing outside my house?" Rick asked the man. The blond stranger—perhaps about thirty—wore a black t-shirt tucked into jeans and was smoking a cigarette. His heavy work boots made him look like an extra out of Grease.

"Wow, this your gaff? Nice. I've been rattling away at the gate for the last ten minutes. Never considered you might be out."

"You weren't rattling the gate just now," Rick commented. "You were just hanging around."

The stranger waved his lit cigarette. "Fag break, mate. Try'na batter down an old iron gate is tiring work. 'Specially after gettin' chased by demons."

Keith held up his iron poker and seemed to examine the dark red blood staining it. "You think they're demons?"

"I know they're demons."

"How?"

"Believe it or not, I once studied to be a priest. Eventually,

I was put off by all those rules they expected me to follow, but I learned a few things." He looked at Maddy and winked. "Those things are demons though, you can bet your hats. I'm happy to tell you fine folks all about it, but I would much rather do it inside this fine mansion, and not out where we might get eaten."

There was something about the guy that Rick didn't like—he was too casual—but he couldn't turn a person away with so much danger going on. They would have to keep an eye on him. It wasn't like they didn't outnumber him.

Rick pulled out his keyring and located the little key that connected to the modern padlock he'd installed on the gate. Before he let everybody in, though, he turned to the stranger and asked for a name.

"Daniel," came the reply. "And very pleased I am to meet you all."

"Nice to meet you too, Daniel. I'm Rick. This is my brother, Keith... Steve, Maddy, and Diane. We're pretty much strangers, but we're bonding quickly. If you want to stay with us then behave yourself."

"Yeah, of course, pal."

They crunched up the driveway while Rick closed and locked the gate behind them, before racing ahead to open up the front door. The alarm beeped, and everyone had to wait in the porch while he disarmed it, but then he invited them all into the lounge where they all sat down—exhausted. It had been a long time since he'd hosted guests, and it made him feel anxious—strange considering the day he was having. It shouldn't have been important.

"I'll get everyone drinks," said Rick.

"Just water for me," said Diane.

"Me too," said Steven.

"I think we should stick to the water," said Keith, although his pained expression made it seem that he wanted a drink as much as Rick. He really had got a taste for it tonight, hadn't he, but unlike Rick, he had the willpower to say no. It upset Rick to realise that he was more like his father than Keith. Perhaps that was why they had always clashed so badly.

"Suit yourself," said Rick, "but I'm having a beer."

He made them all drinks and brought them over on a tray. A silence descended, and everybody's gaze fell on the newcomer, Daniel.

"You're all looking at me like I farted," he said.

"We want to know why you're so sure those things attacking us are demons," said Maddy. She had unzipped the top half of her jumpsuit and let it drop around her waist, revealing a tight black vest and well-toned arms. Everyone appeared hot and sweaty, so Rick got up and switched on the ceiling fan while they continued talking.

"When I was studying to be a Roman Catholic priest," Daniel began, "I spent a little time at the Vatican. There were some interesting books there, I don't mind telling you—many of which were strictly off-limits. But, even back then, I was a bit of a shit, so one night, me and some of the other novices got hold of a book all about Lucifer and the Fallen Angels. You know the story: Lucifer refused to bow down to mankind and went to war against God in Heaven. Got his arse handed to him and was cast down with the other rebel angels, yada, yada, yada. Well, this book was all about what happened afterwards. Lucifer set up a kingdom of his own and named it Abysseus. The Abyss."

"Hell?" said Diane.

"Yeah, darlin'. Hell is exactly what it is. Anyway, God, in all his glory, protected the Earth from this kingdom of Abysseus by creating six thousand Heavenly Seals. Each one protecting a spot where Hell encroached upon the Earth. You see, Heaven and Hell are both tethered to the Earth, a bit like the ropes on a hot air balloon. Heaven is the balloon, it keeps everything afloat. Earth is the basket, it gives us all something to stand on. But hitching a ride on the bottom is Hell. Hell is the ballast; it drags everything down, and drains away all the effort Heaven puts into keeping us all afloat. If Hell gains too much influence, we all go down, you understand? Anyway, to keep everything nice and separate, God created the six thousand seals."

Rick's eyes narrowed. "The black stones are the seals?"

"Yep, them stones are the six thousand seals the book mentioned. Each one protecting a gateway between Hell and Earth. If Hell gains dominion over the Earth, that's a whole lot of extra ballast dragging down Heaven. Maybe that's what this is all about: Another shot at ending God's kingdom. But, hey, this was all stuff I read in a book one time. Make of it what you will."

Rick put his beer down and leaned forward. "If the stones were put there by God, why have they opened and allowed Hell to come to Earth?"

"Dunno."

Rick grunted. "You don't know?"

"Hey, you're asking me to speculate based on a dusty old tome I read as a teenager. My guess would be sabotage opened the gates. Nothing in Hell can affect the seals, so someone on Earth must have had something to do with it. Or maybe God was so pissed off that he summoned the seals and switched them all off himself. Like I said, I dunno."

Keith rolled his eyes. "We don't have any reason to believe your story over any other."

Daniel shrugged. "Nope, you don't. The only thing we need to agree on is that them things are dangerous. We should stick together and hope for the best."

"Good plan," said Keith morosely.

Daniel threw his arms in the air. "It's the best I got, pal." "We should barricade this place," said Maddy seriously. Diane nodded. "Yeah, we should totally do that, like in the black and white zombie movies. We should hammer boards over the windows."

Rick frowned. "This isn't a zombie movie, Diane. Do you have any boards on you?"

"In the films, they used doors."

Rick looked around the open-plan living room and frowned again. "It's all open down here. There's a door on the office and the rooms upstairs, but... Well, I suppose we might be able to work something out."

"What about that big garage you have out there?" asked Keith.

Rick flinched. "No, there's nothing in there." "Probably worth checking out though," said Steven. "No."

Maddy stared at him. "Come on, Rick. We need to find whatever we can. Where's the harm?"

Rick tried to find argument, but couldn't. "Fine," he said. "I'll open it." He stood up and looked at them. "Well, come on then."

They all got up and headed outside and around to the side of the house. The double garage sat beside the property but had rarely been used to park a car. Its main use was as a junk storage shed, and when Rick opened it, he felt his cheeks glow. He knew Keith would be the first to comment, and he wasn't disappointed.

"Are these all your albums, Rick? Oh dear."

Rick looked down at the boxes upon boxes of unsold music albums and cringed. "I've told you before that my record label went bust while I was still in contract with them. This is all the stock from their warehouse. They were just going to chuck it."

Keith sniggered. "And you thought it would be better keeping it in your garage?"

"I didn't know I'd never get another record deal. I assumed I'd sign a new contract and sell this stuff on as signed copies or something."

Maddy studied his face. "Wait... That's how I know you. You're that Rick Bastion guy."

Keith chuckled. "His real surname is Monroe."

Rick shot him a glare. "No, it's not. I changed it." "Shouldn't have bothered."

"I think it's cool," said Diane. "You were really a pop star, Rick?"

He smiled. "Yeah, for about five minutes."

"I have to admit," said Maddy, picking up one of the albums and studying it. "I liked that song."

Steve laughed. "Can't say that I did, but it's still impressive. Well done."

Keith bristled and looked at Daniel. "Were you a fan of Cross to Bear, Daniel?"

"Never heard it. Sorry."

"Oh come on," said Maddy. "You must have heard it. My love for you is just a cross to beeear!" Daniel looked nonplussed.

Rick patted him on the back. "Always glad to meet a non-fan—truly. Anyway, I told you there was nothing in here. I wasn't lying. Unless you think we can pay the demons off with signed copies of my albums."

"I think not," said Keith.

Maddy ran her fingers over the surface of the album and kept glancing between it and Rick. The sight of his pink hair and leather jacket made him cringe. "Could you please put that down," he begged her.

She smiled and tossed it back into the box. "Sorry."

Steven slipped inside the garage and looked around. "You have a few tools in here, Rick. That nail gun could be handy. The stepladder too."

"Take whatever you want. We should start getting the doors off to use as barricades. I think there's a tool kit in here somewhere."

"Where are your keys, Rick?" asked Keith. "I'll park our cars up against the gate; stop anything barging through."

Rick reached into his pocket and handed them over. "Good idea. The iron fence goes all the way around, so it should hold, but the gate is rickety and only held with a padlock."

"Can I borrow your phone, too?"

"Yeah, of course. You want to call Marcy?"

"I'm thinking she isn't answering because it's my number coming up—or perhaps I'm hoping that's the reason. Anyway, it's worth a try."

Rick offered his phone. "Take it. Keep trying her."

Steven started yanking stuff out from the back of the garage and piling it out front. In short order, he had added a hammer, a toolkit, and a garden shovel to the nail gun and ladder. It wasn't much, but it wasn't nothing either. Keith got the cars moved, parked them side by side in front of the gate. Next on the list was getting the bedroom doors off and nailing them against the ground-floor windows. For that job, they all worked together.

"So, Rick," Daniel said to him as they propped a door in front of the office window. "What's the deal with your brother? He's not really the supportive type, is he?"

"You could put it like that."

"Why does he give you so much grief?"

"Don't ask me. I never got on with my dad, but Keith was joined at the hip to him. I think he took over where my old man left off, criticising me all the time. Keith hated when I got a recording contract. Dad had groomed him to be this great businessman, but I went and leapfrogged him by making a couple mil overnight. I can't be certain, but I think he even went so far as setting up a fake account and leaving my albums bad reviews online."

"Yikes, that's a little..." he looked at the door they were holding, "unhinged."

Rick shrugged. "Can't pick your family, I guess."

"A friend loves at all times, and a brother is born for adversity."

Rick held a nail in place and prepared to strike it with the hammer. "What's that?"

"Proverbs 17:17. Priest school, remember? I can't believe I still remember that stuff."

"You really visited the Vatican? What's it like?"

He shrugged. "A bit religious for my liking. Nice buildings though."

They shared a laugh, and before long, they had the door nailed across the window and were off to the next task. Steve was busy in the living room while Maddy and Diane were in the kitchen making phone calls and trying to get help. They got through a couple of times, but only ever received bad news. The Police were tied up, and the Army were concentrated around major cities. Nobody would come rescue a few people in a mansion on the edge of nowheresville. The call operators had started to be quite blunt about that. So Maddy and Diane had switched tact and were now focused on trying to find out what was happening in the country. Rick had loaned them his laptop to aid their research. Maddy had already managed to contact an uncle in Leeds who claimed everything was okay, and Diane had spoken with her mother hiding out at her home in Exeter. People still lived, so perhaps things weren't so bad.

Keith was in the hallway making calls of his own. It was obvious from his expression that Marcy still wasn't answering. Rick felt for him. Not knowing if his wife and son were okay must have been torture. Once again, it made Rick wonder why his brother was there.

A beeping sound brought everyone into the entrance hallway.

Rick knew it was the security system, and he went to the control panel on the wall. The video feed had switched on, activated by the proximity sensors on the gate. The security floodlight bathed the driveway in a spooky yellow-green glow.

It made the dead men look like ghosts.

Rick counted the demons outside the gate and covered his mouth in horror. "There must be two dozen of them out there. Enough to bring down the gate."

"Okay, everybody," said Keith, "get whatever you can to defend yourselves. We're going to keep our heads down and hope they don't find out we're in here."

Daniel elbowed Rick in the ribs and whispered, "Ain't this your gaff, mate?"

Rick shrugged. Nothing Keith said was wrong, but he did have one thing to add: "If they do get in here, there's no way out except the gate, but Steven has put the step ladder in the conservatory. If we have to make a run for it, we can set it up against the back fence and climb over. We might be able to escape without them seeing us."

"We should just run," said Diane.

Maddy was the first to shake her head. "And go where? No, if we can stay hidden, then we'd be stupid to leave. It's the middle of the night. They might not even have seen us."

Keith clapped his hands to get everyone's attention back on him. "We all know about the stepladder. If we need to make a run for it, then it's there, but things haven't come to that yet. The lower floor is barricaded, and we can defend ourselves— we proved that back at the pub. We're okay for now."

"I don't think there's any doubt about them knowing we're in here," said Rick. He prodded the LCD screen with his finger and showed them all what he was seeing. The demons outside, a mixture of burned humans and hunched-over creatures, glared through the bars at the house. They were so unwavering in their focus, so intent on their staring, that there was no question that they knew somebody was inside.

"They're just standing there," said Maddy. "It's like they don't want to touch the gate."

Rick nodded. She was right. The demons were half a foot away from the bars, but would approach no further. It was as if there was an invisible force field keeping them at bay.

Steven leant forward, closer to the screen. "They could climb over it if they tried, but they're not trying. Why?"

"It's the iron bars," said Daniel.

Everybody looked at him.

"What?" Rick asked.

"The seals I told you about in the book. They were forged from iron. God created a substance toxic to anything not of earth and used it to make the seals. He also placed iron in the blood of man to help prevent evil from inhabiting us."

"You mean, like possession?" asked Diane.

"Yeah, possession. Anyway, non-earthly creatures are allergic to iron. They can't cross a barrier made from it."

"The fire pokers are iron too," said Keith, "but it didn't kill them outright."

"No," admitted Rick. "But it hurt them. Perhaps iron is only truly effective as a barrier. It keeps evil spirits out of our bodies, and it's been keeping the demons trapped in Hell via the seal stones. Maybe it's-"

Maddy finished for him. "Keeping the bastards out of your house via the old fashioned fence."

Keith folded his arms. "Well, well, well, it looks like we may have had the fortune to wander into the one safe place in town. I knew there was a reason you wasted so much money on this old house, Rick."

"I obviously knew that somewhere down the line I'd need to seek refuge from an army of demons. Thought I'd be prepared."

Everyone laughed, and Keith bristled again. He was straight-faced as he spoke. "We know nothing for sure, so let's just stick to the plan. Everybody keep their heads down, and be ready. Even if we're safe, we can't stay here forever, unless my brother has a garage full of supplies hidden amongst all of his unsold albums."

Rick wanted to reply with something devastating, but nothing came to mind. Instead, he kept an eye on the security monitor and watched the demons outside. Part of him wished he was stuck inside with one of them instead of his older brother.

~TONY CROSS~
EASTERN PLATEAU, SYRIA

Without vehicles for shade, the men were exhausted within an hour, and they slowed down just a few miles into Syria. Harris had got so hot that he had pulled out his combat knife and cut the sleeves off his shirt. But when night had fallen, they had faced a new set of problems: In the early hours, the desert froze, and the men had needed to clutch themselves to keep warm, hours after sweating profusely. They kept on walking long into the night, trying to put as much distance between them and the gate as they could. Now that it was almost dawn, they were looking forward to the brief window of temperate weather that morning would bring.

"I did not think I would live to see the sun rise," said Aymun, the leader of the ISN trio that now marched side by side with seven British soldiers.

Ellis had been unfailingly polite to the Syrian rebels since rescuing them, and he was no different now. "I thought quite the same for a moment there, Aymun. That was quite a hairy situation we escaped."

Aymun looked confused. He plucked at his dirty black fringe. "Hairy?"

Tony sighed. "He means we were in the shit."

Aymun nodded. "I understand shit. Situation very bad. Allah has sent his servants to punish us."

"Don't start on that," said Tony. "I don't believe your Allah sent a bunch of monsters to kill us in the desert. I'm sure he has more efficient means."

"Allah prefers to test, not punish. If we die, it is because we stop fighting."

Tony grunted. "Do you believe that about your own men? You lost more than a dozen back at the border."

A glimmer of sadness flowed through Aymun's face, but he quickly went back to being expressionless. "They are in the next life, rewarded for their bravery."

"Some reward," said Tony.

Silence followed them for the next hour while the sun rose inch by inch above the horizon. They found a dirt road, and the walking got a little easier, and when they came upon a stream, they decided to set up camp. Ellis quickly upset the men by insisting they share their rations with the three ISN soldiers. Morale had been low ever since.

Tony sat on his own, fiddling with the squad's long-range radio. Ellis had tried it as soon as they'd made it into Syria, but had not been able to get a successful link up. Communication in the desert was never great, but the majority of their unit was deployed less than a hundred miles away and should have been reachable. Yet, when Tony tried to hail them again now, he got zero response. Had another gate opened near base camp? Was the rest of the platoon dead?

Tony wanted, more than anything, to encounter more people, even ISN. He feared what had come through that gate, and he feared what it meant for the world. If nothing else, it answered the question about whether humanity was alone. Either aliens or demons had come through that gate, and it looked like they were here to kill.

Ellis unfolded his map and noted down the coordinates on the GPS readout from his radio. Tony sat next to him to see what the score was.

"We're in the middle of the desert," Ellis told him, never failing to astound with his talent of stating the obvious. "It's not safe for us to stay in Syria. We could head back east, but that would take us closer to that dastardly gate. Or we head south for Israel?"

Tony shook his head. "We'd never make it through Jordan in one piece."

"Then what do you suggest?" "Turkey."

"But that's north, Tony, through the desert and river towns. We could meet resistance. The ISN operate in the northern regions"

"The ISN are everywhere, but we'll be less likely to be attacked that way than if we head south or west. The north is barren enough that we can avoid the towns. We should head for the U.S. airbase in Incirlik. If we can make it to the Turkish border, we should be able to get a ride. We should be able to make it within a week on foot, sooner if we manage to find a couple vehicles."

Ellis rubbed at his jaw. "A week's march across the desert, how are we supposed to manage that?"

Tony sighed. "Once upon a time, armies used to march thousands of miles. If we cut our rations, take as much water from this stream as we can, we'll make it. It won't be a pleasant trip, but any other direction and we risk getting into another firefight. I don't know about you, but I could do without losing another bunch of lads."

Ellis looked at the map for several seconds, eyebrows knitted in concentration. He came up with no alternative, so nodded his head and agreed to Tony's plan. "I will go and let the men know what they're in for."

Tony looked at his Commanding Officer and tried to convey his confidence one last time, hoping it would pass through him and onto the men. "This is how we all get to live, Lieutenant. I'll take hard and safe over easy and dangerous any day. We stick together and we'll be fine."

Ellis nodded toward Aymun who was sitting on a rock with his two men. "What about them?"

"Leave them to me."

Ellis seemed satisfied. "I trust you to take care of it, Staff Sergeant. Carry on."

While Ellis addressed the men, Tony approached the ISN. Aymun nodded to him and said, "Hello, my friend."

"We're not friends, we're enemies. That's why you need to go your way while we go ours."

"You will let us go?"

"Yes, you can even keep your weapons, but you don't head into Iraq and you don't follow us."

"Where will you go? Syria dangerous for British soldier." "Not your concern."

"Only safe place is desert, but you never make in the heat. Summer bad. No time for walking." "We'll be fine," Tony snapped. "I help you."

"Don't want your help."

"You need my help."

Tony studied Aymun and tried to figure him out. He seemed genuine in his offer to help, but here also was a man who believed that infidels should be beheaded and homosexuals hanged. "Why do you want to help, Aymun? We oppose everything you stand for."

"I be very surprised if you know what I stand for. I stand for duty. Your men save my men, so now we help save you. You want out of country. Turkey, yes? I take you across desert, across river. Make sure your men do not burn."

Tony folded his arms, strangely finding himself willing to listen. "How would you help us, Aymun?"

"I lead you to hidden ISN stockpile. Food, water, monies, yes? You can take. Payment for saving my life."

"How do I know you won't turn on my men? You could lead us into a trap. We're enemies."

"I think we are enemies no longer. We have new enemy to fight."

"The demons?"

Aymun nodded. "Allah's test. Perhaps he wish to bring men together by giving them mutual adversary."

Against his better judgement, Tony asked, "You really want to help my men?"

"I swear it in Allah's name. You are not my enemy. Syrian puppet government my enemy, greedy white men my enemy, demons that come through gate my enemy. You are friend."

"Then we should shake hands."

Aymun waved a hand. "Pah, white man's gesture. For Moslem, man's word alone good enough."

"Okay, you have my word that if you get us to the Turkish border, I will let you and your men go free."

"And you have my word that I will not kill you."

Tony smirked. "Good to know, Aymun."

From the demoralised look on the British soldier's faces, Ellis had just delivered the bad news about their upcoming trek. They were sitting in silence, heads in hands and glancing at the featureless desert as if it were some giant, sucking hole waiting to devour them. Ellis had retired to the edge of camp and was trying the radio.

"Still no answer?" Tony asked.

Ellis shook his head. "It's like there's no one on the other end. Do you think something is going on? I mean, more than what happened to us?"

Tony sat down beside his Commanding Officer and crossed his legs. "It seems unlikely there'd be just one of those gates in the middle of nowhere. I assume there're more. Perhaps that's why no one is answering our calls: they're all busy with their own problems."

"I don't want any more of my men to die, Tony."

"No officer ever does. Things could have gone worse, you know? We're lucky any of us got out of there alive."

Ellis sighed and seemed to think about it. "Are Aymun and his men leaving soon? We should depart at the same time, or they might regroup and ambush us."

"No, he's coming with us."

"Pardon me?"

"We saved his life. He wants to repay the favour by helping us through the desert. There's an ISN stockpile. He said we can have it."

Ellis was silent, but eventually he said. "I've known you a year now, Tony, and in that time I've never seen you make a bad decision. If you think we can trust Aymun and his men, then I will back you. Maybe if I had trusted you earlier, the ambush wouldn't have failed so miserably."

"If it hadn't of failed, we'd all be dead. We wouldn't have got pinned behind the hill, and that gate would've opened right behind us. Instead, it opened on top of Aymun and his men. One thing I've learned about war, sir, is that it rarely goes to plan."

"Huh, I suppose you're right. Maybe Allah really does have a plan for us."

Tony pulled around his rifle and started disassembling it to clean it—best to do it now than later. "Well, if that's true, I'd hate to see what He has planned for us next."

***

They rested as best they could during the morning whilst the heat was mild, but it was impossible to sleep, nor were they in any position to stay, so they got moving at noon. Within half an hour of leaving the stream, they were all sweating. The desert seemed to swallow them up, stretching on forever in every direction.

Aymun led the way with his men, Ellis and Tony a step behind. The three Syrians chatted in Arabic, but Tony caught the odd word or two. They were discussing the gate and what had come through. That was good; much better than them discussing a plot against their current travelling companions. Tony reminded himself that the man was an extremist. It would be unwise to let down his guard.

"We must walk one day before we find supplies," Aymun told them. "We go slow like snails, or we will not last out the sun."

"How're you sure the supplies are still there?" Ellis asked him.

"Because only I and my men know about it. They all dead now except Majd and Sayid, so will be more than enough to get us to Turkish border."

"Good, good," Ellis cooed. "Thank you once again for your help, Aymun."

Tony grunted and gave Ellis a look that screamed shut up. It was one thing to accept the help of the ISN soldiers, but another to kiss their arses. The men would lose confidence in their Commanding Officer if they thought he was pandering to the enemy. Although a majority of the ISN had fallen to the monsters from the gate, most of the British casualties had been at the hands of Aymun's men. Nothing would make them friends, however much they acted otherwise.

Tony dragged back a little and fell amongst the men. The best way for a Non Commissioned Officer to learn the state of morale was to mix with the unit. It didn't take him long to discover that the temperament of the men bordered on panic.

"I think it's the end of the world," said Private Harris, his large, square shoulders slumped. He'd been tossing his knife into the air for the last hour, letting it spin, and then catching it. The repetitive action spoke of a taught mind. "Those things came right from Hell. We all saw it."

Corporal Rose, a ginger-headed Scot, agreed. "Aye, they was demons all right. I hope for them they didn't open a gate in the centre of Glasgow. They'll piss themselves and run right back to Hell if they see some of the local split arses on a Friday night."

The men laughed. It was good to have a man like Rose in the unit—a guy incapable of taking any situation too seriously. The corporal could be bleeding from his neck and still crack jokes about not letting the alcohol in his blood go to waste.

Private Harris noticed Tony walking nearby and quickly shut up, averted his gaze. It was bad form to complain on a tour—dangerous as much as it was insubordinate—and one man with a negative attitude could affect an entire unit, demotivate it into a listless squabble of unshaven men. Harris had been caught out, but there was little reason to blame him too much. They had all been through Hell, literally.

"We all know that the situation is fucked up, Harris," Tony said, "but we survived, didn't we? You all went up against a bunch of monsters and lived to tell the tale. We saw them bleed; we watched them die. Don't let them scare you because you don't understand them. Wars are lost through fear. By the end of the Vietnam War, the Yanks were terrified to take one step in that jungle, but that won't happen to us. We're British soldiers, and we have ourselves an enemy. Our job is to kill it. The men we left back there in the desert are relying on us to feed those ugly fucks their own bollocks— and we will, I promise you."

A jubilant cheer roared from the men, which made Ellis and Aymun glance back over their shoulders. Ellis seemed bemused, not understanding what was happening behind him, but the ISN leader seemed to understand, and gave Tony a nod. The men would be looking to Tony for courage. If he was afraid, they would be afraid. It was his duty to show bravery and set an example, but the truth was that he was more afraid than he'd ever been. How long could he keep up the brave face? If he faltered, his men would die—for they were his men, not Ellis's.

Tony patted Harris on the back. "Harris, why don't you tell the lads one of your stories. I swear you've had more lives than a cat."

Harris chuckled. "Okay, Staffie. Did I tell you about the time I ejaculated during a conversation with my mum?"

The men laughed just at the premise.

"No, lad. Let's hear it."

"Okay, well, I was sixteen-seventeen and shagging this bird called Lisa. We was in my bedroom one Saturday afternoon, and she was underneath the duvet giving me head—the best I've ever had. Anyway, I'm just about to get there, getting ready to blow me load. My toes are going, and I start to moan. Lisa starts bopping up and down faster, working my balls with her hand. Then, boom! The bedroom door opens. Lisa leaps up out of the duvet just in time, as my dear old mum comes in. She wants to know what I fancy for dinner. Problem was that I had passed that point of no return. Lisa's mouth had done the trick. So here I am, going off like a sprinkler beneath the sheets—having a giant sodding orgasm—and I have to hold a conversation with my old lady about chicken bloody Kiev. Lisa is laying next to me trying not to laugh her arse off. Anyway, the point of the story is that I blew my load while having a conversation about chicken with my mother. The moral is: always get a lock put on your fuckin' door."

The men bellowed with laughter, and Tony knew he could leave them alone for a few more hours.

* * *

They walked until nightfall, taking water breaks every hour, but even then, they were dry-mouthed and sweating. Now that night had arrived, they were all grateful to see the blazing sun recede. The men had shed their combat jackets and now wore only their webbing over their undervests. Several times, Ellis tried to hail Command on the radio, but within the cradle of the desert, their calls went unanswered.

Tony glanced around. It wasn't the kind of desert that would typically come to mind, with endless dunes of golden sand—only hard-packed dirt beneath his boots, ranging from dark brown to bright orange. There was the odd patch of straw-like grass here and there, but no trees and no shade. Now and then he'd glimpse movement in the distance, but could never tell if it was animal, man, or mirage. They were alone, wandering through sun-scorched oblivion.

"We cross river between Al Mayadin and Boqruss Foqani," Aymun informed them. "There will be trees and water. Supplies are two miles past river. There we rest tonight."

The men muttered contentedly. No sleep in two days had left them looking grey and unsteady on their feet. They had avoided sunburn with the use of the cream in their packs, but the heat had sapped all but their last reserves of strength. Rest was needed, and if Aymun was true to his word, they would get the chance soon. Or they would be double-crossed and murdered. Both were appealing after having marched through a desert.

They walked for about another hour before the hard-packed dirt softened into moist soil and green grass. The river was a half mile ahead and due east of the town Al Mayadin. Tony could see some of the taller buildings on the horizon and even caught the faint sound of a car horn. They had reached civilisation, but heading into the town would be risky. There was no one overtly friendly to the West in Syria and many who vehemently opposed it. It would be too much of a lottery trying their luck there. The British had refused to help the Syrian civilians against the rebels, so why should the Syrian civilians help the British? No, they would stick to the plan and keep heading north into Turkey.

Tony spotted the men gazing into the distance at the town and was quick to distract them. "That's not safety over there, lads. The ISN would be on us before we ever got chance to find help."

The men glared at Aymun.

Tony sighed. "We have an eye on those three and we outnumber them. If they try anything they'll regret it."

The men all nodded defiantly. They were almost beaten, but they would not go down without a fight. A doomed soldier was a dangerous soldier, so let Aymun try something if he dared. Not that Tony had any reason to doubt the ISN leader. So far, Aymun had led them around the settlements and alerted them whenever traffic appeared on the seldom encountered roads. Whenever he spoke, he did so in a friendly manner and showed no sign of contempt. Every bone in Tony's body told him not to trust the man, but somehow he was starting to. He hoped he didn't end up regretting it.

They made it to the river. The moon was full, making the water appear as a twinkling silver strip. Tony stooped down on the bank and cupped water over his neck, giving permission for the men to do the same. They all lined up and cooled themselves down, drinking until they were full. The water was clean and fresh-tasting and led Tony to wonder what the Thames would taste like.

"Should we camp here?" Ellis asked, deferring to Aymun. "No, we cross first, find supply cache."

Ellis needed to show authority, so Tony tried to help him.

"Unless you want to camp here, Lieutenant? It's your decision."

Ellis stuttered. "O-of course... erm, no, I think it would be wise to locate the supply cache first. We can rest after."

Tony saluted. "Yes, sir."

Ellis returned the salute. "As you were, Staff Sergeant. See if you can find a good spot to cross the river."

"No need," said Aymun. "I know place."

Tony found cause for concern. Was this the part where Aymun led them into a trap? But it turned out that the Syrian knew of a raft hidden in the reeds. He and his two men retrieved it from further down the bank and were quick to explain its origin. "In early days of war," said Aymun, "Syrian forces patrol river crossings. Local people make this raft and hide for ISN."

Ellis frowned. "The locals helped you? Why?"

Aymun smiled. "Because they believe in ISN, Lieutenant. You think they side with government? Ha! ISN what they want. We take power and bring back old ways. Ways that best for Syrian people, not rich men and politicians. People in Syria, they starve while others take what they have. The West attack our religion, take our oil, tell us how we must be. ISN say no. We will not be how they tell us to be. We will be Syrian."

Ellis was clearly dumbfounded. "But you people are savages. You behead your enemies, enslave your women, and kill children. Surely people don't want that."

Aymun's eyes narrowed. "We do what must be done to take back our country. In war, bad things happen, yes? How many children has British Army killed? Many, yes? Children die in war. Enemies suffer. Do not judge a man in war, judge him in peace.

Once we have country back, we will feed poor, help weak, and make peace with neighbours, but not while puppet government still lives. ISN fight for Syrian people and Syrian way of life."

Ellis laughed derisively, which led to the Syrians on either side of Aymun to sneer. Neither Syrian spoke English, but they were smart enough to know they were being mocked.

Tony stepped in before the accord between the two groups was shattered. "Aymun, I believe that you believe your actions are just. We believe the same of our own. Right now we're friends, and later we may go back to being enemies, but for now, we must concentrate on what we set out to do. We need to cross this river and get to that supply cache. Whatever differences we have will wait for another time. You gave me your word that you would help us."

Aymun nodded. "I already tell you, Sergeant, that we have new enemy now; is stupid to fight you, but your leader is ignorant man. He stupid man."

Ellis went red in the face. "How dare you. I am a lieutenant in the British Army and you are my prisoners."

Aymun sneered. "We are no prisoner."

"No, you're not," said Tony, glaring at Ellis. "Aymun is here to help us, sir. We made a deal."

"They had the chance to leave, but they chose to remain under my protection. They placed themselves under my command."

Aymun faced Tony. "You give word you let me and my men go."

Tony nodded. "I did."

Ellis glared. "You did what, Staff Sergeant? On what authority do you make deals with enemy combatants? These men are my prisoners, and I decide what happens to them."

Aymun and his men shifted anxiously, and the British soldiers did the same in reply. Fingers slid towards triggers as everybody waited to see what would happen next.

"I have been fair," said Aymun. "You help me so I help you, but if we are still enemies, then say so."

Ellis flapped his arms. "Of course we are still enemies. You're members of the blasted ISN. What would my superiors do if I shook hands with members of an enemy rebel force?"

"Your sergeant wish to shake my hand," said Aymun. "He is better man than you. He see. He see what is."

Ellis frowned. "What do you mean, 'what is?'"

"I mean we all must be as one to fight new enemy. Mankind must be an army. You do not understand. You are fool."

Ellis pointed his finger. "I am no fool."

Aymun sighed and turned his back. "You are fool. I leave, fool."

Ellis pulled out his handgun and pointed it at the back of Aymun's head. "You stop right there. You are my prisoner."

Aymun's two soldiers raised their AK47s and pointed them at Ellis. The British army raised their L85s in reply. A standoff ensued.

Tony threw up both hands and stood between the two groups. The ISN were out-gunned two to one, but they would take a couple of British soldiers down with them before they bit the dust. That couldn't happen.

"Lieutenant Ellis," Tony shouted, "the only priority right now is getting the men to safety. There is precedent for working with the enemy in times of exceptional circumstances, and I believe what happened at the border more than qualifies as exceptional. Over a dozen of Aymun's men are dead. Command will consider our mission a victory, but we will be needed for the days ahead—all of us. We cannot afford to get involved in another fire fight. The ISN are considered an illegally occupying force, but we are not officially engaged in a war with them. Therefore, they are not strictly our enemies. We can work together peacefully as allies."

Ellis continued pointing his gun at Aymun, but his hand trembled. After several seconds, he lowered the weapon and placed it by his side. Everybody sighed with relief—even Aymun.

"Everybody at ease," Tony shouted. "Aymun, that means your men too."

Aymun nodded and muttered something in Arabic. His two men lowered their AK47s.

Ellis was shaking his head and staring down at the ground. "I apologise. This heat... so little water. I am not in my right mind."

Tony groaned inside. Their only officer was hinting at his own incompetency and giving mixed messages to his men about whether they were working with the ISN or not. Things would not go well if Ellis didn't get a handle on things and let everybody know where they stood.

To his credit, Aymun did not linger on the animosity. He smiled at his British colleagues and said, "We must cross river now, yes? Very tired and all must rest."

Tony went to pat the man on the back, but worried about offending him, so he returned the smile and nodded.

They went across the river in three shifts, taking almost an hour in total. The journey was wobbly, and they all got wet, but the night had not yet cooled, and they were all glad of the moist chill.

On the other side, they formed up beneath the glowing moon and got going again. As the temperature descended, they dug into their packs and retrieved their jackets. It would be freezing within an hour or two.

Fortunately, an hour was all it took for Aymun to locate his supply cache. They encountered an outcropping of boulders at a place where the green, fertile river plain changed back to the hard-packed, featureless dirt of the desert. Aymun led them all up the stony hill and waited for them at the top. Tony had his rifle raised, ready for an ambush, but once again, he was glad to find that Aymun had kept his word. It was all there.

The outcropping of boulders was wide and hollow inside, like an inverted cave with the entrance above rather than besides. It was large enough for every one of them to climb inside, and they all gasped in amazement when Aymun lit a gas lamp and placed it at the centre of the room. Stacked up against the walls were numerous rifles and crates of ammunition. There were also piles of clothes and tins of food, along with can openers. Several bedrolls and sheets were bundled up in the corner, and it was pure luxury after what they had just walked through.

"Take whatever you wish," said Aymun, "but please do not touch the Quran. It must not come into contact with ground or be touched by..."

Tony noticed the pedestal in the corner with the holy book placed reverently atop it and nodded. "We understand, Aymun. Thank you."

Ellis looked around. "This is much appreciated, Aymun. I wonder, could I... could I trouble you for..."

Tony caught his superior officer just as he was about to hit the ground. He eased Ellis down onto one of the blankets and propped him up. "Get some water," he shouted.

Aymun pulled a bottle of water from the pile of supplies and hurried over with it. Tony took it and helped Ellis take a swig. "There you go, sir, drink up."

"Oh, thank you, Staff Sergeant. I-I'm afraid I came over rather lightheaded."

"It has been hard journey for us all," said Aymun. "We rest tonight, get strength. Hardest part of trip tomorrow, will take several days to reach Turkish border."

Tony looked at Ellis's grey face and wondered if he could make the journey. The men needed an officer, but Ellis was weak and inexperienced, too recently out of Officer's

Training to possess the grit required to keep going when his muscles begged him to stop. This was still just an exercise to him; he didn't understand the stakes.

Tony took a swig of the water, then gave the remains to Ellis. The men stood around anxiously, so he gave them something to do. "Hydrate, urinate, then get your heads down, lads. We have a lot of walking to do in the morning."

So everyone settled down inside the hidden ISN cave on the edge of the Syrian Desert. Despite the tension inside each of them, tiredness won out easily and they were all asleep within minutes. Tony waited until last to close his eyes.

***

Tony awoke in darkness wondering where he was. He heard rustling, felt the air move.

Then came an explosion.

His hand was on his rifle, and he leapt to his feet. His eyes adjusted enough to see shadows, but it wasn't until someone lit a lamp that he could see properly. By that time, everyone was scurrying to their feet blindly, bumping into walls as they tried to wake up. Ellis was last to his feet, and didn't seem to realise that he should have been the first.

"What the blazes was that?"

"I don't know," Tony admitted. He looked at Aymun accusingly. "What's going on?"

The Syrian shook his head. "I do not know."

Another explosion.

"He's set us up," said Ellis, pointing his finger. "His men are coming for us."

Tony studied the cave, saw no one missing. "If that's true, then who's fighting outside right now?"

"It is not my men," Aymun protested. His foot struck something, and he looked down at it. It was the Quran, knocked from the pedestal when everybody had been stumbling to their feet in panic. Aymun went to pick it up, but Tony saw something that made him raise his rifle.

"Wait! Step away from that, Aymun."

Aymun looked at him pleadingly. "It is holy book. Must not be on ground."

Tony snarled, shoved Aymun away. "This isn't a fucking holy book."

Keeping his rifle on the Syrian, he knelt down and flipped the pages. There was no printed scripture, but instead, handwriting, maps, and numbers—messages scrawled in Arabic. The ink from the most recent messages was still wet.

Tony glared at Aymun. "You're not the only one who knows about this place, are you? The ISN leave each other messages here. What have you written?"

Aymun stayed silent, so Tony pointed his rifle in the Syrian's face. The British soldiers backed him up by pointing their own rifles.

"What a fuck party," muttered Private Harris.

Tony moved the muzzle of his rifle closer to Aymun's face. "What did it say?"

Aymun swallowed, but didn't look away for a second. "I write that we head north, west of Ash Shaddadi. Rescue is needed."

"I told you he would betray us," Ellis shouted.

"I say we shove a wee grenade up his arse," said Corporal Rose.

Tony glared at Aymun, looking into the man's dark brown eyes, and prepared to pull the trigger. "You're a liar. Where is your honour?"

Aymun placed his hands in the air, a placating gesture. "I plan no bloodshed, only rescue. Your captain want to take us prisoner, even after accepting our help. I lead you to safety and escape in night. That was plan."

Tony delayed pulling the trigger. "How can I believe you?"

"Because is truth. You understand, Sergeant. We are no longer enemies. Something has come to destroy all. We are brothers now and must fight. My men will need me and yours will need you. I was going to lead you to safety, then escape. I swear it by Allah."

Another explosion.

Tony kept eye contact with Aymun despite the loose stones falling from the ceiling and into his collar. "You swear by Allah that you aren't betraying us, that the fighting outside isn't you?"

"Yes, I swear it by Allah."

"Staff Sergeant, I command you to take this man prisoner," demanded Ellis.

Tony turned to his captain and sighed. "We have to trust him, sir. There's too much at stake to go off half-cocked."

"I have just given you an order."

"I won't follow it. Not until I know for sure that he betrayed us."

"Then you are under arrest for failure to obey a rightful order." Ellis turned to the nearest British soldier, who was Private Harris. "Harris, please place Staff Sergeant Cross under arrest."

"Fuck you, sir."

Ellis spun on his subordinate with more fire in his eyes than Tony had ever seen in the man. It seemed like a breach in manners was the thing that finally lit his fire. "I beg your pardon, Private? I have given you an order and strongly suggest you follow it."

Harris lifted his chin and showed no sign of backing down.

"With all due respect, sir, I don't believe you're fit to give orders. I will do whatever Staff Sergeant Cross commands until we reach the Turkish border."

Tony considered what was happening. There were few offences more serious in the British Army than mutiny, but as Aymun constantly said: Things had changed when that gate had opened in the desert. Hard choices needed to be made.

Ellis looked around at his remaining men. "Place Sergeant Cross and Private Harris under arrest. That is an order. Disobey me, and you'll all be court-martialled."

Nobody moved a finger. The men's expressions were steely—dangerous. Ellis grew more and more frustrated, growing red in the face, his lower lip quivering.

Aymun was next to speak. "My men believe that a leader should be chosen by his men. You are no leader, Lieutenant—just a fool."

Ellis spun around in a rage and pulled his handgun up and pointed it at Aymun's face.

Bang!

The sound echoed off the cave walls.

Captain Ellis turned to face Tony, who had raised his rifle and fired before he even knew what he had been doing. A pinprick of blood bloomed on Ellis's chest, just to the left of his heart. "Staff Sergeant...?"

The officer dropped to his knees with disbelief in his eyes. Tony reached out to grab him, but reconsidered and let the man fall to the ground where he landed on his back, gave a few quick gasps, and then died.

"Fuckin' ell," Tony muttered to himself, trying not to let himself panic. "Jesus fuck fuck fuckin' 'ell."

He'd just shot his commanding officer. They'd throw the book at him—the whole soddin' library. But what choice had he had? If Aymun had been telling the truth, then allowing Ellis to kill him would have been a mistake. Ellis had no cause to execute the man.

If Aymun really had betrayed them, then Tony had just made the biggest balls up of his life. Please, please, please, let Aymun be on the up and up.

Tony turned to his men to gauge their reactions. A bunch of boys, all of them frightened, all of them tired, but there was something else to them as well. They were hardened. They were veterans. Not one of them seemed to judge him for what had just happened. They were his men.

Tony cleared his throat and said, "Anybody who has a problem with what I just did is free to report me once we're back at a friendly base. Until then I'm going to get you out of this fucking desert and to safety. Stick with me until then."

"I'm with you, Sergeant," said Private Harris.

"Me too," said Corporal Rose.

Soon, every man had agreed to follow Tony, and he found himself in a situation he had never been in before: Solo command.

Aymun moved towards Tony and offered his hand. "Thank you, Sergeant."

"I thought you didn't shake hands."

"I shake hand of man I respect. You are leader, like me. Let us lead together until peace finds us, be it in this life or the next."

Another explosion.

Tony sighed. "This isn't an ambush."

"No ambush."

"Well then, if that racket isn't to do with you, we better take a look."

Aymun nodded. "We must."

They climbed out of the hidden cave entrance and stood atop the boulders. What they saw in the distance shocked them.

Harris groaned. "It was so fucking dark last night that we never even noticed it. Another one of them gates right under our bloody noses."

"For fecks sake," said Corporal Rose.

About a mile away, another gate rose above the desert, monsters pouring out of it. The explosions were coming from a group of militia fighting back against the demons.

"Those are my people," Aymun said.

Tony glanced at him. "ISN?"

"No, Sergeant. Not ISN, just Syrians. They must have been attacked but now fight back to defend themselves. These are the people I fight for. They are brave, and we must help them."

"Then we will," said Tony, realising there was no longer any option to make for the border when the enemy was right here. If you ran away in war, you lost.

Aymun gave Tony a kiss on both cheeks. "We fight together, as brothers, ready to take Allah's test."

Tony turned to his men. "Okay, lads. You know the drill. There's enough weaponry in this cave to make a real dent in the bastards this time, and we'll be the ones springing out of nowhere on them. Those people fighting are civvies, and they're doing a bang up job. Are we going to let them take all the victory for themselves?"

"Fuck no," said Harris.

"No way no how," Rose added.

"Whatever is coming through those gates is here to destroy us, to end our way of life. They want to murder our families, kill our children, and slaughter our women. They came from some 'orrible bleedin' 'ell we probably can't even imagine, and they want to take what is ours. Are we gunna let 'em?"

The men shouted a resounding "NO!"

"Then let's send the fuckers back where they belong." Cheers all around. They were going off to war, and they were ready to kick arse.

~MINA MAGAR~
SLOUGH, BERKSHIRE

THEY LEFT THE CITY OF LONDON BURNING behind them. After the initial attack on Oxford Street, the enemy Army had systematically torn through the city, before backing off to regroup. They waited for the Army to congregate, and then attacked again from all sides. Hyde Park had been a massacre, and Corporal Martin had got a similar report about the Greenwich Park camp. What remained of the British Armed Forces were now regrouping at Colchester barracks to lick their wounds.

Mina watched Heathrow Airport slide by on her left as they sped down the M4 motorway. The thick clusters of shops, factories, and houses faded away behind them as they entered the parklands on the way to Slough. A vast golf course lay to Mina's right, still lit by enormous floodlights. The time on the jeep's dashboard read 4:00. She wondered if people were hiding out in that hotel. In fact, how many people were still alive, cowering in their homes or grouping together at places like the golf club? If everybody fought back, all at once, would they have a chance? Corporal Martin seemed to think so, and she was beginning to agree. The Army could not win this war—that had become clear back at Hyde Park—so the only chance mankind had was if the entire population became an army. Every man, woman, and child.

Both Corporal Martin and David had been making endless calls during the last thirty minutes as they fled the city. The staff of the Slough Echo had locked themselves in the offices, updating the website and posting on the larger newsgroups. At first, they had worked feverishly on this morning's papers, but had abandoned it when it became clear that there would be no paperboys working tomorrow. Now they sought to get information to people through the Web. They had used the information given to them by David and were informing people about what they were up against. The black stones had opened gates, and the legions of Hell walked through them. That was the headline.

Alice had screamed after her brother for a while, but had since gone quiet, staring out of the window and saying nothing. What had happened to Kyle affected everyone, even those who'd only just met him. He'd been a child. A brave boy looking after his kid sister. Mina thought about how many other children were dead.

She took them off the motorway and entered the outskirts of Slough through Ditton Park. The sun had risen, and she was surprised to see people walking their dogs.

"They know something's coming," said David. "It's their attempt to enjoy the normalcy while they still can. Denial can be a powerful thing."

But the denial wasn't true everywhere. Police patrolled the centre of Slough, which looked like it had been turned upside by a whirlwind. Litter choked every gutter, and any shop windows not covered by shutters were now smashed. Mina remembered the 2011 riots and saw little difference. People become intrinsically antisocial in times of crisis. When something bad came their way, they thought only of themselves. People were rioting when they should have been coming together. During World War II, entire peoples came together to support their countries, now people fought their countries even as their countries fought for them. Times had changed. The enemy's attack had come at the worst time possible.

There was a scuffle up ahead spilling out into the road and causing Mina to stop. The Police had gathered, forcing a group of youths to sit on the ground. One of the officers spotted the Army jeep and came over.

"Bout time we got a little help," the officer said.

"I'm not here on behalf of the Army," Martin said. "I'm just getting these two reporters to their offices."

The officer sighed grumpily. "Oh, how are things in the city? Still bad?"

"No, not bad. Finished. There's nothing left in London. The Army got destroyed. I might be the only soldier left from Hyde Park."

The police officer went white. "Shit. What the hell are we dealing with, here? Is it really monsters?"

Mina nodded. "We're at war, and we need to be prepared. Everybody, not just the Police and Army. We all need to be ready to fight."

"Fight monsters? You must be joking. People won't fight. I've just spent half the night trying to stop people robbing each other."

"If we don't start working together, we don't have a chance," Mina reiterated.

"Just do what you can, Officer," said Martin. "Those kids you have under arrest. What did they do?"

"What didn't they do? Breaking into shops, kicking in car windscreens, joyriding..."

Mina looked at the gang of youths and saw beyond their hoodies and baseball caps. She remembered Vamps and at once stopped seeing disenchanted youths and saw potential heroes. She saw young, fit, healthy men with anger inside them that could be put to good use. "You need to talk to those boys," she said. "Tell them what's coming. Give them something to do, and they'll be glad to be of use. I promise you."

The officer sneered. "What? You want me to deputise a bunch of thugs?"

Martin nodded adamantly. "Yes! We just lost an army in Hyde Park. This country needs fighters. You have a bunch of them sitting in the road. This isn't just a news of the week event. This is it—the big summer blockbuster, end of the world, fight for survival type of gig. You have a chance to make a difference, Officer. Get your men and those boys ready, because war is coming to us all."

The officer looked at everyone inside the jeep, then back at Corporal Martin. "You're not joking? This is really the apocalypse or something?"

Martin nodded gravely. "Everywhere is under attack, you probably already know that. It's going to fall on men like you to fight back. There won't be a British Army to sort this all out. It's going to be fighting in streets and dying in pain. It will be youngsters, like the ones you have under arrest, that will fight for our survival. So go tell them what they're up against before it's too late."

The officer nodded. "Okay, I'll round 'em up and get 'em to work. Every able-bodied person I can find will be ready, you have my word."

Martin saluted the officer. "What's your name?" "Richard Honeywell."

"I wish you well, Richard. Stay alive."

"I... Yes, you too."

Mina shifted into gear and got going. She glanced in her rear view mirror as Officer Honeywell stood the gang of youths up and addressed them. He looked like a leader rallying his troops. That was exactly what he needed to be.

Then she headed towards the newspaper offices, comforted by the recognisable streets along which she'd commuted most every day since she'd joined the Echo ten months ago. It'd been her first professional job since gaining her Photography degree from Falmouth. Her father had insisted on her taking a minor in business studies, and she had truthfully found that it had helped her when looking for work as a journalist. It gave her uses beyond taking snaps. Still, her father had not been happy when she went into photography instead of business. Respect and fortune were gained through trade, not by indulging in one's hobbies. Mina's father did not consider photojournalism a proper job.

She wondered how he was.

The last voicemail she'd received from her father had informed her that he was at home awaiting her imminent return. Her absence had forced him to close up the chip shop, and he was extremely disappointed in her. Well, he could go right on thinking about himself. She would do whatever she could to help. Right now, she was the one doing something while her father cowered at home.

"We're here," said David, more for the benefit of Martin and Alice than anybody else. Alice continued staring out of the window, but Martin sighed with relief. He was probably as glad as Mina to finally stop fleeing. They needed to regroup and re-strategize. Running only got you tired.

Mina pulled the jeep up behind Carol's Mazda and switched off the engine. She put the ignition key in her pocket, even though the vehicle didn't belong to her. If Martin asked for it back later, she would hand it over happily, but until then, she liked having access to a vehicle.

"Help me!"

Mina glanced into the road and saw a man lying twenty metres away next to the curb. He looked about thirty-years of age and he reached out to her and pleaded. "I'm hurt."

Martin raised his rifle suspiciously.

"Please help me," the stranger repeated.

Martin took a step away from the jeep and moved into the centre of the road. He looked at Mina and then nodded ahead. "Go, check on him. I have you covered."

Seeing no reason to assume danger, yet possessing nerves frayed to tatters, Mina headed cautiously up the road. The dark-haired man's olive skin gave him a look of the Mediterranean. He wore simple jeans and a white t-shirt stained with blood. As she got closer, she noticed that his nose was bleeding.

"Are you alright? What happened to you?"

The man remained lying on his side and moaned. "Some kids gave me a kicking, took my car, and left me here."

Mina knelt down beside the man and placed a hand on his arm. He was cold. "How long have you been lying here?"

"I don't know. An hour maybe. I... I was afraid to get up." "It's okay now. You can come with me."

The man pushed himself up into a sitting position and winced. "Thank you. My name's Andras." Despite his uncommon name, he had no accent to speak of, plain spoken and bordering on posh.

Mina helped the man to his feet and took him over to join the others. "This is Corporal Martin," she introduced him, "and my colleague, David, and this here is Alice."

Alice didn't bother to look up, but Andras said hello anyway.

"Andras was mugged," Mina explained.

"Not to worry, old chap," said David, patting him on the back. "We've all been through the ringer tonight. We're heading inside, and you're welcome to come join us."

Andras nodded sheepishly. "Thank you."

So they all headed inside the building and went upstairs to the third floor. The lower floors were all unlit, but the third floor offices were glowing with life and buzzing with action. Almost every member of the Echo's reporting staff was present, either at their computers or on their phones—some of them both, typing away with their hands while holding a phone between their head and shoulder. Mina had never seen the office so motivated. Even Carol, usually sitting in her office and violating the smoking ban, was up on her feet, bare-footed in stockings and waddling around on her mahogany cane. Numerous times, Mina had seen that cane waved in someone's face, including her own, but she was glad to see it now. She felt at home again. The world seemed a little less off-kilter.

Carol spotted them and came running on over. "You made it! I'd begun to wonder if you'd ever get here."

"The roads were rather... chaotic," said David. "I gave you all we had on the phone. What's the word this end?"

"It's a bloody shambles. France and Spain have put their Governments on boats and abandoned their own countries in their time of need. America is fighting back, as you'd expect, but they've been hit bloody hard. New York took it right up the arse, poor buggers. China and Russia have killed as many of their own people as they have the enemy. They've flattened Moscow. Africa is doing the best, believe it or not. So many of its countries are heavily armed that their entire populations are effectively armies now. I bet the ugly buggers that came through the gates in Somalia didn't know what hit 'em."

"What about us?" asked Mina. "How is the U.K. doing?"

Carol sighed. "You know the answer to that, luv, because you saw it for yourself. Our Army is mostly overseas, and most of what wasn't disappeared in Hyde Park. What happened in Hyde Park has happened a dozen other places. Army got the shit kicked out of 'em."

"I got word the Army is regrouping in Colchester," said Martin, seemingly wounded by Carol's remarks.

Carol examined the Corporal like she had just realised he was standing there. "That's true, my love, but what's left to regroup? Not a lot. We're up shit creek, not without a paddle, but without a bloody damn boat. We are literally swimming in shit. I can almost taste it. Jesus Christ it's a sodding mess."

Martin glanced sideways at Mina and spoke in a hushed tone. "This woman is your boss?"

Carol heard the comment and pointed her finger. "Yes, I'm her bloody boss, and anybody else who steps inside this office. The Echo is my paper, and we're all working our arses off to get word out to the people about what's happening. You here to help, Sergeant Stiff-neck, or are you going to put the kettle on?"

Martin fidgeted. "It's Corporal Martin."

Carol's eyes bore into him. "Milk, three sugars. Kettles at the back."

Martin frowned, went to speak, but then trotted off towards the back of the office, like a good little boy.

Carol raised an eyebrow at Mina once Martin was out of earshot. "That the fella who rescued you?"

"Yes, he saved our lives."

"Then I'm glad to have him. Now, who's this little beauty?" Carol knelt in front of Alice, who stared at the floor and said nothing.

"This is Alice," said Mina. "We... She lost her brother in Hyde Park."

Carol let out a long, pained sigh. "A big brother, I bet? I had a big brother, too. He's gone now, died of the cancer four years back. Don't know what I would have done if I'd lost him at your age. I want to hear all about him, my love. He might be gone, but the more people you tell about him, the more his spirit will live on. I have chocolate in my office. Will you come share it with me while you tell me all about your brother? I want to know everything, starting with his favourite colour."

"His name was Kyle. He liked blue."

Carol gave Alice an enormous smile. "An American? I love Americans. So, did Kyle like his baseball?"

"No, he liked ice hockey. Clark took him to see the Montreal Canadiens in Canada once."

"Clark your daddy?"

"Step-daddy."

"Right you are. You can tell me all about him too. Come on now, my love." Carol took Alice's hand and straightened up. She turned to David. "Big Jimmy will catch you up on things. I'll be in my office with Alice, but I don't want to be disturbed. Not much else a woman my age can do but calm a child's nerves."

David nodded. "Call me if you need anything."

"I need good news, but don't think I'll get it."

Carol walked away just as Corporal Martin appeared with a mug of piping tea. She snatched it off him as she passed and left him to stand there looking confused.

Mina chuckled. "Come on, Martin. Let's find you something to do other than make tea."

He looked at her and nodded eagerly. "Please do."

* * *

Sitting at her computer, Mina realised that things were as bad as Carol had told them. People in Scotland were fleeing to the highlands, and refugees from the cities flooded the British countryside. There were over eighty gates in the U.K., spread wide enough that nowhere was safe. Likewise, America was under attack far and wide, but had a little more land to work with. Some areas did not have gates at all, and it was to these areas, like the greater Chicago area, where survivors were fleeing. It was also true that Africa was doing better than most other places. As Mina streamed the news channels broadcasting out of Somalia, Zimbabwe, Nigeria, and South Africa, she saw armed militia holding their own against the hordes of creatures. For the first time in history, the whites and blacks in South Africa were fighting alongside each other, instead of against. Mina marvelled at the sight of a little white boy and a black girl holding rifles and standing over the corpse of a demon. Likewise, Al-Jazeera, in the Middle East, gave positive reports of resistance in Iraq, Iran, Jordan, and Israel, but their reputation for propaganda made them less than credible.

The more and more Mina researched, the more she understood that Corporal Martin was right. The nations faring best were the ones where the citizens were armed and fighting alongside the military. Countries with a political climate of unrest, such as Somalia, followed by places like America and Canada where guns were legal, were giving as good as they got. The countries worse off were the ones with the most totalitarian governments, like Russia and China. In those countries, the people at the top seemed happy to scorch the earth to defeat the enemy. Moscow and Shanghai were both burning craters now.

Whatever chance Britain had was unclear, but it was a country famously free of firearms, which meant that it was now almost defenceless. Even the nation's police force used weapons sparingly. The only ones to use them in any significant capacity was the Army, but its majority was overseas, further contributing to those countries like Iraq who were already fighting back.

Exasperated, Mina glanced around the room.

Andras had gone with Martin to try to liaise with the military.

David was working alongside Big Jimmy—an overweight West Country native with a lot of intelligence, but very little personality—to run operations. Mina had taken her orders from Mitchell, the newspaper's System Support Manager, and had been tasked with gaining insight into the situation worldwide to try and form an overall picture. What she really wanted was to find out what was behind those gates—where did they lead? She thought of the creatures as demons now, even though nothing had confirmed it. What did other people think? Did anybody understand what was going on?

The Internet was ablaze with theories—millions of people hiding in their homes and offering opinions. The two main factions were Aliens vs Demons. One forum online operated only with the understanding that the black stones had opened up inter-dimensional portals and that humanity was being invaded by an alien species. Conversely, those who believed Demons were responsible, pointed out that many of the enemy resembled burned human beings, not aliens. What intelligent species would evolve to have burned flesh? The other side would then rebut with the explanation that the burns were from an unforeseen side effect of travelling through the gates. The theoretical victory tilted more towards the demon theory whenever somebody brought up the giants. That they were flawlessly beautiful and possessed scorched wings upon their backs gave credence to the fact they could indeed be Fallen Angels from the depths of Hell. Mina agreed with that theory, then chided herself for believing in something so absurd. Yet, the more she said the word 'demon' the more it lost its potency and supernatural connotations. Now, the word was as real and mundane as 'dog' or 'cat'. It became easier and easier to grasp her new reality every minute, yet harder and harder to accept.

They were being invaded by demons. She listed the things she knew for sure:

Black stones opened gates.
Demons (?) came through.
Giants are in charge of the demons?
Need to fight back. Everyone must fight back. Humanity must fight back.
Fight.
Fight.
Fight.

Mina sighed as she realised that she had so little to offer anybody who might read the newspaper's website. Everyone needed to understand that they were at war, but even if they did, what should they do? This wasn't like watching Iraq on the news and remarking upon the politics of it all. This was war on people's doorstep, outside the local McDonalds. There could be no pacifists in this. Everyone needed to be ready to kill the enemy.

But could ordinary people become killers—soldiers? And would that even be enough?

Mina leaned back over the keyboard and typed a message onto the front page of their website:

NOTICE: Please post anything you know about the creatures. Have you seen one die? How? What do you know that might help others? Please, please share whatever you know, wherever and whoever you are. Please share. We need to help each other.

It was nothing more than a shot in the dark, but just maybe somebody would share something helpful that she could share.

Ring!

Mina flinched as her phone rang. She had forgotten she'd switched it back on earlier to check for messages. There had been a couple of texts from a handful of friends, but most of them just wanted her to tell them what was going on. The only thing she sent them back in reply was: Find weapons. Fight. It was short and a tad dramatic, but there was no time to caress people's sensibilities. Millions were probably already dead, and those remaining would have to go from nought to sixty in a single second. As Mina looked at her phone now, she saw that her father was calling her. It was 7AM, and maybe he'd just woken up. She was the first thing he had thought about. That affected her in a strange way. Made her want to cry.

"Hello, dad. I sent you a text. I'm safe, so you don't need to worry."

"Mina, I will stop worrying about you when you are home. Where are you?"

"I'm at work."

"You need to come home." "No. I'm working." "Bloody goddammit."

"Do you realise what's going on, dad? The world is being attacked. It doesn't matter if I'm at home or work. Nowhere is safe. At least here I can do some good."

"You can do good at home with your father. I need you here."

"For what? To look after you? Don't be so selfish. Do you know how many people have died in the last twenty-four hours?"

"You swear at your own father?"

"Yes, I do swear when you're acting like a moron. I love you, dad, but I'm not coming home. In fact, there's a chance you might never see me again. I was there in London; I saw it all. Maybe that's why I understand and you don't. Now is not the time to argue with the people you love. The office is two miles away; if you want to see me, dad, then come here."

"You order me to come see you? I am your father, and I have bid you to come home."

"You are my father, yes, but not my master. I'll be here if you want me, but if not, then just keep safe and prepare for the worst. I love you, dad. I really do."

Silence.

Mina looked at her phone and realised her father had hung up on her. Exactly when, she did not know. Twenty-four hours ago, she would never have dared speak to him like she just had. Even now, in her mid-twenties, she feared the strict man who was still more than willing to strike her. Yet, gradually, over the years, she had started resisting him, placing just a little more of that distance between herself and his cloying rules. The conversation she'd just had with him was the final snare on her independence being torn away, sped up by the events in London, but always inevitable. She loved her father, but she had also resigned herself to never speaking to him again. She knew that, one day, she would rebel, and that their future relationship would depend very much on his ability to let her go willingly. It was just a pity that, with the way things were, he would have to make his peace quickly, for there might not be a chance later.

Mina stood up from her computer and went to make herself a cup of tea. She needed to wipe her mind and start again.

She met Andras over by the kettle. "Things are bad," he told her. "Corporal Martin keeps shouting and kicking things. I don't think the Army is doing well."

Mina wearily poured some milk and threw in a tea bag. She would need sleep soon, or she'd pass out where she stood. "I don't think wars ever go well," she said. "It's how they end that matters. We need to make sure we do whatever we can to help.

We're in a position of authority. People will look to the media to inform them about what to do. We have to make sure that anyone who finds us gets the best information available. We have to rally people to fight."

"You think they will? I mean, when you found me, I was lying in the road, terrified. I'm afraid I'm a coward when it comes to violence."

Mina thought for a moment, then said, "That was different. When those kids mugged you, you had the option to lie down. When you have to face the demons, that option won't be there. You'll fight. We all must fight."

"Perhaps you're right. Still, seems pretty hopeless."

"You're alive, Andras, same as yesterday and the day before that. So what's hopeless? Hope only dies when we die. So don't die."

"I'll do my best."

"And I'll do mine." She then went on to ask him, "Do you need to call anyone? Everybody has been making calls home to check on friends and family, but I haven't seen you make a call."

"I have nobody to call."

"No one?"

"No one. I'm new here; came to start again. Some fresh start, huh?"

Mina gave him a lopsided grin. "I guess I don't have anyone to call either. Not sure if that's a blessing right now." Andras put his hand on her arm and squeezed. She liked it.

"Better to have loved and lost, they say, but what do they know? The only people I have to worry about are in this room. Thank you for helping me, Mina. I'm so glad I'm not alone right now."

"Don't mention it." She yawned. "Hey, will you find David for me and tell him I've gone to take a nap?"

"He already went and did the same. I saw him sleeping on a sofa in the waiting room."

Mina rolled her eyes. "Nice of him to tell me. Well, you'll find me somewhere nice and quiet for the next few hours, if such a place still exists."

"I'll wake you if anything happens."

"Thanks, Andras." She headed off toward one of the unused offices, of which there were several. Web-based news had led to less and less boots-on-the-ground reporters, and by the time Mina had got the job at the Echo, Carol said she was lucky to find work at all.

There was no soft furniture in the empty office she chose, but that was okay. She nestled down in the corner and closed her eyes as if the worn carpet were a silk sheet. Before she fell to dreams, she hoped against hope that somebody out there would find a way to fight back. She also hoped that her father would call back, but perhaps that was too much to ask.

~RICK BASTION~

DEVONSHIRE, ENGLAND

RICK AWOKE WITH A HEADACHE, BUT IT WAS nothing new. For a few, blurry seconds he lay on the couch his living room and didn't remember that anything was wrong. He was just waking up with a hangover like he had a thousand times before. Then it came flooding back.

He turned and saw Maddy asleep on the floor next to him, and he saw Diane and Steven sprawled out on the other, larger sofa. His new companions, he reminded himself—his partners from last night's battle against the minions of Hell. The thought made him wish he could go right back to sleep. But he couldn't.

He swung his legs down onto the carpet and rubbed at his eyes with the heels of his palms. His head throbbed, his mouth was dry, but before he went into the kitchen to get a glass of water, he wanted to check on something first. Before going to bed last night, he had overridden the alarm to keep it from beeping, but he had left the monitor switched on. When he went over to it now, he saw the creatures still lined up outside his front gate. There were more of them now, standing shoulder to shoulder and filling the entire video screen. And there, right in the middle of them, was a corpse with long, black hair.

Rick narrowed his eyes as he recognised the demon that had killed Sarah. It glared directly into the camera as if it knew Rick was watching it.

Rick felt his fists clench.

"He's been there all morning," came his brother's voice. Keith stood behind him with a mug of tea in each hand. He handed one over, which Rick took gladly. "How's your head?" he asked. "You were blind drunk by the time you fell asleep."

Rick took a sip of tea and shrugged. "I can handle a hangover. I had an expert father to show me how. You were drinking pretty heavily yourself up until we made it back here."

"Difference is: I stopped. Well, at least I did this time."

Rick turned to his brother and saw there was something different about him this morning. His shoulders were lower, his chin raised less proudly. "What is it, Keith? Has something happened?"

He sipped his tea, sighed, then said, "I used your laptop this morning. I had an email from Marcy, sent about an hour after I left to come visit you. She told me she was taking Max to stay with her mother in Gloucester for a few days." He seemed to be holding back tears as he spoke. "Gloucester is hit pretty bad apparently. BBC news is trying to sugar coat it, but when you search the smaller news sites, you get the real truth. There's a newspaper in Slough which has posted a list of the gates that have opened. Gloucester is on the list."

Rick squinted, his head still banging, but now he was confused as well. "I don't understand. Why did Marcy go to her mother's?"

"Because I cheated on her with my secretary."

"Oh God, Keith, seriously? That's so fucking clichéd." Keith's face screwed up in anger, but he seemed to force it away and stared down into his mug of tea as if trying to channel his rage into the liquid instead of his brother. "I've been drinking heavily and… I don't know. I wasn't in my right mind. My secretary ended up causing me all kinds of bother. She called Marcy in the middle of the night and told her I was leaving her and was going to get a divorce. Crazy bitch. All the shit I give you, huh, Rick? Makes me a hypocrite."

This was Rick's chance. The opportunity to finally tell his big brother what a self-centred prick he was. It had been a long time coming, and he savoured the moment.

But he couldn't do it. "I guess there's a bit of dad in both of us. Impulse control has never been a strength of the men in our family."

Keith chuckled, a tear forming in his eye. "You know, I never thought about other women before, but lately I've just started feeling so... unfulfilled. You lived your dream, Rick, even if it was fleeting. What did I ever do?"

Rick placed his tea down on a side table and folded his arms. "Are you kidding me? You've always got whatever you've wanted. You're a rich accountant with a beautiful wife and a genius son."

Keith shook his head. "No, Rick. I'm a rich accountant who used to have a beautiful wife and genius son. Now they're dead, and it's all because of me. If I hadn't cheated, we'd all be together at home now. I sent Marcy and Max to their deaths."

Rick put his arm around his older brother and let him sob into his shoulder. "You don't know they're hurt, Keith. Look at us: We were attacked and made it through okay."

Keith eased away, wiped his eyes with the crook of his elbow. "Wake up, little brother. We're not okay. It's a stay of execution, that's all. Those things have us surrounded."

"The iron gates are keeping us safe."

"You don't really believe that lunatic, Daniel, do you? All that talk about seals and demons. I don't understand what's out there, but it's going to get us eventually."

"For fuck's sake, Keith. Last night, you held everyone together. You were a rock. You've had bad news about your family, I get it, but you need to keep your head straight. Marcy and Max might still be alive, and you owe it to them to make it out of this so you can make things right again."

"Why can't I just give up like you? Last night, you did nothing but drink. You would've died if I hadn't saved you back at the pub."

Rick groaned as he saw the old Keith return. The moment of vulnerability was over. "I'm a sad alcoholic with a failed pop career. You're not me, Keith. You have every reason to go on living. If Marcy and Max are still okay, we'll find them, okay? Maybe not in the next forty-eight hours, but eventually. Until then, we just have to keep our wits about us—me included. I'll try to knock the drink on the head. You're right: It's no good."

Keith sighed. "You're right. If there's a chance, I have to try. Thanks, Rick. You do have your uses."

"You're welcome."

"This place is massive," said Daniel, trotting up behind them. "Took me a half hour to find the lavvy. You might want to give it twenty minutes by the way." He leaned forward and studied the video screen. "Those sods still out there?"

Keith nodded. "Haven't moved an inch. That one in the middle with the long black hair is the one who attacked us at the pub last night. Drove an ambulance right through the door."

Daniel whistled. "Quite the Die Hard villain."

"Makes you wonder, why he doesn't try something similar now?" pondered Rick. "They may be monsters, but they're not stupid. If the iron in the gate is keeping them out, then why aren't they trying to knock the fence down?"

Keith said, "They wouldn't be able to ram it like they did with the pub's door. I parked our cars up against the gate, remember?"

"You think that's the reason they haven't tried to force the gate?" Rick asked, looking at Daniel to see what he thought.

"Maybe," he said. "Or maybe they're waiting for something."

Keith frowned. "Like what?"

Daniel shrugged. "Reinforcements?"

***

"My husband's dead," said Maddy as she stood beside Rick in the master bedroom. They were both staring out of the window at the demons outside. Rick counted over a hundred of them huddled in the road. A crowd of rotting corpses waiting to devour them.

He glanced at her. "How do you know?"

"I left my mobile in the ambulance, but I used Diane's phone to call him. A stranger picked up, told me that my husband died last night in Milton Combe. The demons from the gate in Crapstone have spread out to nearby towns. My husband was on his way home from the hospital when the village was attacked. He tried to help the injured, but he should have run."

"I'm sorry, I didn't know. You're not wearing a ring."

"I have to take it off when I'm working. It's at home. I keep thinking about it, wondering if I'll ever see it again. My husband is dead, and I keep thinking about a silly old ring."

Rick looked at the young women and saw the anguish behind her confident strength. "It's not silly," he said. "Your ring is a symbol of your love for your husband, and his love for you. I think that we hold on to symbols because it makes our feelings easier to tie down and make sense of. I suppose that's why my garage is full of unsold albums—I don't value the CDs, I value the time in my life they represent. Your ring is important. I hope, one day, you manage to go get it."

Maddy closed her eyes. When she opened them again, she seemed a little distant. "Those things outside aren't going to go away, are they?"

"Daniel thinks they might be waiting for something." "Like what?"

"I have no idea. Is Diane still checking the Internet?" "Yeah, things are bad, Rick. The whole world has been hit.

There's even talk of giant angels stomping around the earth killing everyone."

Rick pulled a face. "Angels?"

"Yeah, bad angels—like Lucifer kind of angels. Looks like Daniel's theory about Heaven and Hell might be right."

"Keith doesn't believe him. Not sure I trust him either."

Maddy kept her stare on the demons outside. "I see no reason not to trust him. We're all as screwed as each other. How much food do you have, Rick? I see a lot of beer, but not a lot of stuff to eat."

"I'm a bachelor. I order in."

"I assumed as much, which means we're all going to be dealing with hunger pangs by tonight and feeling pretty rotten within a couple of days. How long will those things keep us penned up in here?"

Rick hadn't even considered it, but Maddy was right, they couldn't stay there indefinitely. "We're going to need to find supplies, aren't we?"

"Or starve to death. It's not a problem right now, but it will be soon. I don't see things going well for us here, Rick. That's why I'm thinking about leaving."

"What? You can't go out there. They'll tear you apart."

"I listened to what you said last night about the step ladder. The demons are all at the front of your house. If I can make it over the back into the woods, I'm sure I can get away. I can find help and bring it back."

"You might get over the gate from the inside, but what if you get attacked and need to get back?"

"I'll figure something out."

"It's a bad idea. What if help comes while you're gone and you've taken the risk for nothing?"

"There's no help coming, Rick. Just take a look on the Internet, and you'll see enough to understand that we're on our own. The Army tried to fight back in London and got torn apart in Hyde Park. Somebody hacked into the CCTV footage and leaked it onto YouTube for all to see. It's devastating. I can accept that we're all going to die, Rick, but I'm not prepared to do it by starving to death. And I don't want to die without my wedding ring."

Rick studied the demons outside the gate and weighed up Maddy's chances. She might be able to slip away unnoticed—maybe they all could—but was getting out really for the best? Yet, how long would they have if they stayed?

The black-haired demon glared up at them and grinned. The malicious intent in his crooked expression gave Rick little doubt that he was not standing there aimlessly. The monster had a plan.

"I think we should all leave," said Rick after having considered things. "Some places are still okay, right? Diane found a couple of areas we could go?"

Maddy nodded. "A few places, yes."

"Then we find the nearest safe place and head there right away. Somewhere better than this—some place where we can survive."

Maddy's face lit up. "Yes, we should all get out of here together. I'd appreciate the company."

Rick nodded and confirmed it to himself, as if he couldn't quite believe it. "Okay, let's leave."

They headed downstairs together and went into the kitchen where Diane was still busy on the laptop. Steven was in the living room, piling up anything they could use as weapons. Knives mostly.

Rick went over to the fridge and reached for a beer, but stopped himself and grabbed a can of coke instead. He pulled the tab and sat down next to Diane at the computer. It was the first coke he'd had in a long time that didn't include whisky. "Hey," he said. "Where's the nearest place that's safe?"

"Torquay. All the South Coast up to Southampton is safe. Plymouth is okay too, but it's so nearby the gate from Crapstone that the demons might reach there soon. I've been reading this website for a newspaper called the Slough Echo. They're trying to list all the information people have found out. I told them about the iron gates and how the demons can't come in—maybe they can pass it on to the army or something. Anyway, this newspaper has listed all the safe towns that they know about. Torquay isn't anywhere near a gate."

Rick looked at Maddy. "If we can get a car, we can be at Torquay in a couple hours. I've always loved the English Riviera."

"I want to go home first and get my ring."

He sighed. "I know you do, but the village isn't safe. Better to stay alive and get it later."

Maddy looked to argue, but ended up nodding. "I suppose you're right. If we're all leaving together, then we should head for the coast like Diane said. If there's any sort of evacuation effort it would be better to be near the ports."

Rick nodded. "Then that's where we head."

"Head where?" said Keith, entering the kitchen with Steven by his side.

"We're heading to Torquay," Rick told him. "It's safe." "Nowhere is safe, Rick. We'd be stupid to leave." "Yeah," said Steven, who had finally taken off his tie and opened his collar. "That gate is the only thing keeping us alive."

"Yes, they gate is keeping us safe," said Maddy, "but we can't just hide in here forever. We need to go somewhere with supplies and food. The longer we stay here, the worse it will get outside. There's a chance to reach safety that might not be there later."

"We'd never make it out," said Keith. "The demons would rip us apart before we even reached the road. You've seen that one with the black hair, Rick. He's just waiting for an opportunity to finish what he started."

Rick shuddered at the thought of confronting the monster again, but he was resolute in his decision. "We go over the back fence like I said last night. The stepladder."

"Oh, wonderful, the stepladder. And what makes you think there aren't a hundred demons waiting for us around the back?"

"Because I've looked, Keith. They're all outside the front gate. We can check things out first, of course, but I'm certain we can sneak away. Torquay is an hour away by car, and it's safe."

Steven shook his head. "It's safe here, Rick. Your house is huge and protected by the gate. We shouldn't leave."

"Don't you get it?" cried Maddy. "We'll starve to death in here. No help is coming, so we have to help ourselves. If we put off now what we won't be able to do later, then we're screwed. We need to leave while there's a chance we can."

"No," said Keith. "I won't allow it."

Rick stood up from his stool and faced his brother. "You won't allow it? Who's asking?"

"I saved your arse last night, Rick. You do as I say."

"Are you kidding me? I thought you'd actually found a little humility after being caught fucking your secretary, but you're the same old control freak. You're not the boss of anyone here."

Keith shoved Rick hard into the kitchen island. "Watch what you say to me, Rick. I've been wiping your arse your entire life, but I'd just as soon give you a good hiding."

Rick was in shock. His brother had never struck him before, not even as a kid. "What the hell is your problem?"

"You're my problem, Rick. You're running away and trying to isolate yourself, just like you always do. I won't allow you to get everyone killed. I've already lost too much. No one is leaving. It's a suicide mission."

"It's not your decision," Maddy muttered.

Keith put his hands up and let some of the aggression leave his face. "Look, I hear what you're saying about the food situation, but we have running water and enough food to get through for a little while longer. Maybe we should wait a day or two before making any rash decisions. We're all in fight or flight mode—and that's understandable—but it isn't conducive to good reasoning. Running for the hills might sound good, but is it wise? I don't think so, and I'm not leaving."

"I'm staying put too," said Steven.

Diane flipped her hair behind her ears and said, "I'm not leaving unless everybody else is. We're fine here, and we have Internet. We should learn as much as we can before we try to escape."

Rick and Maddy looked at one another in desperation. Maddy seemed to have lost her fight and broke eye contact with him. "I'll stay one more day," she muttered, "but after that I'm going home. You people can stay here if you like, but you'll regret it, I promise you."

"I won't regret it," said Rick, "because I'm leaving today."

"You are not," said Keith in a voice cold as ice.

Rick huffed. "Keith, take a hike, okay? This is my house, and I'll bloody well leave if I like. In fact, you can have the place; it's yours. Just stop being a twat."

Keith went red in the face. "Rick, you're—"

"What the hell are you people fighting about?" asked Daniel, wandering into the kitchen. "I could hear you from all the way upstairs."

"What were you doing upstairs?" asked Rick.

"Sleeping, until you sods woke me up. What's the problem here?"

"Rick wants to leave," said Keith. Daniel shrugged. "So let him." "If he goes outside he'll die."

"His place, his rules. If he wants to leave, who can stop him?"

Keith clenched his fists. "I can. And I will."

Rick felt his own face growing red now. He realised, in that moment, that one of the main driving forces of him wanting to leave was to get away from his brother. What was Keith's problem? Whether he was arguing out of genuine concern or just plain stubbornness, it pissed Rick off royally. He had made up his mind and wasn't backing down. The more and more the argument went on, the more claustrophobic he felt, and the more he was certain he wanted to leave.

"Look, Keith. I can't stay in here knowing that those things are right outside the gate. I'd rather take my chances on the road."

Keith shook his head and was actually trembling. "Please, Rick. Don't do something you'll regret."

"You're not the boss of me." Rick went to push past his brother, and to his relief, Keith stood aside.

"I understand, Rick."

Keith grabbed one of the empty beer bottles off the counter and swung it at Rick's head. Rick tried to duck, but ended up on the floor bleeding as Keith stood over him with a look of pity on his face. "The problem with you, little brother, is that you never help yourself. No backbone, just like dad always said."

Before the others in the kitchen had chance to stop him, Keith lifted his foot and kicked Rick in the face, sending him right back to sleep.

~TONY CROSS~

7 MILES NORTH OF THE EUPHRATES, SYRIA

"THERE'LL BE NO ONE LEFT TO SAVE BY THE time we get there," said Tony as he and Aymun led their men across the desert at a sprint. The gate was less than half a mile away, but they could all see the civilian militia were taking heavy losses. The clawed creatures poured out of the gate and cut through men, woman, and children too young to wield a rifle. Blood stained the ground as if gallons of red paint had been spilled onto the dirt.

"If we save only one man or woman then we have done our duty," said Aymun.

The Syrian and British soldiers were all now armed with L85s, AK47s, grenades, and a PKM machine gun that Harris, the strongest of them, lugged over his shoulder. The civilians in front of the gate wielded a mixture of reclaimed assault rifles and pistols, but they were not trained proficiently enough to form a firing line. As they missed shots, or were forced to reload, they were set upon by the demons. In the last five minutes alone, dozens of them had died.

Aymun and his two men reached firing distance first, as they were less unencumbered than the British soldiers clad in full battle armour and carrying the heavier L85s. Aymun dropped to one knee and let off a barrage from his AK47. He hit several of the creatures, even at two hundred metres. His men then overtook him and fired from their knees ten metres ahead. Tony's men caught up and set themselves down a further ten metres before firing. Aymun got up and ran past them all and once again took a knee and fired from the front. They continued this series of firing overlaps until they were only fifty metres away from the battlefield. The civilians saw their arrival and cheered, even as they continued to be slaughtered. It was the first time Tony had ever seen civilians in this region show gratitude to see British soldiers.

The demons outnumbered the militia five to one, but now their flanks were under attack by Aymun and Tony's men. Tony unclipped a grenade from his vest and lobbed it into the air. His men followed suit. Unlike the ones they had tossed at Aymun's convoy, these grenades fell perfectly amongst the enemy and exploded with venom. Mangled demon parts littered the ground along with great clods of displaced earth. The resulting mess was enough to ignite hope. Tony saw the confidence creep onto his men's faces as they advanced further, unloading round upon round into the enemy.

Demons fell in their dozens.

Now that the enemy was split wide open, the militia gained a foothold. They formed up in a group behind their battered vehicles and fired all at once, cutting down another two dozen of their foe in seconds. The battle was turning.

Tony and his men released another volley of grenades, opening up more craters in the enemy's ranks. Any human army would have turned tail after such sudden and devastating losses, but the clawed creatures continued their attack, more than willing to die.

Harris set down the PKM on its bipod and opened her up as soon as it was steady. Its roaring teeth ripped the creatures apart like razor wire, dissecting limbs, torsos, and heads with the precision of a surgeon's buzz saw.

"Send their wee dirty arses to Hell," Corporal Rose yelled triumphantly as more demons fell.

But their advantage waned when Harris's PKM jammed. The decades-old machine gun had been stashed in a cave for God knew how long, and they suffered the consequences. The second thing to go wrong was when one of Aymun's men threw a soviet F1 grenade at the enemy, but didn't bother to cook it first. One of the creatures was proactive enough to scoop it up in its claw and launch it right back again. It exploded mid-air over the original thrower, and Aymun's man hit the ground, clutching his burst eyeballs and trying to pull out the shrapnel. Aymun had no choice but to leave the man where he lay.

The creatures were unbroken, and kept on coming, even as they continued falling to fresh onslaughts of gunfire. Reinforcements came through the gate every second to join the fray.

Harris hadn't thought to bring his rifle with him when he'd picked up the bulky PKM, so he had no way to defend himself when one demon broke away and headed right for him. It fell upon him like a rabid beast and ripped shreds out of his stomach with its claws. At first, only clothing and armour split apart, tatters twirling in the air, but then a spray of blood jetted upwards and covered the demon's snarling face. Tony was too far away to help his man, but Harris wasn't done for yet. The private reached around to his webbing and slid his combat knife from its sheath. He rammed it into the demon's side with such forced that it sounded like somebody had hit a bass drum. He twisted and turned the knife until the creature stopped moving and fell to the ground.

Tony finally made it over to Harris and dragged his injured private back to his feet. It was hard to assess the man's wound while hidden beneath several layers of clothing and torn amour, nor was there time to try, so Tony pulled his Glock 17 pistol from its holster and shoved it into Harris's hand. "You should have brought a backup, Private."

Harris held up his blood soaked knife and gave an ugly grin. "I did."

The civilians screamed as the demons made it through the parked vehicles and attacked the back lines—mostly children and women. There must have been a hundred dead villagers scattered in the desert now, and the militia was down to its last remnants.

"The villagers are falling," shouted Aymun. "We must go to them."

Tony nodded and ordered his men to skirt the edges of battle to where they could form up alongside the militia. They covered each other in turn as they made an overlap toward their ailing allies.

Tony and Aymun reached the villagers just in time. There were perhaps twenty of them remaining, but half were out of ammo, and the other half were wavering. The creatures had pushed them all back to the rearmost vehicles, which meant that they had nowhere further to retreat. A small group of children cowered behind them.

"They just keep on feckin' coming," Corporal Rose shouted, aiming his rifle in a dozen different places and taking well-aimed pop shots. One demon made it through, but he kept his calm and took a leaf from Private Harris's book and stabbed it in the face with his knife.

Tony watched the glowing gate and cringed every time another demon leapt through. It was like they formed out of vapour, coming into existence one droplet at a time, before dumping down into the desert. Were they lined up somewhere on the other side, leaping through the gate one after the other, like lemmings off a cliff?

They would not stop coming.

Tony had an idea. He snatched the last grenade from his vest and coiled up like a spring as he prepared to throw it. When he finally let go, he aimed it right at the centre of the gate. It seemed to sail through the air forever, arcing over the heads of the writhing creatures in slow motion. Then it disappeared. The only proof the grenade had ever existed was a brief ripple in the gate's translucent centres.

The explosion was muted, as though occurring underwater, but a great torrent of flames burst forth from the gate and immolated the demons closest to it. The creatures stopped advancing for the first time, and looked back to see what had happened.

"Attack the gate," shouted Tony. "Attack the bloody gate."

Everyone concentrated their fire on the gate at once, causing the translucent surface to plop and shimmer as bullets hit it like the pitter-patter of rain. The men launched the last of their grenades and cheered each time another muted explosion brought forth another torrent of fire.

But then they were forced to regroup.

While the men attacked the gate, the remaining demons charged. Aymun's last remaining man went down as two creatures grabbed his arms and yanked them off, leaving him to spin around in panic, bleeding into the air like a sprinkler.

Two of Tony's men got isolated and gutted in quick succession. A handful of the remaining villagers went down in a haze of blood.

"There's no more coming through the gate," shouted Tony as he peppered the enemy. "Keep fighting, and we can end this."

The men took heart and kept up the assault, even though the urge to run was in all of them. There were still several dozen creatures coming right at them, but as they spread their fire in a wide arc, they thinned the enemy out.

"We can do this," Corporal Rose cried out. "Kick their lily arses."

The enemy numbers were down to ten, outnumbered for the first time since the fighting began. Harris came up beside Tony with his Glock, popping off shots carefully and exploding heads off demonic shoulders. He emptied his last magazine into a leaping creature and knocked it right out of the sky like a clay pigeon. Aymun fired from twin AK47s now, like some kind of action hero, after picking up the weapon of his fallen comrade. The villagers emptied the last of their ammo and took down another handful of enemies.

Soon there was only one, single remaining demon left alive. It glared at them, and took a step back.

It was afraid.

Tony reached out and reclaimed his Glock from Harris. He crossed the battlefield with it until he was face-to-face with the demon. The oily skinned, coal-eyed abomination snarled at him like a cornered cat, spitting and hissing. Its breath stunk of rotting meat.

Tony raised the Glock and fired a bullet right through the bastard's forehead. For a moment, it remained standing, staring at him through wide, almost-human eyes, but then it teetered and tipped over backwards, hitting the ground with a thump.

The men behind Tony were silent, but then, like a rising tide, their voices rose to a triumphant cry. He turned around to face them, too beat and too weary to smile. What he could do was raise the Glock above his head in victory—the weapon that had fired the final bullet. "We did it," he croaked. "We sent those fuckers straight back to Hell."

The men cheered even more, their voices strained with jubilation. The surviving villagers were crying with a mix of relief and shock. They had done it—they had fought back their deaths.

But then the cheering stopped.

More creatures poured through the gate.

~GUY GRANGER~
CAPE FEAR, NORTH CAROLINA

R EFUELLED, RESUPPLIED, AND REMANNED, THE Hatchet raised anchor and set off from the southeast coast. Guy planned to follow the shipping lanes across the Atlantic as much as possible and avoid the winds by having a senior ensign check the ship's meteorological instrumentation every thirty minutes, but the weather so far was fair. The men were focused. Many had received word of their families and friends being lost in the attacks, but they were turning their anguish into motivation and concentrating on getting to England. Others were just glad to be aboard where it was safe.

"I've relayed a message to Command," Frank told him. "Said we were no longer operational. You understand that if things ever get back to normal we'll all end up in prison for dereliction of duty, and theft of a Coast Guard Vessel?"

Guy nodded. "If things go back to normal I will happily accept full punishment. Until then, I'm going to get my kids."

Frank took his hand and clasped it in his own, an intimate gesture, but appreciated. "I'm sure they're safe. The British Army is no pushover."

"Nor is the United States Navy, but look what happened at Norfolk."

"We'll get them, Captain. I promise you."

"I think the time for calling me 'Captain' has passed." "On the contrary. Now more than ever you need to lead these sailors. The civilians especially will need direction. Give it a day or two, and we will see bouts of seasickness, panic, claustrophobia, and a lot of changed minds. You will have to keep a firm hand to maintain order."

"Firm but fair," Guy corrected. "The former is more important." "Captain!"

Guy turned around to see Lieutenant Tosco hurrying up the ladder.

"What is it Lieutenant?"

"Switch to Naval Frequency 1."

Guy frowned, but gave Frank a nod to do as requested. The ship's main radio squawked to life with the panicked tones of a stranger. "USS Augusta requesting immediate rescue. We are under attack. Our coordinates are..."

Guy raised an eyebrow. "Those coordinates are sixteen miles off the coast."

"We are under attack. All vessels in the vicinity, please respond with immediate aid."

"We can reach them within the hour," said Tosco firmly. "We have to help."

Guy shook his head. "We have our mission, Lieutenant. You agreed to stay on board and cross the Atlantic."

"I agreed to help you find your kids, yes, but I never said I would turn my back on Americans in need. You want to maintain my support, direct the ship towards the USS Augusta."

Frank stepped in front of Guy and faced Tosco down. "How dare you give the Captain orders!"

"No, he's right, Frank. I can't ask the men to save my children if I'm not willing to save the men aboard the Augusta. Lieutenant Tosco, prepare the crew for a rescue operation and battle conditions." He turned and got on the radio. "USS Augusta, this is the USCG Hatchet. Stand by. We'll be with you within the hour."

He turned back to Tosco. "You have your orders, Lieutenant. Go."

Tosco nodded, and saluted as respectfully as Guy had ever seen him. "Aye, aye, Captain."

Once Tosco had left, Frank turned to Guy with concern on his face. "I thought you agreed you would be firm. You just let Tosco dictate our course."

"I said I'd be firm but fair. Tosco was correct in his thinking. Do you disagree?"

"No. It's the right call. I just wish it hadn't come from Tosco. You give that guy's ego a penny and he'll take a pound."

"He's given me his support, Frank. I owe it to the man to trust him."

Frank nodded as if he understood, but then he said, "I would rather trust a man because he earned it, than because I owe it to him."

"Have I earned your trust, Frank?"

"Ten times over."

"Then you'll just have to hope I know what I'm doing. I can handle Tosco."

Frank rubbed at his chin, a day's stubble there for the first time since Guy had met him decades ago. "I worry more about whether Tosco can handle himself."

"Your concerns are noted, Chief Petty. Now, full-steam ahead."

***

When they reached the USS Augusta, they were all glad to see that it was still afloat. That didn't mean it was in good shape though. A battle raged on its decks.

"They're coming up right out of the water," said Frank as he stared out of the pilothouse window. Sopping wet creatures with bloated stomachs and sagging skin were launching themselves out of the water, like dolphins, and landing on the deck of the Augusta. There, they were attacking the sailors as they did their best to stay together.

Guy turned to Tosco. "You know the drill, Lieutenant. Open up the MGs."

Tosco nodded and went to give the orders. A minute later, the rapid fire sprayed across the water and hit several creatures before they had a chance to leap up out of the ocean. The Navy frigate Augusta had far more firepower than the Hatchet, but it looked like its captain had never gotten the chance to use it.

Guy got on the ship's radio and ordered the crew to take to the rails and open fire from their assault rifles. The men— including some of the civilians—lined up along the ship's boundaries and started picking their shots. Guy flinched when he saw some rounds go awry and hit the Augusta's crew, but enough of the bloated, slippery demons went down to make them acceptable casualties. The remaining crew of the Augusta saw the Hatchet now and raised their hands excitedly. Fortunately, they were not distracted too long and could take advantage of the opening they'd been given. They steeled themselves against the enemy and fought for the upper hand. The Hatchet continued to lend support from its two machine guns.

The slippery demons continued leaping up out of the ocean.

Frank clenched his fists, watching the scene without blinking. "Where are these things coming from?"

Guy watched a naval officer fall overboard as a demon swatted him over the gunwale. Seconds after hitting the water, the man was dragged down screaming beneath the surface. Not even the oceans were safe.

There was screaming from the deck below, making Guy and Frank glance at each other in horror. Tosco came on the radio. "The enemy is on board. We're losing men."

Guy turned to the ladder, but Frank stopped him. "We need you here, Captain. I'll go."

"We'll both go. We will need every man we have."

Frank relented, and the two of them raced down the ladder together and sprinted towards the launch deck. What they saw was terrifying. The slimy creatures were horrifying, and a stink of rotting flesh and the sea came off them in waves. Tosco had the crew organised in a line in front of the Jayhawk helicopter, cutting down the enemy with their rifles. Many of the civilians had scattered in panic and had found themselves cut off from safety. Guy watched as Simon— the teenage Avengers fan—backed up into the clutches of a demon stalking him. It grabbed his head and wrenched it right off his neck before he even knew what was happening, leaving behind a spurting stump and a tap-dancing body that flopped onto the deck like a fish.

Frank and Guy both grabbed rifles from the stockpile and loaded them up with magazines. It'd been years since Guy had fired a rifle, and the first time he'd ever needed to shoot to kill. The U.S. Coast Guard were not killers, their weaponry more often a deterrent. Today, they would all become soldiers. Guy picked his shots and nailed a demon right in the back of the head. He aimed again and took down another demon snacking on a civilian's torn-out intestines.

Frank was like a machine, firing shot after shot without seemingly even having to aim. Tosco stood behind the nearby firing line, pointing out targets to the men and shouting motivations. The young lieutenant was in his element, face stained with blood from a slash wound on his neck, and a look of total control about him. He was unflappable.

Guy glanced across at the Augusta. The Navy frigate was under renewed attack now after losing the support of the Hatchet's MGs. Its decks were once again filling up with waterlogged monsters.

"We need to get to those MGs," Guy shouted to Frank. "I'll take starboard, you take port."

They split up, running to opposite sides of the ship. Guy made it over to his MG first, grabbed the handles, and pulled the trigger. The heavy weight of it bucked in his grip, but he kept it steady and drew the bullet stream across the water and took out a dozen demons. The alleviation in the enemy reinforcements allowed the crew of the Augusta to once again recover and start clearing their decks anew. That gave Guy time enough to spin the MG around and face onto the Hatchet's own launch deck. He opened up and cut a swath through the demons attacking the civilian refugees. Tosco kept the rest of the crew organised enough to allow the civilians to creep back into safety where Skip handed them weapons and ammunitions. Everyone needed to be armed and firing. No more being a civilian.

Guy saw that they were winning. Fewer and fewer demons emerged from the water and Frank kept the opposite MG trained to make sure that those that did lost their heads. Many of the demons floated dead on the waves. The men aboard the Augusta were cheering as they swept the last remaining invaders from their deck.

The MG in Guy's hand clunked as it fired its last round— its belt-fed magazine expired. He let go of it cautiously, expecting demons to run straight for him now that they had the chance, but none did. So he did his best to march confidently on wobbling legs towards Tosco who was mopping up the last of the enemy. By the time Guy reached his Lieutenant, the crew was hailing him as a hero. Tosco lapped it up, grinning ear to ear, even as he continued to bleed from the jagged wound on his neck. He looked like the lead in an action movie.

"Are you okay, Lieutenant?" Guy asked his second in command.

Tosco wiped the blood from his neck and looked at it. "Just a flesh wound, Captain. One of them got me when they first came up out the water. Luckily, I'd already taken the safety off my rifle."

Frank left the other MG and came over. "You did well," he told Tosco, although it sounded more than a little begrudging.

"Thank you, Chief Petty, but I can't take any of the credit. The men were warriors, each and every one of them. Let the enemy come, I say. They'll never get the better of the Hatchet."

The men cheered, and were interrupted only by the squawking of a radio. Ensign Bentley brought the unit over to Guy who immediately answered the call. "Captain Granger of the USCG Hatchet. How are you doing over there, USS Augusta? Over."

"Thank the Lord for you, Captain Granger. Thank the Lord. You saved our bacon. Once those things were on board we couldn't stop them coming. It was you cutting them to ribbons on the water that turned the tide. Your men are heroes. Over."

"That they are, Captain. Over."

"Not the captain," came the reply from the Augusta. "Commander Johnson died in the attack, a stray bullet from one of your men, I believe. I'm Lieutenant Hernandez. Over."

"I'm sorry about your commander," said Guy. "My crew did the best they could. Over."

"I understand. Our decks were swamped with monsters. We would've lost far more men if you hadn't been here to help. Over."

"Do you know where those creatures came from, Lieutenant Hernandez? Over."

"Affirmative. Our radars picked up an anomaly on the seabed in this area. The things must have swum right up out of the depths. They were so bloated and malformed that they must have been sunk right down low. Over."

Guy took a moment to reply. "Then it appears these hell gates are beneath the oceans and on land. We should all keep an eye on the radar and steer a clear course. Over."

"Copy that, Captain. We fled Norfolk hoping to regroup, but ran right into another battle. Over."

"You were at Norfolk? So were we. Did you see how things ended there? Over"

"There's nothing left. The USS New Hampshire went under and took a thousand men with her, but several vessels got away. We count our blessings. Over."

Guy slumped back against the port side railing. "At least some of us got out alive. We're not beaten yet. Over."

"Copy that, Captain. Gives us a chance to regroup and head back to coast. Now that you saved us, we'll be able to fight another day. Naval Command is operating out of Florida now, and all ships are to make their way to Jacksonville. It'll be a pleasure to have the Hatchet along for the ride. Over."

"Negative. The Hatchet is crossing the Atlantic. Over." "Why? Over."

"I have a personal matter to attend to. Over."

"We have orders to assemble at Jacksonville. Disobey and you'll be considered a deserter. Over."

"Call it what you want. I'm going to the U.K. to get my kids. Over."

"I can't allow you to do that, Captain Granger. The Hatchet is United States property, and your men have a duty to protect their country. You need to return to coast, or relinquish command to someone who will. Over."

Guy looked around at his crew, each of them panting and ferocious, like blooded wolves. Tosco had his arms folded, but Guy couldn't tell if he was for or against what his counterpart on the Augusta was suggesting. His opinion would be key to persuading the rest of the crew one way or another.

"With all due respect, Lieutenant Hernandez, I don't take orders from you. Over."

"The U.S. Coast Guard has been ordered to relinquish command to the Navy. I am the senior naval officer in this region, and I am taking authority of your vessel. I will have one of my junior officers take command of your crew. Prepare to be boarded. Over and out."

Guy swallowed a lump in his throat. He had already made his mind up about deserting and heading to the U.K., but how far was he willing to go? And how far would his crew be willing to go? Would he allow them to get into a firefight with their own countrymen, just to save his children? No, he couldn't do it. He would have to relinquish command. There was no other option.

I'm so sorry Kyle and Alice.

"Fuck them," said Frank.

Guy looked at his Chief Petty in shock. "You don't agree with them? What about your belief in the chain of command?"

"Fuck the chain of command. The chain of command allowed two-thirds of our Navy to get obliterated at Norfolk. It's you who has kept us all safe. We rescued those goddamn blue dicks and this is how they repay us? Any man tries to board this ship will have to go through me."

The crew looked worried, but none said anything. Guy looked at Tosco, who still had his arms folded. The lieutenant glanced over at the Augusta, then back at Guy. "Those lightweights think they can come aboard and take control of our ship, give orders to my men, they got another thing coming. I say we line up and prevent them from boarding."

"We can't beat them," said Guy, laying it on the line. His crew had earned that much. "They have more guns and a thicker hull. If we get into a firefight, we can't win."

"Don't have to win," said Frank. "Just make it clear that we're more trouble than it's worth. They might take this ship from us, but we can make sure they won't have enough men left to run it."

"We can also make sure that our first bullet takes out Hernandez," said Tosco.

Guy straightened up, pride swelling in his chest. "Okay. Lieutenant, get everyone armed and lined up against the railings. Frank, back on that MG."

"It's out of ammo."

"So is the other one, but the men aboard the Augusta don't know that."

"Aye, aye, Captain."

The men got busy, reloading their weapons and forming up along the rails. Bloated demon corpses littered the deck, but were forgotten for now as the USCG Hatchet had a new enemy: The USS Augusta.

The Augusta drifted in close enough that the hulls of the two ships were almost touching. Its marines lined up along the railing, but they were not pointing rifles—yet. A small man stood amongst them, unarmed. His officer's uniform and Hispanic complexion led Guy to assume that he was Lieutenant Hernandez in the flesh.

"Tell your men to stand aside, Captain Granger. I hereby seize this vessel in the name of the United States Navy."

Guy stood at the railing, also without a weapon—two generals meeting across the battlefield. "Your access is denied, Lieutenant Hernandez. I am the captain of this ship, and my word is law. Be grateful for your rescue and take your men wherever you choose, but they will not come aboard this ship."

"You have American citizens on board. Do you plan on kidnapping them?"

"No man or woman is here against their will. In fact, any who wish to join you now may do so." Guy turned around to look at the civilians, but not one of them stepped forward to leave.

"You have them scared," Hernandez remarked.

"Considering you were all but dead in the water when we arrived, I think maybe it's you they are afraid of. The men on this ship survived the attack on New York, the attack on Norfolk, and now the attack on the USS Augustus. They are safer with me than anywhere else. They are survivors and—as my own Lieutenant called them earlier—warriors. We came to aid you in your time of need when running away would've been easier. My crew is fearless and ferocious. Come aboard if you dare, Lieutenant."

Hernandez laughed like a hyena. "You really think you will win a fight against my ship, Captain? You don't stand a chance."

"Perhaps, but are you willing to lose the men it will take to put us down? I promise that for every one of us you take, we'll take three of yours. We have two machine guns and my ship's main gun aimed at you, not to mention about a hundred rifles. I'm over-manned, you see. That's what happens when you win fights—you get stronger. I look at your crew, Lieutenant, and all I see is fear and exhaustion. They have lost their commander and inherited you. How long do you think they will tolerate your command if you force them to kill fellow Americans? Fellow Americans who just saved their lives. Or perhaps they won't have to tolerate you much longer. Maybe the very first shot fired will be right at your forehead. You're a pretty good shot, aren't you, Lieutenant Tosco?"

Tosco raised his riflescope to his eye and grinned. "Aye, aye, Captain. I can shoot the nutsack off a navy officer from a hundred metres. In fact, I'm ready to pull the trigger right now."

Hernandez tried to respond but tripped over his own words and ended up offering nothing but bluster. He shifted uncomfortably and retreated a step, as he no doubt felt Tosco's sights falling on him. It sent the wrong message to his men, who all suddenly seemed completely unsure of themselves.

Guy didn't want to undermine the Lieutenant too much. The man still had a Navy frigate to command, and his help would be sorely needed back on the coast. "Look, Commander Hernandez, I see you're a good man—a good American—but after Norfolk, it became every man for himself. We all need to do whatever we can in whatever way we can to make a difference. The Hatchet is crossing the Atlantic, and we will lend our help wherever it is needed, just like we did to save your ship, but we will make our own way and decide our own fate. It's survival now, don't you see?

There's not going to be any great war because we've already lost. There's no more United States, there's just us—people. All that is left is resistance, and no resistance ever worked by following empty orders. It will only work by doing what needs to be done when it needs doing. Take your ship, and do whatever you can to help, but if you try to fight us you're only helping the enemy."

Hernandez seemed to mull it over for a long, long time, struggling to find words and scratching at his head. Guy wished the man was more decisive, quicker to reply, for it showed his lack of confidence by thinking so hard in front of his men. Eventually, he found something to say, and it was less rational than Guy had hoped for, but it was sufficient. "I consider you a traitor to your country, Captain Granger, but I will not command my men to fire on fellow Americans. I disagree about the war being lost. It has only just begun. Your country requires your ship and your crew, but I can see that you have brainwashed them to abandon their beliefs—and even stand by while you deny the existence of the United States. I will not risk lives, but when America is victorious, men like you will be strung up for cowardice. If you have any honour at all, you will step down now, Captain Granger, but I don't expect that you will."

Guy sneered. "The last thing anybody aboard my ship is guilty of is cowardice. I wish you a safe journey, Commander Hernandez. Do try to keep your men alive. We won't be there to rescue you next time."

Hernandez turned away and disappeared from sight.

Guy kept his crew lined up along the railings, ready for a fight, but was relieved when the Augusta moved away. Bloated corpses fell into the sea as its crew jettisoned them into the water.

"We should do the same," said Frank. "God knows what diseases these things might carry. Even if they don't, I don't fancy having to look at them."

Guy gave the order for everyone to kick and shove the demon corpses overboard. Their slimy carcasses left behind slick trails of blood and seawater. Many of the sailors gagged.

"Yikes," cried Frank. "This one looks like my aunt."

The men all laughed and gagged a little less.

Guy took a moment to study his enemy close up. The shrivelled up penis dangling between its flabby grey thighs gave no ambiguity as to its sex. Had it been a man once? Its dead eyes were strangely human.

"We got a live one over here!" Someone shouted.

Guy glanced across the deck to see that one of the demons was back on its feet, stalking after one of the civilians. It was badly injured—one arm hanging attached by a thread. Guy had no weapon, but he hurried to help. Frank and Tosco did the same. The creature was missing an eye, but the remaining one bore into them with hatred. In a slurping voice, it spoke to them. "We will drag your souls into Hell and violate your bodies."

Guy sighed. "Will somebody please kill this thing?"

Frank lifted a handgun from by his side. He pulled the trigger three times, and the demon reeled back, spilling over the port side railing and disappearing into the ocean.

"They're here to exterminate us, aren't they?" muttered Tosco.

"Yes," said Guy. "They are."

Frank tucked the gun into his waistband and spat over the side of the ship. "They're welcome to try, but I'm not going down without a fi-"

Frank's head shuddered and his left eye disappeared in a flash of red. He slumped against the railing, exposing the wide-open crater at the back of his skull. A loud crack skipped across the ocean.

"Sniper!" Somebody shouted.

Tosco lunged at Guy and shoved him to the ground just as another shot was fired. The lieutenant took the bullet high up on his body and flipped backwards like an acrobat. Guy was forced to watch, stunned.

Skip was the one to give the order. The old sailor kept his calm and yelled out instruction. "Take cover and return fire. Don't make it easy for 'em."

The Hatchet's crew crouched down at the railings and fired at the Augusta, but the larger Navy vessel was at least a mile away and too far to hit with an assault rifle. The enemy sniper fired a series of follow up shots, but by then, everyone had taken cover and remained there safely.

Guy looked over at Frank and felt a rage bubbling in his chest. His oldest friend shot dead by a faceless sniper on the orders of a jumped up lieutenant. Hernandez would pay for this.

Tosco lay on the deck nearby moaning. Guy crawled over to him and checked for a bullet wound, finding it on his left shoulder—a leaking hole in his trapezius muscle. "You're going to be okay, Lieutenant. It's just-"

Tosco managed to lift himself slightly. "A flesh wound? Yeah, I know... Jeez, hurts like a mother though. How's Frank?"

Guy shook his head and fought back tears.

Tosco cursed, from anger now, instead of pain. "That idiot must have thought we were firing at him when Frank shot that demon."

Guy snarled. "Hernandez was waiting for an excuse. He didn't want to order his men to fire on us without cause."

"He's stopped firing now," said Tosco through gritted teeth. "They're still heading away from us."

A nearby radio squawked. It lay on the deck, and the voice of Hernandez came through it loud and clear. "Men and woman aboard the USCG Hatchet. Your senior officers are dead. Please put me in contact with whoever has inherited command. I wish you no harm, only that you follow the Augusta back to the coast where it will be added to the Navy's relief effort. You are no longer bound to fulfill whatever promises you made to Captain Granger. You are free." A brief pause. "Come in, come in, Hatchet. Whoever is most senior, please respond."

Guy crawled over to the radio and answered it with venom in his voice. "Hernandez, this is the senior ranking member of the USCG Hatchet, Captain Guy Granger. You just killed a man worth ten of you, and I'm going to make you pay for it. You see, when this war is over, they will string men like you up. I will be the one to do it. As soon as I find my kids, I'm coming for you."

There was the mutter of a reply as if someone was about to speak but had changed their mind. The line went dead.

***

Everyone aboard the Hatchet remained in cover until the Augusta was a mere dot on the horizon. Guy shouted for the ship's medical officer, Gonzalez, and got Tosco some help. The lieutenant was in good spirits as a group of enlisted men carried him off to the sickbay. Guy remained on deck, staring out across the vast ocean and feeling the weight of the world on his shoulders. Frank's body lay beneath a blanket at his feet.

The old captain, Skip, came up beside Guy and stared right at him. "Your second in command is quite a hero," he whispered. "Led the men against the demons and took a sniper bullet for you."

Guy nodded. "If more men had his backbone, we would already have driven those monsters back to Hell."

Skip nodded, but exhaled as if something worried him. "What's on your mind, Skip?"

"I worry for you."

"That was always Frank's job."

"Then it's a job vacant for me to fill. He was a good man, the Chief Petty? Your friend?"

"The very best of both, friend and man. I don't know how I would have fared these last few days without him questioning my every move. He was always my conscience, making me consider my actions."

"Well, if I can attempt to fill his boots, I have some advice for you, Captain. Keep Lieutenant Tosco onside. I hate to be the one to tell you this, but these are his men more than they're yours."

The insult was grave, almost unforgivable, but the old captain was right. "I know what you're saying," he admitted, "but he gave me his word he would help me find Kyle and Alice. After that, I'll just have to be ready for whatever happens. Don't worry about me, Skip."

"I always worry about good men. We're back to the old days now, Captain Granger, and in the old days, there was only one way for a captain to lose his ship."

Guy looked down at Frank's body beneath the sheet and thought about his friend's earlier advice. Be firm. He turned to Skip and smiled. "You're wrong, you know? These aren't the old days, Skip. They're the new days. And if Lieutenant Tosco tries to take my ship, I'll kill him."

~MINA MAGAR~
SLOUGH, BERKSHIRE

WHEN MINA AWOKE, THE DAY WAS IN full swing and approaching late afternoon. She felt refreshed for a few moments, but then the grogginess hit her and she craved coffee. She got up off the floor, knees and elbows clicking, and went out into the office. It was as frantic now as it had been when she sneaked off to take a nap. David was in the centre of the room directing things, having apparently taken control away from Big Jimmy.

Andras stood at the kettle, and Mina went and joined him. "You seem to spend a lot of time here. I'd love a coffee," she said.

"Coming right up. It's the only thing I'm good at apparently."

"They won't let you help, huh?"

"Nope." He made her the coffee and handed it over. "It's not that they won't let me help, it's more that I don't really have any way to help. I don't have a network of contacts to call."

"You can help me," said Mina. "I'm used to being treated like a spare part around here. Nobody ever wants help from a photographer."

"So what are you working on?"

"Updating the website with information people can use. We need to get people fighting back. It's our only chance."

Andras smiled at her. "I'm all yours."

Mina had a thought. "Where's Alice?"

"Asleep in Carol's office. Carol's taking a nap too. David's in charge at the moment, I think."

"I'd imagine he is. Go over to my computer, Andras. I'll join you in five minutes. I want to check in with David and see where we're at."

"Sure thing."

Mina interrupted David in the midst of giving orders to the paper's sports editor. The bump on the side of his head had turned a sickly green colour. "Ah, Mina," he said when he saw her. "Back in the land of the living?"

She ignored that he had gone off for a nap too. "I needed sleep."

"The news never sleeps."

"What's the latest?" she asked.

"Much the same as before. The demons—that's what we're officially calling them now—have formed up into three main armies within the U.K. Most of the smaller groups merged together, and the largest army is now currently south of Luton. It's being led by the same giant we encountered in Hyde Park. As such, we've started referring to him as Hyde. The second largest army is based outside Carlisle, on the Scottish border. It, too, is being led by one of the giant beings. We call this one-"

"Let me guess, Carlisle?"

"No, we call it Hex, for the gate it came out of was in Hexham. The third giant has been moving around Wales and is currently outside of Cardiff. We call him Aberdare. His army is the largest by far, and it's yet to meet any real resistance."

Mina filed the names away. "Hyde, Hex, and Aberdare, okay. So the giants are definitely leading these armies?"

"Undoubtedly. We've been gathering reports from all over the country—local police stations, other newspaper offices, et cetera.

People are blogging on the Internet like crazy, can you believe it? The world is at war, and people are sharing it all over the web like the latest Game of Thrones episode."

"People are probably trying to keep themselves occupied. So what have we learned?"

"After the initial attacks, the demons converged to the three main locations I mentioned, each headed by one of the giants. There are outcroppings of smaller groups around, but they seem to be exercising guerrilla tactics—attacking randomly to cause disarray. What's left of the British Army upper Brass believes that the three main armies are intended to destroy us.

Similar armies are gathering abroad too, from what we can gather."

"Are we fighting back?"

"Just trying to rally at this point. The Army made a dent in the enemy foot soldiers, but nothing has scratched the giants. People are calling them angels. If that's the truth, then there may not be a way to take them down unless drastic action is taken."

"Like what?"

"Nukes. The Government is already discussing a scorched earth policy. If it comes down to the survival of the human race, I don't see what choice they'll have. Hope they give us fair warning first. Would hate to look out the window and spot a bomb falling out the sky."

Mina's opinions on nuclear weapons had never changed since learning about them during her college days. The grainy video footage of Hiroshima had convinced her that atomic weapons were barbaric and invited calamity. Now she wasn't so sure.

"Do we have any chance, David?"

"We're still alive, aren't we?" He surprised her by putting a hand on her shoulder. "You and I made it through Hell together.

Oxford Street was the enemy's opening gambit. They won't get a jump on us like that again. The worst has happened, but now we dust ourselves off and fight back. You and I, Mina, will do our part."

Her tiredness wore off. "I'll do whatever I can to make those monsters pay."

David smiled. "Then get people ready. The hits on the website have started to rise. Other websites are linking to us and we're making waves."

"Really? That's great. I'll get right on it."

"What are you waiting for then?"

"Right." She hurried to her cubicle with renewed energy.

Her work was important; people were reading her words and looking at the pictures she'd taken. People might have a chance of staying alive because of her.

Andras was waiting at her desk and pulled up a chair for her. "Ready for your command, mistress."

Mina blushed and giggled. "Thank you, Andras. We need to update the website with anything we learn about the demons. What did we find out while I was asleep?"

"David told you about the three armies?"

Mina nodded.

"Okay, did you know there are three different types of demons?"

She leaned forward. "No, tell me."

"Okay, well, um, there seems to be three different types of demons. There's the extra crispy kind—the burn victims. They are the most common and strong as bulls. They can also talk and use weapons, but they die as easily as us."

"Okay, what are the other two types?"

"There are the corpses—like zombies, except they aren't braindead. They can also talk, but don't die as easily as the burn victims. You can damage them, and they keep on coming. Damage them badly enough, though, and they'll die. The third kind are less like human beings. They're the ones that are hunched over like apes and have those nasty claws. They're as agile as spider monkeys and can disembowel with a swipe, but they die easiest of all. The biggest problem with all three is their numbers. They just keep on coming through those gates. Mankind keeps dying, but the demons keep getting stronger."

"So, to stand a chance, we need to find a way to close the gates. Has anybody tried yet?"

"Nobody has even got close. The gates are the enemy's strong points, and the Army aren't in any shape to stage an attack on them."

"Then that's what we focus on: Closing the gates."

Andras raised an eyebrow. "No big thing then?"

"We aim high, or we lose."

"I understand the stakes, Mina. We all have to do whatever is necessary to survive."

Mina scrolled through the website and saw updates she hadn't put there, as well as some of her photos. The picture she had taken of the stray Labrador had over a thousand views. "I assume David added these extra bits?"

Andras shrugged. "He told everyone to add whatever they could verify. I know Corporal Martin added a few things about how to kill the different demons. David added something about iron being helpful."

"Iron?"

"Yeah, he got an email from some girl in Crapstone." Mina accessed the website emails and located an email from someone called Diane Potter. The subject-heading read: **The demons can't pass iron barriers!!!**

She opened the email and read a hastily typed message from what seemed to be a teenage girl. There was a group of survivors in Crapstone where one of the gates had opened. They had taken refuge at a retired pop star's house surrounded by big iron gates. Apparently, the demons couldn't pass the iron bars or even touch them.

David had already posted about it on the website, and Mina found comments piling up. People cited their own stories of survival, thanks to the tip. A group of survivors in Stockport had fled to a local church after reading the website and were now safe behind its old iron doors. Another group was hiding out at a scrapyard, constructing barriers of their own from the iron junk collected there. People were surviving because of the website.

"It's working," said Mina. "Iron works against the demons and word is spreading. This is how we win, Andras. We find out the enemy's weaknesses, and we spread the word."

Andras seemed troubled when she looked at him, but he changed his expression to a smile. "I guess humanity has a chance after all—especially with a woman like you looking out for it."

A brief flutter of butterfly wings in her belly made Mina blush. "I..."

Andras blushed too and turned away embarrassed. "Not really a good time to flirt, is it? Sorry."

"No, no, don't be sorry. Tell you the truth, it's been a long time since a guy flirted with me. If it takes the end of the world, then so be it."

Andras patted her on the knee and gave it a furtive squeeze. He nodded to her coffee cup. "Time for a refill. Allow me."

Mina grabbed his hand. "Your job fetching the coffee is over. I'll make this one."

Andras smiled. "Milk, three sugars."

"Wow, you like it sweet."

"What's life without the senses?"

On her way to get the drinks, Mina swung by to say hello to Corporal Martin. The soldier looked ready to drop, wobbling on his feet and rubbing at his eyes every couple of seconds. "You look ready to fall into a coma, Martin. You should get some sleep."

He smiled at her. "I keep meaning to call it a day, but something else pops up that I need to deal with and another hour passes by."

"Are you still in contact with the Army?"

He nodded. "I assumed they would call me back to base, but Command has asked me to remain here and pass on any Intel you folks get."

"Makes sense," she admitted. "I'll let you know whatever I find. You know about the iron, right?"

"Yes, I passed it up the chain of command. They're already looking at ways to make use of it. Maybe setting up a central base surrounded by iron fences, or fashioning ammunition out of it, I don't know. If only it wasn't such an outdated substance. Wooden stakes would be better."

"Like in the movies?"

"Yep. We have plenty of wood, but not so much iron. Would make the war a lot easier if people could just grab the nearest chair leg."

"When is war ever easy?"

"I suppose you're right. Still, most wars aren't against supernatural creatures that aren't supposed to even exist. A little help would be fair enough in my book."

Mina's phone rang. She pulled it out her pocket and sighed. It was her father again. "I have to take this."

Corporal Martin nodded. "Of course."

Mina headed away to get some privacy. The newsroom was still a chaotic hive, so she headed out the exit into the waiting area. There was a chair behind the reception desk, so she sat as she answered the call.

"Dad, I didn't expect to hear from you again." "Mina, you are safe?"

"Yes. I'm fine, dad. Are you oka—"

"The monsters are here, Mina. Mrs Patel next door is screaming. I can hear her. Mina, what should I do?"

Mina bolted to her feet, clutching the phone and wishing she could yank her father right through it. "Hide, dad. You need to hide."

"But your website says to fight. Should I go help Mrs Patel?"

Mina almost got stuck on the fact that her father had been reading her website, but she knew there was no time for pride. Her father was in danger. Could she really tell him to hide when she knew it was the wrong thing to do?

"How many are there, dad?"

"Hundreds. They just appeared in the streets, dragging people from their houses. They will be here soon, Mina. My God, Mrs Patel, has stopped screaming. I think they killed her."

"Hide, dad. You need to hide, and I'll find a way to come get you."

There was silence on the line. Then: "No, Mina. I cannot hide. You are out there helping people and facing the evil. How can I hide when my daughter is so brave? I will not hide. I must fight the monsters so that there are less of them for you to face in the days ahead."

"Dad, listen to me-"

"I love you, Mina. I am proud. And I am sorry."

Mina shouted down the phone, but was forced to listen to her father's manic shouts as he entered some unseen battle. She heard the shrieks of monsters, the screams of victims. Then the line went dead.

"Dad? Dad?" She knew it was of no use, but she couldn't help it. She kept on shouting. "Dad?"

"Whoa, what's wrong?" Andras came into the waiting room, two coffees in his hands. When he saw the state she was in, he placed them down on the reception desk and went over to her. "What's happened?"

"My dad. H-he was attacked. I..." She shook her head as tears came.

Andras put his arms around her and pulled her close. "I'm sorry." He left it at that.

"He said he was proud of me."

"Of course. Why wouldn't he be?"

She huffed. "You never knew my father. I've never seen him be proud of me, ever."

"Then at least he got to be proud of you before he died. You're helping people."

"That's what he said."

"Well, it's true. People are already fighting back because of your website."

Mina's phone went again. She snatched it up to her ear.

"Dad? Dad? Oh, it's you, David. Yeah, I'm in the reception area. I... What? No, I didn't. I was just there, and everything was... Jesus. I'll get back on it right away."

She put the phone back in her pocket and looked at Andras. "Did you do anything on my computer?"

Andras smiled. "Like what?"

"David just told me that the website has been deleted. All the information we posted is gone."

Andras frowned. "Weird."

"Yeah, it is. You were sat at my computer when I came out here. What did you do, Andras?"

"Nothing. I... Maybe I did something by accident."

"No, you're an IT specialist. You wouldn't accidentally delete a website. You could only have done it on purpose."

Andras folded his arms. "What are you accusing me of, Mina?"

She sighed, rubbed at her eyes with her thumbs. "Nothing.

Sorry. I need to take a look at my laptop and just hope I can get everything back online. I'll soon find out what happened. Andras, if you did something by accident it could cost people their lives."

"Good."

Mina had been about to walk away, but the comment stunned her. She turned to Andras in confusion. "Good? What do you mean, 'good'?"

He grinned at her, his teeth mouldy, his breath foul. "I mean good that your pathetic attempts to get people fighting are finished before they even got started. You really think you can change anything with a silly little blog? You're all doomed."

The venom in Andras's words was enough to make her stagger back. "Y-you're helping the demons?"

"No, I'm not helping them, you stupid worm. I'm one of them."

Mina opened her mouth to shout for help, but Andras's hand went over her lips and stifled her. His other hand went over her nose, and he forced her down to the ground and climbed on top of her chest. She couldn't breathe.

Andras glared at her as she struggled.

"There will be no resistance," he hissed. "You are all going to die, and this world will be ours. Do you know what it's like to spend an eternity in the fires of Hell? You will find out."

"Mina? Are you out here?"

It was David. He was looking for her. Mina was behind the reception desk—out of sight—with Andras pressing down on top of her. She tried to scream out, to kick at something and make a noise, but she could barely move. She raked at Andras's neck and squealed as one of her nails tore away.

"Mina?" David called out again. "Damn it, girl, I need you to help me get this website sorted. Where are you?"

Mina tried desperately to cry out.

The door swung closed again.

David had gone.

Andras laughed as her vision began to darken. It felt like her head would explode, her eyes bulged out of their sockets. Breathing was so instinctual and automatic, but right now she couldn't catch a single mouthful of air. Every cell in her body panicked. Andras kept on pressing down, squeezing her nose and mouth shut. He bent over her and licked her face. "Sweet dreams, maggot."

Mina hated that the last thing she would see was her murderer laughing at her terror, but that's exactly what happened.

PART THREE

"You must not fight too often with one enemy, or you will teach him all your art of war."

— Napolean Bonaparte

~TONY CROSS~

8 MILES NORTH OF THE EUPHRATES, SYRIA

"WE'RE FUCKED," SAID TONY AS AYMUN and the remaining fighters regrouped behind the vehicles.

Aymun agreed. "Yes, we die here."

Tony looked around desperately. "Where's Harris and that PKM? We need to get it firing again."

Corporal Rose pointed over to a battered old van and shook his head. Private Harris was slumped up against the rear tyre with his chin resting against his chest. "He did'na make it, Staffie."

Tony cursed the air. Harris's wounds had caught up with him, and he had bled out from a torn gut. The PKM was nowhere in sight.

And the demons were coming.

Along with Corporal Rose, only two of the British soldiers still lived. Aymun's men were all dead, but about ten of the villagers remained. Tony had witnessed the death of hundreds of brave men and women in less than forty-eight hours.

What was left of them returned fire, trying to take down the demons before they formed up again in groups. They had the advantage for now, picking off the enemy one by one as they came through the gate disorientated, but the advantage would not last forever. They were running out of ammunition, and trying to keep up with the flow of demons flooding through the gate was already beginning to best them. Now and then, a demon would make it a few feet before going down to a headshot.

"We can't keep this up," said Tony. "We have to retreat." Aymun nodded. "Perhaps that is wise, but I will not go." "Don't be a fool and die here, Aymun. This isn't a test.

Allah doesn't require you to die."

"No," he said. "I require it of myself. I am tired of fighting infidels and invaders. It is time I struck at my enemy in their home."

"What do you mean?"

"I will die having looked upon our enemy truly, so that I may pass on the information to Allah. He needs soldiers in the next life, as well as this one. This is not his work."

Tony tried to understand and thought that he might. "You're going to go through the gate?"

"Yes. Will you cover me, my friend?"

"I..." Tony saw there was no point in arguing. "I'll make sure you get there."

Aymun smiled, seemingly at peace. "Continue the fight after I am gone."

"Damn right I will."

"Good to have met you, Tony."

"You too, Aymun."

Without another word, Aymun broke cover and sprinted towards the glowing gate. Tony gave the nod, and the remaining men laid down covering fire, riddling the gate's entrance with what remained of their ammunition. Demons danced and spun as bullets ripped them apart, but one by one, their rifles ran dry, and the chorus of gunfire lessened. Dead demons continued piling up in front of the gate, but more and more continued coming through.

Aymun ran so fast, he kicked up dirt behind him. He'd thrown down his rifle now, but held a grenade above his head—pin removed, ready to be released. The villagers shouted something in Arabic—numuur numuur—while Tony's last few men gritted their teeth and remained silent.

The last of their rifles ran dry.

The gunfire ceased.

Silence descended upon the desert just as Aymun made it to the gate. A demon came through and dropped right front of him, but before it had time to leap at Aymun, Aymun surprised it by leaping at it first. He tackled the demon backwards, their two bodies took flight and disappeared through the gate.

The gate shimmered. The glowing edges warped and bent while the sound of a cracking whip bounced across the desert.

Something was happening.

The next creature through the gate was on fire. It hit the dirt and spun around, clawed arms flailing. Then it slumped to the ground and went still, leaving the fire to consume its corpse.

Corporal Rose stood up and pointed with a trembling finger. "The gate. It's closing."

Tony saw it was true. The glowing edges of the gate had twisted and contorted, knotting together like a child's tangled skipping rope. The translucent centre darkened. Smoke billowed into the air, and the light started to fade. The shimmering centre solidified into the dark, gnarled consistency of old wood, and then it disintegrated into ash and blew away in the wind.

The gate was gone, and so was the black stone.

Tony drifted out of cover and approached the patch of desert where the gate had been. All that remained was a large pile of ash.

"Martyr," one villager shouted. "Martyr."

Corporal Rose came up beside Tony and whistled. "Aymun did it. He closed the gate."

"Yeah," said Tony. "Not bad for an extremist."

"He was brave."

"He was devout," said Tony. "Never thought I'd ever think it, but we will need more men like him. More men will be needed to sacrifice themselves and close the gates. Aymun's sacrifice has showed us how we can win this war."

"We need to make it to the border," said Corporal Rose. "We have to spread the word."

Tony snapped out of his shocked daze and got to work. He straightened up and gave his corporal a look of urgency. "See if we can get any of the villager's vehicles running. We don't have time for a trek across the desert anymore. We leave in one hour."

The villagers gathered around the pile of ash and began chanting in prayer. Then they all got down and bowed to Mecca. Tony considered joining them, changing his mind about everything he had once thought about a Lord Almighty.

If these gates led to Hell, then somewhere there was a Heaven. So why wasn't God helping?

* * *

Tony, Corporal Rose, and the two remaining privates were ready to go within the hour. They had lost a lot of comrades in the last two days, but each of them knew they were lucky to be alive. That they had destroyed one of the gates would make the sacrifices of their brothers meaningful. The Intel could give humanity a fighting chance.

They still needed to reach the Turkish border.

Tony had tried the cell phones of some of the surviving villagers, but getting through to anybody in authority had been a nightmare. Most of the calls failed, and others laced with interference. It left Tony with no choice but to hand deliver the information. Perhaps the military forces of the world already knew how to close the gates, but if they didn't...

Time was of the essence, so he thanked the villagers who had given him a battered Toyota minivan, and then ordered his three remaining men inside it. The villagers all piled into a Nissan 4x4 like some bad joke—How many Arabs can you fit in a 4x4?—but then they were off, honking their horn in salute as they fled back to their homes. They were simple folk, who had faced an army of evil and lived. They would return to their wives and children as heroes, but it might not be long before they were called upon to fight again.

Tony slid into the driver's seat and clutched into first gear. It was like a furnace inside the cramped vehicle, and the drive would not be comfortable, but the quiet boredom would be sublime while it lasted. There'd be nothing but scrubland for the next many hours, but after that, who knew? Tony dreaded losing more men over the days ahead.

It was the end of days.

As a soldier, Tony had been conditioned for war, but deep down, a soldier needed to have conviction in his heart to operate. A soldier needed hope—however minuscule—that the final battle could be won. He didn't feel that yet, and as much as he knew that the information he had to share was vital, it might only buy the world some added time. Things had changed so much that mankind had already lost. Nothing would ever be the same again, and only darkness lay ahead.

Tony took off across the desert with the last of his men.

~RICK BASTION~
DEVONSHIRE, ENGLAND

RICK WOKE UP WITH A HANGOVER, BUT IT wasn't caused by drink. He fingered his head at the line where his fringe ended and flinched when he felt a wide-open gash. Blood stained the top of his shirt, and he could feel it caked on his face.

That bastard. His own brother had clocked him with a beer bottle, like some thug at a nightclub. Keith had never been violent in his entire life, so what the hell had got into him?

Rick got up off the cold floor and saw that he was in his garage. The only light was from a frosted square of glass above the side door, but it was enough to see all the stacks of unsold albums with his face on. It was the worst place in the world to wake up with a headache, like being surrounded by a manifestation of his regrets. His own face seemed to mock him from the cover artwork, showing him how stupid his pink and silver-streaked hair had been.

A cross to bear. The past.

Days gone by looked good now, considering the current state of affairs. He had no idea how long he'd been out, but there was no doubt in his mind that demons still surrounded his home. The black-haired corpse wanted to finish what he'd started with Sarah.

"Hey, let me out of here," Rick demanded, banging on the side door of the garage. There was a flicker of a shadow across the frosted glass, but no one answered.

"Come on, man. Whoever is out there, stop acting the prick and unlock this door. This is my goddamn house."

The jangle of keys preceded the rattle of the doorknob, and the door opened a tad. Someone slipped inside before Rick had chance to force his way out.

It was Daniel.

"You all right in here, pal?"

"No, I am not. I'm leaving."

"Right you are, but listen to me first, okay?"

Rick folded his arms and let his pissed off expression do the speaking.

"You're probably planning a little pay back against your brother for bottling you," Daniel surmised. "Can't say I blame you."

"Goddamn right I-"

"But my advice is to cool your jets for now. We're all under stress. Your brother is just trying to protect you— although he's a bit of a bastard in the way he shows it."

"Trying to control me, more like."

Daniel chewed at the side of his cheek, then said. "Yeah, you're probably right, but I'm on your side, okay? This is your house, and everyone is alive because of your hospitality. Other people don't see it that way though. They only look at what's in front of them. You've been out a few hours, but your big brother has been rallying the troops during that time. He's got everybody onside, so don't cut off your nose to spite your face. You kick off and your brother will lash out at you again. The others will likely have his back too. The only person who didn't think you were insane for wanting to leave was Maddy, but she's gone quiet."

"I don't give a shit," said Rick. "If I want to leave, then that's what I'm bloody well going to do."

"Actually, I think you're better off staying. The problem you will have now is keeping everyone else from leaving."

Rick growled and pointed his finger, but he let his arm drop and tried to make sense of what he had heard. "Huh?"

"Your brother told me to let you out. He wants to leave before it gets dark."

"What? How long have I been out? What's happened? He was dead set against leaving."

"You've been out less than three hours, Rick, but a lot has changed. Come on, I'll show you."

Daniel opened the garage door and let Rick step through. It was still light outside, but the chill in the air told him it was getting late. "Where is he, Daniel? Where's Keith?"

"Still inside, but wait..."

Rick marched across the gravel driveway towards the house, hands clenched in anticipation of what he would do to his brother. Instinctively, he glanced back over his shoulder at the gate.

But the gate was clear. The road deserted.

Rick stopped so quickly that he tripped and stumbled. By the time he had recovered, Daniel had caught up to him. "They left about an hour ago," he explained. "Just dispersed suddenly."

"What? Why?"

"Diane has been checking the web. According to some newspaper in Slough, the demons have assembled into three main armies. Your brother thinks the demons were recalled to go join their buddies."

"So we're safe?"

"Your brother thinks so."

"But you don't?"

Daniel shrugged. "Maybe, but if we are, then why be in such a hurry to leave? Why not wait a while until we know for sure that all is well?"

Rick nodded. "You're right. It could be a trap."

"I know you wanted to leave, Rick, but that was when you knew the demons were crowded around your front gate. Now, we don't have any idea where they're lurking."

Rick thought about it. "We should all stay put. There could even be help on the way."

"And there's your problem. Your brother has everybody getting ready to make for the south coast. The nearest demon army is north, so he thinks it will be plain sailing all the way down. Ironic, actually, that he's pretty much following the plan you laid out."

Rick looked once again at the gate. Everything Maddy had said was true; they couldn't stay trapped inside forever, but he had a bad feeling about leaving now. The demons were smart, not mindless monsters. The black-haired corpse wanted them all dead. It was personal. Would he just up and leave so suddenly?

Rick decided. "I'm staying here, Daniel, and you're welcome to join me."

"What about your brother?"

"He can leave if he wants. I couldn't care less, to tell you the truth. He's always been a shit, but to do this..." He pointed at the wide gash on his forehead. "Fuck him."

"The others will leave with him."

"So?"

Daniel sighed. "Come on, Rick. You really want a young girl like Diane out there in danger? Maddy and Steve are both good people. They're just a bit lost and following the loudest voice in the room—your brother's."

"What could I do, even if I wanted to? Maddy wants to go home."

"Yeah, she does, but I think she'd rather do it later, and with friends."

"I'm not her friend."

"Rick, all of us are friends now, whether we like it or not. We have mutual enemies, and all we have is each other. You let your brother leave with the others, and you'll be regretting it this time tomorrow. The television has already stopped, and the phones are working less and less. How long before the lights and water die? You want to be alone when that happens? We need to stick together and stay alive. Your brother has the first part down, but I worry he's going to fall on his ass regarding the second."

Rick said nothing else because he was still thinking things through. He went inside the house and found everyone huddled inside the kitchen. They were packing up supplies into a bunch of holdalls that belonged to him.

Keith smiled when he saw his brother. "Rick? I'm glad you're okay. I'm sorry for what I was forced to do, but good news: We can leave now, just like you wanted."

"It's too risky to leave right now. We all need to stay put a little while longer."

Maddy was the first to argue. "Rick, I told you how bad things will get if we stay here. We have to go while there's a chance. The demons are gone."

"But why?" asked Rick. "Why have they suddenly left?"

"Because there are armies forming up and they were called upon to head north. Diane found out all about it."

Rick shook his head and shrugged. "Called by whom? We can't be sure of anything right now. You wanted to stay so badly earlier, I can't believe you're being so stubborn about leaving. You don't know why they left; admit it."

Keith leaned back against the counter and grunted. "Maybe they're telepathic and received orders. Only thing we know for sure is that they're gone, and we have an opportunity to make a break for it. This is a good thing, Rick. If I hadn't subdued you, then you might have been caught right in the middle of them as they left. I saved your life."

The sudden burst of anger was so sudden that Rick snarled like a dog. "You saved my life? Are you kidding? You smashed a bottle over my head like a fucking savage. Who the hell do you think you are?"

"I'm your big brother, and I'm trying to look after you and everybody else here."

"Who the hell asked you to?"

"Nobody. It's a burden I've taken on for myself."

Rick unclenched his fists and tried to calm down. "Look, Keith, if you want to leave, fine, but I'm staying. I suggest everyone else does the same. There's nothing to tell us that this isn't all a big trap. The demons can't get inside because of the iron bars, so they've thought of a way to get us out instead. I'm staying here until I know more."

"Me, too," said Maddy, moving over to Rick's side. "He's right. We could walk right into a trap. Let's wait until tomorrow and make sure the coast really is clear."

Keith slammed his hand down on the counter. "If we don't leave now, there might not be another chance. Do you people not understand what's going on? There's a war. We can't just lie around here hoping help will come. We need to help ourselves."

"I agree," said Steve.

Diane nodded. "Me too."

"And I'm with Rick and Maddy," said Daniel. "So that splits us in two."

There was silence while everyone waited for someone to change their mind, but no one did. Maddy had already taken off her backpack and sat down on a stool.

Keith shoved a bottle of water into a holdall and pulled the zip closed. "That's fine," he said. "We go our separate ways. When I find help, I'll send it to come get you. Hopefully, you'll still be alive."

"Don't do this, Keith," Rick pleaded. His head was still thudding, but he didn't want to see his brother make a mistake.

"I'm sorry I had to hit you, Rick. I was trying to save your life, but it seems there's no helping you." He shouldered the bag and shoved his way out of the kitchen. Diane hurried after him. Steve was a little slower in following and first stopped to speak with Rick before leaving. "Your brother is an arsehole, but I want out of here. It's safe, so I'm going, but I want to say that it took backbone to stay calm after what your brother did to you. I would have smashed his face in. You're a better man than he is. Thanks for letting me stay at your house."

Maddy pulled up a stool for Rick. "They're not leaving for twenty minutes," she said. "Might still change their minds."

"They won't, but why did you?"

She shrugged. "I keep thinking about my husband, and who he would want me to tag along with. He would want me to be safe, and I feel safest around you. You did come try to save me outside the pub after all."

"Yeah, but it was Keith who came out and rescued us in the end."

Daniel chuckled from the corner of the kitchen. "I suppose it's the thought that counts."

Maddy chuckled too. "It mainly comes down to me not trusting a man who can smash a bottle over his own brother's head. I'd rather follow a good guy to my death, than a bad man like your brother. It was different when we were all leaving, but if it comes down to you or Keith, I choose you. Because my husband would have chosen you."

Rick put his hand out to grab Maddy's, which placed on the counter, but he ended up hovering over it awkwardly. Maddy helped him out by standing up and giving him a quick hug. "You, me, and Daniel will have to think about leaving soon ourselves. If your brother gets out safely, we might end up chasing after him."

"I hope so," Rick admitted. "I hope I'm wrong and the demons really have all gone north."

Maddy nodded and exited the kitchen, leaving Rick and Daniel alone together. "You still sure you want to stay now that everyone is splitting up, Daniel?"

"I'd rather we all stay together, but at least you convinced Maddy to stay. Three is better than two. Plus, if it was just us two dudes hanging around together, it would be weird."

"Huh, you still think my brother is walking into a trap?"

"I do, yeah. Diane said the demons were forming up in three big armies, but she also said that there were smaller bands dotted around causing havoc. Your brother doesn't seem concerned about that though. Me, I think that black- haired demon has unfinished business here."

"I can't make the others stay, Daniel."

"I know, but at least you tried. God likes a trier. Idle hands and all that."

"You really think there's a God? How can you?"

"How can I not? In the presence of demons, one cannot possibly deny the existence of God."

Rick rubbed at his throbbing head, loosing several flakes of dried blood. "Then why isn't He helping us?"

"Maybe he was caught as unawares as everybody else. Maybe backup's on its way. Maybe you should pray."

"If I live another day, I just might start. Feel like it would be easier to lay down and die right now."

Daniel went to the fridge. The water had gone into the holdalls, so he was left with nothing to snatch up but a couple beers. He handed one to Rick.

Rick shook his head. "If I start drinking now, I won't stop."

Daniel took the beer back and broke the tab. "I hear you, pal.

There was a time I let myself get carried away with

things that were bad for me. Learned a little self-control since. It's never too late for a man to start changing."

"Not sure if I believe that. With Keith around, I've realised that I'm no different than when I was a kid."

Daniel took a swig of beer before placing the bottle down on the counter. "You've changed since I met you. The guy I met wanted to bury his head in the sand and go sit in the corner and drink himself asleep while everyone else did what needed to be done. The man you are now marched into this kitchen and spoke up for what he believes in, then sat down and refused a beer. You're not a little kid anymore, Rick. Your father's long gone, and your brother's a tit. That pop career you lament so badly can finally be put behind you. The world has changed, and so have you. You have a new cross to bear now, and it's called: Keeping everyone around you alive. Even if you don't see it, people gravitate towards you. That will be important in the days to come. God needs leaders."

Rick smirked. "That religious stuff never quite left you, did it, Daniel?"

"None of us ever loses the Lord, we just sometimes forget that he's there. Believe me, though, Rick, he never forgets about us."

Rick got up from his stool. "We should see the others off."

They went into the entrance hallway and found that the front door was open. Noise came from outside. Keith was busy backing Rick's Mustang up the driveway and away from the gate. Maddy, Steven, and Diane stood by, watching, so Rick and Daniel went and joined them.

"When we leave here, Rick," Maddy told him. "I want to drive your car."

"Be my guest. I was always too scared to put my foot down anyway."

Keith parked the Mustang and got out. Then he went and got into his Range Rover, which he reversed out of the way of the gate as well. It felt like taking the safety chain off a front door during a dark and stormy night.

Keith got out of his car once it was parked and marched back towards the house. "I need the padlock key, Rick."

Rick sighed. "Sure I can't talk you out of this?"

"I've made up my mind. The only chance we have is to leave now."

"I was talking to Steven and Diane."

"Sorry, Rick," said Steven. "I can't stick around while there's a chance to find help."

"Me too," said Diane. "The Internet said the coast is safe, so that's where we need to go. There's a gate too close to here. If more demons come through, we'll end up trapped again."

Rick pictured the gate in Crapstone and wondered if anything was coming through right now. Were there a limited number of demons, or would they continue to pour through forever? Did the Army have any idea of how to close them? Was it even possible?

"Okay," he said with an air of finality. "I'll open the gate for you all."

He walked down the pebble driveway while Keith and the others got in the Range Rover. When he reached the gate he peered through the bars. The coast certainly did seem clear, but the road was too quiet. The cottages down the road were quiet, and trees obscured the farmland further along. There might not be a person alive for ten square miles, or there could be a thousand people dotted around, hiding in houses or in the woods. There was no way of telling what the world was like beyond the driveway.

Rick pulled the padlock around so that he could insert the key, and then unlocked it. Holding his breath, he took one last look through the bars, expecting demons to spring forth from the trees, but none did. The rev of the Range Rover's engine jarred him, and he swung the gate open without further hesitation. It felt like stepping in front of a speeding train.

But nothing came.

Keith's Range Rover crept forwards and almost shunted Rick out of the way. Tradition took him, and he lifted his hand to wave his former housemates goodbye, but Keith kept his eyes pointing forwards. The tinted rear windows kept Steven and Diane from view.

The Range Rover passed through the gate, turned into the road, and sped away.

They were gone.

Maddy and Daniel came up beside Rick. Daniel spoke. "You think we can get that gate closed again, pal?"

Rick took a hold of the gate and began to close it, but stopped when there was an almighty crash.

Maddy's eyes went wide as she looked at Rick. "Jesus! What the hell was that?"

Rick held the padlock in one hand and the key in the other. He thought about putting the two together and going back inside, but he already knew he couldn't. "Keith's crashed the car. The demons never left. It was a trap."

As if to confirm his suspicions, a group of corpses burst from the tree line on the other side of the road and sprinted towards the gate. One of them threw itself at the gate before Rick had chance to fully close it. It struck the iron bars and shunted Rick backwards. His ankle twisted in the gravel and he fell down onto his rump.

Daniel leapt forward and kicked the gate closed, but the demon was half inside and became trapped between the bars. Its skin began to smoke and burn until it squealed in agony and withdrew. Maddy ran up and helped Daniel keep the gate closed until Rick could get back to his feet and insert the key in the lock. His hands were shaking so much that it took him several attempts to get the gate secure, but once he had, the three of them leapt back towards the house.

The dead men and women threw themselves against the gate, even as the iron burned their flesh. They were angrier than before, snarling and hammering at the bars, like angry gorillas.

"They're pissed off," said Daniel. "They had a chance to kill us, and they failed. Maybe they have a boss they're going to have to answer to."

"The son-of-a-bitch with the black hair," said Rick. Maddy looked around. "Then where is he?"

Rick remembered the sound of his brother's Range Rover crashing. "He's wherever Keith and the others are. We have to go rescue them."

Daniel looked at him like he was mad. "Are you serious?"

Rick nodded firmly. "You said your God needs leaders. Well, I'm leading. We grab whatever weapons we can and we go out there. I'm done hiding."

Maddy tried to stop him as he marched into the house and into the living room. "Rick, we can't go out there. They'll tear us to pieces."

"Why? Because they're monsters?" "Well, yeah."

"So we should just lay down and die? They aren't monsters— we've seen them die. If all we do is cower away, waiting for someone to rescue us, then we're all screwed. They'll pick us off one by one. We need to fight back. In the pub, we fought back and won."

"Sarah died," said Maddy. "So did lots of other people."

Rick nodded. "But so did lots of demons. I'm going to get my brother. He's a complete and utter shit, but he saved my life. I don't want to owe him anything."

"Your mind is made up?" said Daniel, standing next to the couch.

"Yes."

"Then I suggest we put all that booze in your kitchen to good use."

"You want to get pissed?" Maddy asked.

Daniel grinned. "Oh, I'm already pissed, darlin', but I wasn't thinking about having a drink. Let me show you some of the things I learned after I left the church."

***

Within ten minutes, the kitchen counter had been transformed into an armoury. A row of spirits—whiskey, tequila, and vodka—sat with dishcloths stuffed into their neck. Keith had taken the iron poker with him, but Maddy had found an old field hockey stick. Daniel had fastened a long chef's knife to the end of a broom handle, producing a makeshift spear. Rick, himself, clutched the long stem of an antique brass lamp he kept in the conservatory.

They all now wore whatever they could fashion as armour. It was hot, but Maddy had put back on her thick paramedic overalls and wrapped a scarf around her neck. The only skin showing was her hands and face. Rick wore a long leather jacket from his pop-star days—the type of thing that looked stupid on anybody who wasn't famous. It was a thick second hide that would hopefully protect him from the claws and teeth of his enemies.

Now that it was time to go, Rick's resolve threatened to leave him. His stomach churned like a blender, and the urge to lurch forward and vomit was hard to resist. When he looked at Maddy and Daniel, reminding himself that they would be with him, he felt a little stronger. It wasn't as if any of them had a choice. The demons were back at the gate, which meant they were once again trapped. Their only choice was to fight their way free, or stay and eventually starve. If they could help Keith, Steven, and Diane, all the better.

"Let's do this," he told the others, who had both taken on the colour of whipped ice cream. They headed out the front door and headed down the driveway. It was now the tail end of dusk, and the security floodlight had come on, bathing the demons in a silvery skin of light. More like angels than monsters, but then Rick heard them growl and knew there was nothing pure or holy about them.

"Let them have it!"

Maddy and Daniel lit two of the Molotov cocktails and let fly. Both flaming bottles smashed against the fence and ignited in a cloud of fire. The demons screeched like tortured children, flailing around like puppets with twisted strings. Flames crackled in the evening breeze, and the smell of burning flesh added to the scents of summer.

Rick followed the next part of the plan and ran to unlock the gate. Once he'd popped the padlock, he yanked the gate open wide enough that the driveway was clear. Maddy hopped into the Mustang and gunned the engine while Rick jumped clear just in time to avoid getting run over.

The heavy American beast struck the group of burning demons and sent them scattering across the road. They seemed to roll and bounce endlessly before coming to rest. There was no ambiguity about their condition. Every one of them was dead, burnt, and battered.

Maddy reached across and shoved open the passenger side door. Daniel was cooped in the back. "Rick, get in."

Rick threw himself into the passenger seat and slammed the door shut behind him. Maddy took off, the car beeping at them to buckle up, which they had to do to shut it up.

"Is this a bad time to say I need a piss?" said Daniel. "Why didn't you go before you left?" Maddy growled. "I should have done. Sorry."

"You can go after we kill the rest of the demons," she said.

Then they all broke out laughing, not because they thought it was funny, but because their nerves were so fried. They had just survived a battle unscathed, and the adrenaline in their veins was like a hit of cocaine. It gave them giddy hope that they might just be okay. So they laughed.

It didn't take but a few moments to get around the bend and find Keith's Range Rover. The vehicle was on its side, windows shattered and axles bent.

"He's still alive," said Daniel. "I'll be damned."

Rick couldn't believe what he saw. He'd felt obligated to come to his brother's aid, but had possessed slim hope that there would be anything left to rescue.

Keith was holding his own. He popped up out of the Range Rover's side window, which was now facing the sky, and swung his iron poker at any demon that got too close. They tried, in vain, to drag him out of the wreckage, but he picked his swings and made sure every one counted. Several of the demons lay dead in the road, their skulls caved in.

Steven was dead. He lay on the tarmac, face down after having apparently launched through the windscreen. Keith's older vehicle must have lacked the nagging seatbelt alarm that Rick's Mustang possessed.

Diane was nowhere to be seen.

Maddy repeated the manoeuvre she had performed at the gate and ploughed the big American export right into the group of demons. Some of them got up, but most stayed down.

Demons still surrounded Keith's Range Rover.

Maddy pulled on the handbrake, and Rick leapt out of the car. Maddy and Daniel were right behind him, running at the enemies with all the fierceness of barbarians. They swung their weapons with everything they had. Daniel stabbed a demon in the guts with his spear, before pulling it free and using it to pluck out the eyes of another. Maddy swung her hockey stick like a baseball bat and caved in several skulls. Rick bludgeoned demon after demon with his antique lamp.

But the demons kept on coming, attacking like a pack of hyenas. The dead men and women were joined by hunched-over creatures with long, twisted claws. Rick caught one in mid-air, smashing it in the side of its face before it had chance to return to earth. Maddy hit another so hard with her hockey stick that its lower jaw detached and rolled across the road. Atop the Range Rover, Keith fought with renewed energy. He saw his rescuers and dragged himself out of the broken window, fending off demons with one hand, while he climbed with the other.

Rick fought his way over to the Range Rover and helped his brother down. "Sorry about your motor," he said.

Keith shrugged. "Least I can say I owned one. A dream fulfilled for a while is better than a dream out of reach."

Rick frowned. "Sounds like something I'd say."

"Look out!" Keith shoved his brother out of the way as a demon slashed the air with its talons. Keith jabbed out with his poker and impaled it right through the mouth, then lifted his leg to kick it away. The next demon that attacked fell afoul of Rick's lamp and hit the floor with a broken spine.

"We make quite a team," said Keith.

Rick nodded. "If only we'd found out sooner."

Keith stared at his brother and let out a laboured sigh.

"Let's leave the past where it belongs, huh?"

"You mean like you being an arsehole most of my life, culminating in you breaking a bottle over my head and locking me in my garage?"

"Yeah, stuff like that."

Rick patted his big brother on the back. "It's forgotten. Now, come on."

Maddy and Daniel were back to back in the middle of the road, demons coming at them from all sides. Rick was about to wade in and help them, when Keith grabbed his arm and stopped him. "Diane," he said. "She's still inside the Range Rover."

"What?"

"She was in the front with me. Her head hit the dashboard. We have to get her out."

Rick turned back to the Range Rover and leapt up on top of it. As he looked down inside the broken windows, he could see the pale shape of Diane. Unconscious.

Keith climbed up beside Rick to help. The whole time they were up there, Maddy and Daniel continued to fight for their lives.

"Hold on to me while I lift her out," Rick told his brother. Keith nodded.

Rick lowered onto his stomach and reached an arm inside the window while Keith kept a tight hold on his belt. Diane murmured when his hand brushed her face, and it was a relief to know that she was still alive, but she didn't wake up. A shadow cast across her face, and as Rick's eyes adjusted, he saw it was blood from a wound hidden beneath her blonde hair. He fondled between the shadows and shafts of light and located her wrist. When he pulled, Diane slumped back in her chair and her eyes fluttered open. She moaned. Ignoring her pain, Rick heaved her upwards; a dead weight, but just about manageable—the girl couldn't have weighed over eight stone. There was still life in her legs, and once he pulled her up into a standing position, she kept herself there.

"Diane," he urged. "Diane, wake up. You have to—Jesus!"

Rick was jerked backwards by his belt. He twisted around

and saw his brother stumbling across the top of the car. From the road, the black-haired demon snarled, a massive gash in his torso pouring with brown sludge. Keith slipped off the edge of the car and disappeared out of sight.

Rick turned back to Diane. "Diane, wake up!"

Her eyes fluttered and eventually stayed open. Her gaze fell upon Rick, and she panicked.

"Diane, it's okay. It's me, Rick."

She stopped struggling and took a hard look at him. "Rick? I... I thought we left you."

"You did. It was a trap, but you're okay. Come on."

Diane reached up with both arms and allowed Rick to drag her up onto the side of the car. She was unarmed and disorientated, so he told her to hop down and run to the bushes at the edge of the road. Rick, himself, dropped down and went to join the battle. He retrieved his brass lamp and smashed in the brain of a nearby demon. Keith was right ahead, being beaten half to death by the black-haired, dead demon.

Rick shouted. "Leave him alone!"

The demon raised his fist to strike Keith again, but held it in the air and looked at Rick with a sickening grimace. "Wait your turn, worm."

"That's an ironic thing to say for a maggot-riddled corpse."

The demon wasted no more time with trash talk. It dropped Keith to the pavement and stalked after Rick. Rick clutched the lamp, but felt as if he were holding an inflatable mallet. The creature coming towards him was massive, and the gaping wound in its torso had not been enough to stop it.

Rick leapt forward and took a swing, but the demon was too quick. It backhanded Rick across the cheek hard enough to send him down to the ground and see stars. The loose stones on the road bit into his palms as he tried to right himself. Keith staggered back to his feet and leapt at the demon's back, but he too was swatted away with a cruel backhand. He ended up on the floor right next to Rick, and the two brothers crawled backwards together. The demon stalked after them with the plodding ferocity of a rhino. His gnarled hands were thick, and perfect for breaking bones.

In the background, demons surrounded Maddy, while Diane cowered in the bushes at the side of the road. Daniel was nowhere to be seen.

"Why are you here?" asked Rick.

The demon stopped his approach and seemed to answer after careful thought. "Because the alternative is remaining there."

Rick shook his head. "Where?"

"Hell. Do you know what it is like to finally be free from there? To return home to the place that allows us the pleasure of life?"

Rick saw sadness on the demon's face and made an assumption. "You were people once. You were a man?"

The question seemed to enrage the demon. "Not just a man—a prince. My family's kingdom stretched from the Euphrates to the Tigris, and all we wanted, we took. Now I am a prince once more, here to take what I wish and answer only to the Red Lord himself."

"So, it sounds like you're still somebody's bitch," said Rick.

"I am a prince!" The demon's face screwed up in fury, but, having stalled sufficiently to recover his strength, Rick was able to spring up and wallop the demon around the head with his lamp.

There was a resounding crack and Rick shouted triumphantly, "We already have a monarchy, thanks!"

The demon reeled backwards on its thick legs, face distorted from the large dent now in the left side of its skull.

But the black-haired dead man did not go down. "Fuck sake," cried Rick. "Don't you die?"

"Princes die when princes choose to die."

"Do they choose to go to Hell? Because that's where you've been rotting."

The demon tried to backhand Rick again, but this time, he ducked and gave his enemy's knees a hefty blow with the lamp.

The demon bellowed and stumbled sideways. "I will tear you into shreds and feed your remains to vultures."

"You'd need to go someplace else for that," said Rick as he smashed the demon in the hip. "No vultures here, I'm afraid."

"There will be nothing left when we are done with it. We will destroy all."

"Except vultures, apparently." Rick took another swing, but his luck ran out, and he missed. The demon caught the lamp stem, yanked it away from him, and threw it to the ground.

"Now you die, worm." The demon punched Rick in the stomach, and his ribs cracked like twigs. He slumped to his knees, able only to catch half a breath.

Keith raced to help, but Rick put his hand up and waved him away. "No... Keith, go... help Maddy and Diane. Get them out of... here."

The demon grinned. "Yes, Keith, run while you can. I'll deal with you later."

Keith kept on towards Rick, but slowed down, and then stopped. "Rick, I can't-"

"Just go!" shouted Rick, clutching his ribs in agony. "Get the hell out of here."

Keith swallowed, then turned and ran. He called Diane out of the bushes and they went to Maddy's aid—just in time to save her from being torn apart by a demon creeping up behind her.

Rick coughed and tasted blood in his mouth. Every breath he took was shallower than the last. The effort of even staying upright on his knees was too much. He slumped onto his side.

The black-haired demon stood over him, deep, guttural laughter coming from deep down from its dead insides. "A valiant display—braver than a thousand other worms we have slaughtered in this village. It will be a pleasure to add you to our ranks, once your time in Hell is over."

Rick flailed, no longer able to take another breath. His vision fizzed with swirling rain drops, and he tried to find the strength to get back to his knees and face his death with his head held high, but he only felt himself getting lower and lower to the ground. Eventually, his head rested against the cold tarmac. He looked up at the sky and saw the moon shining down on him. It was pretty.

That was when the demon raised his foot into the air and stamped Rick's skull into pulp.

~DAVID DAVIDS~

SLOUGH, BERKSHIRE

"MINA? MINA, WHERE ON EARTH ARE YOU, girl?" David had tried Mina's cell, but it only ever rang out to voicemail. The last couple times, the call hadn't even connected—it appeared the nation's cellular network had started to fail. Whatever contingencies were put in place by the networks could obviously only last so long without human intervention. David imagined call centres and hub offices lying empty, employees all fled, or ripped apart by demons. Inside the offices of the Slough Echo, things seemed almost normal, but he knew that was likely an exception. It was just a busy news day as far as the staff of the Echo was concerned. Everybody had been tasked with the same jobs they would have been given if a local celebrity died. They were somehow outside of the situation, as journalists so often were. It was hard to realise that the current situation affected them as much as the people they were reporting the news to.

The last time he'd spoken to Mina, she'd said she was in the waiting area, but when he stormed out there to find her, she had been nowhere to be seen. Her whole website had been erased—didn't she care? People had been funnelling through to the landing page in droves over the last several hours, and there was evidence that it was directly helping people survive. How on Earth had it been deleted?

David headed back out into the waiting area, returning there to check, even though he'd already inspected it once. It was the same thing he did with his car keys some mornings. Whenever he misplaced them, he'd go to the sideboard in the hallway again and again because that was where they were supposed to be. Mina said she was in the waiting area, so that was where he went once again.

He never expected to bump into Andras.

"Do you know where Mina has wandered off to?" he asked. "She's needed."

Andras nodded and looked rather sad. "She got a call off her dad. I think he's gone."

"Gone?"

"Yeah, you know... dead."

"Oh, poor Mina. Is she okay?" He felt for her. From what he'd witnessed, Mina's father was a controlling man, but still her father. He could tell she loved him, but lots of people were dying in the world, and no one had the luxury to mourn them. They needed to keep working.

"Do you know where she went, Andras?"

"For fresh air, I think. I asked her if she wanted to talk, but... well, she doesn't know me, so she just went be alone."

"Of course. I'll go look for her, and see if she's okay." Andras nodded. "I'll make myself useful inside."

"Yes, please. Little Alice is awake, so Carol will no doubt be back on the floor ready to give out tasks."

"Great, I'll get right on it."

Andras walked away, but something occurred to David that made him call the man back. "Andras?"

He turned. "Yes?"

"You were at Mina's computer last. Do you know what happened to the website?"

"Don't ask me. Everything was fine when I left it. Maybe it was hacked."

"By whom? Who out there would want to stop us giving out information about the demons?"

"The demons, for one."

David thought the idea of tech savvy demons was ridiculous, so he gave a thin smile and walked away. There was something off about Andras. They had found him cowering in the road outside the building, but since then, the man had shown little fear or concern. Nor had he made any phone calls to friends or loved ones.

Mina had probably gone out to the front of the building to get fresh air, but David would rather her be inside. The army south of Luton had been spotted moving west by a middle- aged postal worker trapped in a Chinese restaurant. He had been providing typo-ridden email updates from an iPhone attached to the building's Wi-Fi. The updates had stopped about fifteen minutes ago.

David opened the door in the hallway that led to the stairwell. He wasn't about to trust the lift—the power could go at any minute and he didn't fancy being trapped inside a metal coffin. Despite the mugginess of the summer night, the stairwell was chilly, and a draught whistled up the central gap between the levels.

He started down the step, his ears picking up a rhythmic thudding, like a tree branch tapping against a window in the wind. It seemed to come from the floor below, and as he looked down the central hollow of the spiralling stairwell, he saw something flashing in and out of view. What on Earth was it?

He quickened his steps. He had a bad feeling, and was eager to find out he was wrong. But he wasn't wrong. The bad feeling was completely warranted.

Mina swung from a long length of telephone cord attached to the safety railing, her neck broken. The thick, grey cord bit so deeply into her windpipe it looked like her head might pop off at any minute and send her decapitated body plummeting to the bottom floor lobby.

"Mina!"

David panicked. He reached out and grabbed Mina's legs and tried to hoist her back up onto the landing, but she was too heavy. Her body swung wildly around on the end of the cord. The only thing he could think to do was call for help. So he screamed until his throat hurt. "Somebody, help me! Please!"

Before he knew it, he was sobbing. Nobody came. Nobody could hear him.

***

Eventually, David's thinking prevailed, and he pulled out his phone and dialled Carol. When she heard what had happened, she appeared in the stairwell within minutes. She stood beside him now, looking down at Mina where they laid her down on the landing. Getting her down had been much easier with two of them.

"The silly girl," said Carol. "She was so bright."

David was light-headed, so he leaned up against the railing and dropped his head as he spoke. "We survived so much together, to end it like this? It makes no sense. She wouldn't do this, Carol."

"Of course she would, David, my dear. In fact, it takes more courage not to kill ourselves right now. You know the demon army is heading this way?"

David nodded.

"Corporal Martin thinks it might be planning to head down to the South Coast, maybe attack Portsmouth. The Navy is there, rounding up people into a refugee camp."

David rubbed at his temples, fingers moving in clockwise circles. "They're trying to exterminate us."

"Looks that way, which is why it's such a sodden' shame that young girls like Mina are making their job easier for them. We needed her. Silly girl."

"She didn't do this, Carol. I know her. She was strong. I listened to her stand up to her father, I watched her run into a burning building to save a girl—she wasn't in a vulnerable place. She was motivated, and she wanted to help."

"Andras told me her father might be dead. That's likely what tipped her over the edge, David."

He'd been a reporter for thirty years, and something didn't feel right. "Andras was at Mina's computer right before the website got wiped. He was in the waiting area when Mina went missing. Who is he?"

"He's just some chap, David, trying to survive like the rest of us. He isn't up to no good, I promise you."

David looked down at Mina's body and sighed. "Perhaps you're right. Give me a minute and I'll be back to work."

"Okay, I'll see you in the office. Alice wants to see you now that's she's awake."

"Alice? See me?"

Carol shrugged. "She wanted to see you and Mina both, but we'll have to break the news to her. She likes you."

David frowned. "Heaven knows why."

"You and Mina saved her life. I don't blame her for wanting to stay close to you. You've done well, David. Don't lose yourself now. I need you."

"I'll be back to work in a minute, just want to put Mina somewhere quiet."

Carol squeezed him on the arm and smiled. Then she left him alone with Mina. He was able to pick her up into his arms, and he took her down another level into the offices of an accountancy firm that sub-let part of the building. He took her into the boardroom and placed her down on the long desk where he straightened her legs and put her arms by her side. It was nice to see her at peace, but strange that he already missed her so. Before the chaos that erupted in Oxford Street, David had thought nothing of Mina—just another youngster with a camera, naively hoping she could make a mark on the world. Now he knew different. Mina had been a brave and kind woman, and he'd been lucky to know her. He'd been so consumed with his career for so long that he'd forgotten how to make a friend. In Mina, he had at least found pleasant company, and a person he respected. Now it was too late to appreciate her, and he regretted it more than ever.

He felt so alone. There had always seemed to be time for a wife and kids later on, and even at fifty, he hadn't felt his options were closed. He was selfish at heart and had wanted to be free for as long as possible. Now he wanted nothing more than for someone to sweep him up in their loving arms and hold him. Just a friend would do.

David wept over Mina's body.

Perhaps she really had killed herself. If he was drawn to such dark introspection, perhaps she had been to. It still didn't feel right, though.

He ran a hand over her cheek. "Sorry, kiddo. I hope you're some place nice."

He was about to move away, when he noticed a spot of blood on her shirt. It could have come from her broken neck, but when he looked at her throat, he saw no breaks in the skin, not even where the cord constricted her flesh. He examined her more closely, until he eventually discovered the source. One of her fingernails had torn away.

A defensive wound?

David had once reported on a murder case in Essex where he'd seen the body of a woman close up. She'd been raped and strangled. Her fingernails had been broken too.

Did somebody attack you, Mina?

Andras?

David couldn't bring himself to trust that man. Something was just off about him. Somebody had done this to Mina; he was sure of it.

It was time to do some investigating.

He headed back upstairs and into the newsroom, acting calmly while remaining suspicious. Alice waited for him with a cup of tea and handed it over. "I've never made tea before," she said. "Everyone in America drinks coffee."

David took a sip. It was weak and lukewarm. "Perfect! You're a natural English lady if ever I saw one."

She smiled, but then fell back to sadness. Obvious survivor's guilt—a brief glimmer of happiness followed by shame as memories of her brother's death returned. He did something he was unused to and gave the little girl a hug. "We'll get you home to your mummy soon, sweetheart, I promise. Let's just get this mess sorted out first."

"It's okay," she said. "I know I'll never go home."

"You don't know that, Alice. We'll do everything we can." "I heard Corporal Martin say that America is just as bad as

here. My mommy might already be dead."

It hurt David's heart to see a child so devoid of hope, and he did his best to combat it. "There are lots of people still very much alive, Alice. We are fighting back. Your mummy might be okay. Your father too. He's a Coast Guard, isn't he? He'll be safe on his boat."

"I don't see my daddy much. He'll be too busy to come and get me."

"I don't have children, Alice, but believe me, I know your father will be doing everything he can right now to get to you."

Alice nodded, but didn't seem to believe him very much. "He doesn't know that Kyle is dead. Corporal Martin has been trying to reach my mommy, but she's not answering anymore. That's how I know she's dead. She said she would stay indoors with Clark, so why isn't she answering?"

"The phones are playing up, sweetheart. Corporal Martin will keep trying her. Why don't you go ask him to call again now for you?"

She sighed. "Okay. Tell me when you want more tea."

"Will do." He took another sip of the lacklustre brew and smacked his lips. "Mmm."

Once Alice had gone, David went and grabbed Mitchell, one of the Echo's system administrators. The pasty-faced spindle of a man had a look of constant illness—with perpetual dark bags beneath his eyes. "Hi, Mitchell. I was wondering if you could do something for me."

"What's up, David?"

"Is there any way you can go on Mina's computer and find a history of what was done on it?"

"You mean like a list of user actions?"

"Yes, that's it exactly."

Mitchell nodded. "Piece of piss. There's black box software on the entire network. It records every single keystroke. Carol had it installed after we got accused of phone hacking last year. She wanted to know exactly what was going on under her nose. You thinking somebody in the office deleted the emergency website on purpose?"

David nodded and kept his voice low. "I do think that, yes, and I also think that someone used Mina's computer to do it."

"Makes sense. The backup was on Mina's laptop, and that got deleted too. I've been trying to restore it for the last hour. Where is Mina, anyway?"

David decided not to confuse things for the time being, so he lied. "She's gone to get some air."

"Okay, well, let's go take a look at her computer."

They went on over to Mina's cubicle, where Mitchell sat down and opened her laptop. David leaned over his shoulder while he tapped away. "How long will this take, Mitchell?"

"Ten minutes. Leave me to it."

"Okay, I-"

Somebody bumped into the back of David, and he was unnerved to discover it was Andras. He held two steaming mugs of tea out in front of him. "I saw Alice made you a cuppa earlier, so I thought I'd get you one a little stronger. Bless her socks, but she goes a little overboard with the milk."

David tried to smile, but only a grimace appeared on his face. Standing in front of Andras, he was even surer that something was odd about the man. Maybe Mitchell would find the answers that proved his suspicions were well founded.

David reached out to take one of the mugs, but as he did so, Andras thrust out his own arm. Their hands collided, and the mug bounced up into the air. It flew over Mitchell's shoulder and landed right on top of Mina's laptop. There was no fire, or even sparks. The laptop's screen simply flickered for two seconds, then went dark.

Mitchell leapt up. "Damn it! You clumsy idiot."

Andras covered his mouth in horror. "I'm so sorry. I... It was an accident."

David looked down at Mina's laptop and groaned. "Is it okay? Can you fix it, Mitchell?"

Mitchell picked the laptop up and winced as it drained steaming hot tea from its vents. "It's gone to digital heaven."

"Then the black box recording is lost, too?"

Mitchell shook his head. "No, I can still get it from the network. It'll just take me a bit longer. Give us an hour."

David caught a flash of concern present itself on Andras's face at the mention of the black box. Perhaps he hadn't counted on that.

David turned to face him. "Did you do that on purpose, Andras?"

"Do what?"

"Ruin Mina's computer."

"What? No, of course not. It was an accident. My nerves are fried. I'm jittery."

"No," said David. "You're the least jittery person in this office. If it was you who deleted the website, just come clean about it now. You might be able to help us get it back online."

"I swear, I did nothing. Mina was on my back about the same thing."

"Mina's dead," David said it so that only Andras heard it. He also added a hint of aggression to his tone. He wanted Andras to know that he was on to him.

Andras took a step back as if the shock of Mina's death had dealt him a physical blow. It could easily have been a reaction he'd rehearsed. "What do you mean she's dead? I just saw her an hour ago."

David nodded. "In fact, you were the last person to see her alive. Strange how bad things keep happening around you."

Andras looked confused, but it was as if a mask fell. He leaned in close to David and spoke in a growl. "I don't know why you have it in for me, David, but I suggest you back off. I would hate for you to have an accident too."

"Are you suggesting you had something to do with Mina's death?"

Andras stepped back and put on a bright smile as he pulled back and dropped into a practiced, defensive face. "Of course not. I had nothing to do with it."

It was then that David noticed the ragged scratch mark on

Andras's neck, right below his ear. The small incision looked exactly like the kind of wound a woman's fingernail would cause.

"We'll talk again later, Andras. I have some things to attend to."

Andras moved, but made sure to bump into David and shunt him out the way. "Go do some reporting, David, while you still can."

David glared at the man's back as he walked away and spoke only to himself. "Oh, I plan on it, you son-of-a-bitch. I'll find the truth. I always do."

~RICK BASTION~

DEVONSHIRE, ENGLAND

WHEN RICK OPENED HIS EYES, ALL HE SAW was red. He tried speaking, but his jaw seemed to open and close in strange ways. He was cold, could feel nothing at all but the chill on his skin.

"Hold on, Rick. I haven't finished with you yet."

Rick tried to move, but managed only to shift his legs from side to side.

"Hold your horses!"

Something clicked. Rick felt pressure inside his skull, and he was able to move his jaw again. He screamed. "Help me!"

"I am helping you, pal. Just stop wriggling like a worm."

The red drained from Rick's vision, and the world returned. Daniel hunched over him, staring.

"D-Daniel?"

"Yeah. Sorry for running out on you all, but me and the black-haired gent have some history. I was hoping to get the jump on him, but by the time I got around back, things had already taken a turn for the worse."

Rick blinked, took in a deep breath that felt divine in his lungs. "I... was hurt?"

"You were dead, pal, but no worries. I brought you back."

Rick shot up into a sitting position and looked down at himself. Blood covered him.

He fingered his skull and felt it move.

"Give it a few moments to set," said Daniel. "Your head was cracked wide open."

Rick glanced around. He was sitting in the middle of the road, right next to his brother's wrecked Range Rover. All the demons had gone, except for the corpses they had left behind.

"I-I... I don't understand."

"Khallutush stamped your head into pulp. I wasn't sure I could mend you."

"Khala...Khala?"

"Khallutush. The black-haired demon. He used to be a—" "A prince," Rick finished for him. "He told me. Right before he... You really brought me back to life? That's impossible."

Daniel chuckled, but the sound was phlegmy, as if he was ill. "You should know by now, Rick, the rules have changed. Demons and angels walk the earth."

"Who are you, Daniel?"

Daniel moved into a cross-legged position, where he propped his elbow on his knees. He looked sick as he spoke, like he was going to throw up. "My name is Daniel, The Watcher."

Rick frowned. "Huh?"

"Thought that might confuse you. Don't you people read your bibles anymore? I am Daniel, one of the twenty Watchers fallen from Heaven."

Rick's expression remained blank, but a bout of hysterical laughter wasn't far off. What was he listening to?

Daniel tutted when he saw no understanding on Rick's face. "I'm an angel, you numpty. One of the Fallen who fought beside Lucifer in the Heavenly Wars. I fell from grace with two hundred of my brothers after God's faithful prevailed— Michael and Gabriel and all them good eggs. You must have heard of them?"

Rick nodded.

"Well, it was all a long time ago now. A really, really long time ago."

Rick tried to follow along. "So you... fought against God?"

Daniel nodded. "I was young, stupid. Lucifer swept me along in his mad adventures before I even knew what was happening. One minute all was well, the next I'm fighting a war against my own brothers. Lucifer lost, and we all fell, lost our wings and ended up in Abysseus."

Rick shuffled backwards, moving away on his butt. "You're... You're one of them?"

Daniel sighed. "I came through the gates, yeah. Of course I did—nobody would voluntarily stay in Hell, would they? I saw the seals break, and I scarpered. Doesn't mean I want anything to do with all this. I'm not one of them."

"What are they?"

"You already know that, Rick. They're just people. Or at least they were. They're the sinners sent to Hell throughout all of human history and even from times before. Some of them had only been in Hell a single second when the seals broke, but others, like Khallutush, have burned in Hell for millennia. The very worst beasts don't even understand the concept of time anymore; their suffering has been so long. The Fallen have suffered since Abysseus first came into being—our pain was used to forge its walls at the dawn of history."

"Why are the demons here?" Rick couldn't believe he was asking the question. "What do they want?"

"A new home," said Daniel. "Somewhere a little less fire- and-brimstony. At least, that's what most of them want. The Fallen, though, they want to force God's hand and finish what they started. Lucifer and the Red Lord want to see Heaven crumble. The Fallen lead their armies and intend to scourge humanity from the face of the earth and finally put an end to God's finest creation. If God does not act, his work will be undone, his existence undermined. If humanity doesn't fight back, He will have no choice but to intervene, and then he'll be vulnerable."

"So this is a war on God?"

Daniel nodded "And all He created. The Red Lord would rather see everything burn, than suffer in Hell one moment longer."

Rick actually believed what he was hearing—after all he had seen and done, how could he not?—and wanted to learn more. "Who is the Red Lord?"

"I don't know," Daniel admitted. "Few in Hell have ever seen him, but he pulls Lucifer's strings—always has. He might even have been the one who convinced Lucifer to start the war in Heaven in the first place. He-" Daniel broke off and started coughing and heaving. It went on for almost a minute. Once he caught his breath, he brought the back of his hand away from his mouth and saw blood.

Rick grabbed him by the shoulders and steadied him. "Are you okay?"

"I'm fine. It just took a lot to bring you back."

"Why did you?"

He shrugged. "Dunno, really. Suppose I must like you. We need to go."

"Go where?"

"To get a little payback. Khallutush went after your brother and the others. They took off in your car, but I don't know what happened to them after that. They might have gone back to your gaff."

"They'd be better off making for the coast."

"And they probably will have, but we need to get off the street. I need to rest."

"Okay, then we'll head back to mine." Rick got up to his feet and helped Daniel to his. The self-proclaimed Fallen Angel had gone ghostly white, and his nose dripped with blood.

"Daniel, are you sure you're okay? You look bad."

"I'll be fine. You're the one who just had his skull crushed. Come on."

They started down the road, allowing Daniel to take slow steps. There were more dead demons lying around the bend, crushed and broken, most likely, by the 19inch wheels of his imported Mustang.

"I hope they got away okay," said Rick.

"Even your brother?"

"Yes, even him. Daniel, if you're an angel, where are the others? I mean, the good ones, from Heaven."

"Huh, been wondering that myself. The Fallen are all here—over two hundred in total. They all lost their wings when they fell, cut off from Heaven and God's divine spirit. They're driven by nothing now, except madness and anger. Lucifer had indoctrinated them long before they fell, and over the millennia, he has got them slavering for a new war, a War of Chaos and Ending. They want to wipe every living thing off the face of this planet, and then laugh in God's face. They will show no mercy, for none was afforded to them. So, yeah, the Heavenly angels could do with making an appearance right around now."

Rick felt sick in his stomach, but he kept probing for answers, even though each one he got made him more desperate. "Why aren't you like the other Fallen, Daniel? Where are your wings? Why are you... human?"

"Because this isn't my body. When I opposed Lucifer's grand plans for a new war, he threw me into the lowliest pit in Hell. But nothing ever dies in Hell—my body still smoulders there now. When the seals broke, I projected my soul upon another."

"You said demons couldn't possess people because of iron in their blood."

"I didn't say it wasn't possible. The man whose body I took was in a coma. He was anaemic, and I was able to force my way in. It was he who spent all that time at the Vatican. I have all his memories, but don't know his name. Isn't that odd? I even talk like him."

"So, you're here to help? You want to fight Lucifer? Why?"

Daniel looked at Rick like he was an idiot. "Lucifer dragged me along in his first war and got me sent to Hell for all eternity. I'd say that's reason enough to hold a grudge."

They carried on down the road. All was quiet, everything still. Even the trees were devoid of motion—no breeze rustled their leaves. The entire stretch of road was dead, and only Rick and Daniel walked it.

The world had ended.

Rick's house came into view around the next bend. The gates were still hanging wide open, but there was no Mustang parked in the driveway.

He couldn't help but smile. "The others aren't here. They must have made for the coast. Good on them."

"Shame," said Daniel. "It would have been nice for us all to stick together."

"If you're an angel, why can't you just magic us to wherever they are? You brought me back to life, so why can't you do something as simple as that?"

"I lost my wings when I fell. I'm not really an angel anymore. I have a little residual power, just enough to bring you back, but I can't teleport, or shoot fire from my eyes. Lucky for you, neither can any of my big brothers currently stomping their way around the earth."

"How do we fight back?"

"By doing what you've been doing. I don't know if you noticed, Rick, but we just passed about two dozen dead demons. Maddy must have killed five or six by running them down in your car. They die as easily as you do. If people realise they can fight back, humanity might have a chance. Men are animals, but they've forgotten. People need to rediscover their claws before it's too late."

"I think it might already be too late."

Daniel stumbled and almost fell. His nose bled again, and Rick had to steady him. When he looked into his eyes, the irises had turned a solid black.

"What's happening to you, Daniel?"

"The iron in my blood. There's only a trace amount, but it's keeping me from healing. Bringing you back, it... it..."

Daniel's legs folded, and he fell into Rick's arms, shuddering and moaning.

"I've got you. I've got you." Rick knelt down and heaved Daniel up onto his shoulders. He hurried through the gate and staggered up the driveway. The front door hung open too; he hadn't closed it when he'd left—he'd not expected to return. There was something sad about returning home now—an emptiness of knowing it was no longer a house, but a tomb. It was destined to deteriorate into a neglected ruin. Still, it was the only thing left that reminded Rick of what life had been less than a week ago.

Things had changed in the blink of an eye.

Daniel trembled across Rick's shoulders, having a mild fit as he hurried inside and went into the living room. He threw the wounded angel down on the couch, and then he turned to go get water from the kitchen.

"Worm! You live still?"

Rick lurched backwards in fright, colliding with the glass coffee table in the centre of the room and cracking it. The noise brought more demons rushing into the room, and he found himself encircled.

The monsters had invaded his home.

"What are you doing in my house?"

Khallutush bared his rotting teeth. "Looking for things to kill. I get to crush your skull all over again, worm."

Rick remembered what Daniel had said about fighting, so he didn't back away, even though he wanted to. Not intending to get pinned down, he clambered up onto the couch and launched himself over the back of it. He collided with a nearby demon and sent it crashing into the wall. It stumbled to its knees, which gave Rick chance to viciously stomp on its head. Another demon tried to grab him from behind. He thrust his head backwards and broke its fragile nose before spinning around and clubbing it in the side of the head with his fist. It fell down unconscious.

More demons attacked, but Rick kept them at bay with fists and feet, stomping them whenever he could knock one down. He eventually found himself face to face with Khallutush, who stood before him, laughing like a towering hyena.

"Lie down, worm, my foot is ready to reacquaint itself with your skull."

"No, thanks."

Khallutush roared and swung his giant fists at Rick. Rick ducked and delivered a punch of his own, hitting the festering gut wound caused by the iron poker. His fist came away caked in foul smelling gore, but Khallutush bellowed in pain and doubled over.

Rick raced into the kitchen and yanked open a drawer. He pulled out the biggest knife he could find and—

Khallutush rammed into Rick from behind, knocking the wind out of his lungs and sending him sprawling across the counter top. He barely slipped away before Khallutush could hit him with a follow-up blow.

Another demon ran into the kitchen and tried to leap on Rick while he was off balance. He ducked and buried his knife into its guts, pulling it free with a sickly pop. Then he dodged behind the kitchen island and used it as a barrier between him and the monstrous Khallutush.

Khallutush laughed. "You reek of desperation."

"And you reek of ancient dead person."

"You speak to a prince of Hell."

"You're in my fucking kitchen." Rick picked up a bamboo chopping board from the counter and hurled it at Khallutush. It hit the demon in the chest and made him grunt, but then he laughed. With impossible strength, he reached out a giant hand and swept aside the heavy granite-countertop island. Rick stumbled out of the way before he was crushed, but found himself cornered at the back of the kitchen with no way to get out.

Khallutush approached.

Rick threw a punch, but Khallutush caught his hand and squeezed. "Worthless maggot. You will be forgotten before your body even cools."

Rick moaned as the bones in his hand creaked in the demon's vice-like grip. He beat at Khallutush's chest with his free hand, but it was like punching brick. Every second the pressure increased. Khallutush seemed to savour the agony on Rick's face.

Rick screamed.

"Yes," Khallutush purred, "Beg. Beg for mercy. Beg to be forgotten."

Rick bit down on his tongue as the tiny bones in his hand snapped like twigs. The pain was so unbearable that he would do anything to make it stop. It took everything he had not to give in. "I'm a one-hit wonder. I'll never be forgotten."

Khallutush snarled, and clamped his fist closed, crushing Rick's hand flat and breaking every tiny bone. He screamed so hard that something in his throat ripped. He coughed, spluttered, and vomited.

Khallutush let him collapse to the floor and stood over him. "Time to die, and stay dead, worm." He lifted his huge foot over Rick's skull. "You have the honour of dying at the foot of a prince twice."

Rick clutched his hand and moaned on the floor, waiting for death—welcoming it.

"Didn't anybody tell you?" came a voice from across the room. "Your kingdom fell to ruin a long time ago. You're a prince of nothing."

Still perched on one leg, Khallutush glanced back over his shoulder and seemed confused.

Rick craned his neck and saw Daniel standing in the entrance. The wounded angel held the severed head of a demon under his arm, like a basketball.

"Daniel the Watcher?" Khallutush snarled. "You should be burning in Hell."

"I'm on vacation." Daniel bowled the severed head into the air, and it ignited. When it struck Khallutush, it engulfed him like a human torch. His thick arms flailed as he spun on the spot and screamed defiance. "You will all burn!"

Daniel raised an eyebrow. "Says the one who's on fire."

Khallutush flailed across the kitchen, flaming hands reached out towards Daniel, but he slowed down half way and slumped to his knees. He kept his focus on Daniel the entire time, his wicked eyes shining through the flames. "He will never forgive you, Daniel."

Then the ancient prince collapsed onto his front and died.

Rick clambered to his feet, clutching his mangled hand against his chest and trying not to black out from the pain. He stared at Daniel in amazement. The angel still looked at death's door, sweating profusely, but he'd killed the demons in the living room and had turned one of their severed heads into a blazing cannonball. He was anything but meek.

Rick bent down and righted one of the kitchen's fallen stools. He dragged himself on top of it and looked at Daniel. "I thought you didn't have a lot of power left?"

Daniel placed his hand down on the side counter and tried to catch his breath. When he did, he said, "I have a couple of parlour tricks when needed. I dealt with the rest of the demons in the house. If you get that gate closed, I think we'll be safe for now."

"Maddy had my keys, but I think I have a spare set somewhere. I'll go find them."

"Great," said Daniel. "You go do that while I pass out."

Rick opened his mouth to speak, but was interrupted as Daniel collapsed face first on the floor, right next to Khallutush.

~DAVID DAVIDS~
SLOUGH, BERKSHIRE

D AVID STOOD WATCHING AT THE EDGE OF the room. He watched little Alice hard at work, doing whatever the adults gave her to do, so that she didn't have to face the anguish inside her head. No child should face what she had. Her brother had been far too young to die a hero.

Carol was a hero too. The tireless old bird hobbled about on her cane, shouting orders like a drill sergeant, keeping everybody on task. She was there to keep them all motivated and unafraid, but she had nobody doing the same for her. It was her toughness alone that kept everyone going.

Mina might have been the biggest hero of all. She had faced danger at every turn, but had never shied away from doing the right thing. She had been unwilling to turn away from any person in need, but nobody had been there for her when she'd needed it. In David's line of work, he rarely met 'good' people, but Mina had certainly qualified. Since Oxford Street, he had cared only about getting the story and furthering his career. With all the death he had seen, he realised how vain and petty his life had been. It all seemed like such a waste. Mina's death highlighted how fragile life was, and how easily it could slip away. It made no sense that her death had affected him so much, but it had. He couldn't get the image of her swinging body out his head.

It filled him with rage.

Mina hadn't killed herself, he was certain of it. She'd been murdered. Andras had a scratch mark on his neck, and he had been the last person to see Mina alive. That was evidence and a connection to the victim. The only thing left to prove was motive. David intended to do that right now.

He went on over to where Mitchell was tapping away at his keyboard and leaned over the man's shoulder and whispered,

"Please tell me you have the black box data for Mina's computer."

Mitchell started at the sudden voice in his ear, but he recovered and nodded. "Just finished compiling it. You want me to open it?"

"Yes."

Mitchell zipped around with the mouse and opened a couple of folders. He double-clicked a text file, and the contents popped up on screen.

"What am I looking at?" asked David, as he examined the crowded mess on screen.

"It's just code. Let me scroll down... Here—the last few actions before the website went dark. Someone definitely deleted the whole thing."

"How?"

"They deleted all the files off the local server, and then uploaded through Mina's FTP manager. They basically uploaded a blank slate to the website. That's why there's nothing but a white screen—there's no data to fetch."

"You have a backup?"

Mitchell nodded. "Yeah, I can access the revisions on the server and roll things back. Should be easy enough."

David was relieved and let it show, but there were still other questions he wanted answered. "Anything to tell you who deleted everything?"

"Yes, it was Mina."

David frowned. "She wouldn't have."

"You're probably right, but it was her logged in at the time."

David folded his arms for a moment and thought it through.

"She was updating the website when she was last sitting down. Do you have that data?"

"It's here—4.57PM. I saw her sitting there myself. She got up a little after five. According to this... the data was deleted at 5.06PM. It was right after Mina left the office to take a phone call. I know who deleted the files."

David already knew the answer as well. "Andras."

Mitchell nodded. "Yeah, he stayed at Mina's desk for at least ten minutes after she left. It could only have been him."

"Then I have what I need. I suspected Andras was the one behind the sabotage."

"Sabotage? You don't think it was an accident then?"

"No, I do not."

"David, what exactly is going on here? Where's Mina?"

"She's dead, Mitchell. I strongly suspect that Andras killed her, right after he deleted the website."

Mitchell shook his head and looked bewildered. "Mina's

dead? Man, why would Andras do anything like this? It makes no sense."

"Murder rarely makes sense, Mitchell, but I'm certain it was him. Mina had a broken fingernail, and Andras has a scratch on his neck. She tried to fight him off."

Mitchell flopped back in his chair and put his head in his hands, seemingly close to tears. "God, David. We're fighting for our lives here, and there're still monsters like him running around. I still don't understand why he would do it."

"Me neither, but now I have everything I need to demand an answer."

Mitchell nodded. "I'm right behind you. Where is he now? Andras?"

David looked around. He had assumed Andras would be somewhere nearby, but he wasn't. Damn it. Had he realised David was on to him and scarpered? He couldn't be allowed to get away.

David took a few steps, then grabbed Corporal Martin as the soldier went to walk by. "Hey, Martin. Where's Andras?"

"I haven't seen him, but listen to this. I just spoke to a colleague based out of Camp Bastion. They've been monitoring areas of the Middle East with satellite surveillance and they—"

"Not now, Martin. I need to find Andras."

The soldier shrugged. "Fine. I was only going to tell you that someone closed a gate in Syria, but if you need to rush off, then by all means..."

David gawped at the corporal. "Somebody's closed one of the gates? Really?"

Martin grinned. "I promise you. The MOD satellite only gave a bunch of still images, but there's evidence of a firefight, and the gate is gone. Looks like somebody fought back, and won."

David slapped him on the arm. "Hooray for mankind. We will not let those bastards walk all over us."

"Hell no, we won't. They're going to wish they never stepped foot in our territory."

David felt the smile trickle from his face as he regretted Mina not being there to share the good news. "Andras. Where did you see him last?"

Martin shrugged. "He headed out to get some fresh air, I think."

David looked towards the exit and growled.

"You okay, David?"

He didn't reply. He marched across the office, shoving Big

Jimmy out of his way in the centre of the room. Then he barged through the exit and went out into the waiting room. It was empty, but something in David's bones told him he was heading in the right direction. Andras was out here, somewhere; he knew it.

He took the stairs downward and detected the tang of blood in the air. Despite her being dead, David wanted to check on Mina. He headed to the accountant's office where he had placed her, and the smell of blood got even stronger. It made no sense because Mina had not been wounded. Whether it was paranoia, or a subconscious eye for detail, David noticed the furniture in the office had moved. The reception desk had been piled high with stacks of paperwork, but some of those piles now lay on the floor. It could have been a breeze, but it was hot and still. He could already feel the sweat on his back just from taking the stairs down.

A shuffling sound came from one of the smaller offices. It was too dark to see in through the room's windows, and horizontal blinds broke up any would-be shadows, but he knew somebody was inside. David considered shouting out, but reconsidered. He was here to find that bastard, Andras, so he didn't want to give himself away.

The shuffling stopped, replaced by a faint whispering. The words made no sense, a jumble of consonants and few vowels. David kept low and crept towards the door to the office. He placed his ear against the wood and tried to listen.

A man inside was chanting—"Grlaw grlaw, hmdar veri vesta. Larix van doth."

It was Andras, David was sure, but what language was he speaking? He knew a little Latin from his university days, but it wasn't that. He knew German from a brief spell as a war correspondent, but it wasn't that either. It was gibberish—the guttural snaps of an angry dog.

Andras was insane.

The thought of getting his hand on Mina's murderer was too much to resist. David barged through the door.

Andras stood half-naked over Mina's unclothed body. Her hands and feet were removed, placed in each corner of the room, and the brown flesh of her stomach was sliced open to reveal a gaping hole. Congealed blood coated Andras's bare chest.

"You... you fuckin' monster!"

Andras saw David, but he didn't seem to care. He held his bloody hands up in front of him as some kind of grizzly taunt.

David felt weak. His stomach's meagre contents dredged up, and he vomited. Mina had been his friend and colleague. Now she lay, defiled, on the floor. "Why would you do something so unspeakable?" he demanded once he could get a hold on himself.

Andras's answer was: "To send a message."

"A message to whom? Me?"

"Ha! You are insignificant. The message is for my brothers. You may have heard of them; they are currently crushing your world beneath their glorious feet."

David drew a blank.

Andras grunted. "The Fallen are my brothers, and they will destroy all. The time of man is over."

"You're talking about the giants?"

"They are not giants. Men are puny ants."

"You're a loon," said David. "Do you think you're some kind of demon helping the other side? Fantasy or delusion, I don't care which. You're finished."

Andras laughed. "You don't get it, do you? This is just a meat suit. Some drug addict I borrowed as he choked to death on his own vomit. You could not bear to look upon the glory of my true form. I am here to see you all burn."

David glared. "You killed Mina."

"I will kill millions before I am done."

"Then why are you hanging around a regional newspaper office?"

"You are one of the few news gatherers left. You have provided me with data from all over the world, highlighting areas that my brothers need to address. I deleted your pathetic website, and I will help delete mankind's existence."

"We're helping people," said David. "You won't stop us."

"Mina thought the same. Such an enthusiastic, brave girl. She might actually have made a difference, but you? No, you are too self-involved to ever be a hero."

"You will lose. We've closed one of your gates."

"One of thousands. My brothers will defend the others; I have already warned them. You have no chance. Humans are weak and mushy. The Fallen are eternal."

David looked around the room, saw that, in addition to Mina's scattered limbs, there was also a series of bloody sigils smudged onto the walls. "Who are the Fallen? How did you send a message to your brothers?"

Andras grinned. "Like this." He dropped to one knee and shoved his bloody hands into the open cavity of Mina's stomach. A bright light filled the room, and a sudden concussive force threw David against the wall and knocked the wind out of him. A shimmering puddle appeared in the air above Mina's stomach, and an image projected onto it. David saw one of the giant's up close—a blond man with crystalline-blue eyes.

Andras kept his hands buried in Mina's belly as he spoke. "Qemuel, He who was destroyed by God, but has risen, it is I, Andras, The Discordant."

A booming voice returned. "Brother Andras, what say you?"

"I am compromised and must move on from this place. What would the Red Lord have of me?"

"Take back your form, and join us in battle. Shed your fetid shackles, and rise in your glory. Human vulnerability does not suit you. Make rivers of human blood."

Andras sighed euphorically. "Yes. Yes, I will bring forth my body and lay waste to all I see. Screams will fill the—"

David tackled Andras to the ground and terminated the conversation. As soon as the demon's hands left Mina's body, the portal blinked out of existence. Andras growled as David straddled him. David was no fighter, but he was a man, and he was angry. He pummelled Andras with punch after punch.

Andras was not a man though, and that was clear when he snaked a hand onto David's face and cooked his flesh.

"Glat glat comna hartis."

David screamed as his skin blistered and boiled. He could not escape the crushing, searing grip. His vision blurred and blackened.

"Burn, maggot," Andras growled.

David reached out his hands desperately. His fingers found Andras's face, and he pointed his thumbs at where he hoped a pair of eyes would be. There was a moment of resistance, followed by a wet squelch as David's thumbs disappeared inside Andras's eye sockets.

The demon bellowed.

Andras's searing hand slipped away from David's face and went to his own mangled eyes. The burning stopped, and David collapsed backwards onto the floor, trying to cradle his face, but recoiling in agony as his fingertips caused sparks of agony, like white hot pokers. It hurt to blink, and his lips flared with unbearable pain.

Andras rose to his feet at the same time David did. Both men moaned and staggered around in pained confusion.

"I'll tear out your insides," Andras spat.

David was in danger of passing out, but he focused on staying upright and readied himself for a fight. "Come and try it, you fucking monster."

Andras attacked, but it was clumsy and in the wrong direction. He hit against a desk and stumbled.

"You're blind," mocked David.

Andras glanced in the direction of his voice, bleeding eyes pierced like grapes. "No matter. I will return to my own body soon and see more clearly than ever."

David crept to one side, moving around to Andras's side. "Until then, you're a blind, little mouse."

Andras spun around. "I'll kill you."

"Then come on. Better yet, why don't you go get your big giant body, and stomp me into puddles."

"I will show you pain you cannot imagine."

David chuckled. "I'm thinking you can't get back to your true body without doing another one of your nasty spells, but how are you going to manage that with no sight?" He moved around behind Andras. "Am I right?"

Andras spun around, getting frustrated. "I will bathe in your blood!"

"Your brother's name was Qemuel?"

"Qemuel, The Great and Risen."

David moved around behind Andras again. "He said you were vulnerable in a human body."

Andras swiped at the air, but got nowhere near hitting David. David crept back towards the front of the office. A coat rack stood beside the door. Somebody had left a long golfing umbrella hanging from one of the arms, and David unhooked it carefully.

Andras swiped at the air again, but was still nowhere near. He'd begun to rave and rant like a maniac. "I'll grind your bones into dust, you maggot. You seek to mock me? I am Andras, Marquis of Hell."

"And I'm David Davids, reporting to you live." He used the umbrella's crooked handle to hook Andras's ankle and yank the demon off his feet. He hit his head on the desk hard enough to leave him stunned."

David's face still flared with agony, but he couldn't help but grin as he swung the umbrella like a golf club and struck Andras under the chin. The demon moaned and grabbed his face.

"That's the problem when you inhabit a human body, Andras, dear boy: We're all so weak and mushy."

Andras clawed at the air blindly.

David hit him again with the umbrella. "If I kill you, what will happen?"

"You cannot kill what cannot die."

"You'll go back to your body, won't you? If I kill you, I'll release you. Wouldn't want to be doing that. Would be a terrible waste of intel. I think you owe us after all the spying you've been doing."

Andras leapt to his feet like a cat and swung for David, almost hitting him this time. "Let's finish this," he hissed. "I cannot bear the stench of humanity any longer."

David swung the umbrella at Andras's head, but this time, Andras snatched at it and yanked David towards him. When Andras dug out one of his eyeballs, he screamed so hard he almost lost consciousness. In desperation, he forced the umbrella upwards under Andras's chin, hard enough to bury itself in his neck. It was enough to get the demon to retreat.

David staggered backwards, palming at his ruined eye, which was now an empty socket.

"An eye for an eye." Andras sniggered over by the door. David choked back his torment and reminded himself what would happen if he gave up. "I took both of your eyes, you son-of-a-bitch, so you're still the one losing."

"Then I have work to do." Andras came forward again, but stopped when the door to the office opened.

"David?" came a meek little voice.

David's heart leapt into his chest when he saw Alice standing there. "Alice, get out of here, now!"

"But Carol is looking for—"

Alice screamed.

Andras grabbed her around the throat and held her in front of him. "Just what I needed," he said. "I can use her guts to make a spell and get me back to where I belong."

"Let her go," David warned.

"I don't think I will. In fact, I think I'll let you watch with your one good eye, while I twist her head off."

"Just let her go!"

Alice stopped screaming and went completely silent, like she had after her brother died. She looked at David with her lower lip trembling.

David smiled at her, despite it causing him agony and his ruined face no doubt scaring her. "Don't you worry about me, sweetheart. Everything is okay."

"No," said Andras. "The time has come for little children to learn about the horrors of the world. There are no heroes, only blood and death."

Alice panted, not fear in her eyes, but anger. "Yes, there are heroes."

Andras chuckled. "No, there isn't, child. There are only monsters, like me."

"You're wrong. My brother was hero. His name was Kyle." She lifted her foot into the air and stomped hard on Andras's shin.

He let go of her and hopped on one foot as his hands went to his injured leg.

"You little shit!"

David reached out his hand. "Alice, come to me. Quick!" Alice ran to his side, and once she was safe, he sprinted

forward and drove the metal tip of his umbrella right into Andras's open mouth. He shoved the demon backwards, through the main office, and into the reception, driving the umbrella deeper and deeper into his throat as they picked up speed.

Out the office's exit. Across the hallway.

The open stairwell lay just ahead.

Andras tried to get his balance, but David kept on shoving him back until he struck the safety railing over the stairwell. They had enough speed that Andras went right up over it. He managed to cling on for a moment, but David was the one with all the leverage and grabbed a hold of the demon's wrist. He glared into his face. "Back to Hell with you."

Andras laughed, and actually threw himself backwards. He wanted death, wanted the release that would send him back to his true body. He fell from the second floor and hit the ground below, letting out an endless wail as the air escaped his compressed lungs.

David turned to find Alice coming out of the office behind him. "Get back to Carol," he said. "I'll be right up."

Alice nodded and ran up the stairs.

David headed down to where Andras lay at the bottom, gasping for breath. The demon's body was twisted and broken, and the pain on his face was a joy to behold for David.

"Hurt's doesn't it. I broke my wrist once when I playing badminton. Ached like buggery for almost two years. I can only imagine what a broken back must feel like. Next time, throw yourself from a little higher up to get the job done."

Andras struggled to move, but could barely even lift his neck. "M-maggot."

"You're the one on the ground."

"I will-"

"Yes, yes, I know: You're going to do unspeakable things to me. I'm terribly frightened, but right now, you're all but paralysed. I'm thinking, with a little tender loving care, we can keep you alive for some time yet. I'll make sure you're right at home. You can have a front row seat, while we help save the world."

Andras struggled, but could only flop like a beached salmon. "Let me die."

David sneered, ignoring the sharp pains coming from every inch of skin on his face. "Now why would I do that? I'm not a monster." He stamped on one of Andras's lifeless legs and broke the shinbone. "Well, maybe just a smidge."

He grabbed Andras by the arms and dragged him up the stairs, being as clumsy and careless as he could. By the time Andras reached the top, he was begging for mercy.

~RICK BASTION~
DEVONSHIRE, ENGLAND

NIGHT FELL, AND ALL WAS QUIET. RICK HAD JUST dragged the last of the dead demons into the driveway, and had returned to Daniel, who still slept fitfully on the couch. The Fallen Angel was in and out of consciousness, and Rick wasn't sure he would ever wake up. Daniel was one of the good guys—had all but proved it—and if he died, then Rick would be left alone and clueless.

He sat down at his piano and placed a glass of water on the lid. The whisky had all been used to make Molotov cocktails, but even if he'd had some left, he would have chosen water.

He thought about his brother, and Maddy, and Diane. He hoped that they had made it someplace safe, but whether there even was anywhere safe to go was a major question. His laptop had been in the kitchen during his fight with Khallutush and hadn't made it. Nor did the phone or television work anymore. The power and water were still on, but he expected to lose them eventually too. Whoever was in charge of such things, had probably died or scattered—no blue-collar worker would stick around and do their job while the world ended. Everybody had a family to get to, somewhere. Everyone, that was, except for Rick. His only family was a brother, whom he rarely even liked and would most likely never see again. He didn't specifically mourn the loss of his brother, but the bond of having somebody close would be missed. Rick was used to loneliness, but he'd never endured what he was feeling now: Abandonment. The world had left him. The one thing left in his life that could bring him comfort was his piano—but he only had one hand with which to play. He looked at his crushed fingers and wept, but then he looked at his trembling right hand and realised that he was blessed to be left with anything at all.

Fingertips of his good hand resting on the keys, Rick held his breath. Always a twinge of excitement before playing the first note, and now was no different, but there was a feeling of trepidation also—he would have to play one-handed for the first time in his life, and wasn't sure he could do it. A single hand with which to create something living, amidst all of the death. One hand to breathe life to music.

He started playing.

House of the Rising Sun.

He played flawlessly.

The melody took him away, carried his mind to that ethereal place where all great music comes from.

"That's pretty good. Ever think about doing it professionally?"

Rick's fingers leapt off the keys and hung in the air. He spun around and saw his brother standing in the living room. "Keith?"

"Yep. I didn't think you'd made it."

"I kind of didn't," said Rick. "What are you doing here?"

Maddy and Diane walked in and joined Keith. All three of them looked weary and tired.

"Hi, Rick," said Maddy. "We came back."

Rick didn't understand. "Why?"

"Because there's nowhere to go." Keith let out a heavy sigh. "We tried to make for the motorway, but there are wrecks everywhere. People are fighting in the streets, and there are still demons all over the place. We'd never make it to the coast. We thought our little battle was special, but it's happening everywhere."

Rick glanced at Maddy. "Your wedding ring?"

She shrugged. "I thought it was important, but after what I saw out there, I've realised that there's no point holding on to the past. My husband is gone, but I'm still here. There are better ways to honour him than getting myself killed."

"We came back here to stay safe behind the gates," said Keith. "Never expected to find you home."

"I never expected visitors."

Maddy came over to the piano and hugged him. "I'm so glad you're okay, Rick."

"Likewise. Does anybody have a plan on what to do next?"

"We managed to get some supplies at a corner shop," Diane answered, "but not much."

"We have a few days," said Maddy. "I just want to rest for now, figure it all out in the morning. Try to find some answers."

Rick glanced across at Daniel, still unconscious on the couch. The only answers they could hope to get would likely come from him—one of them—so they should all pray that he made it through. For now, Rick decided to keep Daniel's secret. Let the poor angel sleep.

"It's nice to have company." Rick waved an arm. "Make yourselves at home."

"I'll put the kettle on," said Diane, heading towards the kitchen.

Maddy followed. "I'll help her."

"Excuse the mess," Rick warned them.

"Looks like a whirlwind hit this place," Keith commented as he looked at the broken furniture and bloodstains in the living room.

"Yeah, it's been Hell, and I think I lost my hand. Hey, speaking of hands, what's that in yours?"

Keith looked down at the slim object in his hand like he'd forgotten he was holding it. "Oh, yeah, well... The garage was still open, and I thought you were.... Well, you know. There were plenty, so hope you don't mind."

Rick stared at the portrait of his face on the album cover in his brother's hand and frowned. "You took one of my CDs? Why?"

Keith blushed, shuffled his feet. "I didn't think I'd ever see you again. Wanted something to remember you by."

"A picture of me with pink hair and a cheesy grin?"

"A picture from when I was proud of you."

"You've never been proud of me, Keith."

"Yes, I have. Just never wanted to admit it to myself, until now. I'm proud to call you my brother. I think losing Marcy and Max has put things into perspective for me. Family matters. We survived the end of the world together, Rick."

"Not yet we haven't. And you don't know Marcy and Max are gone. We'll find a way to get to them."

Keith nodded. "Bring it on, I say. Those demons will have to be crazy to mess with a chartered accountant and a fading pop star."

"And a paramedic," shouted Maddy from the kitchen.

"A barmaid too," came Diane's voice.

Rick and Keith looked at each other and chuckled.

"Then I guess we have our team," said Rick. "Now we just need some theme music." He turned around and placed his fingers over the keys. "Any suggestions?"

Maddy and Diane came in with the piping hot brews. "Surprise us," said Maddy.

Rick thought for a moment, then came upon the perfect song for the situation. He put the electricity in his fingertips to work and started to play. The melody was perfect.

The Final Countdown.

~TONY CROSS~
INCIRLIK, TURKEY

CIVILISATION SEEPED INTO VIEW ON THE horizon, and the featureless browns of the desert started to share the landscape with patches of green and the straight lines of sun-baked concrete. It had taken almost twenty hours of continuous driving, but they had made it across the Turkish border. They found the country in disarray. Word had arrived that Istanbul was under siege, and Ankara, in the North West, was assumed to be next. The Turkish armed forces were everywhere, a disorderly mess that fought side by side with local militia, police, and the bravest civilians. The whole country was ready for war, but no one seemed to know quite what to do.

Tony and his men ran out of petrol just south of Osmaniye. Seeing the roads clogged with traffic and wrecked vehicles, they headed west on foot, until they found a couple of civilians on scooters. It pained Tony to do it, but he threw the young men to the ground and took their vehicles from them. The four soldiers doubled up on the two bikes and took off as fast as they could, dodging around the crawling traffic whenever they could see a gap. Many of the civilians walked barefooted, climbing up buildings or hanging from streetlights. It was a free for all. Everybody wanted to find somewhere safe to dig in. High ground seemed to be most desirable, and people fought to get to the rooftops. They did not understand how little good it would do them when the demons arrived.

With the underpowered scooters, the journey to Incirlik Air Base took a little over six hours. When they passed through the green pastures and farmland and finally reached the Air Force installation, it was like witnessing a miracle. Planes flew in and out of the runways with amazing regularity, splitting the air with their deafening roars every couple of minutes. American soldiers hurried about, like worker ants, carrying weapons or loading up vehicles. The place was alive.

Tony was halted at the gate and had to give the names of him and his men, along with their ranks and service numbers. They were British soldiers, not American, which meant it took over thirty minutes for them to get clearance to enter. Once they had, they were warmly welcomed by a United States Air Force Colonel. The officer had unkempt grey sideburns peeking out from beneath his cap, and a fuzzy brown moustache.

"Colonel Chase," he said. "A pleasure to meet you fine gentleman. You told my sentries that you closed a gate. We got word of it yesterday, but we were unsure whether to believe it or not. Is it true?"

Tony nodded. "It opened in the Syrian Desert, but it's closed now. How many more are there?"

The colonel wore a grave expression as he spoke. "Over six-thou of them. It's bad, Staff Sergeant."

"I gathered that. Sounds like we're pretty much fucked."

"If you know how we can close those ungodly gates, then we have a fighting chance at least."

So Tony told the colonel what he knew—explaining how Aymun had thrown himself through one of the gates, and that the next thing anybody knew, it was collapsing in on itself like a faulty firework. The colonel remained silent the whole time he listened, expressionless but for the fleeting excited movements of his bushy eyebrows. When Tony finished, the U.S. Air Force Officer let out a long, weary sigh and shook his head. "So, to close the gates, men and woman must give their lives? I've spent the last decade fighting martyrs and suicide fighters, and now that's exactly what we need. Lord, if life isn't ironic."

"People are already giving their lives," Tony remarked. "Every second, by the sounds of things."

"That they are, Staff Sergeant, but not voluntarily. I'm not sure there'll be many queuing up to sign on for such a task."

"They won't," agreed Tony, "but in the heat of battle, you'll find your heroes. My men did, and it was a Syrian named Aymun. As long as we spread word of how to close the gates, you'll be making sure people know what to do when things are hopeless. Aymun died so that the rest of us have a chance to turn things around. There'll be others like him."

The colonel lifted his chin and nodded proudly. "I hope you're right, Staff Sergeant. I'll get you and your men back home as soon as I am physically able, but I hope you can appreciate the difficulty that entails at the present moment."

Tony waved a hand. "We'll go wherever we're most needed. I think home just got a whole lot bigger. Time to stop thinking in terms of boundaries and realise that we're all in this together."

"Men fight for flags better than they fight for their fellow man," said the colonel.

"It's time for a change," said Tony.

"Perhaps you're right—in fact, I hope very much that you are. For now, make yourself comfortable. You and your men are my personal guests, so present yourself to the Administration department as such, and they'll find you somewhere to rest up. I imagine you're starving."

"Bleedin' famished, sir."

The American colonel looked bemused and let out a hearty chuckle. "You and your lads are safe, for now, Staff Sergeant, so make the most of the rest. I'm sure there'll be more battles ahead. Let's hope we can win them."

Tony looked back at his three remaining, battle-beaten men and grunted. "Or lose well enough to make the enemy regret winning."

"I'll catch up with you later, Staff Sergeant. I have duties..."

"We can sort ourselves out. Thank you, Colonel. Get that information spread to every corner of the world. More of those gates get closed, the better."

The officer saluted and Tony did the same. Then the American turned on his heel and marched away. Tony joined his men, who were sitting on top of an ammo crate. There was a group of U.S. airmen nearby whispering amongst themselves. Word had already got out that these were the British soldiers who had closed the gate in the Syrian Desert. The Yanks were looking at them like revered war heroes.

Corporal Rose got up and stood to attention. The two privates followed suit.

"Stand down, men. I'm not a bloody officer, nor shall I ever be. I'm a squaddie like the three of you and damn proud I am, to have crossed the desert with you lads. We just left Hell lying in our wake. We kicked a bunch of demon's arses and wiped our boots on their faces—and there's gunna be a fuck-load more arses need kicking in the days to come, so we need to be ready. The world is at war. Not World War III, but the war that will decide whether mankind finishes its run right here and now, or if it lasts another ten thousand years. Our enemy is terrifying, and worse than anything mankind has ever faced, but we can make it bleed, and we can make it dead. Our enemy is strong, but we are stronger— we are men. Our enemy is demons from the pits of Hell, but we are British soldiers, and we are men. The world needs heroes, and I'm looking at three of the best right now. Don't lose heart, and don't think too hard. England is waiting for us, but there's a war to win first. I will stand beside you in the fight ahead, and I ask that you stand by me."

"Fucking aye, ya crazy bastard," said Corporal Rose. "I'll follow you straight to Hell if you ask me to, Staffie."

The two privates said much the same thing.

"Good," said Tony, "then let's go find out where the Yanks eat their grub and stuff our faces full of their hamburgers. It might be the last good meal we have for a long time. We'll be dining on our enemy's blood before long."

What Tony didn't voice out loud was: Either that, or they'll be dining on ours.

The four British soldiers crossed the American Air Force base, focused only on their appetites. There would be time enough to worry about the fate of mankind tomorrow, for tomorrow, they would fight again. Tonight, they would rest.

~GUY GRANGER~
ATLANTIC OCEAN

T HE COAST OF THE UNITED STATES WAS three hundred miles behind them, and the vast, blue ocean seemed to stretch on for eternity. Guy didn't know what he would find in England, but there was no doubt in his mind that things would be tough. The U.K. had been hit as badly as America, but its citizens lacked the freedom to bear arms. The citizens of the U.K. would have only their bare hands to defend themselves against the demons. But Alice and Kyle had been with the British Army, as safe as they possibly could be. There was a chance, and a little hope was all a father needed.

He strode across the launch deck and stood in front of his old friend, Frank. They had covered his body with the Hatchet's Star Spangled Banner and placed him onto a plastic gurney. He had been positioned at the rear edge of the deck so that he could be slipped off into the sea, where he belonged.

The men had assembled, a mixture of sailors, civilians, and a handful of children. Guy wasted no time in addressing them. "Men, women, and children, the days past have taken their toll, and even a piece of our souls. The part of us that was innocent is no more, and our days of peace and pacifism are behind us, replaced by pain and war. You are all a part of something greater than each of us. Each of you represents humanity's fighting spirit. All of you have survived horrors and faced intolerable nightmares. The human race will survive too, as each of you has survived. This ship is a weapon, and every man and woman aboard it, a warrior ready to wield it. Together, we will strike the enemy down and take back our world. We will make it safe again for our children, and resign this terrible period of history to textbooks and memory. John F. Kennedy once said, 'Mankind must put an end to war before war puts an end to mankind' and that has never been truer than now. I trust each and every one of you, and I will die to protect you. You must also be willing to die to protect others. It is not a choice, but a sacred duty. We are a part of mankind's army, and we will win back peace. While the blood in our veins is warm, humanity will keep on fighting."

A brief cheer rippled through the crowd, but Guy halted it with the wave of his hand. "For now, we put to rest a great man; a man who devoted his entire life to serving his country and protecting the innocent. My oldest friend, and a man I will always look up to—Chief Petty Officer Frank Theodore Jacobs. I would like to read you all a poem that I know Frank would have liked." Guy unfolded the piece of paper in his hands and began to read:

"Sunset and evening star,

And one clear call for me!

And may there be no moaning of the bar,

When I put out to sea,

But such a tide as moving seems asleep,

Too full for sound and foam,

When that which drew from out the boundless deep Turns again home.

Twilight and evening bell,

And after that the dark!

And may there be no sadness of farewell, When I embark;

For tho' from out our bourne of Time and Place The flood may bear me far,

I hope to see my Pilot face to face

When I have crost the bar."

After a moments silence, Guy directed the men to tip Frank into the sea. He didn't blink until his old friend had disappeared completely beneath the waves. The reason he shed no tears was because his sadness was propped up by pride—pride to have served with a man as honourable as Chief Petty Officer Frank Jacobs.

Eventually, Guy headed to the pilothouse where a skeleton crew had remained to keep the ship on course. They all saluted him when he arrived.

Tosco stood at the console, plotting their course.

"Are we all set, Lieutenant?"

Tosco nodded. "The journey should take us about four days, if we keep a decent speed. We've fallen too far south to make it any quicker."

"Four days is acceptable. I would like it to be four minutes, but I'm realistic. Thank you for joining me, Lieutenant."

Tosco chewed his lip as if he wanted to mention something. Eventually, he did. "Do you know what you'll do when we reach England, Captain? Will you disembark?"

"I'll decide when we get there."

"I will stay behind. Perhaps, head back home, if we can refuel again."

Guy sighed. He didn't want to have this conversation now, but it wasn't going to go away. "Let me make one thing clear, Lieutenant. The Hatchet is my ship. If you head home, it will be because I ordered you to, not because you take the ship while I'm off doing other things. When I find Kyle and Alice, I will be bringing them home, so the Hatchet will wait for me to return."

Tosco looked embarrassed for a moment, then sniffed loudly and lifted his chin. "I think we both understand this ship is stolen from the U.S. government. Who it belongs to now is a matter of interpretation. I want you to find your children, Captain, but the Hatchet cannot sit around and wait for you. What if you take weeks to return? We all have jobs to do, and do them we must. Helping to rescue your children is a courtesy, not an obligation."

"Be very careful, Lieutenant. I made it clear when we embarked that anybody coming along would be expected to help me find Alice and Kyle. Whatever happens afterwards will be my decision."

Tosco smirked with all the confidence in the world. "If it comes to a popularity contest, Captain, you'll lose."

"Then let's not make it one. Just do your job, Lieutenant, and we'll all get along just fine."

"I always do my job, Captain, and will continue to do so." With that, the disgruntled Lieutenant left the pilothouse, leaving Guy to endure the sideways glances of his men. He was tired of having the same conversation with Tosco, but it would eventually come to a head. When it did, he just hoped he had Alice and Kyle safely in his arms. Then Tosco could do whatever the hell he liked.

Guy looked out at the Atlantic Ocean and wished he could stretch his arms out across the vastness and touch his children's cheeks. He longed to hold Kyle and Alice so badly that it hurt his chest. Please let them be alive, he prayed. Just let them be alive.

buffer had filled it previously, but now, it made the perfect cell for a paralysed demon.

"Hello, Andras. How are you feeling?"

Andras scowled, both eyes still useless and blind. "You think you can keep a Marquis of Hell prisoner?"

David chuckled. "In a dirty broom closet, no less. Such audacity, I never thought I was capable of."

"I will gut you."

"Perhaps, but not now, and not today. Today, I get to be the one doing beastly things to human flesh."

"There is nothing you can do-"

David pulled the steak knife out of his pocket and buried it in Andras's collarbone, making him scream. While the pain was still fresh, he grabbed a bottle of bleach and emptied it onto the wound. "So fortunate you still have some feeling left. Makes this a lot more fun."

Andras squealed like a stuck pig.

"You and I are going to become very well acquainted, Andras, dear boy. You're going to tell me all about The Fallen and the dreadful monsters that serve them."

Andras grunted, got on top of his pain enough to curse and swear. "I will never!"

David grabbed the steak knife and pulled it free, before burying it in Andras left ear. Once it slid in, he twisted it and sliced the flap of skin in two.

Andras bellowed so loud that it made David flinch, but it was music to his ears, and he ended up grinning. "Another thing you need to know about humans, Andras: We don't cope terribly well with pain. What was it you said? We're all so weak and mushy. I am going to teach you all about pain, one scrap of skin at a time, and for every life that your abominable colleagues take, I will

~DAVID DAVIDS~
SLOUGH, BERKSHIRE

DAVID SAT AT MINA'S DESK WITH HIS LAPTOP open, ready to hit 'upload'. Corporal Martin just got word from what was left of British Intelligence that somebody destroyed a gate in Syria and stopped the demons pouring through. It was hope. But hope was only as good as the amount you spread it. Closing a gate required a human sacrifice—someone to jump inside and break some kind of cosmic rule that short-circuited the portals. Mitchell posited that a living person could not enter Hell, and whoever had done so in Syria, had been the equivalent of a computer virus, corrupting whatever code kept the gates open. Typical of Mitchell to use such a technical metaphor, but what mattered most was the message—that the gates could be closed. Just so long as a person was prepared to step inside and end their lives. It would take a brave soul to make such a sacrifice, but David had faith that there were heroes out there. It was his job to give the world the opportunity to find them.

Carol tapped him on the shoulder. "What are you waiting for, David?" She, and everybody else in the office had gathered in a semi-circle around him, waiting for him to update the new website with all the information they had gained so far. News of refugee operations and safe areas, sightings of enemy armies, and a warning that demons could take human form—like Andras. The main thing they needed to know was how to close the gates. The gates were the demon's means of reinforcements. Closing them would be vital to gain a foothold in the war.

"I'm just a little nervous," David explained, reaching up and adjusting the bandage over his missing eye. The cotton had stuck to his burned face and made him wince every time he moved. "This could be the moment the tides change. We hold the information on how to fight back. It's... Momentous."

"We're not the only ones who know," said Martin. "British Intelligence is getting word out wherever it can."

David looked at Mitchell. "How many subscribers does the website have?"

"Ninety-three thousand."

David nodded. "Enough to make a difference. Our entire careers have been about giving people the news, letting them know what they need to. For the first time in my life, I feel like I'm about to achieve that goal."

"Just press send, you daft apeth," Carol urged.

David clicked the mouse and uploaded the website. Then he sat back and sighed. "It's done."

There was silence in the room, and nothing happened. They hadn't expected anything right away. The amount of comments on the website had been tapering even before Andras had deleted it, but there were still thousands of subscribers who were paying attention. Hopefully, some of them would make use of the information.

David glanced around the room until he located whom he wanted. "Corporal Martin, let me know the moment we receive word of any more gates closing. We need to pray that the one in Syria was not a fluke. We need to pray that people fight back."

Martin nodded and got to work. Carol went back to giving orders, and David just sat there at Mina's desk. He had just finished what she had started. He was proud of the work they'd done together. We did it, Mina. We got something useful and sent it out, just like you wanted.

Little Alice wandered over to him a couple of minutes la[ter,] carrying a mug of tea. She gave it to him, and he took a sip throu[gh] his ruined lips; it was much stronger than before. "You're getti[ng] very good at making tea, Alice. You were very brave yesterda[y] when you helped me fight Andras."

She nodded, looked afraid, yet brave at the same time. "He was one of them, wasn't he?"

"Yes, he was. You did the right thing. You could have run away, but instead, you fought. If all people are as brave as you, we'll be okay."

"Kyle didn't run. He fought."

David sighed and put his arm around the girl. "I'm sorry I didn't get to know the lad better. I think I would have liked him."

"Mom and dad will be upset when they find out."

"They still have you, and for that, they will be grateful, trust me. Is Corporal Martin still trying to reach them?"

"I think he's busy."

"Well, I'm sure your mummy and daddy are waiting to hear from you. We'll try them again soon."

Alice looked at him like she didn't believe it, but she trotted away obediently. Of all the tragedy David had witnessed, seeing that little girl lost in a foreign country and watching her brother die was the saddest. He would do whatever he could to see her reunited with someone who loved her.

For now, he left his seat and headed out of the office. He had something to attend to, and was very much looking forward to it. His face was a ruined mess, and he had witnessed the death of thousands—the man he had once been was gone, and it was time to do what was needed.

Andras was still tied up when David entered the storage closet outside in the waiting area. Cleaning supplies and an old floor

extract retribution on you. You might have come from Hell, but you have seen nothing yet. I'm going to be the biggest monster you've ever met."

David got to work, mastering the various ways to make a human being scream. Even if the demons conquered the world, this one would pay dearly. If mankind had a chance, they would have to lose a part of their humanity and become more like the monsters.

Blood covered David within minutes, and he embraced it.

VAMPS

LONDON

"YO, VAMPS, I CAN'T DO ANOTHER DAY, MAN." Vamps looked at his boy, Gingerbread, and shook his head. "You've seen what's happening to our streets, Ginge. We don't got no choice but to help out. Things are fucked up. People need us."

Gingerbread had grown pale, as he always did when he was tired. It made his red hair stand out even more, especially his beard. His expression was the same as Vamps five-year old nephew, Bradley, when he wanted sweets but got cabbage. "Vamp, man, we ain't heroes. We gangsters."

"Yeah, we gangsters, and another gang is moving onto our turf."

Ravy joined the conversation. "They're monsters. I never signed up to fight no monsters."

"Me either," said Mass.

Vamps turned to face him. "We never signed on for nothing. We were born and raised, yo. This fight came to us. We go out and we help, just like we did yesterday. We stopped some bird from getting raped. Do you not get that? She's alive because of us."

Mass stood up from the floor and nodded. His grey hoodie was badly torn where he had fought with a demon. His MMA skills had in handy and his strong arms had allowed him to throttle it until it was dead. "Vamps is right. I like how it feels... I mean, what's going down is shit, but I liked the feeling when we helped people yesterday. I felt all respectable."

·331·

Ravy was the smallest of them all, and pretty useless in a fight, but he had done his part. "Fine, but eventually we gonna die. This ain't the boys from West Ham, this is some serious shit."

"Way I see it," said Vamps. "The chances of us dying are pretty high anyway. Least this way we take some of those ugly bitches down with us." He looked at Gingerbread.

Gingerbread sighed. "Alright, I'm in. What's the plan?"

Vamps grinned, glad that his boys were sound. "We go out and head towards the first scream we hear. Arm up, boys, today ain't gonna be the day we die."

They grabbed their guns and knives and headed out of the Boots Megastore where they had holed up during the night. The fighting in the city had continued, but only in small pockets now. Before finding sanctuary, they had encountered a group of Chinese tourists in Leicester square. They were surrounded by hunched over demons and fighting back as best they could. One of them even knew Kung Fu, which had been amusing. The small Chinese man had been swooping and swirling amongst the demons like a ferret and breaking their arms and legs. Before they finally fell on top of him, he had killed at least a dozen. It had bought the rest of his companions some time—time enough for Vamp and they boys to come to the rescue.

Vamps had led the vanguard, popping off shots from his granpop's Browning. The boy's had added fire from their own pieces, and in the matter of minutes, the fight was over. Their numbers had been growing less and less, not because they were dying, but because they seemed to be heading out of the city. Only a few smatterings had been left behind to terrorise survivors like the Chinese tourists.

The city was quiet and cold, the dawn sunlight not enough to bring warmth. Dead bodies littered the streets and begun to smell. The scent of blood was not as strong as the scent of shit. Vamps had never seen a dead person before, but it seemed that they all shat their kegs before moving on. It wouldn't be long before the streets were stinking with disease. He would have to get his boys out of there soon. Perhaps tonight they would head out and make for the coast.

Right now though, they had to patrol the streets. When this war was over, and if they lived, they might just get some respect. No more being kept down by society because they were young and broke, and crew up in council-owned flats. They would be warriors, respected by all. When the shit went down, the upper classes were nowhere to be seen. There were no middle-class heroes in a ground war.

"Hey," Gingerbread pointed. "Something's going on down there."

Vamps put a hand over his eyes to shield his sight from the rising sun. There was definitely movement. "Piccadilly Circus," he muttered. "The place was clear last night when we passed through."

"It isn't now," said Ravvy. "There's a bus coming."

Vamps frowned. "If there's a working bus, why the hell isn't it trying to bounce? They should be fleeing as fast as the wheels will take them."

They picked up their pace and hurried towards the bus. The brightly lit signs on the corner of Piccadilly Circus were scorched and blackened from a fire in the shop below.

The bus up ahead stopped. It was not a city bus, but a plain white bus with darkened windows. The air brakes hissed and then the door folded open. A man in a grey suit exited and lit a cigarette.

Vamps street senses acted up. There was something wrong about the bus driver. He was too calm, the way he stood in the street smoking like nothing had happened. There was a pile of torn-up bodies not ten feet away.

"Hold back, yo." Vamps put an arm up and slowed his boys down. He moved to the side of the street, sliding in and out of the alcoves to keep his approach hidden.

Somebody else was getting off the bus. It was another man in a suit, this one younger than the other and stocky as a wrestler. He had long blonde hair like a young Hulk Hogan. In his hand he held a length of chain, and as he yanked on it the first in a line of handcuffed men and woman spilled out of the bus. When the last prisoner stepped off, there was a line of a dozen of them.

"Is it a prison bus?" Ravy asked.

Vamps shook his head. "No, way. Travelling prisoners wear matching uniforms to stop 'em running and blendin' in. I remembered when they moved me from Belmarsh to Brixton after some fuckers were trying to off me. They had me in this shitty grey tracksuit. Those people are wearing their own clothes."

"Then who are they?" Gingerbread asked.

"Who are the dudes in suits?" Mass asked.

"I dunno," Vamps admitted. "Let's crash over there and watch what happens."

They moved over to a delivery van and stooped behind its large rear compartment. Vamps stuck out his head to see what was happening up ahead.

The two suited gentlemen brought the line of prisoners into the middle of the road and then had them kneel down. At the same time, a sleek black Mercedes pulled out of a side street. It parked up and a chauffeur stepped out and opened up the rear door. Vamps covered his mouth when he saw who exited.

"No freakin' way!"

Gingerbread frowned. "Who is it? You know that dude?"

Vamps turned to his boys and nodded. "Yeah, man. That's the fucking Prime Minister."

Mass whistled. "That skinny fucker is the PM? We should go over. If we help him, we'll have it made, yo."

"Innit," said Ravy.

Vamps turned back to watch and was absolutely certain

that the man was John Windsor the Prime Minister. He was wearing an open collar shirt and straight black trousers. His jet-black moustache was a dead giveaway.

He walked up in front of the line of prisoners and began talking to their warden. The men and woman all pleading and begged when they saw their Prime Minister, but he acted as though they weren't there. One woman sought to rise to her feet, but the chauffeur hurried over and kicked her kneecap. She screamed.

"What the fuck, yo," said Mass.

Vamps clutched his Browning, making sure it was still there. "This shit smells wrong man. We need to go help."

"Yeah," said Gingerbread. "We should go pop that stuck up motherfuckers. He cut my nan's benefits last year."

Vamps was just about to break cover and go sort shit out, but he leapt back down when he saw demons spilling into Piccadilly Circus.

Mass looked like he was about to freak. "What the fuck, man? There're hundreds of 'em. We need to bolt."

Vamps agreed, but he couldn't help but watch. The Prime Minister and his companions seemed unafraid, even as the line of prisoners screamed and begged. The demons surrounded them and Vamps could no longer see what was going on."

"I'm fucking off," said Mass.

Vamps nodded. "I'll meet you at the Lyceum where he saw those rickshaws we can use. I'll be right behind you."

Gingerbread frowned at him. "What are you talking about? We need to get out of here."

Vamps waved his hand. "Get the hell out of here, boys. I'll be there. I promise."

They didn't seem to like it, but the boys got going, leaving Vamps hiding behind the van. Once the others were around the corner and out of sight, Vamps turned and climbed up onto the vehicle's roof.

Once again he could see what was going on, and once again he did not like it. The demons were not attacking the PM, and in fact the PM seemed to be addressing them. One of the demons – a burned man at least a foot taller than the others and sporting singed dreadlocks stood directly in front of him and was nodding his head as if receiving orders.

Then the strangest thing of all happened. The warden in charge of the prisoners handed over the chains to one of the demons who, instead of attacking, began leading them away. The demons filed away, back into the side streets, taking the sobbing men and women with them. The PM remained behind with his companions and seemed to be smiling. Vamps had been a dealer most his life, and he had just seen a deal go down for sure.

But what the hell was the trade?

And what the fuck was the PM doing out here trading the lives of innocent men and women. The anger associated with the questions made Vamps look down at his gun and think strongly about using it. But it would be suicide. The demons had only just left and the PM knew shit that made him dangerous. It was time to bounce.

Vamps moved over to the edge of the van and was about to climb down when he heard a shout. It wasn't his boys behind him. It was the chauffeur. He'd been spotted.

With no time to waste, Vamps through himself from the top of the van. As soon as he hit the pavement he felt the pain. His ankle folded sideways and electricity ran up to his knee.

He picked himself up of the floor and began hobbling away. He glanced back over his shoulder and saw the PM diving back inside his Mercedes. But his two companions were giving chase. With two good legs, they were faster than he was. The fact that he had a gun was not going to help, because he quickly realised that his pursuers had guns too, bigger ones.

The only question now was who would get to him first— his boys, or the bad guys behind him. No way did he wasn't to end up in chains like those people.

Vamps had no clue what was happening, but he knew one thing for sure: Shit just got worse.

THANKS FOR READING

Iain would love for you to join him online on Twitter and Facebook.

TWITTER - @iainrobwright

www.facebook.com/iainrobwright

And don't forget to check out his website for all the latest news and updates.

www.iainrobwright.com